MAROON & COMPANY

Carrye,
Thank you for the support
of Maroon & Company
Relax and enjoy!!

written by:
Vetella A Camper

Vetella A. Camper

6.30.13

First published by Dog Ear Publishing
4010 W. 86th Street, Ste H
Indianapolis, IN 46268
www.dogearpublishing.net

ISBN: 978-1-4575-1452-4

This book is printed on acid-free paper.

This is a book of fiction. Any real places, events or persons--living or dead--referenced in this movel are used solely to give an authentic feel to locations and chracters. Every other situation or resemblance to actual persons--living or dead--is coincidental.

Printed in the United States of America

For Christian, Jeremiah and Orion

The grands

Chapter 1

(Chandler)

"Chandler, remember when we met?"

"How could I forget? When I heard there was a new girl in the office that was so attractive and so nice, I had to see for myself. I figured you couldn't be pretty and nice, too. And I was right." Our laughter melted into the noises and sounds on the outdoor patio at the Innkeeper's Tavern. "Then when I came into the office, instead of me checking you out, you sized me up."

"I did not."

"Yes, you did, Stevie Michelle."

"Okay, but you did the same."

"Of course I did. That's what I came in to do. I wanted to know who the new person was on the block. And then when you said you had looked for the shade of hose I had on, you sounded like my kind of person. Anybody who takes interest in coordinating her stockings with her clothes has some style about her."

"Yeah. Angie said I had to be someone special for you to notice me, because you never talked to anybody."

"I never talked to her. Those girls in the office bore me. All of them. Their conversations consist of lost loves, divorces, their kids and what they're having for lunch to finish filling out their fat thighs. You looked and sounded like a breath of fresh air."

"You, know, that's what I thought, too!" Stevie Michelle exclaimed. "You seemed umm . . . ahh . . . inventive, if that describes it, while the rest of the office was trying to reinvent the toaster."

"Yeah, and look at me now. I'm talking about the very things that drive me crazy with them. Lost love, divorce . . ."

"Okay, so you are. But even your divorce has a plot."

"Stevie Michelle, what are you talking about?"

"You know. Will she get the house? Will she get the car, the stocks, the time-share in the Bahamas? All they get are the bills, the kids and the dog."

"I never thought I'd go through this." I hung my head slightly. "Especially not at this stage of my life. Just when I think I've got some stability, *bang*! Wade says in that deep, diplomatic voice of his, 'You know, Chandler, I think you should consider seeing a lawyer. I have.' I asked him, 'You're considering it, or you've seen one?' I should've been suspicious when he encouraged me to quit my job and go to the Culinary Institute in New York. People asked me what man would let his wife go to school out of town for two years. I said, 'Oh, no sweat. Wade and I have talked about it and I'll be home on the weekends and he travels, too, so if I can't get home, he'll come to New York. It'll be romantic, so everything'll work out fine. The two years'll fly by.' They flew, all right, and so did he."

"Come on, Chandler. We both know that's no excuse for him. You said you've always suspected Wade of being a womanizer and you had to keep a tight rein on his flirting."

"And when I think about it like that, Stevie Michelle, I'm glad it's happened the way it has. I got tired of Wade's flirting. He was wearing me out. A marriage shouldn't be based on a woman worrying about what her man is doing every time he walks out of the door. I had become so paranoid that when the phone rang and there was a hang-up, I'd keep track of the times and dates to see if there was a pattern. I should've known that having difficulty pronouncing his name meant trouble. Why would a mother name her baby Wade Reece Webb, anyway? Try to say that three times. But, oh my God, the first time I saw him, I didn't care if his name was Wee Willie Winkie. He was fine."

"He still is, Chandler. You've taken very good care of him. And yourself. Wade looks the way he did when I met him eight years ago. You both do."

My head tilted back slightly, the sun drenching my skin, I sat at the table rewinding the reel in my mind. Wade was taking a continuing education course at Cleveland State University and I was completing my bachelor's in business. We met in the computer lab and I was impressed that he was not only handsome, but also educated and intelligent. Ruggedly handsome, engineering fit him well. He was the type who looked good in jeans and dirt and sweat, but could also be transformed into the executive via a navy double-breasted suit. His smile, when he flashed it, with those perfectly even teeth, was charming. And Wade's hands had me captivated because they were large, yet slender, graceful, dramatic and dexterous. The piano was a breeze for him. He played, but sporadically.

Embarrassed, he had asked if I could help find the on switch for the computer. After I learned he was an engineer, I thought, *But he can't even find the switch on the computer*. On our first date I asked Wade if the computer was his way of approaching me. He confirmed that he honestly couldn't find the switch, but he was glad he couldn't. A year after my graduation, we were hot and heavy, and decided to get married. I knew I was taking a risk with such a handsome man, but I was willing to take it. I didn't love Wade for his looks, but for his charm and our ability to talk about anything. We had great conversations and when we made love, his hands used to dance a wonderful ballet over my body.

"Chandler, you want anything else?" Stevie Michelle asked.

The waitress was waiting for my answer. "I'll have another sparkling wine, please."

"Remember, you're driving and I can't drive a stick," Stevie Michelle said.

"Don't worry, I'm all right."

In concurrence, Stevie Michelle told the waitress, "So then, bring two of those."

The patio at Innkeeper's was quaint with an enchanted alfresco setting. The people who surrounded the bar were either sitting or standing under a dark green canvas awning. The patio tables, some topped with green umbrellas, stood on concrete squares. The planters hooked to the wrought-iron fence were filled with yellow, hot pink and purple flowers. I could hear the flow of the Chagrin River at the bottom of the hill. As Stevie Michelle sat under the umbrella, hiding from the sun, I exposed as much of my body as I could. The September Saturday was wonderful for Innkeeper's, shopping and my convertible 1984 Alfa Romeo. The car was a third anniversary gift from Wade and I had asked for it in the divorce. While driving on the open road, my little red car allowed me to feel free, and the stick-shift gave me a feel of control. Driven exclusively in the summer and early fall months, it was in impeccable condition.

"You know, you should learn to drive a stick, Stevie Michelle. How can you be a designated driver when I get loaded? And I plan to get loaded one of these days."

"It won't be long before you'll be driving the Volvo again," Stevie Michelle said.

I said, "Yeah. Summer's gone and as far as I'm concerned, wasted." A yellow-jacket settled on my plate. "You know, the bees are bad this year." I didn't disturb the little scavenger, but watched it sample the remains of my lunch. "Maybe it's because I didn't have children."

"What, Chandler?"

"Maybe Wade wanted a divorce because I didn't give him a baby?"

"Stop it, Cawthorne!" Using my last name was the start of Stevie Michelle getting on my case about something. "Children don't have anything to do with this," she said, "so stop blaming and doubting yourself. Wade is Wade. He's charming, but at the same time he doesn't give a damn."

"Hey, hold it. That's my ex-husband you're talking about," I said, laughing.

"Yeah. I know. It's just like me and Carl. We didn't talk about children before we got married and I didn't think to tell him that I wasn't planning to have anymore, and I guess he took it for granted that I was. I grew up in a house where there were too many mouths to feed and too many butts to clothe. Maybe that's what made me gun shy? All of us never got the love and attention that we needed. Nelson was happy and I really saw no need to change that."

"The number of children in a family sometimes has nothing to do with the amount of love that goes around, Stevie Michelle. Didn't you want to share a child with Carl?"

"I didn't want to share Carl with anyone."

"That's strange."

"What is?"

"You said you divorced Carl because he was too jealous, but then you say you didn't want to share him with anybody. Who was the jealous one?"

"Chandler, it's like this." Stevie Michelle drained the last of the champagne from her flute. "There's a difference between obsession and jealousy. Carl was obsessed and as time went on, the more obsessed he became. I think it had something to do with him being older. On the other hand, I was jealous. And it took me a long time to develop an understanding, a distinction of the two—jealousy and obsession. Also, that combination between us was lethal. Carl fixated on me as a possession, like one of his cars or antiques, and though he adored Nelson, he wasn't his flesh and blood. I had Carl, I had Nelson, and that was enough for me, and I was selfish about it. They were all I needed."

"Speaking of Nelson, how's he doing?"

"He's handled college better than I thought he would. I'm the one who needed to let go, and I didn't know how at first. I didn't feel he could handle being out of town, but it was me having the trouble. Nelson's adjusting well."

The waitress returned with the champagne. The bubbles stayed contained within the glasses as she poured.

"How about dessert, Chandler?" Without my answer, Stevie Michelle asked the waitress, "What's for dessert?"

As she recited the delicacies, I stopped her to say, "The gingerbread with the caramel-chocolate sauce sounds good. What do you think, Stevie Michelle?"

"That sounds good to me, too. I haven't had gingerbread in years."

"One of those and two plates and forks, please," I ordered. "We'll share." Stevie Michelle and I always shared dessert, unless it was PMS week for one of us; then it became every woman for herself.

"I'll be right back with your dessert," the waitress said as she swatted at a bee.

"Stevie Michelle, this has been a good day. Thanks for coming with me. I even found that camel blazer I wanted."

"And on sale," she added. "I'm still thinking about that tangerine suit I tried on. I liked it."

"I didn't. It's not your color. The style is nice, but that orange made you look jaundiced or something."

"Chandler, jaundice is yellow. The suit is orange."

"I don't care. It made you look sick. Orange is not your color. Maybe because you're yellow."

"Don't you start, Chandler. If you're out in the sun one more day, we can just pour barbecue sauce on and serve you for Labor Day."

"What are you saying?"

"You're done. Time to come off the grill. That's what I'm saying."

"You got something against black people?"

"Only when I remember them being three or four shades lighter."

Our humor was personal—our own. And I loved our world when we were in it together. Stevie Michelle listened, rarely judged me and often had advice. Good or bad, she had advice and cared enough to share it.

Dessert was placed on the table and I took the liberty of putting half on the other plate for Stevie Michelle. Tasting it, I said, "This is wonderful. I would've never thought of serving gingerbread this way. Maybe with apples and a cinnamon glaze, or something like that."

"It amazes me how you get so excited about food. You're really into it—making it, dissecting and guessing what's in it," Stevie Michelle said.

"There's nothing like preparing a dish that's a piece of artwork. It's so satisfying. Definitely more satisfying in the long run than a relationship." Sighing, I said, "I shouldn't've said that. I'm feeling sorry for myself. There's no comparison or substitute for a good relationship. The right man could be as delicious as a side dish to beef tenderloin with a port wine sauce." I waved the thought away and said, "And I don't want to get on the 'man thing'. *Okaay*?"

"Hey, you started it," Stevie Michelle playfully retorted. "Listen, Chandler, you've got a master's in business and an associate's in culinary art, so what's up now? What do you plan to do with all your talents?"

"I wish I knew," I said, savoring the gingerbread and caramel-chocolate combination as I ate. "I had planned to work in a restaurant for a while, you know, to get a little experience. But living alone, I couldn't survive on eighteen or twenty thousand a year. Hell, I can spend that on perfume, stockings and gasoline. That's why I'm back at Creative Solutions. I know they were shocked to see me in the employment office." *The woman who's forty, who's making the drastic career change*, I thought. "I'm just glad they were able to find a position for me. Customer relations ain't exactly what I had in mind, but something is better than nothing."

"Well, at least you're supervising the department."

I dropped my fork onto the plate and said, "Hell, I'm not supervising a *damn* thing. I do as I'm told like everybody else. I could kill Wade. He's ruined everything." Grimacing, I added, "But don't get me wrong. Don't think I'm not grateful."

Licking her fork, Stevie Michelle said, "Hey, you promised me you wouldn't do this to yourself, girl."

"You're right," I said, smiling. "You know, so far you're the only thing that's been consistent in my life for the last five years. You're here no matter what. You're perfect for me. Maybe I should've married you?"

"Don't pretend you haven't done the same. You came in on the tail-end of my divorce from Carl, but you were right there when I married and divorced Jeff."

"Yeah, Stevie Michelle, but a real friend wouldn't have let you marry him."

"And how were you going to stop me? There are two things you don't keep a woman from doing—having the man she wants and getting to a Sak's sale."

The champagne made us silly, but it felt great.

"How long did it last?" I asked.

"Six months, two days and fifteen hours. And Chandler, wasn't it nice that Carl agreed to handle the divorce for me?"

"I don't know how you had the nerve to ask him."

"It was easy, because I was desperate. It was like I woke up from a bad dream and there was a two-hundred-twenty-pound dumb jock in bed, looking dumber and jockier as I kept staring at him. I called Carl while Jeff was asleep next to me and said I had to talk to him. Begging, I admitted I had made the worst mistake ever. And Carl made me beg for his help. Really beg. He tried to play the how-much-is-it-worth-to-you game. I reminded him of who he was talking to, so he knew the galaxy wasn't a limit. Besides, who could I trust more than the lawyer and the man I was married to for almost twenty years? He was great getting me out of my first marriage, so I knew he was capable."

The champagne continued to induce the laughter.

"Yeah, go ahead, laugh," Stevie Michelle said, "but I've escaped attorney fees twice out of three divorces. You know of any other woman who's done that?"

"Maybe we should send your name into the *Guinness Book of World Records* for the most divorces without paying," I said.

The sun was directly over our table and I soaked it up like a sponge. Stevie Michelle and I finished our dessert and stared after the waitress as she moved like the bees from table to table. I asked Stevie Michelle, "You ready?"

She glanced at her watch, pushed back her chair and in a raspy voice said, "You think we can make it to the car? I'm stuffed."

"Me, too."

The waitress put the check on the table. I asked her to wait while I looked at the bill. I placed the credit card down on top of it. As she walked away, Stevie Michelle whispered, "You don't feel guilty about doing this?"

"No. I don't," I said. "When Wade gets the charge, there're two things he can do. He can either cancel the card or demand that I give it back."

When the waitress returned, I knew something was wrong. "Excuse me, Mrs. Webb, but this card isn't going through."

Stevie Michelle and I looked at one another and burst into laughter.

"See, I told you," I said. "Either he'd call me or cancel the card." I looked at the waitress without embarrassment. "Give us just one minute. We'll get this taken care of." Stevie Michelle and I went into our purses and counted out the amount of the bill in cash, including the tip. I handed the money to the waitress, and Stevie Michelle and I gathered our packages and floated across the patio. The sun was at our backs as we headed for the exit. A path of benches, impatiens and marigolds in baskets and pots lined the walkway. When we got to the sidewalk, I could see my Alfa Romeo. It patiently waited, like an obedient pet. Stevie Michelle and I crossed the street and put our packages inside the trunk, then got into the two-seater. The convertible top was left down, so the seats were warm, almost hot, from the sun. Starting my little red toy was a pleasure. It had such a polite disposition. It didn't roar and it didn't purr. It had its own distinct start, its own sound, and when I turned on the ignition, it returned the favor. I shifted into reverse, backed out of the space and headed up the street, stopping at the light before turning left onto Chagrin Boulevard.

From first to second gear, I headed up the steep hill, still bathing in the sun's rays. When the road leveled, I settled into fourth gear and cruised at forty-five, allowing the car to effortlessly handle the curves.

"Have you talked to Lorelei?" I heard Stevie Michelle ask over the noise of the wind, the car's engine and the radio.

"I got a letter from her Thursday. She's not too happy back home. She says things have changed a lot since she last lived there. She wrote that what used to be vacant, open land is now either developments, golf courses or shopping centers. Except for her family, she says most of the people she knew had left Little River. But, the kids are enjoying the beach.

Stevie Michelle looked dreamy when she said, "She has the three most beautiful children. She and Walter made the most beautiful kids."

"They did, didn't they? Oceanna is gorgeous. She looks so much like Walter and Lorelei that you know she had to have been made from the love of both of them. Three is as handsome as Oceanna is pretty, and Topper's not running far behind Oceanna, either. She's still got some little girl features to shed, and then she'll be a heartbreaker, too. And, Stevie Michelle," I said, taking my hand from around the stick-shift and pointing at her, "I'm telling you that was a divorce that should've never happened."

"Why do you think so?"

"Because Walter and Lorelei still love each other. I know they do. Walter is Wade's best friend. I've listened to what Wade said Walter has said to him, and I know what Lorelei has told me. I think they could have worked their problems out. I feel they are two people that should be together until they leave this earth." Reaching a steep decline, I shifted down to third and felt the Alfa pull back with obedience. Then, in second, the car obeyed my command again. The engine gently roared. "She said she went home to Little River to get herself together, but I don't think she'll be happy anywhere except here, with Walter. Her letter was indicative of that. Though she tried to sound upbeat, I read between the lines. Something isn't right with her. I don't know—" Shaking my head, I said, "Do you realize that for the last two and a half, three hours all we've talked about is divorce and ex-husbands. Let's break this up. We sound like real losers and that ain't good, and that ain't us."

"Okay. What should we talk about?"

"Oh, God!, this is sad; I don't know."

"I know!" Stevie Michelle squealed. "Let's talk about . . . what's the name of the restaurant?"

"Maroon," I whispered.

"Yeah. Let's talk about Maroon. It's been awhile since we've done that."

The road leveled out again. I responded with the stick shift that was under my power. The air, the serenity of the open road, and having my best friend on the other side of me was therapy. I needed that.

"What will the dining room look like?" Stevie Michelle asked.

"Small, but not too small," I emphasized. "It'll have 15 or 20 tables covered with white linen and lots of fragrant flowers around. The lights will be dimmed just right and the candles on the tables will make even the ugliest woman look sexy. The special will change weekly, if not daily, and I will select the best wines and beers."

"You don't like beer," Stevie Michelle stated.

"Well, I've got to have it anyway."

Stevie Michelle coaxed, "And what about the waiters?"

"Oh, yeah. They'll recite their names and say, 'It's my pleasure to serve you tonight.' And then a call will come in that Anita Baker heard about the restaurant and wants to reserve it for a private dinner party after her concert. And the next time the president visits, he'll decide to have stuffed portabella mushrooms with shrimp and crab instead of perogies."

Only Stevie Michelle could play the dream game with me and not make me feel silly or childish. When Lorelei tried to play, she just didn't have the right questions and the knack for it like Stevie

Michelle. Stevie Michelle knew how much I wanted to own a restaurant, and there weren't many that I hadn't eaten in within a sixty-mile radius. I would watch for the restaurant reviews in the local newspapers and magazines and, if they were good, Wade and I went. We even talked about writing our own critic's column, "The Cooking Critic's Corner". I could feel the adrenaline whenever I thought about becoming a restaurateur. If Wade never missed anything else about me, he'd miss my cooking. I knew that. He didn't have plain spaghetti on Mondays or pork chops and mashed potatoes on Thursdays. He'd get penne pasta, grilled chicken breast, sundried tomatoes and garlic with pine nuts, or grilled pork chops stuffed with shitake mushroom and walnut dressing, and cranberry relish with garlic and chive mashed potatoes.

"And opening night will be by invitation only," I said. "The guest list will consist of the mayor, important execs, anybody else that I think's important, and, of course, the disbelievers of my dream."

"In that case, maybe you should have two openings. The disbelievers list will be a pretty long one. But remember, I believe in you."

Taking my eyes off the road and glancing at her, I said to Stevie Michelle, "I know you do. But even I know it will take more than the dream game and us believing in me. It's going to take cold hard cash and concrete plans. Restaurants are the first to fail and most investors don't want to hear about them."

Like a man's erection after an orgasm, my dream deflated with the facts of restaurant ownership.

"There will be bottles of—What's that champagne—I mean sparkling wine—I like?"

"Gloria . . ." My hesitation to answer was out of frustration. "I don't want to play anymore, Stevie Michelle. Let's just drop the subject." Tears floated in my eyes as I tried to gain control of my emotions.

"You okay over there?"

"Hunh huh. Just got something in my eye."

"I know. They're called tears."

Rolling out as I began to laugh at Stevie Michelle, the tears instantly dried.

"It will be okay, Chandler. Don't worry."

"It's all so scary. I've been on my own most of my life, but for some reason you just don't get used to it, because we always have that need for the comfort zone with someone. Wade had become my comfort zone, regardless of my insecurities with him."

"You're intelligent, you're strong and most important you're gifted with the talent of persuasion, Chandler. That combination will come in handy one day when you need it. But right now take it one step at a time. You're newly divorced. You've got to get used to your maiden name again, for starters. I used to hyperventilate at least three times a day when it hit me that I was actually going to be on my own for the *first* time in my life. After Jeff, I had no alternative. Who showed me? Who told me I could do it? My girlfriend. Remember? I've been lucky, Chandler, but even luck runs out sooner or later. Carl was generous in our divorce and when I got rid of Jeff, who was too stupid to give me a hard time, Carl was there for me again."

The road seemed endless as the Alfa cruised with comfort. Stevie Michelle's long-legged five-foot, ten-inch frame fit inside just as well as my five feet, six inches. When we zoomed up and down the roads, we joked about being the black Thelma and Louise—me being Louise, of course.

"You got a date with Marvin tonight?" I asked, chuckling that Stevie Michelle always had a date; it was a matter of with whom.

"When I talked to him this morning we did."

"What's that supposed to mean?"

"The last two times he's canceled on me. I don't know what kind of game he's playing, but I got news for him. I'm too old and too tired for the games. Besides, I'm not that crazy about him anyway. He's just something to do."

Chuckling, I said, "What if that's how he feels about you?"

I could see out of the corner of my eye the stare Stevie Michelle was giving me as she said, rolling her eyes, "I doubt that. Remember, I am Stevie Michelle Parks."

"Oh, so you're using your maiden name again?"

"Yeah. I thought I should drop the last names of my husbands after divorce. Otherwise, I'd be known as Stevie Michelle Parks—Bean—Wilkes—Grayson."

I cut our Chagrin Boulevard tour off when I turned onto Lander Road, heading for Stevie Michelle's house.

"Chandler, do you think you'll marry again?"

"I asked myself that not too long ago and I decided that now is too soon to say. I liked being married, and the problem isn't marriage, but who you marry."Pulling into her drive, I looked around the yard and said, "It is so beautiful out here."

"Yeah, it is and I better appreciate it while I can."

"How long do you have to sell it?"

"In the divorce decree it states within three years, which is fine with me, because it's not the same without Carl here, believe it or not. I remember the first time I saw this house. Carl was so proud of it, and

I was proud of him. Maybe that's why we never talked about selling it—and buy what? Chandler, I'll tell you something. I don't think it's to the extent that you talk about Lorelei, but I've come to the conclusion that I'll always love Carl. He's a mellow man." Stevie Michelle reached between the bucket seats to give me a hug. "Thanks for a great day."

"You, too," I said, putting my arm around her.

I popped the trunk latch from inside the car as Stevie Michelle got out, getting her packages. "I'll talk to you on Monday," she said.

"Okay. Talk to you later." I gently backed out of the drive, attempting to avoid scraping the bottom of the car on the steep apron. I tooted the horn and drove off.

My ride home was one of constant, fast and uncontrollable thinking and wondering if things would be okay like Stevie Michelle said. I was usually the one who told her not to worry, or take it one step, one day, at a time. It was unfair of me not to believe her. She was right when she said I was a survivor of so many adverse conditions. Why should it be any different this time around? It would take some adjusting, that's all. I adjusted when the alcohol finally destroyed Mommy. I adjusted when Daddy died, leaving me with a not-quite-an-adult sister; and when Kennedy had that bad car accident that almost took the last of any family I had, I adjusted. I worked, stayed in college and helped Kennedy get better. I adjusted and grew stronger. I thought, *My shoulders are pretty strong. Bruised, but strong.*

The house was a welcoming sight. Rolling into the driveway, I noticed the leaves needed raking and the grass cutting. I ignored the idea of doing it just as fast as I acknowledged it needed to be done. Wade used to cut the grass. *I'll get Jason, the boy down the street, to do it for me*, I thought. The "For Sale" sign in the front yard had started to look authentic under the sixty-year-old oak tree. The beautiful colonial in the background served as the invitation to come look inside. Each day I saw the sign there I became more accepting of it. It wouldn't be long before someone would buy the house. Property in the Forest Hill area sold fairly quick and with the economy being decent, that was a plus. I was definitely anxious to get it sold. Like Stevie Michelle said, it's not the same when the people who used to live in a house aren't there anymore.

I pulled the Alfa into the garage and felt the cool of the shade as I entered. Shutting the car off, I didn't bother to pull the top up. The car's fan automatically came on as it cooled the engine. *That's right, you're home for the night. Cool down and rest*, I thought. I got my packages out of the trunk and went inside the house.

Chapter 2

(Chandler)

Tuesday, September 24, 1996 - 6:00 p.m.

Dear Lorelei:

I'm sorry it's taken me so long to correspond. I started to call, but I know how you like letters, so I decided to write. To answer your question, yes I'll visit you as soon as I can. As a matter of fact, I think November would be a good time for me—somewhere around the first or second week, before Thanksgiving. I want to be home around then to spend the holiday with Kennedy and Cornelius. You know, they're expecting their first baby. I'm finally going to be Aunt Chandler to someone. It feels great.

How are your kids doing? It's good to hear that Oceanna's at Spelman. Now she's closer to you. I miss you, Lorelei. Stevie Michelle says hello. We went on a shopping spree Saturday. Well, it wasn't as much of a spree as it was therapy. It's finally hit me that I'm on my own, once again. I'm not whining, but just plain scared—not about the future, but not knowing what the future is. Stevie Michelle actually told me not to worry. Can you believe that?

Well, enough about me. I could read the unhappiness in your letter. If there is anything I can do, please let me know. It'll help me. You know, sometimes when we're concentrating on someone else, we're able to worry less about ourselves. Write to let me know how things are going and if there are any eligible bachelors down there. I'll need one soon—as soon as I get myself together so I don't scare him away (smile).

Remember, this is home for you, too, if you decide to come back. Don't forget to write. This letter stuff is catching on with me. When I read the letters you send it seems you're right here with me. It's cool. It's reassuring.

I love you and hope to see you soon, and hear from you sooner.

Love,

Chandler

The phone rang just as I was addressing the envelope to Lorelei. "Hi, Kennedy. How are you feeling? . . . The morning sickness will pass . . . I know. It can make you crazy being hungry all the time and then throwing up after you eat . . . Sure, I can go shopping with you Thursday evening. I went with Stevie Michelle on Saturday. We had fun. She's crazy as ever. How's Cornelius? . . . Did you remember to tell him that there's some gardening tools over here that he can have. I don't think I'll need them anymore. And if I do, I'll borrow them from him . . . Okay, I'll talk to you on Wednesday to confirm . . . Love you, too."

It was a blessing that Kennedy found Cornelius. Kennedy's personality had changed after she and Mommy had a fist fight one day when Mommy was drunk and had pushed Kennedy to the floor and to the breaking point. The abuse had taken its toll on Kennedy and she decided to inflict some of her own. Fortunately, but unfortunately, I was no longer a resident of the Cawthorne household and was unable to intervene. Mommy pressed assault charges and Kennedy actually did twenty-nine hours in jail. She was eighteen and I was celebrating my quarter-century birthday in New York with a guy I was dating that I can't remember his name. Flying home, I had an uneasy urge to phone my family. As a rule, I called only once a week and truthfully, sometimes I'd let it go for a week and a half, maybe two. As soon as what's-his-name dropped me off at my apartment, I made the call and learned about the trouble. Through the details, Mommy's words dragged with intoxication. I wondered how long she'd been drinking—hours, days? Was she coherent regarding what had happened? When I got to the house, I saw on her face the years of abuse that Kennedy had suffered. Mommy had a black eye, with a cut above it, a swollen lip, and her forehead had a bump on it the size of a small kumquat. My heart sank. The abuse had created a monster in my little sister that pushed her into beating our mother.

Daddy had gone with Kennedy's boyfriend to get her out of jail. She came into the house only to get her things. She moved in with her boyfriend for about three months, then got two jobs, setting up her own living space. Mommy died approximately six months later from liver failure and Daddy a year after that from a massive heart attack.

On several occasions, Kennedy and I tried talking about what happened "that day" and all she would say was, "I just clocked, Chandler. The bell rang and I came out fighting. Mommy kept pushing and shoving and yelling, and when she pulled my hair, I just clocked." Kennedy and I were victims of child abuse and not until I was older, did I understand how much. And not until Cornelius came into her life did Kennedy begin to trust someone.

Cornelius wasn't a fine, fancy man. He was average looking and didn't mind shopping at the discount superstores for what he needed, including his clothing. He was a loving husband. He was a driver for UPS and his hobby was model trains. Cornelius' train collection was impressive—awesome, even. He taught me the scales of the models and not on Christmas, but on Easter, he took the trains out of their boxes and set them up with the miniature trees, people, animals, buildings, including miniature telephone poles and lines. He grew up in Youngstown and after a few years in a factory there, he moved to Cleveland, where he met Kennedy at a wedding reception. Shortly after they were married, Cornelius asked me, in confidence, why Kennedy never talked about our parents. I just said, "Because she really didn't know them." Cornelius, at that moment, probably thought I was weirder than my sister. I knew he wanted to ask how can a daughter live with her parents and not know them, but he didn't ask and I didn't elaborate. After all, I never questioned why he set up his trains on Easter, so I thought we were even.

Kennedy and I didn't talk about our feelings much, but I had learned to process and express my thoughts. Even at the age of thirty-two, Kennedy continued to hold onto the silence. She had great freedom of expression with Cornelius. Totally supportive of her, his personality was conservative, calm and consistent. The three C's, as Kennedy and I had labeled them. He wanted her to stay home to be his wife and the mother of his children, and she was fine with that.

She loved the tranquility. So, two years into their marriage they were going to have a family. Kennedy didn't know how proud I was of her for waiting until she was married to get pregnant.

Double checking the address on the envelope with the one on Lorelei's letter, I licked the stamp and stuck it on. I'd take a walk later to the mailbox.

Chapter 3

(Chandler)

The house was noiseless as I went to the front hall closet to get a box that held the last of Wade's things. I looked inside at the contents—a few reference books, a clock and an old camera. Those were the last of the "miscellaneous" things that he wanted. I practically dropped the box at the door. The clock inside made a protesting sound. Wade was coming at seven o'clock. I hadn't seen him in about three weeks—since the divorce had been final. What would I say to him? *Hello, Wade, how are you?* Or, *your shit's at the door; get it and get out*. I was angry. The house was empty. I felt empty, and the phone company called to say a fifty-dollar deposit was required before the service could be transferred in my name. I was paying for my recovered independence. Wade said the transfer had to be done soon or one day I'd pick up the phone and it would be dead.

Still standing at the door, becoming more disgusted with my new marital status, I raised my eyes to the ceiling in respect to the deity above. A cobweb blew in the draft. *That would drive Wade insane*, I thought. I felt the need to cry. I hadn't cried for at least ten or twelve hours, and I had about a half hour before Wade was to come, and he was always late, so forty-five minutes were probably mine to do whatever I wanted, and I wanted to cry. As my face contorted for the occasion and the tears filled the reservoirs in my eyes, blurring my vision, the phone rang. "Shit, a helpless soul can't even get time to purge the self-pity," I mumbled as I wiped away the tears, walking to the kitchen. "It's probably Wade, with an excuse of, 'I'll be a little late,

Chandler, because it's taking me longer than I expected to get Mary, here, off.'" I was talking to myself again. It had become a habit.

"Hello," I said into the phone, simultaneously chuckling and crying.

"What's so funny?" Stevie Michelle asked.

"If I told you, you wouldn't believe me."

"You got company?"

"No. I'm just waiting for Wade to come get the rest of his junk. What's up?"

"Hey, listen. I've got two tickets for the Luther Vandross concert."

"Oh, Stevie Michelle," I whined, "this is not the time in my life where I need to see or hear Luther. He'll either make me cry or cream in my pants. Either way, I won't appreciate it."

"Come on, Chandler. You know how I love Luther."

"Why don't you ask Marvin, or somebody."

"Because Marvin, or somebody, ain't worth the cost. Come on. It's free—my treat."

"You're going to be sorry when you've got a whimpering, craving-for-love divorcee sitting next to you, screaming, 'Oh, Luther, my thighs would love to have you between them tonight. Oh, baby!'"

"Hey, the tickets are paid for; you can yell whatever you want."

I didn't know who was out-laughing who. I said, "Okay. When is it and what time?"

"Saturday. Eight o'clock. We've got great seats, too. Sixth row from the stage."

"How'd you get seats in the sixth row and the concert's Saturday?"

"It's all in who you know."

"Or is it all in who you screw? Who gave you those tickets, Stevie Michelle?"

"Chandler, I can't believe you're talking to me like this. I'm hurt."

"Yeah. Right. Where'd you get the tickets?"

"Remember Byron from Polygram Records?"

"No, I don't. Which season was he?"

"You're going to be a bitter, lonely old woman, Chandler. The kind where the next time you're on your back with a man looking down into your face, he'll be the mortician scraping your guts out, preparing you for embalming."

"Oh, you're mean."

"Yes, I am. So, you want to get some dinner before the concert?"

"Yeah. Usually my love comes down better on a full stomach."

"Where do you want to go?"

"Stevie Michelle, I hadn't expected to make so many decisions tonight. I don't know. How about . . . Hmmm, how about . . ." The doorbell rang. "Shit. That's probably Wade. Let me think about where to eat and I'll call you back after he leaves."

"Wherever you decide, make the reservations, too."

"You are so lazy," I said. "I gotta go. Talk to you later." Hanging up, I took in a deep breath and exhaled. The bell rang again before I got to the door. I looked through the single-pane window. Wade's strong, sturdy frame was there. He was staring back over the front yard and I knew he was thinking that I hadn't taken care of it, but I didn't give a damn what he thought. I was a perfectionist, but Wade was a perfection nut. I opened the door and he quickly turned to face me.

"Chandler, the grass needs attention."

"Jason down the street is going to do it tomorrow," I said as I felt my nerves burn. I couldn't believe myself. I was being polite to him. It was none of his business what the grass looked like.

"If the place is going to sell, it's got to be immaculate—manicured."

"I know that, Wade. I said it'll be done tomorrow."

"Has anybody been to look at the house?"

"Not today. There's an appointment for Thursday."

"How many, so far?"

His peppery questions were irritating. "Wade, you can get that information from the realtor. You have her number. Call her. As pretty as she is, I'm surprised you haven't already."

"Chandler, you don't stop, do you?"

"Look, I don't want to argue, Wade. I'm sorry." I thought, *What the hell am I apologizing for*? "Your things are in the box. Check'em out. Make sure everything's there before you go." I took one last glance at him before I turned to walk into the kitchen. Then it registered that Kennedy had asked me to go shopping at the same time as the house was to be shown. "Oh, shit, Wade!"

"What now, Chandler?"

"I've got something to do on Thursday and the house is going to be shown then."

"Well, you'll just have to cancel your date. The house is more important."

"I don't have a date. I promised Kennedy I'd go shopping with her."

"Haven't you done enough shopping? I got the bill from the charge card you stole."

"I didn't steal anything. You left it, so I used it."

"You know what I mean, Chandler. I could have you prosecuted."

"You won't. It would take too much time. Besides, it wasn't that much. It would cost you more to take me to court."

"You call eight hundred dollars, not much? Your concept of money has always been distorted."

"I handled our money very well, Wade. It didn't become a problem until you needed excuses to leave. You amaze me."

"It's nice to know that I entertain you, *honey*."

"Wade, the bottom line is I'm not available on Thursday and someone has to be here. I elect you."

"Look, I don't feel comfortable with that."

"Why? You used to live here. I'm not asking you to move in. I just need you here for the showing. What, an hour or two of your time is too much? You want the house sold as much as I do. It's our last tie to one another, Wade. Just think, you'll be rid of me forever. It won't kill you to be here. They'll be in at six-thirty and probably out by six forty-five or fifty."

"I don't have keys."

"I'll leave them under the flower pot by the garage. Just remember to put them back when you leave."

"All right. But from now on, coordinate your time appropriately."

"Wade, I've got things to do before I get to bed. If everything is there," I said, looking down into the box, "then I'll talk to you some other time. Don't forget Thursday." I walked into the kitchen.

I was exhausted. Talking to Wade was like trying to go up a down escalator. I could hear the things in the box clank as he picked it up. Then the door slammed. I waited fifteen seconds or so before I walked into the hall to see Wade and his 'miscellaneous' things leaving. Locking the door, I looked out the window. He was backing out of the drive. The license plate on his car read, "Webb 1". I thought, *It should read, #1 ass. You'd think he'd be more discrete.*

With my arms folded, I walked to the threshold of the living room and stood there. I looked around at where everything stood and where things used to be. The sofa, covered in forest-green chintz, still held its place against the cream wall between the two windows. Missing were the end tables, but I didn't like them anyway. The crystal lamps were gone, also. The tan carpet had what looked like golf-course holes where the two Queen Anne chairs used to sit. I always meant to put coasters under the legs, but never got to it. I walked over and rubbed one of the indentations with my foot, attempting to fluff the carpet. I had a feeling those impressions would be there for a long time, if not forever.

The hooks remained on the wall above the mantel where Wade had taken down one of my favorite oils. It was a scene of a little girl sitting on a stool, peeling potatoes, staring with large, beautiful, sad brown eyes at whoever would stare back. I watched the empty space and listened to the old Westminster tick with a double rhythm. It would chime soon. I walked into the dining room, hearing my shoes make the sound shoes make in an empty room with hardwood floors. I had opted for cash in the divorce and Wade made certain that I kept very little of value in furniture and assets. He also got the timeshare in the Bahamas. But the one thing I fought hard and long for was the Knabe piano that stood bold and confident in the den. I would have given up anything necessary to have it. It was because of me that we acquired it in the first place, and I wasn't letting it leave my possession. The sun was setting and I could see the piano in the shadow of the den. I remembered it, as if everything transpired yesterday, but it was actually right before I went to culinary school. I had taken a day off from work. I'm sure it was a Thursday. It was a day when I went to a few estate house sales that had been advertised in the *Sun Press*. A couple of the estates belonged to prominent Clevelanders and the decision of which one to stop at first was tough. The house off Shaker Boulevard on Montgomery already had a line of people waiting when I arrived, and I took my place with the rest of the treasure seekers. The sale was conducted by "The Movers"—a group of old ladies that ran a no-nonsense liquidation business and took no offers, nor pity. They were old and cantankerous. I think the prerequisite for membership was to be wrinkled, age spotted and have a bitch's attitude. I was used to them and knew they strictly wanted the money and no conversation.

Only so many people were allowed in the house at one time, and I must have been in the second or third group. While being patient in line, I watched the goods as they were moved out, like ants transporting crumbs to the colony. Rugs, lamps, chairs, silver and books. I finally made it through the door and the house looked as I had imagined. Maintained, but an outdated French Tudor, there was room after room, and each contained things that looked to belong in a museum. As I walked around, I touched and gazed at everything. Then I walked into a room that appeared to have been added to the house in afterthought. There seemed no need for it other than to possess the piano, which was so sinfully beautiful it would captivate anyone who dared to look at it. The instrument was poised atop an oval oriental rug that was as gorgeously gracious as the piano. Had the room been built for the piano, or was the piano built for the room? I got close and ran my fingers over the cabinet.

I quietly opened the lid of the keyboard and there was a business card. "Sold" was written on it. When I flipped it to the other side, the card read "AAA Piano Company." I placed the card at the end of the piano and started a little tune that Wade had taught me. Although my playing was definitely amateur, almost juvenile, the magnificent boldness of sound of the instrument was evident. I played for a few minutes or so when a woman came to the door and said, "Excuse me, but that piano is sold and you shouldn't be in here." It was one of "The Movers", looking as old and fearless as the rest of her pack.

"I'm sorry," I said. "I was just admiring it."

"It's sold," she repeated.

I eased off the bench, closed the lid and slid past the woman through the door. I continued looking around when an armchair caught my interest, but I didn't want to buy it before I went to the other sales. Although I left the house, the piano stayed on my mind. I stopped at the other estates and bought a game table, a waffle iron, and a silver-plated candy dish. It was a long shot, but I went back for the chair on Montgomery. When I walked in, the house had been emptied except for a few knickknacks and trash. "The Movers" were completing final paperwork. Unable to restrain myself, I maneuvered my way to the room where the piano was, expecting it to be gone. Not only was the piano there, but a tall and rich-looking man and a woman were in the room. They seemed to be having a heated discussion. I stood to the side of the doorway and listened. Glancing at the woman, I assumed she was one of "The Movers", but I didn't know who the man was. I heard him say, "If they were supposed to be here this afternoon, then why haven't they come. You told me it was understood the piano had to be moved out today. Today, Frances! As of tomorrow, this house and anything left in it belongs to the new owners and I don't have time to fool around with it anymore. My plane leaves tonight and I'm going to be on it. Have you called?"

"Yes, I did, Mr. Denison, but I didn't get an answer."

Hearing them, the wheels in my head turned. I listened a little longer.

"I'll try calling again."

Before she caught me eavesdropping, I quickly slipped into one of the rooms close by. "The Mover" walked out, leaving the man with the piano. I went into the room. I didn't know what to say, but something told me to inform him of my interest in the piano. "Oh, I'm sorry. I seem to be a little lost in this massive house. It's like a maze. Can you point me in the right direction?"

The man, appearing impatient, tapped his nails on the piano. "If you walk down that hall, to your right is the way out."

"That is a beautiful piano. Did you buy it?"

"Contrary. I'm the one selling it. As a matter of fact, I thought it was sold, but the presumable buyers haven't come to get it."

"Do you mind me asking what it sold for?"

"Seven thousand."

My heart fluttered when I heard the deal. The intricate legs alone were worth that. Whoever was lucky enough to swing that price was stupid not to have carried it out on their back before somebody came to their senses. "You seem a little nervous that they're not going to come for it."

"I am. This is the last big item to be moved. This piano has been more trouble to me than it's worth. I have a Steinway in California, where I live, so I don't need it, and each time I try to sell it, the deal, for some reason or another, falls through. I wonder if my mother is trying to tell me something."

"Is this your mother's house."

"It was until she died."

"I'm sorry to hear that."

"She suffered for a long time, so I'm relieved that she's not suffering anymore."

"I understand. My mother suffered a long time before she died, too. Aaah, Mr. Denison, if someone else offered to buy the piano, would you sell it to them?"

"How do you know my name?"

"Oh, I heard the ladies out there talking and I figured since you seemed to be the only man in the house, you must be Mr. Denison. Am I correct?"

"Yes, I'm Chuck Denison."

"So, Mr. Denison, if I offered to buy it, would you sell it to me?"

"Are you serious?"

"Very." I began to breathe with fierce excitement and my heart was vibrating my insides as it beat ferociously.

"I did tell you the price, didn't I?"

"Yes sir, you did, but I don't have quite that much."

"How much do you have?" he asked, brushing his medium-length blond hair away from his face, suspiciously awaiting my answer.

"Well, understanding that it has a cracked soundboard and some strings need replacing, and usually if you replace some, the rest should be replaced also, and seeing that it would cost me a lot more to do all that than it would a dealer if he bought it, I would think it fair that I should be allowed to have it at forty-five hundred." While catching my breath, I could hear my words echo in my ears. I couldn't believe that I was standing with a man, obviously successful and knowledgeable, negotiating the price of a piano. What was I doing? How was I going to explain it to Wade if he accepted my offer? Oh Wade, you'll never guess what little item I picked up at one of the house sales today . . . and it was a bargain at—

"That's too low. I can't sell it for that. The lowest I'll go is six thousand."

"Fifty-five hundred and I'll have it picked up before your plane leaves tonight."

"How did you know—Never mind. Five thousand, five hundred cash?"

"Ummm, credit card. The Movers accept credit cards. Is that okay?"

"If they'll accept it, then it's fine with me. I just want this monstrosity out of here. I want to go back to California with everything finalized and this is the last of it," he said as he hit the side of *my* piano.

I heard footsteps coming down the hall. "Mr. Denison, I can't get anyone," the Mover, Frances said as she walked through the door. "It's like they've disappeared off the face of the earth."

"That's all right, Frances. This woman—"

"My name is Chandler."

His smile was an apologetic one. "Chandler just bought herself a 1959 Knabe limited edition for five thousand, five hundred dollars. Is that what we agreed upon?" Mr. Denison asked me, for Frances' sake.

"Yes, sir."

"But, Mr. Denison the dealer made a larger offer and I'm sure they're on the way."

"Frances, you're not sure of that," Mr. Denison said. "You just told me there's no trace of them by phone or smoke signal, so help this—Chandler, please." His gesture less anxious, he said to me, "Oh, by the way, the soundboard is in perfect condition, although all the strings should be replaced, but good try. You ought to be in sales." Mr. Denison smiled at me and told Frances to do whatever she does to get the sale processed.

Frances, The Mover, gave me a mean stare; the stare I'd seen others receive from her pack. My mind quickly went from her unfriendliness to the unfriendliness I would receive dealing with Wade. I had to call him. I took out one of the credit cards in my purse, hoping it was the one with the ten thousand dollar limit. I also hoped that there was nothing, if very little, on it. I handed the card to Frances and followed the old woman into the room where they had the cash box and credit card paraphernalia. While looking around for a telephone or some type of a communication device to get in contact with Wade, I thought of things to say.

"Is there a phone I can use?" I asked.

"It is not a policy of The Movers to provide telephone access to the public."

I could have choked her, but instead I remembered I had a phone in my car that I had *access* to any time I wanted it. As she was sliding my credit card through the machine, my mind kneaded over what to say to Wade—my dear, understanding, patient, unruffled, considerate husband. He was going to kill me.

I had to do some fast thinking and even faster talking. How was I going to get a seven-foot piano out of one house into another in a matter of an hour or two?

After the slip was filled out and I signed it, I quickly ran through the front door and down the long drive to my car. Dialing the number, I unconsciously pushed the send button and the phone began ringing. "Please be there," I mumbled.

"Hello."

"Hello, Wade. Look, I don't have a lot of time to do this, so I want you to listen to me. And don't say anything."

"Chandler, what have you done now?"

"I asked you not to say anything, Wade. Just listen." I took a deep breath and prayed for the best with what I was about to spring onto a man that could be explosive if surprised. "Wade, I just bought something bigger than a bread box, but smaller than a Yugo. No, maybe a Honda Civic."

"You know I don't like riddles, Chandler."

"Wade, wait a minute. Just listen."

"All right, but hurry up. I'm getting nervous."

I blurted, "I bought a piano!"

"You bought what?"

"I just bought a piano. It's the most beautiful thing I've ever seen, Wade, and—"

"How much?" I heard his voice echo in my ear.

"It's got the most beautiful legs on it."

"How much?"

"It's made of mahogany and the cabinet is in good, almost excellent condition, with a few scratches on it. But they're repairable."

"How much, Chandler?" Wade bellowed.

"Fifty-five hundred."

"What!!?"

I jumped from the loudness of his voice as I moved the phone away from my ear. Then calmly I said, "Five thousand, five hundred, but it's worth every penny and more."

"Oh my God, Chandler. I can't believe you're serious. Tell me you're not serious."

"I'm serious, Wade, and I need you to help me get it home. You can holler at me later, but right now I've—we've—got to do some fast thinking."

"I think you're going to tell those people that you are insane and you didn't know what you were doing, and you want your money back."

"I can't do that, Wade."

"Yes you can!"

"Then I won't do it! Now, are you going to put your authoritative side away for awhile and help me? Because I want this piano and I'll stop at nothing to have it."

There was silence and I felt my adrenaline spew in spurts.

"What is it you want me to do?"

I sighed, deflating my lungs. "I need you to help me move it. It's a seven-foot Knabe—"

"A Knabe, hunh? Where'd you find that?"

I could hear the enthusiasm in his voice, but that had to wait at least until we had a plan.

"Yeah. It's a Knabe, Wade, but I've got approximately an hour to have it moved."

"Chandler, you're asking the impossible. I don't know anyone that can move a piano, especially one that size."

"Wade, you're an engineer; think of some way to get it out."

"Chandler, I'm an engineer, not a piano mover. And I don't know any."

"Use some of your connections, Wade. I want to get that piano out of there. They're giving me an hour. I can probably stall for another half-hour or forty-five minutes, but that's all. Come on, Wade, think."

"Babe, I don't want to sound pessimistic, but that is a job for professionals or it can be a disaster."

"Okay, let's call a professional."

"Chandler, think about what you're saying. Nobody's going to come pick up a piano without an appointment."

"Wade, I want this piano. I've got to get it moved." My voice was pleading. "Hold on," I said. I reached in the back of the car, picked up the telephone book I kept on the floor and lifted it to the front. People asked why I had a telephone book in my car and I always answered, "I've got a phone, don't I?" I flipped through the pages, looking for movers, piano movers. As I looked, I said to Wade, "This is what I want you to do. Call around to see if you can get a U-Haul truck and see if John, Walter and Calvin are home. If they are, tell them you need their help moving a piano."

"Chandler, what are you doing? They don't know anything about moving pianos."

"I know that, Wade. But it's a chance we'll have to take. In the meantime, I'll try to get in touch with a professional mover and see if they have someone who can talk us through moving the piano. It'll be like talking to a 9-1-1 operator while administering CPR."

"Chandler, you get nuttier the longer I'm married to you."

"Will you do it, Wade?"

Reluctantly, he said, "Yeah, I'll do it."

"I think the address here is 2890 Montgomery. It's off Shaker Boulevard. My car will be in front. Call me back when you find the truck and the guys." Before I hung up, I said, "Hey, you've got to admit that there's never a dull moment with me around." I heard him chuckle and the phone go dead.

I ran back into the house to give a report. "Someone will be here to move it," I said to three of The Movers standing behind a table. Then I went back into the room with the piano and Mr. Denison, but he wasn't there. He must have been somewhere in the house, because I hadn't seen anyone leave while I was outside. I ran back to my car. I called four moving companies before someone answered. "Hi, my name is Chandler Webb and I need someone to help me . . . Yes, I need a piano moved. Could you do it for me today? . . . I thought not, but then could I ask a favor? . . . Could you coach amateurs on how to do it by telephone . . . No, I'm not kidding . . . This is an emergency and I need all the help I can get . . . They're not here yet, but hopefully they'll be here soon . . . It's a seven-foot 1959 Knabe, limited edition . . . Yes, the cabinet is made of mahogany . . . What type of building is it being moved from?" Looking up the drive to the house, I said, "A big Tudor with what seems like hundreds of rooms and hallways . . . Yes, I think the doorways are standard . . . Yes, it's on the first floor . . . You'll help? Thank you, sir . . . Okay, I'll call you back as soon as they get here. What's your name . . . Herman. Okay, Herman. Thank you."

I didn't know if Wade was trying to call me while I was on the phone. I paced outside the car waiting for the phone to ring. A minute went by, then two. If Wade couldn't get a truck, then the plan would die. The anticipation was killing me. I called him. The line was busy.

I quickly hung up, hoping he was calling me. The phone rang.

"Chandler, I've been trying to call back, but your phone's been busy." "I was talking to a mover, Wade. He's agreed to walk us through it over the phone. He told me the first thing to do is unscrew the legs. He said they should come off easily, so bring a screwdriver."

"What kind? What size?"

"I don't know, Wade. Bring'em all. He said that model is very heavy and we need some strong arms. Did you get the guys?"

"I got in touch with John and Walter, but Calvin wasn't home."

"That's okay. I think we can do it with the two of them. How about the truck?"

"I got that, too, Chandler."

"So, you'll be here soon?"

"Yeah. John's picking up the truck on his way and Walter will meet us. It should take everybody no more than thirty minutes."

My smile was enormous. We were about to pull off the biggest legal heist I'd ever been involved in. I once bought a solid silver platter at a garage sale for fifteen dollars because the seller thought it was silver plated, but this bargain had nervous adrenalin flowing through me.

I wouldn't relax until the piano was in my house. I sat in the car, waiting and thinking. I was going to give Wade the biggest kiss when he arrived. He had helped with little resistance. I thought, *Maybe he's mellowing*. I turned on the radio and slid low into the car seat, closing my eyes, attempting to recover some of the energy I had expended. My thoughts drifted as the easy sound of Joe Sample cooled my burning nerves. A noise was destroying the tranquility. When I opened my eyes, a truck was pulling into the driveway. It wasn't a U-Haul. It was a truck that had "AAA Piano Company, Sales, Moving and Restoration" on the side. My heart hesitated. That was the company on the card. They had come for *my* piano. I nervously fumbled with the car door handle that I had effortlessly opened thousands of times in the past. Upon getting out, I beat the truck up the drive as I ran into the house, panting. The Movers had packed up their operation and ignored my presence. They weren't who I wanted to see, anyway. I was looking for Mr. Denison. "Excuse me. Is Mr. Denison still here?" They all stared at me as if they had never seen a frantic black woman before. "Is he here!?" I insisted.

"I think he's upstairs," one of the old biddies volunteered.

"Mr. Denison," I yelled as I found the stairs. "Mr. Denison?"

"I'm in here."

I heard his voice, but because the upstairs was as filled with rooms as downstairs, I had no clue of where *here* was. "Where?"

"I'm in here. The master bedroom." Him saying the master bedroom was like someone telling me, 'I'm somewhere in Texas; find me.'

"Where's that?" I shouted.

A blond head poked out of a room before me. I ran toward him. "Mr. Denison, they're here. They've come for the piano."

"That's good. So, you'll be moving it out?"

"No! You don't understand. It's the company coming for it. The people who were supposed to be here earlier today. They're here now."

As I approached Mr. Denison, I hesitated before I said, "Are you going to let them have it?"

"You bought the piano."

"But I don't know if they put a deposit on the piano and if they did, then it's rightfully theirs."

"That's not necessarily so," he said, coming out of the room, heading to the first floor. I followed close behind. With his hands in his pants pocket, Mr. Denison skipped the steps with familiarity. At the bottom, he confidently walked toward a man wearing work boots, jeans and a dark navy t-shirt with muscles bulging through. His blue cap had the company name in white lettering on the front. He was talking to Frances.

As he approached the man, Mr. Denison extended his hand, announcing, "I'm Chuck Denison."

The man shook his hand. "How'ya doin? I'm George Arnanopolis."

"George, what can I do for you?"

"I'm here to pick up a piano. I believe it's a Knabe."

"Yes, but I have to inform you that it's been sold."

"I know. To us."

"No. I sold it to this woman about an hour ago. You were supposed to be here in the afternoon and when you didn't come and we were unable to get in touch with anyone, I took the liberty of accepting her offer."

"But Frances guaranteed me the piano. I've got the truck and crew with me."

"Did you leave a deposit?"

"No. But Frances knows that when I say I want an instrument, it's only a matter of picking it up and writing a check."

"I apologize, George, but Chandler's already paid me. Like I said, we tried to get in contact with you before I sold it. I have to leave tonight and I needed to tie-up everything before I left."

"This is real shitty. I mean, I've taken the time to come all the way here to find out—"

"Chandler, there's a truck in the drive. We can't get in." It was Wade. I hadn't noticed him come in. Mr. Denison and the piano mover looked at Wade with curious stares.

"Mr. Denison, this is my husband, Wade."

"Nice to meet you, Wade. I was just telling Mr. Arnanopolis—George—that unfortunately he got here a little too late to purchase the piano. I sold it to your wife."

The man from the piano company looked disgusted and like he wanted to punch somebody, but he kept his cool.

"Well, would you mind moving your truck so I can pull in?" Wade asked.

"Yeah. Sure. Just give me a minute," the piano man said, cutting Mr. Denison a look of angry defeat. The man turned on his heels and stomped out the door.

The wheels in my head were turning again. I wondered how much the piano man would charge to take the piano to my house. After all, he was the professional and he did come to move it, although it wouldn't be going where he expected. I caught him and explained what I needed. He looked at me with disbelief and said, "You want me to take the piano to your house?"

"Yes. For a price, of course. A reasonable price," I added.

"Lady, I just lost a good piano with great resale value and now you want me to move it for you?"

"Well, what does one have to do with the other? The move could at least pay for your travel, time, your crew and put gas in the truck. That's what business is all about, isn't it?"

"Where do we have to go?"

"About four miles from here."

"Is it a house?"

"Yes."

"First floor?"

"Yeah. So how much?"

He rubbed his hand on his thigh and looked over the yard. "Three hundred."

"Oh, come on! I had another company quote me two-fifty. You're trying to rob me."

"Like you did me?" He showed me a coy smirk.

"Look, I did nothing of the sort. I offered to buy the piano, not knowing that there was a prior offer for it. I just happened to be here at the right time."

"How much did you pay?"

"What?"

"How much did you give for it?"

"I don't think I have to disclose that information," I said.

"No you don't, but I thought I'd ask. What would it hurt for you to tell me? You got the piano. It's yours and there's nothing I can do about it other than make you an offer that hopefully you can't refuse."

I smiled at the piano man and thought, *This could be a fun game, although I'll never sell.* "Eight thousand."

His smirk became a full-blown grin. "So what would it cost me to take it off your hands?" The piano man was a businessman.

"What's your offer?"

"I'll give you ten for it. I can write the check right now. You've just made two thousand dollars."

I was grateful Wade wasn't standing there. He would have tried to make me take it. The piano man's offer was better than any stock market I could have invested in. But before Wade joined us, I wanted to stop the game. I had no intention of selling and as much as I was interested in the pursuit of business, I didn't want Wade to make the fun I was having become serious. There would have been no way he would have let me walk away from a five-thousand-dollar capital gain. He would have choked me right there on the spot. "I'm sorry, I can't part with it right now. It's perfect for me. So, can we agree that you'll move it for say, two-hundred and seventy-five?"

His grin immediately disappeared. He sighed, rubbing his thigh again. It must have been a habit of his. "Eleven."

"No. The answer is still no."

"Where's the address?" he said, dispirited.

I got a pen out of my purse and took the liberty of pulling a business card out of his shirt pocket. I wrote my address on it. I told him that my husband would stay while the piano was being moved onto the truck. I would be at the house waiting for them. I wanted Wade to follow so that they didn't make a getaway with the piano. After all, there was nothing on paper to say I existed.

I explained everything to Wade while Walter was standing with him.

"But Chandler, I've already gotten the truck. And how much is he going to charge?"

"Wade, he's a professional mover. You're the one who told me that we were taking a big chance to move it ourselves. So, this way we can relax, knowing a professional is handling it. And if you take the truck back now, you'll probably get most of your money back, if not all of it." I looked at Walter. "Walter, if you follow John back to U-Haul, I'll fix dinner for everybody tonight. Grilled swordfish and my famous herbed corn and Caesar salad." Then I planted every man's weakness in his mind. "And ice cold beer."

"You're nothing but a tease, Chandler."

"That's not fair. When have you ever known me not to deliver, Walter? Teases don't deliver. I plan to satisfy you." Walter had me all wrong. I wasn't a tease, just a big flirt. Wade had taught me how.

"Okay, Chandler," Walter said. "I'll tell John what's happening. We'll meet you back at your house." John sat inside the truck, waiting for the big job. I had wanted Kennedy to meet him before she met Cornelius, but everything worked out for the best.

"I'll see you later, guys," I said, giving Wade a kiss with plenty of tongue action. As I walked away, I heard Walter say, "Wade, *mannn*, that is one intense woman."

* * * * *

Appreciating that the piano was still with me, I walked into the den, gave the Knabe an admiring stare, and lovingly caressed my bundle of mahogany and ivory. I brushed my hand across the top, leaving a small circle clean of dust. *I'll dust tomorrow*, I thought. I sat on the bench and opened the lid. Tapping the middle C several times with my thumb, I spontaneously started playing Moon River. I hadn't played for about two months, and my fingers and mind weren't cooperating with one another. I closed the lid and gently stroked one of the legs, feeling the detail. I whispered, "Some things are worth the trouble." The sun had disappeared behind Mr. and Mrs. Baines' house. I put on my jacket and walked to the corner to mail my letter to Lorelei.

When I got back, I took a hot shower and called Stevie Michelle. "I made an ass of myself with Wade tonight," I said, lying across my bed with only a towel wrapped around me.

"Well, you're bound to do that a few times before he's out of your system. What you need, Chandler, is something else to concentrate on, something else to distract you, like another husband."

"You're crazy, Stevie Michelle. And I know you're serious, too."

"No, I'm not. This year I'm concentrating on our independence."

"Woman, do you know what you're saying?"

"Yes, I do. I'm saying screw the male gender and let's get on with life."

"I'm with you on that, especially when I'm horny," I said.

"Oh, that too shall pass," Stevie Michelle said.

"That's it! I know there's an imposter on the other end of this phone. Stevie Michelle, did you fall, hit your head and now you've got amnesia?"

"No. I've just— How do you say it— Evolved," she said so calmly and convincingly.

"Yeah, until you get horny, too."

"Well, Chandler, it's like being an alcoholic; take it one day at a time."

"I don't know why I talk to you, woman," I said.

"Because you love me?"

"Probably. But anyway, it's past my bedtime and I'll talk to you later."

"Okay. Sweet dreams."

CHAPTER 4

(Chandler)

I stood at the tiny window in my small office at work. I had tried to make it as personal, yet as spacious as I could, but I still felt trapped. Creative Solutions wasn't where I wanted to be, but I needed the money and the health benefits. The six girls I supervised were as motivated as a chef in an automotive repair shop. But who would motivate me first, so I could motivate them?

I would sit, daydream and put off assignments until I couldn't put them off any longer, only to do enough that was acceptable. It had become almost impossible to hide my discontent with work. And my boss, a woman, was another minus in my dilemma. I craved for the kitchen and all that went with it. The expertise of keeping the eggs from curdling in a béarnaise; developing a crust for a pan-seared tuna or halibut; creating a dessert that would be my trademark, were all apparatuses of my contentment. I could smell the garlic, basil and nutmeg. I loved the scent of fresh chopped herbs and ground spices. I couldn't pretend. I ached, itched, hungered, thirsted and starved for what felt as natural as breathing. I needed to work with a Henkel instead of a BIC pen.

"We've got to get this report over to marketing by the afternoon. Do you have the figures?" Julie Macklin, the boss, asked as she barged into my office. She was in her early thirties and was sure she would be president of the company one day. She was aggressive, a know-it-all, invincible and on a mission, and none of those characteristics were a problem until she invaded my space.

"You asked for those late yesterday. I haven't gotten to it yet. It's only ten o'clock. I had to finish the—"

"This takes priority, Chandler. I told you that yesterday."

"I don't remember you saying the word 'priority', Julie, but if you say you said it, then you said it. Give me an hour and I'll have the figures for you." It would have taken me twenty minutes maximum to get it done, but I wasn't going to let her know that.

"If I'm not in my office, just put it on my desk."

I mumbled, "Yes'em boss," as she flipped her hair and walked out. I knew she was only doing her job, the one she lived for and loved so much. I was the rebel, and an angry one. I leaned over my desk, picked up my BIC and began creating a recipe using fiddlehead ferns, morel mushrooms, and lots of garlic and butter.

* * * * *

Activity in the mall was slow and lazy as Kennedy and I walked, my arm inside hers. "You know, Chandler, I was lucky finding Cornelius."

"I don't think luck had anything to do with it. It was your destiny and his. He needed someone like you to love and vice versa. You two have a quiet kind of relationship. No pressures of being the best or having the best, or being envious of who has the best. I wanted a relationship like that with Wade, but I guess we were both competitive and guilty of eccentricities. We worked hard to maintain our habits. Right now I'd pay big bucks to have the marriage you and Cornelius have."

"Oh Chandler, you know better than that. We're sisters, but that's as far as our personalities cross. You've always been outgoing. The standard—the norm—is not normal for you. I had a dream the other night where you had taken the baby on vacation with you. Instead of going to Disney World to ride the Teacup and listen to *It's a Small World After All*, you had him on an island, strapped to your chest, above a boat, parasailing, while you sang, *Reaching for the Sky*, by Peabo Bryson. I think before I went to bed that night I ate half of that nectarine cobbler you brought me, so my dreams were a little wild. In other words, big sister, you will not be a typical aunt and I'm looking forward to it. Cornelius won't understand, but he'll get with the program sooner or later."

"Do we know what we're having?"

"No. And Cornelius and I have decided we don't want to know until the good Lord shows us. That's part of the excitement. Besides, we don't care."

I touched Kennedy's belly. *She's small for seven months*, I thought. But what did I know? She was healthy. The doctor said the baby was healthy and I was waiting to be an aunt. It was like waiting for a soufflé to rise.

"What about names?"

"Alexandria if it's a girl or Alexander if it's a boy."

"Either way, Alex, hunh?"

"Yes."

"No Cornelius junior?"

"Chandler, please. I love my husband, but his name stops with him. He understands. So how have you been coping with the single life?"

"Hey, let's get ice cream," I said, somewhat dragging Kennedy by the arm to the stand.

"Chandler, are you going to answer me?"

"Kennedy, I don't know how to answer that because I don't know yet. I've been too busy to think about it or make an assessment."

"You don't want to answer me?"

"It's not that. I just want this time with you to be on the upbeat. We're shopping and talking about a new member of the family, and then you bring up my dismal life. I don't think it's the time. Maybe one night when I can't sleep and you're up raiding the refrigerator, but not now. What flavor do you want?" I asked, looking at the waitress behind the ice cream stand, wondering how much they paid her to wear that ridiculous uniform. She looked like a candy striper with a bad home perm that resembled straw.

"Do they have chunky monkey?" Kennedy asked.

"Whoa. You *are* pregnant!" I said.

The waitress said, "No, but we have chocolate chip or chocolate, chocolate nugget."

"I'll have the chocolate, chocolate nugget," Kennedy said.

"Whoa. One or two scoops!?" I asked.

"Just one."

"That's good. I was going to ask where you put the suicide note. Go ahead, give that baby a chocolate rush."

"Chandler, don't make me laugh. My stomach moves funny when I laugh. I don't know how people with big bellies twelve months out of the year do it."

"I'll have a plain old-fashioned scoop of butter pecan, please. See, I'm not so eccentric. Could you top that scoop with a couple cherries, too."

Kennedy's belly, as she held onto it, jiggled under her top. I started laughing, too. We sat on the bench across from the ice cream stand, and then there was silence. That kind of silence where it felt like deja vu. It was the silence when one of us would reveal an inner thought—a personal inner thought. A thought when once revealed, the person you revealed it to would understand, or there was no reason to reveal it.

"I'm scared, Chandler."

"About what?"

"About being a mother. I have these dreams sometimes where the baby slips out of my hands while I'm bathing him and he drowns. I try to pull him out of the water, but he keeps slipping. I've had that one a number of times. Then there's the one where one minute he's in the car seat and when I look into the rearview mirror, he's gone."

"Is it always a boy when you dream?"

"Yes. But what does that have to do with anything?"

"Nothing. I just wanted to know." I looked into my little sister's face. "You still don't know how to eat ice cream without dripping it." It ran down her chin. I took my napkin and dabbed at the chocolate. "Don't worry, Kennedy. We had this conversation, I think about seven months ago, and look how well you've done so far. You're healthy and so is the baby. You're a good mommy already. Think of it this way—you may not know what to do or how to be, but you know what not to do and how not to be. Just remember the examples we experienced and do the opposite. I'm in the same dilemma. I've got to be a good aunt. I think about that, too. I want to be fair to the baby and myself. I can see me over compensating, which will not be good for either one of us. We're going to do okay. I know it. And about those dreams; I think you're calling for them. Don't let them prevail. Have pleasant thoughts and think of pleasant smells when you go to bed. Then your dreams will be pleasant, too. I promise you." I didn't know what I was saying, but my concept was worth a try and I thought Kennedy would buy it. So, if she believed me, then I believed the bad dreams would stop.

Kennedy took my hand and placed it on her stomach. "Can you feel it?" she said.

I could. I felt our baby move. "It's all that chocolate you sent down there. He's doing somersaults."

"Don't make me laugh," Kennedy demanded. "So, if I asked you to make me a German chocolate cake, would you? I thought the ice cream would stop my craving, but it hasn't. I wish you'd go home right now and make it."

"We're going to have to commit you to a fat farm once this baby is born."

"Oh, Chandler, please. The baby's asking for it, too. He's been wanting it since yesterday afternoon. And I've only gained twenty-seven pounds. The doctor said I shouldn't start worrying until I go over thirty-five."

"There are some rewards to being pregnant. If I gained thirty-five pounds, it would be all in the ass."

"So when can I expect it?"

"By Saturday. I'll make it for you by Saturday."

Kennedy tried to reach over to hug me, but she had a package in her lap and her body had become large and cumbersome. I met her the rest of the way.

She looked down in her lap and on the floor around us. "Chandler, I can't believe all this stuff you bought. When I have my baby shower the only thing we'll need to request are donations to his college fund. Everything else is here. I think you went a little overboard with the daily journal. He probably won't be able to write until he's about seven or eight."

"That's not for him, silly; it's for you. The day he's born, I want you to start logging activities—things that occur."

"Are you crazy? I'm not going to have time for that."

"Yes, you will. Just a few lines, Kennedy. It'll be fun. Then we can look back in it later. You know. Writing down his first smile, the first time he follows you with his eyes, with sound."

"Chandler, that's what baby books are for."

"No. This is different. You also write down your feeling to the things he does. It'll be fun. Really!"

"And I suppose you keep a journal, big sister?"

"Actually, I do."

"Really?"

"Yeah. I started about two years ago. I got turned onto the idea by one of the girls at the institute. She wrote down everything that happened each day, from how she felt, to what she cooked, to how it tasted. I got a diary and wrote in it every night before I went to bed. It became a habit and now every night it's a part of getting ready for bed. I wish I had started it as soon as I learned to write."

"You're really serious about this, aren't you?"

"Yeah. Just try it. Okay?"

"Okay." Kennedy stared at her feet. "I think we'd better go now. My feet are swelling. I can feel my shoes bursting at the seams."

I looked down and her ankles were larger than I had ever remembered them. "Now you've finally got legs."

"Don't make me laugh, Chandler!"

I took Kennedy and her packages to her house. When I got home, Wade's car was parked in front. It was eight-twenty. What was he still doing there? All the lights from the basement to the second floor were on. I guessed since he didn't live there anymore, or pay utilities, he had no respect for energy conservation. Walking through the side door, I cut off the light to the basement. When I walked into the kitchen, I could hear voices. I knew Wade's, but I didn't recognize the other. There was a half empty bottle of wine on the counter. I stared at it for a few seconds and then went into the living room. Wade and the real estate agent were sitting on the lone piece of living room furniture that I had retained in the divorce. They looked cozy on the sofa. I cleared my throat and Wade looked up. Beverly, the agent, was next to him on the sofa. "Hey, Chandler," he said. "Good news. We got an offer for the house tonight. Beverly says everything'll be written up tomorrow. Isn't this great?"

"Are you celebrating?" I asked, my tone and mood teetering on annoyed.

"Well, we were waiting for you to get home so we could tell you the good news, and I thought a glass of wine would be nice."

"Then, if you're buying, please buy me a glass," I said.

Wade quickly got up from the sofa and followed me into the kitchen. He knew I was agitated and he didn't want a scene.

"How dare you have me come home and see you having a private party. How dare you take it upon yourself to open *my* wine. If there's an offer on the house, you two could have phoned me—from her place or yours, Wade. I don't care, but to see you here, acting like some animal in heat, I can't—"

"Chandler, don't start any bullshit. It's a friendly glass of wine."

"Don't tell me what to do, mister. I want you to put the glass you have in your hand on the counter and tell Ms. Thang in there that the bar is closed and you're taking the party to your place."

"What the hell are you so upset about?"

Through clinched teeth, I whispered, "I don't expect for you to get it. I don't care if you get it. Just get out and leave the keys." Wade sat the glass on the stove and dropped the keys next to it. He was still so divinely handsome and I still loved him. I had to stop loving him or I wasn't going to survive. I don't know what he said to Beverly, but she walked out with Wade without saying a word to me.

I went around the house turning off lights and crying. My negative, paranoid imagination percolated. Getting rid of the house was the best thing. I hoped the offer was good and within forty-five to sixty days I could start over, like the new moon.

Chapter 5

(Lorelei)

Three was such a beautiful child when he was sleeping. The first night in the new house had him a little frightened. Standing with my arms folded and one leg crossed over the other, I leaned against the door jamb and stared at him as he slept. The light from the hall illuminated his room precisely so I could watch him. Sometimes he was the strangest child. He didn't want a nightlight in his room because he said the monsters could see where he was, but at the same time he was afraid of the dark. As a compromise, I turned the light on in the hall, leaving his door open. I had hoped he'd sleep through the night.

Although he was eight, Three hadn't adapted well to being away from Walter. He had asked for, and talked about, his daddy everyday since our move to Little River. Aunt Ruby said he'd get better, but standing there, looking at him, it had been his worst night. It had to be the new house. Aunt Ruby wanted us to stay with her a little longer, but she had taken care of enough children in her lifetime that weren't hers. Besides, everybody needed their space.

I rented a three-bedroom condominium—there were plenty of them in Little River since the new upswing of golf courses and tourists. I had hoped to make the condo a temporary dwelling, because Mrs. Donahue's house was for sale. It was a seven-bedroom, five-bath, deep red burgundy, brick house with stone trim and many, many windows. The backyard was covered with beautiful shades of pink and yellow roses that bloomed from late spring all the way past autumn. I had admired her house as a child and I wanted to buy it.

Topper wasn't a problem. She was self-sufficient—too self-sufficient. At thirteen, she was fixing meals and doing laundry for herself and Three, but I still felt they needed me to be readily available. I blew my sleeping son a kiss from across the room and went into Topper's bedroom.

"Hi, Mom."

"What you doin' awake, Topper?"

"I heard Three. Is he all right?"

"Yeah. Just a nightmare."

"Still missing Daddy, hunh?"

"He was gettin' better when we were at Aunt Ruby's, but tonight . . ."

"It's the new place, Mom, but once he goes to the pool and the game room, he'll be okay."

"How you doin'?" I asked, sitting on the bed next to her.

"Me? I'm fine. I think I made a new friend in school today."

"Oh, yeah? What's her name?"

"She's a he, Mom."

"Oh, yeah? Okay. Then what's *his* name?"

"Jimmy."

"He's in yo' class?" I asked, curious—no, nervous, about my daughter having a 'Jimmy' friend.

"No. He's a grade higher than me in the eighth. Oh, by the way, Mom, could you call me Olivia in public instead of Topper?"

What had gotten into my daughter? Not only did she not want to be called by a name that she had been called all her life, she's met a boy. If she was awake thinking about him, I had reason to be nervous. And he was a year older. It wasn't because she was my daughter, but Topper was a beautiful girl. As a baby, people would stop us to stare at her, commenting on how pretty she was. She got her nickname because when Walter would look at her, he'd say, "Lorelei, I don't think we can top her." And somehow we started calling her Topper. Olivia Antoinette Scott was her birth name and finally she wanted it to be acknowledged. She still looked like Topper to me.

"Well, I'll try, but it ain't goin' to be easy. I mean, I been callin' you Topper for a very long time."

"I know, Mom, but please try. And it's 'is not', Mom, not 'it ain't'."

"Okay, *Olivia*," I said. "I'll do my best, although it *is not* going to be easy." We giggled. "I think you need to get some sleep. School tomorrow."

"Mom, when you asked me how I'm doing, I said fine, but I kinda miss Daddy, too. I tried making that sausage omelet this morning like he makes and although I did it exactly the way he does, it just didn't taste the same. Three said so, too."

"You probably left a spice out or didn't put enough in. Maybe you didn't use enough salt or pepper."

"Mom, I'm telling you, I'll never make it as well as Daddy, and that omelet is my favorite breakfast."

"You'll be with him soon, so he'll be able to make it for you." I looked into my daughter's beautiful shiny eyes. The nightlight caught them just right. I had been told that she looked like me, but Topper was Walter, and Walter was her, and I loved them both. "Give me a hug," I said, reaching for Topper, surrounding not only her physical presence, but also her vanishing innocence and youth. Topper easily slid out from under the covers and wrapped her perfectly slender arms around my neck. I kissed her cheek. "I love you, baby."

"I love you, too, Mom."

Patting her back, I said, "Get some sleep. Everything's goin' to be fine."

"When Three and I go to see Daddy, are you coming?" she asked.

"Topper, I can't go. Yo' father and I are divorced."

"*Duhhh*, Mom. I know that, but I thought you could come and spend some time with Miss Chandler."

"It just so happens that Miss Chandler is comin' here. As a matter of fact, I'm goin'ta write her tonight and ask if she'll come aroun' the time you and Three will be goin' to Cleveland. That way she can ride back with you on the plane. I'll worry just that much less."

"*Jeez*, Mom, I can take care of me and Three."

"I know. But it ain't you and Three that I'm worried about. I'll feel better. That's all." Looking at the clock on the table, I said with a firm tone, "All right, young lady, snuggle into bed. We'll talk some more later." I got up and helped her with the blankets. "Sleep tight. Don't let the bed bugs bite," I said, instantly wondering where that saying came from. As I thought about it, it wasn't pleasant talking about bed bugs. I shrugged away my thoughts and said, "Good night, baby."

"Good night." As I reached the doorway, Topper said, "In your letter, say hello to Miss Chandler for me."

"Okay. I will."

Topper always did like Chandler. They would talk and giggle about things that they wouldn't share. Topper used to go shopping with Chandler and once she came home with a beautiful bouquet of flowers. I thought they were a gift for me, but Topper said they were for her room, because, "Miss Chandler said every girl should have fresh flowers around. They help her feel pretty." I think Topper was ten then.

When I walked into the hall, I realized that everything in the condominium was either gray or beige. The carpet was gray and the walls were a shade or two lighter than the carpet, but gray just the same. I walked down the gray steps into the gray dining room, through the gray hall into the beige kitchen. At the table, I started my letter to my friend that I missed very much.

Sunday, October 6, 1996 10:00 p.m.

Dear Chandler:

You won't believe the weekend I've had. We moved into the condominium. It's another adjustment for Three. Topper seems to be doing okay, but she misses Walter, too— and, of course, right now Oceanna is in her own world at Spelman. Tonight Topper asked that I start calling her Olivia. My daughter is growing up, I'm afraid. She also told me that she has a new friend. A boyfriend, Chandler. His name is Jimmy. I'm going to lose my mind watching my children grow up.

Anyway, things are starting to fall into place. How long have I been here now? Six months and the kids and I are still adapting. Work at Kingston Plantation resort is boring. I don't even like the name. Here we are in the 90's and white people still want to have plantations. There's the Rutherford Plantation, the MacDougall Plantation, the Richards Plantation, the Denton Plantation, etc. But anyway, I won't get into that except to say the accounting department at Kingston is so rigid that I actually looked in a book the other day for a reference. In other words, they are strictly by the book. (Smile)

I might as well tell you what I'm thinking of doing. There is a house here—old Mrs. Donahue's house—that's for sale. It has seven bedrooms and five baths, and I'm thinking about buying it and turning it into a bed and breakfast. The income would help pay the mortgage and before you say I'm crazy, right now it's a thought. I can't explain it, but things are different in this town. Maybe it's me or maybe it's just like they say, that everything must change.

My Uncle Simon is finally retiring and my brothers, Manny and Aussie, are going to run the shop along with their construction company: Garris Construction. They've got fifteen employees. Not too shabby. Mike Ray, my other brother, is running the satellite office in Atlanta. Development is pretty big there, especially since the Olympics. I can't wait to maybe take a weekend to go visit. It'll have to be a weekend, seeing as I don't have any vacation yet.

I can't wait to see you, Chandler. In your letter, you said that if I needed anything to let you know. It's not big, but it is a favor. I was hoping that you could come down here around the time for Topper and Three to go to Cleveland to visit Walter, so that they can ride back with you on the plane. Knowing that you are with them would make me happy. They're leaving on the 26th. I know it's a little later in the month than you said you wanted to come, but you'll still be home for Thanksgiving. Give it some thought, okay?

There have been nights that I just want to sit and talk with you. That's kind of hard long distance, but I think of you all the time and how we used to dig out the old albums, listening to memories and sipping wine. Walter and Wade would leave and go God-knows-where. They would come back and we would still be sitting there singing and laughing, sipping wine. I wish you were coming tomorrow. It's been raining all week and that hasn't helped my mood any. I know what you are thinking, and no, I'm not depressed. I'm just lonely. Even with family here, I'm lonely. If it wasn't for being distracted with Topper and Three, I'd spend a lot of time thinking about my future, but for now, they are my future. And yes, not knowing what the future is, is scary, but it would be scarier if we didn't have one—and we do have one, Chandler. You were asking about bachelors in your letter. Well, if I find any, I'll have to keep the first one for myself. (Smile)

I'm going to call you in the next week or so. For two reasons: First, to tell you what fun things I've set up for your visit and most of all to hear your voice. Maybe we can get Stevie Michelle in on the conversation. That would be hilarious. Tell her I'm thinking of her also.

Kisses, kisses,

Lorelei

P.S. Topper says hi.

The rain tapped and the wind was breathing at the window as I folded my letter. Getting up from the table, I closed the window and inhaled deeply. Back at the table, I stuffed my letter in the envelope. I thought that it would have been nice to have a friend like Chandler in Little River. I turned off the light.

Chapter 6

(Lorelei)

It rained so long and so hard, I anticipated Noah's ark floating by, but finally after four days, the sun was shining. Although Aunt Ruby had a clothes dryer, she still occasionally hung clothes outdoors. She was taking them off the line, folding and putting them into the basket, as I walked into the yard. "Some old habits never die," I shouted.

"How you feelin', honey? I was just thinkin' about you," Aunt Ruby said. "You got the kids with you?"

"They gettin' out of the car." I started helping her with the clothes. "You would rather stand out here hangin' clothes than usin' the dryer?"

"There's nothin' like clothes after they done hung in the fresh air and sun, Lorelei. And besides, what else I got to do? All the kids are practically grown now. I just need to stop a squabble now and then, and fix lunches here and there, but overall . . ."

"Hi Auntie," Topper and Three squealed.

"There they are," Aunt Ruby said, grabbing both Topper and Three, hugging and kissing them. I watched as they wiped their faces. Aunt Ruby still had wet kisses.

"Mom, I'm hungry," Three announced.

Before I could say anything, Aunt Ruby was giving instructions for food in the kitchen. "I fried some fish. It's in the oven. There's string beans and potatoes, too. And Topper, slice you and Three some cornbread. That fish was caught this mornin'. Simon brought back a whole mess of'em, so help yo'self. There's plenty."

I watched my children disappear into the house.

Looking after them with admiration, Aunt Ruby said, "They outstandin' babies, Lorelei."

"They ain't babies no more, Aunt Ruby. I wish they were."

"Naw, you don't. Watchin'em grow is the best part. Watchin' you and the boys grow was the best time for me. I'm glad I had the chance."

"Too bad My Mother didn't feel that way." While I spoke, I wasn't sure why my thoughts of her surfaced. I hadn't regarded My Mother for a long time and I mentioned her to my children only once. I felt that was enough. Regretting that I spoke of her, I watched Aunt Ruby's happy expression sink. "I'm sorry, Aunt Ruby. I didn't mean to—"

"Oh, that's all right. You ain't done nothin'. Whether you know it or not, there ain't a day that goes by that I don't think about Octavia. I always have. I used to could look forward to her letters, but when you turned eighteen, even the money in the blank sheets of paper stopped. They just stopped, Lorelei. I don't know if it was a coincidence or if somethin' happened. I wanted to see her just once before I died. I wouldn't ask her any questions; I'd just look at her. Stare at her for hours if I could. From what I can remember, you two identical." Aunt Ruby dropped the clothespins she had in her hand into the bag that was hanging on the line and softly touched my hair. "And I do try to remember."

I was thankful for Three's interruption. "Aunt Ruby, when I'm finished eating," he said as he ran out of the house, "can I have some ice cream? Please?"

The exuberance that had escaped her returned when she looked into my son's face. She said, "How you know I got ice cream?"

"I saw it in the freezer. Topper got some ice out and there was the ice cream. Strawberry! Strawberry's my favorite."

"Yes, you can have ice cream, but you gotta finish yo' food."

"Thanks." Three ran back toward the house.

"Just one scoop," I shouted after him. "Aunt Ruby?" I timidly said.

"Oh, I know that tone," she said, smiling at me. "What is it, baby?"

"Remember when you tried to give me my inheritance and I told you to keep it 'cause I didn't need it?"

"Oh, Lord. You tellin' me you want it? Well, it's about time. The last will me and Simon had done, I made sure the lawyer put in there that money belongs to you. And feelin' that you was never goin'ta ask for it, I also put in there that if you wasn't aroun', it was to go into a trust for yo' kids. I mean, after all, you never know what will happen. Only the Lord knows for sure."

"Aunt Ruby, you the most amazin' woman. You a saint. I love you so much." I hugged her tight. I could feel the fragility of her aging body. I needed her to be on earth forever.

"So, what you goin' to do with it?" she asked in a canny tone.

"Well . . ."

"C'mon, tell'ya old Aunt Ruby."

"I'm thinkin' about startin' a bed and breakfast. You know, they very popular now, more so than hotels."

Aunt Ruby's baffled look confirmed she wasn't enthusiastic. 'With all the hotels aroun' here now, you think that's a good idea? I mean, the few motels left are havin' a tough time."

"That's just it, Aunt Ruby. They havin' a tough time 'cause they ain't modernized themselves. What people want now is service, not just some place to sleep. The hotels offer service and so do bed and breakfast establishments, just with a personal touch. Those motel rooms are just that, *rooms*."

"Where you goin' to have this place?"

"I want to buy old Mrs. Donahue's house. The location is perfect. Right on Highway 17, it can't be missed, bein' along that strip of beach shops and restaurants." My excitement and optimism grew as I talked to Aunt Ruby.

"Honey, that sounds like a lot of work. People comin' and goin' all the time. You'll never have no time to yo'self or for the children."

"But just think of the people I'll meet. They'll be from all over the country. That's an education within itself. And I know you'll help me."

"Oh, no. Me and my Simon goin' to enjoy our golden years. I'm finished workin'. We thinkin' about sellin' this place and gettin' us one of them condos, like you got, and doin' a little travelin'." Aunt Ruby couldn't hold back her smile.

"But won't you help me get started?"

"If I'm in town. I'm goin' to be like them white folks we see all through Myrtle Beach. Wrinkled and barely able to walk, but they enjoyin' the little life they got left."

Aunt Ruby didn't have a wrinkle in her face, and the silver hair on her head almost looked out of place. She and Uncle Simon had taken good care of each other.

"Okay. Would you at least look at the place with me?"

"I know you didn't think I was goin' to let you see it by yo'self, now did you?"

"No. But I thought I'd ask anyway. When's a good time for you?" I asked. "I'm goin' to call today for an appointment. I'm so excited,

Aunt Ruby. I'm doin' this on my own. I don't have to worry about what Walter thinks or wants."

"Oh, you think about it all right." Aunt Ruby's point-blank words were impacting. "You ain't got to listen to what he thinks, but *ohhh* how he still talks to you."

My smile let Aunt Ruby know that what she said, I understood.

"It's one thing to be divorced," she said, "but it's another to be spiritually and emotionally separated. He's still a main artery to yo' heart, Lorelei.'

"It's not like that, Aunt Ruby. Honest!"

"You keep tellin' yo'self that. One day it could come true, but I just don't think so. Not to bring up the past, especially one not so pretty, but I know what kind of love you had for him to put yo'self and the family in the straits that you did. Yo' reputation was tarnished and the respect for this family was jeopardized. You loved him that much then and you love him now."

"After two decades, you still refer to Walter as *him*," I said, chuckling.

"But, that don't mean I ain't got respect for'im. He's the father of my grandnieces and nephew, and he takes good care of'em. It's a shame to see twenty years flushed." Aunt Ruby sighed.

"I don't think of our life together as flushed. We got three children and had a good marriage when it was good. But if there ain't no trust, you can't have a decent life together."

"After twenty years, Lorelei, what is there not to trust? You never told me why you divorced'im. But since we on the subject, I wanna know. You just called me up one day, tellin' me, 'Aunt Ruby, Walter and I'm gettin' divorced.' I didn't believe you. Say I'm nosey, think anything you like, but I want you to tell me what was so bad that you gave up the man you love."

It may have sounded ridiculous to the rest of the world, but Walter's distrust hurt me. I would have never jeopardized our trust, or our marriage, but he accused me of stealing and that hurt worse than anything else he could have said or done. "It was the idea that he didn't trust me after all the years we spent together, Aunt Ruby."

"That ain't no answer, Lorelei."

With a direct stare, I bellowed, "He accused me of embezzlin' money from the company. All right!? I ain't never stole nothin', Aunt Ruby. And if I was goin' to steal, it wouldn't be from my family. He might as well have slapped my face or thrown me in front of a bus, 'cause that's what his accusin' felt like."

"And you hurt so bad that you couldn't accept an apology and move on?"

"That's just it, he didn't apologize and I couldn't live with feelin' he thought of me that way. I had taken care of the books for Scott and Son for over sixteen years, and all of a sudden I would start takin' money—what, from myself? There ain't nothin' I *needed* money for that I didn't have money for. Walter took good care of us. It hurt, Aunt Ruby. I was hurt enough to feel that there was nothin' left between us." I blinked back the tears. Aunt Ruby got one of the dish towels from the folded laundry and handed it to me. I dotted at my eyes.

"You may be hurt, but you also still in love. I think I told you a long time ago that love is stronger than pride, Lorelei."

"And so what if it is!? We divorced and that's that. It don't matter no more. Walter has gone on with his life and I'm tryin' to get on with mine. Now, let's change the subject. *Pleeez.*"

Aunt Ruby moved the clothespin bag down the line, unpinning a sheet. "That's fine with me. What you wanna talk about?" she asked. I helped her fold the sheet.

"Oh, nothin' in particular. And I'm sorry if I got a little huffy."

"Lorelei, nothin' means more to me than the happiness of my family. And I tried to make sure of that when you and yo' brothers were children. But I ain't got no control over yo' happiness no more. What I'm tryin' to say is, I don't want to think about life without Simon and if the good Lord decides to take him away before He summons me, I can accept that better than havin' to accept Simon walkin' away."

A breeze fluttered the clothes on the line. The hair at the nape of my neck stood as I thought of Walter and how Aunt Ruby explained losing someone you love. She was right; I would never accept it. "I think I'll get some ice cream, Aunt Ruby. How about you; you want some?"

"Sure, why not? But make mine two scoops."

Chapter 7

(Lorelei)

"Hello, Chandler."

"Oh, my goodness, Lorelei? I was just on the phone with Stevie Michelle and she asked how you were doing. I told her instead of asking me, to give you a call. Oh my goodness. It's so good to hear your voice."

"I finally got you. I been tryin' for a couple days, but I didn't leave any messages, so it ain't no fault of nobody's but mine that you didn't call me back."

"What's going on, girlfrien'?" Chandler asked. "I have your letter and I've already made plane reservations, but I'm going to need your help with the hotel."

"No way, Chandler. You goin' to stay with me. I'll have Three and Topper double while you here. Topper'll have a fit, but she'll get over it."

"Really, Lorelei, I want a hotel. I want to be waited on hand and foot for a little while. Like when you leave the bed unmade, someone will come in and make it for you. I want to be able to order tea and a croissant, and they'll bring it to me."

"Well, if you want all of that, then it sounds like a job for the Hilton or Marriott. The only thing I could be able to guarantee is the tea and croissant, and that's on Sunday mornin'."

"Lorelei, my goodness, you've only been home, how long?—six or seven months and your accent is thicker than ever."

"You think so?"

"It's thicker than the pineapple milkshakes I used to make for you."

"It's funny you should mention those milkshakes. I wanted one yesterday, but I didn't know how to make it."

"It's easy. Got a pencil?"

"Hold on." I ran to the other side of the kitchen, looking in drawers for a pencil and notepad. "Okay, I got it," I said into the phone.

"It's real simple, Lorelei. First take either fresh pineapple or canned, but you know I prefer fresh over anything else. Put about a half cup into a blender, add about a cup of orange juice and blend until smooth. Then add a half teaspoon of vanilla extract and keep adding vanilla ice cream and blending until the shake is the thickness you want. If it's not sweet enough, put in a little powdered sugar. I know how you like sweet drinks."

"That's it?"

"That's it. I told you it was easy."

"I'm goin' to treat myself tonight. I used to drink Coke floats all the time until you started makin' those shakes for me."

"And if you really want to treat yourself, turn it into an adult drink by adding a little rum," Chandler said, laughing with that familiar sharp, broken sound I remembered so well.

"It sounds like you right here, Chandler. So close that if I could, I'd hop in my car and drive to see you."

"I wish I was that close. How's the weather there?"

"Sixty-five and sunny today, but tomorrow's only supposed to be in the fifties."

"It's forty here today and gloomy, so your sixty-five would feel like the tropics. Enough about the weather. Everything else okay?"

"Yeah. I guess. Remember I wrote you about the house I want to buy?"

"Hunh huh."

"Well, my Aunt Ruby and I are goin' to see it tomorrow. Chandler, all I can say is I'm so excited."

"So you're intent on this bed and breakfast thing, hunh? I was hoping you'd come back to Cleveland."

"You serious?" I asked, not knowing any way I could go back.

"Why not?"

"Why don't you come to South Carolina?"

There was a pause before Chandler said, "I don't know why. There definitely isn't anything holding me here. I hate my job. The house is sold. I've got about forty-five days to find someplace to live and most of all, I don't have anyone in my life to stay for. Kennedy and the baby maybe, but I'm only the aunt." Chandler seemed to be talking to herself rather than to me. "Remind me to give it some serious thought when I'm down there. I've been upper north, mid east, far west, to the islands, but I've never been to South Carolina. Yes," she said, her voice concrete with her thoughts, "remind me to take a good look at South Carolina while I'm there."

"Okay, 'cause I decided that while you down here, we goin' to spend a couple days in Hilton Head. It'll be a mini vacation for me, too. I thought Saturday and Sunday would be good. We could leave early Saturday morning. It's about a three- or four-hour drive from here."

"I've heard that's a nice place."

"This'll be my first time, too. So we can experience it together. Aunt Ruby said she'd take care of Topper and Three while I'm gone."

"All right. You've got a deal." Chandler yelled into the phone, "South Carolina bound, I am! I'm really starting to feel good about this trip. Thanks, Lorelei."

"Hey, this is as much for me as it is for you, Chandler. So, when will you be here?"

"My plane lands at the Myrtle Beach airport at twelve-thirty-six in the afternoon on Tuesday, the nineteenth."

"Damn, Chandler. I'll be at work, but I think the hotels have shuttles for pickup. I'll call to make sure. It's hard for me to take time off, bein' new. But I'll see you as soon as I get off."

"Don't rush. I'll want to go to the hotel and rest anyway."

"Hey, let's get Stevie Michelle on the phone," I said. Stevie Michelle and I weren't as close as me and Chandler, but I missed talking with that horny toad of a woman with all her craziness.

"Okay. Hold on. I hope I can do this right." Chandler clicked the line and it went silent. A few seconds later I heard, "Hello." It was Stevie Michelle. I'd recognize that voice anywhere.

"Oh, cut the sexy voice," I said. "It's only me."

"Lorelei!!?"

"Yeah."

Then Chandler said, "We're on three-way."

"Chandler!?" Stevie Michelle screeched.

"You got it. The one and only."

Then the three of us attempted to talk at once. "Hold it," I said. "We got to take turns. Okay, Stevie Michelle, you first."

"This is fantastic. You know miss bossy Chandler told me to call you and I was going to, really. Because, you know, Nelson is in Atlanta where Oceanna is. He's attending Morehouse and I thought they might want to get together. You know, someone from home."

"My brother Mike Ray is there, too, workin," I said.

"Stevie Michelle," Chandler interjected, "listen to that accent."

"Yeah, I hear it. Can't miss it. That drawl is heavy, man. Goes on forever."

"Y'all go to hell."

"Hear her, Stevie Michelle? *Y'aallll* go to hell". Our harmonious laughter was a musical trio. The sound jarred memories of us in the park, learning to rollerblade and Stevie Michelle skating straight into a pond; and the time Chandler was making pina coladas for us at her house, the blender lid came off and her kitchen smelled of coconut milk for a week, not to mention it took that long to get it off the walls and ceiling; and the night the three of us dressed in black clothes to go steal rocks from an empty lot for Chandler's rock garden. Chandler's plan—bright idea—was for us to drive into the lot, pretend we had a flat tire and jack up the car like we were changing the tire. So, I took the jack and the spare out, and leaned the tire against the side of my old station wagon. Then we put rocks inside the bed of the wagon. While we loaded the rocks, the spare that had been leaning against the side of the car rolled off the curb into the center of traffic. It rolled like a bowling ball down an alley, heading straight for a strike. The tire fell flat in front of a Camry. Luckily, the light was red. I laughed so hard, I almost wet my pants. Stevie Michelle went to get the runaway wheel and the guy's car that it stopped in front of tried to convince her to let him change the tire. He had no idea he was witness to a rock heist.

Stevie Michelle's voice came over the line. "You know, I'm a little upset with you two. How dare you make vacation plans without including me?"

"I told you, you were welcome to come," Chandler quipped.

"Yeah. C'mon," I reinforced.

"Seriously. I know I can come, but Nelson will be home for a few days around that time and I want to be here. Next time, I'll make the plans."

"Deal," I said.

Chandler mumbled, "Yeah. Right."

"As a matter of fact," I said, "why don't we try to make plans for the New Year? That's if nobody's got anything better to do. I mean, like be with the man of their dreams."

Chandler said, "I'll meet you December 31st. Just tell me where."

"I'll make the reservations and bring the champagne," Stevie Michelle chortled.

"Then it's a deal," I added.

Somehow the three of us were paddling in the exact same boat, navigating toward some semblance of completeness and happiness.

"Okay, listen up, girls," Chandler commanded. "I think we should spend the New Year in the Bahamas. What do you say?"

"Are you planning to ask Wade for his time-share?"

"Very funny, Stevie Michelle. Real funny," Chandler said. "We better make reservations now."

"You know the rule, whoever makes the suggestion makes the connection," Stevie Michelle claimed.

Chandler said, "Stevie Michelle, you are so lazy. And I think that's another one of your rules you've made up."

"Well, who would be better than you for this project, Miss Bahama Mama?"

"I'll do it, but not because you said so."

"Whatever."

Chandler and Stevie Michelle would kill a rock over one another, but they also had thrown a few pebbles amongst themselves. They sometimes were like children and I would get caught in the middle.

"Listen, you two," I said, "I got to help Three with his homework, so I'll talk to the both of you later. And the Bahamas is definitely on. Chandler, don't worry, I'll take care of the hotel reservations for either the Marriott or the Hilton before you get here, whichever's got the best rate. Talk to you two crazy women later." I hung up the phone thinking that the three of us in the Bahamas, unescorted, unchaperoned would be worse than a troop of unsupervised boy scouts at a girl scout camp. The smile on my face was devilish and the thought of us together again reminded me of when I was a little girl and our neighbor, Mrs. Clarke, had a puppy that used to lick my face. I began to giggle just the way I did back then.

CHAPTER 8

(Lorelei)

I went to pick up Aunt Ruby at ten-fifteen. The appointment to see Mrs. Donahue's house was for ten-thirty.

"Lorelei, I been givin' this bed and breakfast thing some thought." I turned the car radio down so I could hear Aunt Ruby. "And what I been thinkin' is, what do you know about runnin' a place like that? I still keep wonderin' if you know how much work it's goin' to be for you. I'm more than willin' to help, but I ain't for bein' a maid to nobody."

I spouted with laughter. "Aunt Ruby, you ain't goin' to be doin' nothin' like that. When I asked that you help me, I meant with reservations and makin' sure the guests are happy. We'll have people come in to clean and take care of the rooms and yard." I placed a hand on her shoulder. I took a few quick glances at her, while I gave attention to the road ahead of me. Aunt Ruby was a stern, sturdy woman and I loved her sensibility. "I need you aroun' to make sure that everything runs smoothly. Just the way you did with Uncle Simon's business."

Aunt Ruby took a piece of hard candy out of her purse and unwrapped it. She said, "Okay then, I'm with you on this."

"You got another one of those?" I asked. She gave me a butterscotch as we pulled into the drive of Mrs. Donahue's house. The real estate agent was standing outside her car.

"Good morning, Mrs. Scott. Nice to meet you. I'm Phyllis O'Keefe and I'll be showing you around the place. Is this your mother?"

"No. This is my Aunt Ruby." The woman was a tall blonde. Her hair was layered past her shoulders and big curls flopped up and down as she talked. The lipstick on her mouth formed two, thin, pink horizontal lines. The shade of blush on her cheeks matched. I glanced over at the car. She drove a dark blue Mercedes Benz. She looked to be forty-five or fifty, but it was hard for me to tell white peoples' ages. They were always younger than what I guessed.

"Well, hello, Aunt Ruby," Phyllis O'Keefe said in a counterfeit tone. "I was thinking we'd start upstairs and work our way down. So, shall we go in?" Walking ahead of us, I noticed she had a nice figure with shapely legs underneath her beige suit that was identical in color to the interior of her car. "The history on this house is that it's seventy-five years old and Mrs. Donahue and her husband were the second owners," she said. "The owners before them were the Atterburys, who were cousins of Mr. Donahue."

As she talked, Phyllis O'Keefe fumbled with a ring of keys. I would've bet that she didn't get them made at Swails Lock and Key. Aunt Ruby and I stood close behind her. Finding the key she was looking for, Phyllis O'Keefe unlocked the front door of the house. The door swung inward and an unexpected, musty pungent odor rushed out like a thief running from the scene of a crime. Aunt Ruby and I moved aside as the foulness escaped.

Phyllis O'Keefe continued talking as if her sense of smell was immune. "This house has seven bedrooms and five baths, all on the second floor. There is also a powder room on the first." She walked in and Aunt Ruby and I hesitantly followed.

From what I could see, all the windows, curtains and blinds were closed. Phyllis O'Keefe turned on a light switch that allowed us to see the odor, as well.

I unequivocally asked, "What is that smell?" Aunt Ruby nudged me.

"Almost a year of being locked up and unattended. And there's been some water damage," Phyllis O'Keefe volunteered.

We walked the narrow staircase up two flights to an even narrower hallway. The house was bare, but the shadows remained where pictures and other ornaments hung on the walls. Looking at the second floor, the house hadn't been updated in many, many years. Phyllis O'Keefe found light switches with familiarity as we walked through the hall into one of the bedrooms. "This is the master bedroom," she said. The damask wallpaper was water stained on the outside wall. The odor was very prominent in that room. When I looked up into the corner of the ceiling, I could see clear through to the sky. My eyes followed down the wall to the floor where it buckled. The water had damaged both.

We quickly walked through the other six bedrooms and the baths. The standing water in the toilets had grown a grayish-black film that smelled of rot. I began to feel sick. The staleness of the house was permeating. I could feel a headache tempering and my skin crawled.

"Aah, Ms. O'Keefe," I said as we were going down the stairs to the first floor, "I think I've seen enough. I don't want to waste no more of yo' time or mine."

Phyllis O'Keefe looked at me with surprise. "Oh, I see. Well, the first floor is in better shape. That's why I start on the second, so people understand the condition of the house. Why don't you look at the first floor? You might be surprised."

I was feeling sicker by the second. "Well, if you can open some windows or somethin'?"

"Come on into the kitchen." Phyllis O'Keefe began walking, flipping light switches as she went.

My nausea came close to the feeling I would get when I was pregnant with my babies. Phyllis O'Keefe quickly opened the kitchen door. The outside light beamed in. I walked onto the porch. With short breaths, I inhaled fresh air through my nostrils into my lungs.

"You okay?" Aunt Ruby asked.

I shook my head. "I don't know what's worse, the nausea or the disappointment."

"Not what you expected, hunh?"

"Not at all." I looked from the concrete floor to the concrete ceiling, where there was a wasps nest securely attached between the brick and concrete. I said, opening my arms to the fact, "This is so deceivin'. How can the outside of the house be better taken care of than the inside? I mean, that's where you live."

"Lorelei, you got to remember that Mrs. Donahue was put in a nursin' home when she left here. She couldn't take care of this big house by herself. So, it got neglected. And it takes a lot to destroy brick. The inside ain't brick." Aunt Ruby put her arm around my shoulders and squeezed.

"It would take too much money just for repairs," I said. "Then you could start on the decoratin'. That's another fortune. And I don't want to think about the things we can't see."

Phyllis O'Keefe stuck her head out of the door. I wondered how she stayed inside. "Is everything all right out there?"

Walking back into the kitchen, I reluctantly raised the grey shade at the window. The instant light exposed the floating dust that I had disturbed. I looked at all four walls. I sighed. The missing tiles on the walls and floor from the water damage, the old-fashioned cabinets and sagging window sashes were more than I wanted to tackle. It would be at least eight months to a year before my children and I could move in.

Aunt Ruby must have been reading my mind when she said, "Lorelei, Manny and Aussie could probably work wonders with this place. It would take a while, but—"

"Manny ain't had a conversation with me since I been back in Little River. How am I goin' to ask him out of the kindness of his hard heart to help me? Besides, he and Aussie are too busy."

"You won't know 'til you talk to'em, Lorelei."

Facing Phyllis O'Keefe, I sighed again and said, "Thanks for yo' time, but right now I'll have to think about this. It ain't what I expected."

The disappointment on her face was greater than mine. Her reflex was to pull a card out of her pocket and hand it to me. "Call if you change your mind or want to see something else."

Aunt Ruby and I walked out of the kitchen onto the porch while Phyllis O'Keefe pulled the shade and locked the door behind us. At the car, I said to Aunt Ruby, "Nothin's goin' right. That ain't a house, it's a disaster. Did you hear her? 'Well, the first floor is in better shape.' That ain't sayin' much when the second floor should be condemned. Aunt Ruby, I could see straight through the roof to the blue sky. That hole gave new meanin' to sky lightin'. Nothin's goin' right," I repeated.

"It's yo' imagination, sweetie," Aunt Ruby assured me.

"I hope so. What do I do now?"

"You look for another house. That's what you do."

"There ain't no other house. Not for what I want to do and certainly not on Highway 17. And truthfully, Aunt Ruby, I ain't sure I want to look for another house."

Chapter 9

(Lorelei)

The rates were better than I expected, both at the Marriott and the Hilton. Probably because it was off season. Chandler called me from the Hilton to say that she had gotten in and would be waiting for me to get there. She said to take my time, because she wanted to relax after her flight, but I couldn't wait to see my girlfriend. I went home straight from work, showered, gave Topper and Three instructions for the evening, and promised my daughter that she would see Miss Chandler no later than the next day, if not that evening. I wanted to spend some time with her first.

Easing my car underneath the overhang of the hotel, a valet opened my door. "Would you like valet parking, ma'am?" he asked. I nodded and he handed me a ticket. The doors of the hotel parted and I walked straight to the elevators. Pressing the button for the sixth floor, I anticipated the full smile of my friend. I imagined her perfume. Three once said, "Mom, Miss Chandler always smells like flowers." I felt my son was in love with my girlfriend, because whenever she was in his presence, he would stand tall and stare at her. For long periods, my son would be mesmerized with Chandler.

Looking at the numbers on the doors, Chandler's room was around the corner from the elevator. I took a deep breath and knocked.

"Who is it?"

That was no imposter behind the door. It was the voice of the divine Ms. Chandler Cawthorne. It's resonance was as distinguished as her laugh, her smile, and her appearance.

"It's me, the southerner, come to see the Yankee."She swung the door open and Chandler was standing in a beautiful, cream hand-knitted sweater, a pair of jeans, and to my shock, wearing her hair in a short sassy cut with curls flowing to her face."*Loook* at you!" I squealed. "When did you do it?"

"Two days ago. I needed something different, Lorelei. And I still do, but I'm just not quite sure yet what the hell the other is. Do you like it?"

I raised my hands like a painter to frame her face, and said, "It's you. It's definitely you."

"Good. I'm getting used to it. I was worried for a minute."

Inside the room, we gave each other a big long hug. I stepped back to take another look at Chandler. "Other than the hair, you ain't changed. Not that I expected you to."

"I don't know if that's good or bad."

"What?"

"Me not changing. I need to change, Lorelei. Or is it that I need *a* change?" Chandler then held up her hand and said, "I'm sorry. I'm going to stop this right now. It's just that I've had a lot of time to think on the plane and being in this beautifully serene room . . . whatever is on my mind, we'll talk about it later. I want to hear about you."

"You sure?" I said, not because I was worried about Chandler, but because I wanted to help someone that was always there to help me. It would have done me good to do her good.

"Sure, I'm sure. Now please, come into my humble surroundings, have a seat and I'll order up some snacks and may the bullshitting begin. I can't get over the view, Lorelei. You did good, girlfrien'. Right on the beach."

Chandler called room service and her chef instincts easily took command. She ordered things that weren't on the menu. I kept hearing her ask, "Can you do that? Do you have that? Would it be possible?"

"What did you order?" I asked. "It's a surprise, Lorelei. But I hope you like it." Sitting on the bed, facing me in the chair, Chandler said, "I know you know that I'm dying to hear about this bed and breakfast endeavor of yours. I want to hear it all."

Solemnly, I said, "There ain't no bed and breakfast."

"What!!?"

"It fell through, Chandler. The house was a total disaster and I don't see anything better comin' along. Not in Little River, anyway."

"*Aaah*, honey, I'm sorry to hear that. I know how excited you were." If anyone had a concept of entrepreneurial enterprise, it was Chandler Cawthorne and I knew she felt my distress.

"I wish I could say it's all right, Chandler, but I'd be lyin'. Everyday, the disappointment crumbles my passion."

"Lorelei, you can't let that happen. If you think hard enough, you'll come up with another idea. It might even be the same one, but on another, different scale. Just stop worrying about what didn't happen and think about making something else happen. That's what I've been trying to do. As God is my witness, I've been trying real hard."

There was a knock at the door.

"Who is it?" Chandler lilted.

"Room service."

She made a slight bounce on the bed. She untucked her legs from underneath her and took sprightly steps toward the door, opening it. The waiter rolled the cart into the room and stopped it at the end of the bed. Chandler lifted lids off the plates and nodded her head.

"Will that be all?" the waiter asked.

Chandler smiled. "Yes. It looks wonderful. Just a minute." Going into her purse on the dresser, she took out money and handed it to the man. "Have them charge it to the room, please."

"Yes ma'am." The little man shut the door behind him.

"Get over here, girl," Chandler demanded. "There's some interesting stuff beneath these lids." Lifting the first one, Chandler recited, "Chilled asparagus with a lemon dill sauce." Under the second lid, she said, "Bruschetta with a sun-dried tomato, kalamata olive and pine nut tapenade. Beneath this third lid, Lorelei, is crab, shrimp and sweet corn salad with bell pepper confetti. And last, but not least, a bottle of sparkling wine." Chandler held the chilled, dripping bottle high above her head. She looked like the Statue of Liberty. Her grin was infectious and I began smiling also. "This wine is guaranteed to give us great ideas about the future, Lorelei," she said, laughing her familiar, sharp, broken laugh.

"Pop the cork," I encouraged. She did and I could smell the grapes and the earth. I held my flute to the bottle and tilted it just the way Chandler had taught me to do. She then poured herself a glass and made a toast. "To two women finding their way."

"I'll drink to that," I added. The first sip encouraged me to take another and then another. Before I knew it, my flute was empty. "These things don't hold much, do they?" I said.

"Better to keep filling it with the sweet nectar, my dear." Chandler's smirk was mischievous. "Enjoy, girlfrien'." She placed the plates of food on the table and we sat across from one another nibbling.

"Do you think my idea was even a good one, Chandler? I mean, my Aunt Ruby was probably right; I don't know nothin' about runnin' a bed and breakfast." I was beginning to feel the wine. It felt good.

"You had the desire. That's the first step. You would've had to work out the rest, but you're smart, Lorelei. You're a CPA. You've been behind the scenes of businesses. You know what works and what doesn't. That's a very good start. That's a good foundation." Chandler's gaze went from plate to plate as she said, "I'd like to meet the chef here. This stuff is very good."

"See? You a good example, Chandler. You been talkin' about a restaurant for a few years, now. What's stoppin' you?"

"You really want to know?" Chandler was looking over her upturned glass.

"Yeah, I do. I really wanna know."

"Fear. That's what I've been thinking about, Lorelei. The whole trip across the sky to South Carolina, I've been thinking I have a fear. A strong one. But I'm grateful for that fear, because it has made me stop and think, and I think I've got to go for it. I'm so unhappy with my job and with my life that I feel it's the only thing that will save me." I could tell Chandler had been wanting to spill out her feelings for some time. "I'm dying, Lorelei. The worst kind of death. The kind that has a cure. I only need to get to the antidote in time."

"And you believe the restaurant will do it?"

"I *am* food, Lorelei. And food is me. I believe the world deserves the best of it and I can create some of the best. I know I can. I graduated one of the top in my class. My classmates learned to respect the little black woman beneath the chef's hat. So did the instructors. Oh, the students gave me a hard time at first, but I made the grade. They even pulled pranks on me. Lovingly, of course, but they were pranks just the same. But I still endured, Lorelei. During one of my final exams, I utilized some of our heritage of soul food cooking along with their French and Italian ancestry of cooking and I blew them away, Lorelei. I blew them away." Chandler's excitement had her bouncing in the chair. "You hear me? I blew them away!!" I could see that the wine was helping her feel the future.

"Then let's do it!" I blurted.

"What?"

"The restaurant. Let's do it. You and me, Chandler. Let's do it!" The wine was helping my future, also.

"No, Lorelei. I can't bring you into something so risky. If this is going to be done, I've got to do it alone. Maybe after I'm sure it's working, then it may be a different story."

"Don't try it, Chandler. That's what business is all about. Risk and havin' the resources to make it work. You got enough capital?"

"Not all of it."

"Where you goin' to get it from?"

"Borrow it."

"From who?"

"The banks. Investors."

"What's the matter, my money ain't good enough for you?"

"Your money is designated, Lorelei. And I'd feel the worse if your investment went rancid. So I can't do it. I can't take your money."

"Yes you can, dammit! 'Cause I want you to. I hate it where I am, too. Kingston Plantation is killin' me the same way Creative Solutions is poisonin' you. You said I know all the ins and outs and back doors to the accountin' business, and I'm a CPA, Chandler. Just like you one of the best chefs, I'm one of the best accountants. All you got to do is take care of the cookin' and I'll take care of the bankin'. You keep the customers comin' through and I'll keep countin' the money they bring in. It's as simple as that."

"Lorelei, it's not as simple as that. There's licenses, insurances, taxes . . . all of that."

"As Topper says, *duhhh*. I know." I dug my heels into the carpet and leaned over the table. "Listen, Chandler, I've ate yo' food. I rave about it to everybody, wantin'em to taste it because my descriptions don't do you or yo' food justice. As a matter of fact, I was goin' to be selfish and ask you to cook a meal for my family. Aunt Ruby, Uncle Simon and my brothers and their families. But I know that would be selfish, so I scrapped the idea."

"Why? I would love to cook for your family. I was planning to do something for you before I left, anyway. But the more the merrier. What day?"

"I was thinkin' Friday, since we leavin' Saturday for Hilton Head."

"Okay. I'll do it Friday. Anything in particular you want?"

"Yeah. Yo' good cookin!" The bottle was empty and our spirits were full. I wasn't going to let Chandler off the hook. I wanted to finish our conversation about the restaurant. "Chandler, I seriously want you to think about me investin' in yo' restaurant. I know Maroon could use a partner like me."

A fixed smile graced Chandler's high cheeks and enhanced her glowing eyes. "You remembered the name," she said.

"I can't forget the name of the business I plan to invest in, now can I?"

"Oh, Lorelei—it's crazy. Everybody will think you're crazy. I can't let you do it."

"Everybody already thinks I'm crazy and who cares what they think? I certainly don't and I have proven in the past that I don't care.

It's my money and I can make my own decisions. And I have decided that I want to work with you. You keep fifty-one percent, if that's what you nervous about. You call the shots."

"That's not it. I really am worried about your money."

"I'll tell you what. You think about it and by the time you are ready to leave Little River, you make a decision. A final decision and I won't bring it up ever again. Okay?"

Chandler squirmed in her chair and I could hear the wheels in her head turning. "Okay. Deal. I'll give the idea thought and let you know by the end of my vacation."

We reached across the table and shook hands like two big shots.

CHAPTER 10

(Lorelei)

Friday came around so quickly, it still felt like Wednesday. Winifred had volunteered to drive Chandler to get the ingredients she needed for the dinner she was preparing. When I called Chandler later in the afternoon, she kept apologizing for all the stops Winifred had to make. She had taken Chandler to a little specialty shop in Myrtle Beach for some of the things. She wanted to buy something there she called almond paste. Chandler said it was part of the dessert she was making. Then they went to two different grocery stores to buy mushrooms and to a butcher's shop, because the meat at the grocery store didn't meet her standards.

When Aunt Ruby answered the phone, she said, "Lorelei, this chef friend of yours is a serious cook. I asked her if I could help and she said, 'No offense, Ms. Ruby, but you can clear out of here. You are now a guest in your own house.' She's been in that kitchen all afternoon and I don't hear much of anything and don't smell nothin'. The only thing she's asked for is the barbeque grill. I'm relieved she ain't plannin' to bring it into the kitchen. I don't know what she's fixin' up in there."

"Aunt Ruby, don't worry. Chandler is silently creatin' a food masterpiece in yo' kitchen. When she's done, you'll probably ask her to autograph it for you. Then you can say, 'I had Chef Chandler Cawthorne in my kitchen.' So, just leave her be."

After the events of the day, I was finally headed to Aunt Ruby's with my children to have dinner. When I pulled into the drive, Aussie's and

Winifred's cars were there. And although they were older, their kids were in the yard running and playing. I guessed the excitement of something new and different had them giddy also. I had informed the whole family of my friend and her food creations.

When I walked into the house, Winifred and Aunt Ruby were setting the tables. The family had grown so, there was the rented table that had been put lengthwise between the dining room and the living room. The kids usually ate there.

"Lorelei," Aunt Ruby, said, "she ain't let nobody in there, but at least now I can smell the food."

I eased by Aunt Ruby and stuck my head inside the kitchen door. "Can I come in?" I humbly asked.

"Only for a minute. This sauce is temperamental and I've got to keep my eye on it."

"Okay, Chef Chandler. I only want to say hello and thank you."

"Hello. And what do you want to thank me for?"

"For bein' my friend and what you doin' here and now."

"Lorelei, if you're trying to get sentimental and syrupy on me, save it so I can pour it over dessert. Now, I love you, too, but I have people out there waiting."

"Yeah, you do. Includin' me. You sure there's nothin' I can do?"

"I'm positive. Unless before dinner you can find another brother that has the personality of, and looks like, your brother Aussie."

"You sound like Stevie Michelle, Chandler."

"I never said I was original. From time to time I even borrow recipes."

Chandler could always make laughter. I backed out of the kitchen and met Uncle Simon as I turned around. "Tell Miss Chandler that the grill is ready," he said. My mouth hung open. I couldn't believe my ears. She had everybody hopping. Even the master key maker. I laughed. "What you laughin' for, Lorelei? This is serious business. She wanted the fire a certain way and I think I got it. Now, you goin' to tell her or do I have to?"

"Oh, Uncle Simon, I'm sorry. Of course I'll tell her. Pushing the kitchen door open, I yelled, "Chef Chandler, the fire is ready, says yo' assistant, Uncle Simon." When I pulled my head out of the door, I grinned at him and he smiled back.

The inside of the house was as chaotic and as in a frenzy as the children running outside.

Aunt Ruby walked past me and said, "Yo' chef friend said this is buffet style, Lorelei."

I don't know when it started, but my sense of smell picked up the charcoal scent of meat grilling. I inhaled a deep breath. "Smell that, Aunt Ruby? It's our dinner on the grill."

Aunt Ruby took in a breath also and let it out slowly. "Yeah, it do smell good. Lorelei, this friend of yours ain't one of them weird chefs is she?"

"It all depends on what you call weird, Aunt Ruby. Chandler taught me to eat some things that I can't even pronounce, but it all has been good."

"You know what I mean, Lorelei, like squids and fish eggs."

"Aunt Ruby," I said, patting her on the shoulder, my attention searching past her, "you goin' to love it. I promise."

Looking through the house, I had hoped to spot Manny. I knew Mike Ray would not make it from Atlanta, but Manny should have been there. It was almost dinner time. Chandler said six o'clock and she was always prompt. Glancing at my watch, it was five-forty. I walked over to Winifred, and asked, "Where's Manny?" She just stared at me. "Is he comin', Winifred?" She shook her head. I looked away, not staring at anything in particular. I felt like I was seventeen again and at my engagement party. Manny had shunned me then, too. Except now, at forty-one, I needed to dispose of my feelings of guilt and shame, once and for all. I automatically looked for Aussie. Then I stopped. I said, "No," to myself. Aussie could no longer fix things for me, especially with Manny.

I went outside and called Three over. "Honey, Mom will be right back, if anybody asks."

It felt the same as when twenty years before I backed out of Aunt Ruby's drive to seek out my brother's whereabouts. The only difference was that I was driving a Taurus instead of a Malibu.

As I drove, the combination of anger and hurt depleted my oxygen supply, and I couldn't seem to breathe. I rolled down the window. When I got to Manny's house, his pick-up was in the driveway. I didn't pull in behind it. I parked on the road. Getting out of the car, my knees were unstable. I stood there a few seconds and then walked to the house, knocking on the side door.

"Come in; it's open," Manny said.

He was standing at the kitchen sink with a wrench and a pair of pliers, laboriously working at the faucet.

"Hi, Manny. Remember me? I'm Lorelei."

An unwanted smile emerged. "Yeah. How you doin'?"

"I don't think you really care."

"Sure I do." He went back to working at the sink.

"Manny, whatever it is, why don't you just say it? What's got you so pissed off that you can't stop what you doin' to talk to me?"

"I didn't know that you wanted to talk. I thought you came to see Winifred."

"We both know where Winifred is, so why don't you cut the crap, Manny, and talk to me man to woman?"

"What you want me to say?" He kept working, tightening the faucet.

"Anything that will let me know why you hate me."

"Don't be dramatic, Lorelei. You always were a little actress. One that imagined things and made things up."

"And you were always the one that made everybody uncomfortable with who they were, so they had to be actors and actresses."

I jumped as I heard the wrench hit the sink. The sound was harsh and rang in my ears.

"You responsible for who you are, Lorelei. Nobody else," Manny yelled. "You made the choice of bein' a slut."

"A slut!!?"

"Yeah. A slut! As far back as I can think, I been deceived by women. You even conspired with my wife to betray me. The both of you thick as thieves."

Manny's focus was on me and on saying all that had been inside of him for a number of years. Winifred never told me that Manny knew about her and Russell. Although I stood as tall as I could, I felt my knees swaying.

The veins in his neck pulsated as Manny's voice blared, "You don't know what the hell I went through when our mother left. I was just a kid, fightin' for the reputation of a woman that didn't give a damn about me. Then my wife betrays me and my only sister runs off with her lover, carryin' on the tradition of her mother."

My knees suddenly strengthened and my thoughts evolved into words. I hollered, "That's it, Manny! It's always been about you. You ain't gone through no more than Aussie or Mike Ray. They decided to live with the disappointment and humiliation and embarrassment without blamin' anybody. I ain't once heard you mention our father. He left, too, you know! He was just as much our father as Octavia was our mother. I ain't heard you talk about how wrong he was. How he abandoned his family, includin' our mother. Nobody's perfect, Manny, not even you. You go aroun' with yo' nose in the air, judgin' and condemin'. As far back as I can remember, I spent half my life tryin' to please you and little did I know there ain't no pleasin' you." I had to catch my breath. My eyes burned from straining back the tears. "You didn't want me to marry Russell—for yo' own selfish reasons, of course—but, when I divorced him, 'cause I actually found someone that made me happy, somebody that I loved, I was the worst walkin' creature on this earth. I never thought I'd have the courage to say this, Manny, but you full of shit, big brother. Big time. I ain't little Lorelei no more. I'm a woman with children, two ex-husbands and a wheelbarrow of feelin's and emotions that I ain't got no place to dump. I'm actin' my life out with everybody watchin', includin' you, and that ain't easy, Manny, 'cause there ain't no retakes. I'm out on stage and there ain't no retakes." I inhaled a cleansing breath. "And regardin' Winifred and me stickin' together as thick as thieves, as you call it, you too stupid to realize that we were tryin' to protect you. 'Cause we knew you couldn't handle it, big brother. You and I ain't got no right to be judgmental. They did what they did when they weren't committed to us. Russell and Winifred owe us nothin'. I didn't then, but now I understan' why I didn't freak out when Russell told me. It wasn't about him and Winifred havin' sex, it wasn't about what they did, but how I felt about Walter. I had fallen in love with another man and what he did and felt was more important to me. Two months after Russell and I were married, I wanted to run to you to say that I had made a mistake. But I was afraid that you'd condemn me forever, so I kept my feelin's to myself. While you standin' there actin' like the world owes you so much, think about how much you already been given. Yo' wife loves you, and yo' boys are wonderful and adore you. Yo' business is thrivin' and you healthy. So, Manny, if you loved Winifred one-quarter as much as I loved Walter when you asked her to marry you, then you wouldn't have cared if she fucked twenty men before you, 'cause from what I heard, a whore makes the best wife."

My brother's expression was priceless—his mouth dropped like the mouth of a ventriloquist's dummy and his eyes widened to the point of splitting at the corners. My hurricane attitude had subsided to a heavy rain. "Manny, what happened with our mother was better than forty years ago, and Russell and Winifred was more than twenty years ago. So what I'm sayin' is when you goin' to let go? Even if you can't forget, at least try to forgive. I have. We all live in a world that we didn't choose, Manny." Pleading with him, I said, "Listen. My best girlfrien' is here all the way from Cleveland to visit, and I want her to meet my *whole* family. When you goin' to be done punishin' me? I tried to convince myself that it don't matter that you ain't at dinner, but it does, 'cause if it didn't I wouldn't be here. I remember when you and Winifred were gettin' married and you were nowhere to be found the day of yo' engagement party. I didn't just stand aroun' like everybody else, wonderin' where you were. I came lookin' for you." My thoughts drifted to that day in the yard. "By the way, those Mimosa trees are doin' great," I said, visualizing him planting them. "That was the first time in my life, Manny, that I felt you approved of me, that I contributed to the togetherness of this family, and that I was worthy. Yes, I embarrassed you, and in the eyes of the hypocrites in this town, I embarrassed Russell, Aunt Ruby, Uncle Simon, Aussie, Mike Ray and probably more people than I can recall. I left you all sufferin' with my sin. Maybe Russell drank himself to death because I left him or maybe he was goin' to do it anyway. But, I ain't responsible for that, nor am I a coward, and most of all, I ain't goin' to condemn myself or let nobody else do it. I was in love with Walter and I couldn't imagine bein' without him, and I wasn't for twenty years. Regardless of the present or the future, Manny, if I had to do it all over again, I'd do it again. I never told nobody this, but if our mother felt anyway like I felt for Walter when she ran off the porch to that man, I can understan' her runnin'. The only thing I can't understan' is how she left us behind. When I think of my babies, I . . ." I turned away. I didn't want Manny to see me cry, so I walked out of the house. I squealed as I almost bumped into Winifred. We stared at one another. "How much did you hear?" I asked, not worried one way or the other, wiping my cheeks.

"All of it," she admitted. "I didn't mean to eavesdrop, Lorelei, but I also didn't want to interrupt. You were saying things that should have been said a long time ago."

"I know. Thanks for thinkin' so, too."

"When Aunt Ruby said you left, I had a feeling you were coming here."

"Well, I'm leavin' now. I said all I got to say. Chandler's probably lookin' for me."

"Okay. I'll be back soon." Not much older than me, Winifred's hair had grayed significantly. And the southern sun exposure had added permanent melanin to her skin. She went inside the house.

I sat in my car and finished my cry. A good cry is like a summer shower. The rain rinses the dust from the atmosphere, and the tears rinse the hurt and guilt from the soul.

I made it back to Aunt Ruby's in my record time. When I walked in, Chandler was wearing her chef's coat with her name monogrammed in black script above the breast pocket. The black piping on the cuffs, down the front and back, and the knotted-rope buttons added style to the jacket. Standing in the dining room, she described what was on the buffet, but the aroma was indescribable. It was ineffable.

"What's this, Miss Chandler?" Uncle Simon asked.

Her hands on her hips and with authority, Chandler said, "Sweet purple cabbage with fresh corn from the cob."

"I ain't never seen it together like this."

"I think you'll like it, Mr. Swails."

"For some reason, I think I will, too." Uncle Simon put a huge serving on his plate.

Chandler looked in my direction. "Lorelei! Come over here, girl." She held onto my waist as she testified, "I think I did good. Everything came out the way I planned. I'm a little worried about dessert, though, because I don't have my little black recipe book that I should always travel with. There are some recipes in there that I created myself. I can see it now, on the butcher block. But anyway, I want you to indulge. Just let me explain everything first."

Chandler took my hand and led me to one end of the buffet. She pointed at a platter. "The meat," she said, "is beef tenderloin that I sliced to a medium thickness and grilled. It's topped with a thick, rich port wine sauce. It's as good as a pan gravy, if not better." We smiled purposely at one another. "In the platter next to that one is basmati and wild rice with herbs, and sautéed shitake and cremini mushrooms. As I just explained to your Uncle Simon, in the bowl there is purple cabbage that I simmered in chicken stock, brown sugar, white vinegar, butter and a good'ol bay leaf. Then I tossed in fresh corn from the cob. You know, to add a little contrasting color. It's pretty with the purple broth. I think you'll like it a lot. And then, last but not least, corn cakes made with buttermilk, corn meal, flour, jalapeno and red bell peppers. I cook them like pancakes. They add a little spice to dinner. I also included some plain dinner rolls for those that don't want to venture."

"Everything looks so good, Chandler. Can I eat now?"

"Sure. I've already prepared Three's plate for him. He insisted that I do it."

I looked between the two rooms and saw my son eating everything except his napkin. "Chandler, thank you."

"No. Thank you. This is the best time I've had in a very, very long time."

"Hey, Chandler?" Aussie's voice soared above all the others.

"Yeah."

"If dessert is as good as dinner, you ain't goin' to escape Little River. I'm goin' to see to it. You a cookin' gold mine."

Joyce was sitting next to Aussie smiling and shaking her head. He leaned over and kissed his wife's cheek. When they got married, Joyce confided in me that Aussie convinced her to have premarital sex by saying he wanted to make sure they were a perfect fit for one another. She said that was the only proposal he made and she made the announcement of their engagement. I would have expected something like that from Mike Ray, but not sweet, sensitive Aussie.

"Dessert!!" Chandler, in a panic, ran into the kitchen. I didn't follow her because if she had screwed up, there was nothing I could do, and if she had screwed up beyond repair, there was definitely nothing I could say.

"Lorelei." Aunt Ruby was sitting at the head of the table when she called me.

"Yes?"

"When you finish getting' yo' plate, come sit next to me." She told Aussie to bring a chair.

I methodically placed some of everything on my plate. Even a corn cake. I sat next to Aunt Ruby. She had cramped a piece of roll between her fingers, circling the plate, sopping the last bit of sauce. "This is the best food, Lorelei. She can come and cook in my kitchen anytime. Is she available for breakfast?"

"No, Aunt Ruby. We goin' to Hilton Head tomorrow. Remember?"

"Oh yeah. I been meanin' to ask if you want the kids to spend the night? That way you ain't got to drag'em out so early in the mornin'."

"Could they?"

"Sure honey."

"I'll drop some clothes over later tonight after I take Chandler back to the hotel." I finally cut a piece of steak and ate it. It was like eating warm bread and butter. It melted and the flavor of grilled beef, herbs and spices lingered. The rich, dark, reddish-brown sauce was as smooth as the inner thigh of a young woman. "Aunt Ruby, Chandler's done it again. Have you ever tasted anything like this?"

"No, I ain't. She ought to package this meal and sell it for a million dollars."

"She is and I'm goin' to help. I'm goin' to be a partner."

"You goin' to do what?"

"Well . . . She ain't agreed yet, but I know she will."

I ate another bite of steak. I didn't know what had me more in a trance, the taste or the idea of that very taste being available for anyone from anywhere to experience.

"Lorelei, you want to explain better?" Aunt Ruby had the same look when I told her about the bed and breakfast.

Just as I was about to give her the details, Aussie's voice again echoed above the family's multiple tones. "Oh well, there goes my plan to eat Manny's portion. *Heere's* Manny," he said, imitating Ed McMann on the Johnny Carson show. Winifred let go of his arm as Manny walked toward me. At the same time, Chandler came out of the kitchen with a large pan, holding each end with oven mitts. "Hot stuff," she announced into the room. Her forehead met Manny's nose as they almost collided.

"Oh, my goodness. I'm sorry," she said. "I didn't see you. This is hot and I didn't want to burn any—You must be Manny." Chandler placed the pan on the buffet.

"How'd you know?"

"Because the notoriety of my cuisine hasn't yet reached the population of Little River that weren't invited to this little private party. And anyway, you're exactly how Lorelei described you. Tall, dark and stubborn. You're late for dinner, mister."

I didn't know how Manny was going to react to my girlfriend's deficiency of finesse, but to my surprise, he smiled at her and said, "So, you the famous chef?"

"So far, only in this household. The critics here have been generous with their rave reviews, but the most important one is from the man I hear is so hard to please."

The smile on Manny's face disappeared. "What else did my little sister tell you?"

"That it would have broken her heart if you weren't here today. But, despite the consensus, I can see you're not a heartbreaker."

His smile reappeared. "Is there as much spice in yo' food as there is in yo' personality?"

"Try it and see."

Chandler was the second northern woman to read Manny his rights. If Winifred had been listening, she would have been impressed with my girlfriend.

Chandler took on her favorite stance of resting her hands on her hips and with her strong voice, she said to the dining room, "I've prepared one of my favorite desserts. One that I created myself. It's an almond nectarine cobbler. Please help yourselves."

I thought there was going to be a stampede to the buffet. Everyone got into a line except me and Aunt Ruby. Chandler handed Manny a plate and was going to explain what was on the buffet, but almost everything in the dishes had been devoured. She and Manny went into the kitchen, and when they came out, he was carrying a plate with the rim barely visible. The steak was literally at risk for falling off the edge. Chandler came over to where Aunt Ruby and I sat.

"You're not having dessert?" she asked.

Aunt Ruby looked at the line. "As soon as there's room for me," she said.

I had never seen so much commotion. Everyone was eating and having a good time. That day, Chandler's culinary expertise had turned my aunt and uncle's house into a banquet.

"Miss Chandler?" Uncle Simon was towering over us with a plate of Chandler's cobbler. I could smell the spices—nutmeg, cinnamon and butter and something else that smelled candy-like, sweet. "You call this nectarine cobbler?" he asked.

"Almond nectarine cobbler, Mr. Swails."

"Is it a secret recipe of yours?"

"Well, not exactly. Whomever I would give it to I'd swear them to keeping it among us."

"Then that's what you do, Ruby. You'll take the oath, 'cause you got to get it."

"Simon, this lady's a chef. That dessert is probably too hard for someone like me to make."

"Nonsense, Ms. Ruby. The hardest part is finding the almond paste. I finally found it in a tiny gourmet shop in Myrtle Beach. Thanks to Winifred. She's been incredibly wonderful."

I watched Manny at the other end of the table as he ate. I could tell he was enjoying Chandler's cooking. Every so often he'd say something to Aussie. I wanted to choose the right time to talk to him. Maybe even apologize. I didn't deserve his silent treatment, but he didn't deserve my blasphemy either.

Aunt Ruby got up and followed Uncle Simon to the buffet. Chandler took her place in the chair. "Lorelei, there is no need to hold back what's on my mind. While I've been in the kitchen, I've been thinking."

"You been talkin', too."

"Hunh?"

"You talk to yo'self when you cook, Chandler. Ain't you noticed?"

"No. Not really."

"Well, you do. I don't know what you be sayin', but you talk."

"Okay, so I talk. Does that make me crazy, because if it does, then that will confirm how crazy I am for saying what I'm about to say."

"Just say it," I coaxed.

"Lorelei, I've been giving your offer some thought and . . . even though I think your . . . even though I don't believe you understand the risks of a restaurant and although I told you I'd let you know before I left . . ."

"For Christ's sake, Chandler, just say it!"

"I'm going to accept your offer, Lorelei. If you're willing to take the risks, I am, too. But there will be some rules to our risk taking. The first one is I'll take more than you will."

My skin felt warm all over. The blood was dancing in my vessels. Chandler may not have understood that the risks she was talking about felt like a sure thing for us. She didn't know that I would totally dedicate myself to our business.

My squeal was loud and everybody's eyes were on me. "Chandler, I was prayin' you would say yes. You just tell me what I need to do!"

"First, Lorelei, calm down. Don't get excited until after everything is in place, which is going to be a while. At least eight to ten months, the way I calculate it."

"But just the same, it's goin' to be, Chandler. It's a goal. Somethin' we can look forward to." I leaned over to hug my girlfriend. Chandler's smile was tentative. "Don't worry," I said, "I understan' what I'm gettin' into. I do."

"I hope you do, because like I said before, I've got a great fear—a fear bigger than the both of us. But when I have times like today, watching people enjoy the universal language of food, then I'm in the right world." Chandler looked around the room and then back at me. Also, I better tell you now that I'm going to do it in Cleveland. I don't think a new business in a new place is such a good idea."

Without searching for the words, I said, "Chandler, I'm ready to go home." Although I loved the south, the south hadn't changed since the day I left. There were new developments, new names and new money, but the division of the races and cultures remained the same. "I think I know why I came back here and it's done. There's just a few loose ends, but overall, I'm finished here. I'll come back to visit my family, of course, but I've changed."

As I talked, Manny leaned between the two chairs. His deep, low voice chortled, "Chandler, I like the spice in yo' food and the amount in yo' personality is pretty good, too."

"Thanks, Manny. Coming from you, I'm flattered."

"Don't be flattered. It's the truth. All of it." Then turning to face me, he said, "And for you, little sister, if you give me a moment of yo' time later, I would appreciate it. I got some apologizin' to do."

"We both do, Manny. We both do."

He stood tall. "I want some of that dessert before it's all gone. I hear it's out of this world. Too bad Mike Ray ain't here. He would have appreciated this. He loves good food and pretty women." Manny walked to the buffet.

"He's not so mean, Lorelei. As a matter of fact, he's rather charming." Chandler was grinning and blushing.

"Down girl. He's married to my favorite sister-in-law."

"I'm not planning to steal him. I admire a good-looking, charming man. No harm done, okay?" Chandler held up her hands in innocence. "It's just too bad they're all married, and to nice women."

Once dinner and dessert was finished, the women, including the famous chef, went into the kitchen and washed dishes and pans. But that was okay, because we also capped the night off with some of Aunt Ruby's homemade cherry wine. Chandler wanted the recipe.

Chapter 11

(Lorelei)

We started out for Hilton Head an hour later than our original planned time. We were both tired from the day before, because Chandler went with me to take the children's clothes by Aunt Ruby's. Then when I took her to the hotel, we walked on the beach. The night air was brisk as the water teased at our feet, catching us by the ankles. We wrapped ourselves in sweaters to keep warm, and walked and talked long after dark. We had some catching up to do.

I drove the distance to Hilton Head. Highway 17 was serene at six in the morning, as nature was awakening to the day. Chandler was mesmerized with the flight of an eagle. She said it looked like a 747 coming in for a landing. She was like a child with her first experience. "I've only seen them on television, Lorelei. It's an awesome creature. So large, yet so graceful, yet so intimidating."

"Yeah. And just think how their habitat is bein' destroyed. Another one of God's beautiful creatures bein' destroyed. That eagle ain't the one that's intimidatin'. All that developed land you see behind those pine trees is where they used to live and fly. Now you see'em landin' on the sides of highways. And it's because of the white man and his greed. That's who's intimidatin'. Before I moved away from Little River, you could see woods for miles. Now there ain't nothin' but condos, resorts and golf courses. Where we goin' today used to be owned by black people until white people moved'em out, Chandler. They took their land and moved'em out."

"Now, Lorelei, this is the twentieth century. I think it's against the law just to take property from people."

"All depends on how you do it. The way it was done on Hilton Head is through the taxes. Most of the land that those people lived on was either given to their ancestors by ex-slave owners and the properties were handed down from generation to generation, or they purchased it for little of nothin' 'cause a lot of it was swamp. Those black people lived off their land. They fished, grew their fruits and vegetables, and had no reason to leave. Then white developers came. Filled in the swamps that led to the ocean and developed right on top of it. The black people that didn't sell their land for little of nothin' were eventually put off it for non-payment of taxes. The white people raised the property taxes to the point where those poor black folk couldn't pay and then they were thrown off their land. Imagine yo' previous tax bills bein' six hundred dollars and then gettin' a bill for six thousand. Those damn white people foreclosed on their properties. So, now where they used to commute from Hilton Head to Charleston to work, they now commute from Charleston to Hilton Head— Workin' for the very people that stole the property they used to own. They say it's survival of the fittest. I say its legal murder." I didn't want to bombard Chandler with my disheartenment. Walter used to tell me that talking about my prejudices, my dislike of white people, was like discussing religion and politics. It wasn't to be done. But sometimes I had to do it. It was like too much would get bottled inside and I had to let it out. I had to vent. "Truthfully, Chandler, I want to go to Hilton Head to see what white people stole. I know it sounds silly and—"

"No, Lorelei. No, it doesn't. We all have our prejudices and we all have our anxieties about discrimination. That's one of my worst nightmares about the restaurant. I contemplate many obstacles because we are black and because we are women. How am I supposed to concentrate on the success of a business when I have to anticipate the barriers of running it? There will be fences that we'll be on the wrong side of, that we won't have control over. There's the barrier of people not patronizing us because we're black. Not because our food is lousy, but because of the color of our skin. Prejudice and discrimination is as alive and well in the north as it is in the south, Lorelei. You know that. And sometimes it doesn't matter what you offer and how well you present it. If you are black . . . Well, you know. We've been accepted in sports and entertainment, but even in that we're limited. Our theater and movie roles are scarce. Personally, I know I'd never make head chef working for someone else. It will happen only if it's my own restaurant, and what does a title mean if we don't have the customers? It's almost like I don't want the public to know who owns Maroon. I want to remain anonymous, behind the scenes, and only present what's important—the good food. I mean, as a race, we even discriminate amongst ourselves."

Chandler and I rode in silence for a few minutes. I felt I had started a downward spiral of our spirits and I wanted to lift them. "Have you thought about a location for the restaurant?"

Chandler was slow to respond. "*Yesss*, I think so. I've been looking at this empty little shop by the rapid station. It's ideal. Bay windows with a curving walkway to the door. It has ivy growing over the brick. On each side of the walkway, in front of the bay windows, are two patches of grass about ten by ten feet. I've visualized islands of yellow and purple crocuses opening up to the first sunny days of spring. Then in the summer we'll have large red clay pots on each side of the door with big beautiful bouquets of flowers spilling over. Yellows, pinks, purples, blues, whites . . . and some of the flowers can actually garnish the plates. Like nasturtium."

"I ain't got used to eatin' flowers yet, Chandler. Like all those crazy mushrooms you cook with. Sometimes I think you goin' to cook with the wrong one and we'll be found, all dead, right where we sittin'."

"Lorelei, I don't know where you come up with all your nutty ideas. It would be different if I went out picking them myself, but those mushrooms are grown on farms and then sold."

"Well, it still takes some gettin' used to. The only mushrooms I was familiar with were those white ones that look like doorknobs."

Chandler laughed with heartiness. "Those are just plain domestic mushrooms, Lorelei. Full of water with no flavor other than the taste you give them when cooking. But they have their place, too."

I realized that we had been driving with the radio off. I turned it on, leaving the volume low. Luther Vandross was singing in his smooth, seductive voice.

"Stevie Michelle and I went to see him not too long ago."

"How was he?" I asked.

"As pretty and talented as ever. When he sang *Too Proud to Beg,* I almost cried. And when he sang *Superstar*, I did cry. That man's style and voice is phenomenal. And everything was fine until this guy sat down beside me. He smelled of stale cigarette smoke. He was alone and didn't seem like the type to come see Luther, but I guess he bought a ticket, so he had the right to be there. But that wasn't the icing on the cake." Chandler adjusted the seatbelt and shifted her weight so that she could face me. "Then *boyfriend* pulled a cheap bottle of wine out of the other pocket and turned it up to his mouth. The smell was horrendous. I told Stevie Michelle what he was doing and all she said was, 'I'm glad he's sitting next to you'."

My eyes watered from the laughter Chandler had created. If she wasn't a chef, she could have been a comedienne.

The sky had opened to the sun and it was a cool, bright and beautiful day. "Is that baby's breath growing on the side of the highway?" Chandler asked.

"Hunh huh. It grows wild out here. You want to stop and pick some?"

"Naw. Let's leave everything intact. I don't care how much you say it's changed, so far, I love it down here. Things are so green and vibrant. By now, everything at home is brown and ready for hibernation."

"It gets that way here, too; it just takes a little longer."

"The longer, the better," Chandler declared.

A lighthearted conversation rode with us from Highway 17 to Interstate 95. "Look at the map, Chandler, and tell me where our next exit is."

Unfolding the map so she could see more of it, Chandler ran her finger down the length of Interstate 95. "We're taking 95 to Interstate 278, which should run us smack dab into Hilton Head."

Chandler suddenly became quiet. I glanced at her. Her forehead was wrinkled as she faintly vocalized.

"What you sayin'?" I asked.

"Oh, nothing much. Lorelei, have you ever talked to me about Bluffton?"

"What? What is it?"

"It's a town on this map."

"I ain't never even heard of it. So, I know I ain't said nothin' to you about it."

"Well, I have heard of it, but I don't know when or where. According to the map, it's not far from Hilton Head."

"So what you sayin'? You wanna go there?"

"I have no reason to go, Lorelei, if I don't know what I'd be going there for. It's just baffling me where and why I've heard of the place. That's all."

"Well, if it's important, it'll come to you."

Chandler sighed. "I guess so."

We crossed the Wilton Graves Bridge into Hilton Head at approximately ten-twenty. The boats appeared to skate on a tinted sea-green sheet of glass. "There it is, Chandler. On the other side of this bridge is the paradise island of Hilton Head, South Carolina."

"I just love it down here, Lorelei. It's one of the most beautiful parts of the country I've seen."

After driving over the bridge, we continued along the William H. Hilton Parkway. On both sides of the foliated strip that divide the road were malls, motels, banks, corporations and restaurants. I had to remember to keep my eyes on the road.

"Look at this, Chandler. They got everything. They got brokerage firms, real estate companies, furniture stores, McDonald's and Wendy's."

"What did you expect?" Chandler asked, still peering through the car window.

"I don't know, but nothin' so modern and metropolis. This place is boomin'. Look at the traffic."

The shiny, expensive foreign cars moved in a processional fashion. Hilton Head expressed money and power, and the money and power exuded.

"Where are we supposed to be going, Lorelei?"

I snapped from my awe and told Chandler to take out the Hilton Head map that was in our packet and look for Shipyard Plantation.

She nervously fumbled with the small accordion-folded sheet. Her eyes roamed the map before she said, "Here it is!"

"Where should I be goin'?" I asked.

"Stay on this road and you'll come to what looks like a big circle. Then Plantation Drive should be beyond that."

Although the peak vacation season had ended, the traffic on Hilton Head island was congested and slow to move, but that gave us an opportunity to look at our surroundings. When I reached the point that Chandler had indicated on the map, there was a gate and a "keeper of the gate" that apparently protected the part of Hilton Head that I wanted to see the most—the living and playing areas.

"May I help you?" the man in the tan and brown uniform asked as I pulled the car up. He reminded me of a pudgy-face, rosy-cheek, park ranger. I estimated his age to be over eighteen, but under twenty-three.

"Yes," I said. "I'm here for an overnight stay and I'm tryin' to get to my hotel."

"Which hotel is that, ma'am?"

"The Crowne Plaza."

Hanging onto the doorway of the shelter, he pointed straight ahead. "Stay on this road and at the next traffic light, turn left. About a mile down, the Crowne Plaza will be on the right."

"Thank you," I said as the yellow and black-striped gate raised, wondering if I should have told him his fly was open. Chandler and I rode through.

"We just entered into their private world," I said.

The left turn that I was told to make, made a difference in scenery. The street was residential and had modern homes that were stained in different shades of earth tones of grays and browns. The properties were secluded by large oaks with moss gently swaying from them. Children and adults were cycling, jogging and rollerblading over the narrow asphalt paths. Peeping through the dense foliage, pools and tennis courts were unoccupied. Reddish-brown pine needles served as neat ground cover throughout the manicured community.

"What you think, so far?" I asked my girlfriend.

"I'm impressed. It's so peaceful and comfortable. I can't wait to see more of it, especially the beaches."

"Yeah. We goin' into what's called Harbour Town later to take a look aroun' after we have lunch. And then we'll head down to Forest Beach. But let's get to our room first, rest until aroun' one and then see some of what this island is all about."

"Sounds wonderful to me." The hotel was where I was told it would be. When we entered the room, I immediately fell across the double bed, closest to the window, letting out a deep sigh. Chandler took care of the bellman, although we could have carried our small bags ourselves.

"I'm exhausted," I said. "I still ain't recovered from yesterday."

Chandler closed the door behind the bellman. "Nothing that a quick, warm shower won't cure." She grabbed her bag and headed into the bathroom. A few seconds later, I heard the water running. I closed my eyes and felt my body float above the sound of the shower and the soft croon of Chandler's singing.

For some reason, my thoughts drifted back with Walter when we finally got the honeymoon that we had talked about for years after we were married. He had surprised me with Disney World. It was the most romantic week of our marriage. Topper was conceived there. One night we went to Epcot to see the fireworks and laser show. Everything was so beautiful that Walter and I went straight back to the room and made passionate love, forgetting all preventives.

I put the little trinkets, photos and autographs that I brought back from our trip into a separate scrapbook. I stored it in the same box where I kept the books My Mother sent. For weeks, I looked at the books and the scrapbook before I went to bed. I was going to get the box out when Chandler and I got back to Little River.

"You ought to try it, Lorelei."

Chandler's voice returned me to Hilton Head. She came out of the bathroom wearing a towel around her slender torso. She was forty, but she was in damned good shape. Her skin was taut and rich with a brownish-red hue.

"You feel better?" I asked.

"Much. Go ahead and try it. The water will relax those tight, tense muscles."

"Chandler?"

"Yeah?"

"Is it okay for me to miss him?"

"Miss who, Lorelei? Three?"

"No. Walter. Is it insane for me to miss him?"

"I think it would be insane for you to say you didn't. I think it's okay, because I miss Wade, too. And until somebody comes along to fill the void, that space will always feel hollow and will only fit the man that used to occupy it." Chandler was searching through her cosmetic bag with intensity when she said, "I predict that you and Walter are not finished yet. You may be divorced, but you are not forgotten."

"Oh, now you ain't only a chef, but you a psychic, too?"

"It doesn't involve being psychic, but only using common sense to observe," she said with apt confidence.

"Observe what?"

"Observe you and Walter. Lorelei, just like you're lying there thinking about him, Walter is somewhere doing the same. We can't spend the majority of our lives with someone and then expect the thoughts to cut off because we've signed the divorce papers. That's only the beginning."

"Well, what about you and Wade?"

"I think about him all the time. But Wade and I are different."

"Different how?"

"For starters, he asked me for a divorce, and right when I thought we were working things out. I have a bitterness that makes me think of him with a little more animosity than you think about Walter. Besides, although they are best friends, Walter is less condescending and egotistical than Wade. That makes for a better chance at reconciliation. And I believe that Wade thinks about me in his own pompous way, too."

I sat up on the bed and pulled my sweater off over my head. "You right, a shower will help." Walking into the bathroom, I said, "I spent all my life with someone; now I just want to get to know myself."

Chapter 12

(Lorelei)

The Village at Wexford was a quaint shopping area of Hilton Head with one-story buildings and restaurants. Chandler and I went into Damon's Restaurant and ordered all kinds of fattening food. French fries, onion rings, chicken and ribs. The frozen strawberry daiquiris were the best. After we ate, we went in and out of the stores. Chandler bought some kind of kitchen gadget that grated cheese and I bought perfume. Then we drove to Harbour Town. We were fascinated with the docked boats. They were expensive and showy. Our next stop was Forest Beach. We rented three-wheeler bikes and raced up and down the shore. Crazy and wild tire tracks trailed behind in the wet, compressed sand. The late afternoon, early evening air was brisk and salty. When I licked my lips, I could taste it.

Before the sun descended into the ocean, Chandler and I walked and talked about Maroon and how we would take the first steps to make it happen. The evening tide drew closer and closer, cautiously warning us that it was time to leave. While we rode back to the hotel, we continued our discussion about Maroon.

"Lorelei, I'll work the business plan and projections first. Then we'll start an account for the restaurant. And, of course, you'll set up the books. We've got to decide to incorporate or remain a partnership. But, let's take one step at a time."

Chandler's business aptitude transformed her into someone to be taken seriously. She projected with gentle, easy persuasion that she knew what she was saying, what she wanted and how to get it done.

She once helped Walter with a problem he had installing some carpet. He accepted a job that was literally, at the time, too big for Scott and Son, but it was a profitable and prestigious job. Chandler convinced Walter to consider subcontracting with a competitive company, offering a profitable piece of the action. Under the subcontract, the job would be handled strictly through Scott and Son, and the subcontractor would not bring vehicles, tools or workers on site that displayed their company name. Walter was skeptical that anyone would accept the offer. Chandler said, "Money is money, Walter, and every company needs it, especially if it's clean, legal money." The Carrier Carpet Company accepted the deal through Chandler's negotiations. She was a natural and I admired her zeal.

Exhausted and feeling the autumn chill, the warmth of our room felt blissful. We pulled out our uncensored nightwear and got ready for bed. I sported a pink oversized T-shirt, a pair of lime green socks, and my bedspread robe that Walter had given me at least three Christmases before. But, I was shocked to see Chandler exit the bathroom wearing a floral printed flannel nightgown and white socks with a solution on her face that glistened in the dim light.

I commented, "Where's the fancy lingerie?"

"Where's the man?" Chandler answered, opening the closet, looking inside. "Just as I thought," she said, "he's not here." She fell on her bed, rolled over and stared at the ceiling. "Lorelei, I think we should cap the evening with hot herbal tea and dessert. Something disgusting." She didn't wait for my recommendation before she picked up the phone. "Yes, what are your desserts . . . oh, the chocolate brownie with hot fudge and raspberry sauce sounds perfect. One of those and a large pot of lemon herbal tea, and two cups, please. With lots of sugar."

When Chandler hung up the phone, with no provocation, we began giggling and laughing. I looked at her and said, "Don't get cold feet on me, Chandler. We're really goin' to do this."

"What, eat the dessert?"

"No, silly. We goin' to start the restaurant. I mean, I don't want you callin' me when you get back home sayin' that you changed yo' mind. I'm serious and ready. I'm goin' to give my all with this business. So tell me now if you havin' second thoughts, 'cause I'm serious. Real serious."

She stopped laughing, sat on the side of the bed and Chandler said, "I don't have a choice. My heart pounds with excitement and alarm at the same time. I may never feel comfortable with the decision, but I feel confident in it. I won't back out, Lorelei. I'm going to collect all my resources, which includes you, and I'm—we're—going forward.

There ain't nothing to do, but to do it." She gave me a thumbs up and I gave her one back.

The knock outside the door halted our talk. "Who is it?" I asked.

"Room service, ma'am."

"I'll be there in a minute."

I took two single bills from my purse and answered the door. Taking the tray, I made sure there was plenty of sugar on it. "Thanks," I said as I gave him the tip. "Have them charge it to the room." The waiter pulled the door shut for me.

"Chandler, this looks disgustingly awesome." I placed the tray on the table by the window. "I think we should send announcement letters out," I said.

"Lorelei, this isn't a wedding. We're starting a business." Chandler came to the table.

"Well, it kinda is. I mean, Chandler, we mergin' into business, you and me. I think the world should know that."

"We'll tell them soon enough. We don't need any well-wishing or skepticism, so it's best to keep it to ourselves for a while. I don't even know if the location is available. And we know the most important thing is location, location, location."

We stuck our forks into the dessert at the same time. The brownie and fudge were warm, while the raspberry sauce was chilled.

"Oh, my God, this is as good as an orgasm," I said.

Chandler rolled her eyes at me. "Don't push it, girl. There ain't nothing better than an orgasm that I've eaten, driven or worn, so I'm not convinced, but it is good."

We ate dessert, drank tea and afterward decided that we had run out of conversation and steam. Turning out the lights, I went to bed with the warm confidence that we were the best of friends and partners. The sea air had relaxed my senses and I thought about being an entrepreneur. It definitely was morale bustling. I had a goal, something to work toward. I began constructing a mental list of things I needed to do to get ready. First, I had to tell the children. Oceanna would suck in air between her lips and say, 'Mom, is it that difficult to figure out what you're doing? Dad will think you're crazy, especially after all you went through getting to Little River.' Topper and Three would be thrilled. The closer they were to Walter, the better. My children loved me, but they had a connection with their father that was extraterrestrial. I was very proud of that fact and would have—

"Now I remember!" Chandler shouted as she jerked upright in the bed.

"What's wrong?" I asked. The vexation in my voice was more of concern. I turned on the light. My girlfriend was wide-eyed and slightly startled.

"Bluffton, Lorelei. I remember where I heard the name before." Chandler slung the covers back and sat at the edge of the bed. "I was young, Lorelei. About sixteen or seventeen. But, anyway, my first love, Spoon—" Chandler smiled and became starry-eyed, "had a teacher. He was an English teacher—who was retiring. He said he was going home. Home was Bluffton, South Carolina, Lorelei. I remember. It was Bluffton. He told me to look him up if I ever was in the area. I never thought I'd get here, but I'm in the area."

Chandler got up and began pacing between the two beds, back and forth through the short, narrow space. She was making me dizzy.

"Lorelei, tomorrow before we go back to Little River, we've got to stop in Bluffton."

"Do you know where you goin'?"

"No. But he said that if I ever got here just to ask anybody for the Van . . . the Van . . ." I thought Chandler's head would explode over the pastel peach walls, she was thinking so hard. She snapped her fingers. "Van Horn!! Sam Van Horn was his name." Then she plopped down on my bed. She looked me straight in the eyes. "But suppose he's dead now? I mean, he was retiring when I met him. That was twenty, twenty-five years ago."

"But it could be a possibility that he's still alive, Chandler. It won't hurt to go. Why do you want to see him anyway?" I asked, feeling that there was some deep connection.

"He helped me once with something that would have haunted me for a long time, if not the rest of my life. He helped me bury it, settle it in my heart and mind. And he was genuinely nice. I'll never forget that." She was smiling again. "He had the nicest voice, Lorelei."

"Did you have a crush on'im?"

"No. I was impressed. You know. I looked up to him because he was—*welll*—so impressive."

"Well, if it's that important to you, then we'll go. It ain't like it's out of the way. We'll have breakfast and head to Bluffton. Now, can we get some sleep?"

"Sure. Sorry I bothered you." Her smile was honeyed.

"Good night," I said, shaking my head. I pulled the covers to my jaw. Chandler turned off the light.

* * * * *

Chandler was in the bathroom running water as I lay thinking about the night before and that there was never a dull moment with her. When they were married, Wade must have experienced many exhausted days dealing with Chandler's intense personality. She was dynamite and she lit a fire under everyone that was connected with her.

"You think somebody else could use the bathroom?" I yelled.

"I didn't know you were awake. I'll be out in a minute." Chandler came out fully dressed in a white blouse and a faded red cotton sweater that was too big. I guessed it used to be Wade's. She wore a pair of jeans that fit her forty-year-old body impeccably and tan buckskin shoes with white socks.

"Oh, ain't we preppie this mornin'."

"First, Lorelei, good morning. Second, go to hell. And third, get up. We've got to go to Bluffton."

"You a real slave driver, girlfrien'." I yawned and eased out of bed snail-like. "We at least goin' to have coffee first? If I got to deal with you today, I got to have the energy."

"Yeah. We can do breakfast. For some reason I'm hungry this morning."

"Okay, give me thirty minutes. I looked down at myself and said, "No, give me forty-five. You think you can hang on that long?"

"Just get ready, Lorelei. And in the meantime, I'll give you the story of Sam Van Horn."

Chandler went into more detail than I had expected. I anticipated something a little more lighthearted than drugs and murder. But she kept talking and I attentively listened. I didn't interrupt her with questions, because I knew she would answer any I had if I kept listening.

After I got dressed, we had breakfast in the hotel's restaurant. Chandler talked more, and we ate pancakes, sausage, fruit and I drank coffee. She refused to touch the java, because she said if she had caffeine, I would probably throw her out of the car while it was moving. She systemically sipped her herbal tea between sentences.

"So, that's the story of how I got to meet Sam Van Horn," she said. "For some reason, the sound of his voice has never left me. It's strong, yet lyrical. If you can imagine a James Earl Jones and an Ossie Davis voice combination, then you've got Sam Van Horn's voice."

"Chandler, that's impossible."

"No, it isn't. That's how he sounds."

"No silly. I mean me bein' able to imagine it. Nobody's got the imagination you do."

Our booth filled with laughter.

Chandler insisted on paying for breakfast and gas when we got onto the William H. Hilton Parkway. At the pump, she took the map from the glove compartment and once again found Bluffton. "We take 278 to Highway 46 straight into Bluffton," she said, handing me her credit card that I gave to the station attendant.

Traffic was as bad leaving Hilton Head as it was going in, as we cruised the William H. Hilton Parkway. I stopped Chandler from turning on the radio because I wanted to talk to her about a decision I had to make. "Ms. Cawthorne," I started, "I need you to listen. I'm goin' to explain this the best I can, 'cause I ain't talked about it in over twenty years. And it ain't easy for me to talk about."

Chandler stared at me, wearing a smirk. "You don't have some seedy past full of gossip, do you?"

Leeringly staring back, I said, "Chandler, this is serious. Okay?"

She loss the grin and said, "Okay, I'm listening." As I drove west, the sun's rays crammed the interior of the car. I inhaled and let the air out fretfully. "Like I was sayin', I ain't never talked about this to nobody. And the only people I think know are Walter, my family and Russell, my first husband. But, I'm probably wrong about that. And the reason I want to tell you is it involves Oceanna and while she spends more time down here in the south, there's a chance that she'll hear about it, especially if she spends any time in Little River." I tried gathering my thoughts before I continued. "I told you that I was married before Walter, right?

"Hunh huh."

"Well, before I left Russell, I was havin' an affair with Walter."

"Hunh huh. But, you never told me that part."

"I know, Chandler. But, if you *shuddup*, there's more that I ain't told you."

"Okay. I'm sorry." Chandler leaned back in the seat and I drove, thinking of how to explain.

Inhaling again, I said, "Durin' the affair, before I divorced Russell, I got pregnant by Walter and the only person I told was my Aunt Ruby. She swore me to secrecy 'cause she said that would be best. So, I didn't tell Russell I was pregnant by another man—Walter. He thought Oceanna was his. And he thought that 'til I left him. Then there was the changin' of Oceanna's birth certificate. I had to come down here to do that, and at the same time face everybody, includin' Russell. Anyway, to make a long story as short as I can, the paperwork was filed and Oceanna's new certificate was issued with her true last name of Scott. But the whole thing is, Chandler, I ain't never told her the truth. And I ain't sure if the right thing is to tell her. She called the other day to say she was comin' to Little River on her Thanksgivin' and Christmas breaks. That means she'll be exposed to what goes on aroun' Little River, includin' all the gossip. If she's goin' to hear it, I want her to hear it from me—her mother—not some malice-strickened old biddy. I'm just relieved that she ain't got to face Russell. That would be a hard meetin'. Not that I'm happy that he's dead, but—"

"He died?"

"Yeah," I moaned. "He always drank heavy, and I guess when I left he never came out of the bottle 'til the alcohol killed'im." My hands started to tremble. I grabbed tighter at the steering wheel. "Right before I left Little River with Walter, I told Russell that Oceanna wasn't his. But truthfully, deep down, Chandler, I think he always knew. And I never had the guts to ask."

"Lorelei, is this adultery thing really bothering you because you believe Oceanna will find out in an unscrupulous way? Or is it because you can't live with your conscience anymore because you feel guilty about Russell drinking himself to death?"

"Chandler, I feel I need to set the record book straight with my daughter. And, I got to do it now, 'cause I got this gut feelin' that she's comin' closer to the truth the closer she gets to Little River. And yes, sometimes I do feel guilty. I don't want to believe that leavin' Russell had anything to do with him dyin', but if I hadn't left, he'd probably be alive today."

"Oh, girlfrien'. You can't think like that. I believe what happens is meant to happen. I know it sounds rudimentary, but that's how I see it. Russell's untimely death was meant to be, just like Spoon's, because I believe our destinies are chosen for us. Russell didn't have to be an alcoholic. He could have just as easily been hit by a train. Would you have blamed that on your leaving him?"

"No."

"So there it is. You said he drank heavily while you were married. So did you commit murder or did he commit suicide? Alcoholism is a slow suicide. I know. My mother died that way. She had a choice, Lorelei, and she made the decision to drink. Russell could have just as well gone on with his life alcohol free and if he felt he had a habit that he couldn't control, there was help for him. He chose to drink and not get help. Don't you beat yourself up about something that only he had control over. I used to batter myself something fierce, also. Then I thought, for what? I couldn't change whatever happened and if I'm to be judged and punished, then I know whose job that is—not yours, not mine or anybody else. God will take care of it."

Chandler was my best friend and I respected her opinion and decisions. "So, what do I do about Oceanna? She don't even know who Russell is. I never wanted to face it before, Chandler. And now it's starin'at me."

"Okay, so you tell her. The worst that can happen is she'll never talk to you again."

I took my eyes off the road and looked at Chandler with surprise.

Gently rubbing my shoulder, she said, "I'm just kidding. Don't panic, Lorelei. I don't think she will hate you. Oceanna is a mature young woman and if you explain it to her the same way you explained it to me, with sincerity and love, I know she'll understand. Walter is her father and I think he's the father that she would want. It's all right to let her know that you are human and that you made a mistake. You'll feel better once everything is said and done."

"Thanks, Chandler. I believe I'll feel better, too."

Highway 46 was a short journey from the Wilton Graves Bridge. The sign read: Bluffton, five miles.

"Oh my God, Lorelei. This is exciting. It's like being detectives solving a case. Walking up to people with a picture, saying, 'Have you seen this man?'" Chandler laughed. "Doesn't it feel like that to you?"

"I told you I ain't got the imagination you do," I said, feeling doused in Chandler's make-believe. "Did you have such a big imagination when you were a little girl?"

Although I couldn't see them, I could feel the intensity of her thoughts when she said with heavy emotion, "I wasn't allowed to. I guess that's why I do it so much as an adult. I missed it as a child and I think I missed the most important part of my childhood. I don't mean to embarrass you, Lorelei. I know it seems crazy that I do this at such an old age, but— A good example is: Did you ever play dress-up as a little girl?"

"Sure. Didn't everybody?"

"No. See that's it. I didn't. While you were playing dress-up, I was probably washing clothes, doing the dishes or just trying to be quiet, so my mother wouldn't notice me, because if she did, then I'd be reprimanded or given another chore to do. So, I didn't play pretend, but I did dream and they are two different things. Pretend is just that, pretend. But a dream is reality. Do you understand what I'm saying?"

"I think so." It was difficult thinking like Chandler. Her core was different from anybody else I had ever known. She had a mystique. One that drew me in, because she always provided another perspective; a perspective that if you thought about it long enough, it could mean more in the future than at the present.

"Slow down, Lorelei," she said. "I think we're here. I think we just rode into a town called Bluffton."

"How can you tell?"

"On your right is a fire station. Most towns have one."

I pulled off the road onto the small graveled lot. A glistening red fire engine sat on most of it.

"Lorelei, look. Look how the trees hover and bend over the road. See the way the light grabs the leaves and the moss, making them shimmer like silver? And look how the narrowing dark asphalt road winds ahead of us like a black serpent, as if there's no end to it. It's so mysterious."

"It does look enchantin'," I added.

A man came out of the fire station's garage. Chandler rolled down the window.

"Can I help, ladies?" he asked. His crew haircut, the pants with suspenders and the short-sleeve t-shirt with muscles bulging through, made him look official.

Chandler leaned out the window slightly. "Yes. We're from out of town and all I have is the name of someone I'm looking for. He told me that if I ever came to Bluffton to look him—"

The fireman politely interrupted her. "Even with just a name, I may be able to help."

When it finally came time for Chandler's debut, she choked up. "Ahh, ahh."

I leaned over and said, "Sam Van Horn. His name is Sam Van Horn."

"Yeah," the fireman chuckled. We call him 'Snow' because of his white hair."

"You know him?!," Chandler squealed. "Is he still alive? Is he still around here?"

I was embarrassed for the both of us. Chandler dropped the map out the window. The fireman picked it up.

"You know where we can find him?" I asked.

The fireman reached for the pen between Chandler's fingers and began writing something on the map. As he wrote, he said, "Take the road you're on now to Bruin Street. Turn right. When you come to Burnt Church Road, make a left and drive about a half mile. Turn left onto Post Lane. Pointing a precautionary finger at Chandler, he said, "But you got to be careful that you don't miss the road that goes to

Sam's place. It'll be on your right. It don't have a name, but there's a wooden gate with a carved black and red woodpecker on it."

The fireman handed Chandler the map and she thanked him. We pulled back onto Highway 46 and followed the directions we were given. There was nothing on either side of us but nature and the subtle smell of pine and earth. We came to Burnt Church Road and I made the left the fireman had indicated. I watched the odometer as I drove to measure a half mile. Then we saw it: Post Lane.

"There it is!" Chandler squealed.

I had to admit, but only to myself, that I was becoming as excited as she was. I didn't know Sam Van Horn, but when the fireman said he lived in a log cabin, that ignited my interest. I had always wanted a log cabin as a summer getaway. I thought once the children were all grown, Walter and I could build one, someplace down where Chandler and I were. Some place secluded and on a road with no name. But that was just a dream. Or was it pretend?

"Slow down, Lorelei. Remember, he said we'd miss it if we're not careful."

"I know."

We both looked out Chandler's window as I slowly drove. Although it was November, the vegetation was thick and verdant. As the car eased up the road, Chandler and I couldn't help but notice a tall Victorian house that was painted a stark white. It looked totally out of place there. A woman was perched on the banister with a paintbrush, stroking one of the massive pillars. There was scaffolding and ladders all around her.

I stopped the car in front of the house. "Excuse me," I yelled out the window.

The woman put the brush down and as if she was thankful for the interruption, unhesitatingly walked to the car. She was a small white woman wearing a washed-out V-neck sweater, a pair of old painter's pants and worn deck shoes. Her hair was a soft blonde underneath the red bandana she had tied around her head.

"Yes?" she said as she approached the car.

"I'm sorry to bother you, but do you know Sam Van Horn?"

"Sure I do," the woman said in a thicker drawl than my own, chuckling afterwards. I wondered why people chuckled when they were asked about Sam Van Horn. She raised her arm and pointed down the road. "He's not far from here on the right," she said. "Look for the woodpecker on the gate."

"Thank you," Chandler and I said together.

"You're getting into this, aren't you?" my girlfriend asked.

I didn't say anything.

"C'mon, Lorelei, admit it. You're as interested in meeting Sam Van Horn as I am?"

"Chandler, don't be ridiculous. I don't even know the man. I'm doin' this for you."

"Yeah. But you're having fun."

"Okay. You got me curious."

The gate, and most of all the woodpecker, were where we were told they would be. I turned onto the road with no name. The gravel was dry and the dust stirred. I looked over at Chandler. I could tell that she was not used to the rural environment in which some people in the south lived. "It's amazing what can be found off the main path, ain't it?" I asked.

"It's so out of the way and quiet. Look at all this land, Lorelei. He had mentioned that he had acres. I guess this is part of it."

"I guess so."

Then like something out of a fairytale, the thicket opened to bright sunshine, blue-green grass and a beautiful knotty-pine log cabin. Giant pine trees were spread sporadically throughout the yard. Chandler and I both gasped. The only thing that indicated we weren't transferred onto the little house on the prairie was the blue minivan that sat close to the cabin. Everything else looked and felt authentic.

"This is beautiful," I said.

"I know. Now it makes sense why twenty years ago he couldn't wait to get back here. I would have never left."

I stopped the car a distance from the cabin, turned off the engine, and Chandler and I sat there. As we looked at the land and the cabin, pointing out things as our eyes discovered them, a tall white-haired man walked out the cabin's door.

Chandler gasped. "That's him, Lorelei. I know it is. From here he looks exactly like I remembered. Oh, my goodness. Now we've got to get out. Oh, I hope he meant what he said about looking him up if I was ever down here."

"Why wouldn't he have meant it?" I opened my door. "Come on, Chandler. We bein' silly. There ain't nothin' to be nervous about. He's big, but he looks harmless."

Chandler opened her door and got out. We walked together to the cabin. She kept whispering, "That's him. That's him, Lorelei."

We stopped at the three steps that led to the porch. Up there, Sam Van Horn looked really big.

"Hello, ladies," he said. Chandler had been right. His voice was of an indescribably distinguishable tone.

"Hello, Mr. Van Horn?" Chandler managed to get out.

"Yes."

"You probably don't remember me, but my name is Chandler Cawthorne and you used to teach English in the north, in Cleveland, and you taught a boyfriend of mine."

A huge smile crept onto Sam Van Horn's face. Then he said, "Clarence Witherspoon."

I had seen a lot of movies, and I had experienced some dramatic, emotional times myself, but Chandler had not prepared me for her performance. When Sam Van Horn said, "Clarence Witherspoon", Chandler grunted with emotion, dropped to the steps of the cabin, raised her hands to her face, and began to cry. She sobbed like a lost, frightened child. If I hadn't been there, no one could have convinced me of the moment ever happening. I felt I was intruding on an event that needed to be documented only by the two people experiencing it.

Sam Van Horn stepped off the porch and sat next to Chandler. He put his huge arm around her shoulders. "I didn't mean to upset you," he said.

"You didn't," Chandler said into his shoulder. "Forgive me, Mr. Van Horn. I didn't know I would do this. I didn't know I would be here. Not now, not ever." Then Chandler looked at me. "Oh, I'm sorry, this is my friend, Lorelei."

I handed her a tissue from my purse.

"Nice to meet you, Lorelei. I'm Sam." He reached out and firmly shook my hand. Then looking at her, he said, "Chandler, you're as pretty as you were those twenty-odd years ago. And you really haven't changed." He got up from the step and said, "Come here. I want to show you something." Chandler followed him onto the porch and looked to where he pointed. "See this birdhouse? It's the one Clarence made. I keep it up here, hanging from the porch, so the birds won't nest in it. I take it down every couple years and add a little paint and some nails and glue where they're needed. I've kept it all these years."

The birdhouse hung low enough that Chandler could touch it with her fingers. She turned to me and said, "Spoon made this house, Lorelei."

My insides fluttered with sentiment.

Sam Van Horn invited us to sit in the two rockers that seemed to be made especially for his porch. They were the most beautiful rockers

I'd ever seen. The wood, same as the cabin, was pine and they were stained with a lacquer that reminded me of a shiny, smooth caramel dipped apple.

"Where did you get these rockers?" I asked.

"Ernest Lee Carter. He makes them. I don't think there's anyone within a twenty-mile radius that doesn't have one or two. It's his hobby. He keeps making them and people keep buying them."

"I'd like to have one myself," I said.

"He'll take your order and in about six weeks, you'll have a custom-made rocker."

"Do you have his number?"

"Sure do. Before you leave, I'll make sure you get it."

"Thanks."

As we talked, Chandler's eyes would occasionally drift to the bird-house. She would stare for a few seconds and then rejoin us.

"Mr. Van Horn, it is beautiful out here. Who takes care of all this for you?" she asked.

"I do. I have a tractor I use to cut the grass and a guy comes around to keep the trees trimmed."

A large, light-brown dog came from around the side of the cabin.

"Where have you been, Buster?" Sam Van Horn asked.

The dog was wet. He walked onto the porch and flopped in front of Sam Van Horn. He ignored Chandler and me. Sam Van Horn reached down and patted the dog on its side with firm, manly thumps.

"He's part Lab and part Collie, and like me, doesn't have much of a social life," Sam Van Horn said. "There's a creek that runs behind the cabin that Buster likes to swim in. That's why he's wet. He eats, sleeps and swims in the creek. I'd like to show you around the place, if you'd like to see it?"

"Yes. We would," Chandler said.

Sam Van Horn got up from the banister and Buster got up, too. Chandler and I followed them down the steps onto a trail that had obviously been created by Sam Van Horn and Buster walking the same path many, many times.

"We've got six acres. Most of it undeveloped."

At the back of the cabin there was another porch, almost identical to the front, with garden tools leaned against the banister and a small Formica and chrome kitchen table and two chairs. There was a bowl, a knife, and onions and potatoes on the table.

"Did we interrupt your lunch?" Chandler asked.

"I was just going to fry chicken and cook some potatoes and onions," he said. "Not that I need it." Sam Van Horn rubbed his belly.

He was a big man with a small gut, and if he did all the work to keep up the place, he needed his energy.

"Want to join me for lunch?"

Chandler and I looked at each other.

"Oh, come on. There's plenty. I've got some sun tea brewing and some homemade ice cream for dessert. You would make me and Buster happy. My son left Wednesday to go back to Chicago and it's sort of lonely since he's been gone. So don't deny a lonely old man lunch with two beautiful women."

Chandler and I agreed to stay. Sam Van Horn completed our tour down by the creek. It was a beautiful scene. The water flowed over rocks and moss, winding through the acreage as it disappeared into the woods. Buster put on a swimming show for us. Chandler and Sam Van Horn talked about the previous years that took our stroll to the foot of an impressive vegetable and herb garden. Chandler was in heaven. She picked and smelled all the ripe herbs and insisted that Sam Van Horn allow her to prepare lunch.

The inside of the cabin was neat throughout. The loomed rugs had been dropped without sequence and country furniture filled the rustic spaces. Family photos were arranged on tables and above the fireplace. There was a loft that stretched across the living and dining rooms that could be accessed by either stairs or a ladder. There were hundreds of books stacked in a built-in bookcase. The recessed lighting made the titles readable, even to a blind man. A giant fan that looked like it could cool an arena, hung from the ceiling.

Sam Van Horn brought another chair from the kitchen onto the back porch. He took in a deep breath of air. "She's cooking her butt off in there," he said. "This is a pleasant surprise. Not only do I get lunch prepared, but by a chef. What a treat. What a treat!"

He sat at the table with me and we drank sun tea. "I told her not to forget to go to college," he said, "and she didn't. She went to two colleges. So, you girls are starting a restaurant?"

"Yes sir," I said shyly.

"I'm definitely impressed."

Sam Van Horn was making me blush. The concept of the restaurant had to be official if we were telling people. Other than my Aunt Ruby, he was the second.

Chandler came out of the cabin with three platters. She did a balancing act with the trio, one on her arm and the other two in each hand. "Lunch is served," she announced.

Sam Van Horn rubbed his large, mature hands together. The sound was rough and scratchy. Then he helped with the platters. "What do we have here?" he asked.

That was Chandler's cue. "I hope you don't mind, Mr. Van Horn, but I deboned the chicken and pan fried it with a little oil and butter, garlic, and fresh basil and rosemary from your garden. I roasted the potatoes and onion in the oven. And the string beans looked so fresh on the vines, I plucked some, blanched and marinated them with red bell pepper strips in a little Italian dressing. And I whipped up some cornbread—which I'll bring right out.

Mr. Van Horn said, "Look at this!"

I proudly stated, "She's one of the best. Just the day before yesterday, she cooked dinner for my whole family and they ate everything except the plates and platters. I think a few forks were swallowed."

When Chandler came back with the cornbread, it was cut neatly in squares and I could smell the butter she had spread on top and between the slices.

"Okay, we can eat now," she said.

She handed the chicken platter to Sam Van Horn. I spooned some of the aromatic potatoes and onions on my plate. The string beans were a bright green and tender. I ate three slices of cornbread. When we finished, there were two pieces of chicken left and no potatoes or string beans. I think Sam Van Horn hoped that nobody claimed the chicken, because he had dinner plans for it. Buster watched every mouthful Sam Van Horn ate, in hopes of a sample, but he never got one.

Sam Van Horn officially dropped his napkin on the table, indicating that he couldn't go another round. "Can you stay for dinner?" he asked.

Our laughter aroused Buster. He stood on all fours and barked for the first time.

"See, Buster wants you to stay, too."

Chandler humbly said, "Thank you, Mr. Van Horn, but Lorelei and I hadn't planned to be here this long. And please understand that the invitation sounds tempting. I could stay out here forever. I've come to the conclusion that I love the south and I'd love to have a vacation spot just like this one day. I know it's a wild dream, but right now it feels real."

I said, "But it ain't pretend." Chandler looked at me and nodded twice.

"It may not be as wild a dream as you think," Sam Van Horn noted. "I plan to sell some of this land right beyond the creek. You may want to buy and build a cabin like this. Having a neighbor like you would be great. Maybe I could get invited to dinner."

"I'd cook for you anytime, Mr. Van Horn, but I'm about to sink my life into a restaurant. There's no room for frivolities or luxuries. It may be a struggle to keep a roof over my head in Cleveland."

"Well, if you want it, the offer will stand. Both my sons like the cities. I have one in New York and the other in Chicago. I don't think they'll ever come back here to live. Unlike you, they don't like the south. But even if they do plan to return, this will be plenty for them."

"Ain't that the way it always is?" I said. "They got it, but don't want it. We want it, but don't have it."

"I went to visit the son in New York and his apartment is the size of this porch, if not smaller, and he's as big as I am, if not bigger. It was so small in there I told him we would have to take turns breathing."

Buster barked again with our roar of laughter.

Still giggling, Chandler got up from the table and began clearing it. Sam Van Horn and I helped. Buster followed us into the cabin.

Sam Van Horn pulled a plastic container out of the freezer. "I promised dessert," he said. "I made ice cream from my mother's recipe and I think it's the best."

"You made it yourself?" Chandler asked.

"I sure did. The best kind. The fattening kind. I've tried those low-fat, no-fat ice creams. I hate them. This ice cream is sinful. Loaded with fat and calories." He scooped out three stoneware bowls full.

"Vanilla bean," Chandler chortled. "Not only is it full of calories, but rich flavor. I haven't tasted vanilla bean ice cream in years. Mr. Van Horn, thank you for a relaxing afternoon." Chandler's tone was breezy and carefree. "And I hope you liked lunch?"

"I loved it. Thanks." Sam Van Horn put a scoop of ice cream into Buster's bowl. He licked it like he was human. "I know it's not good for him, but he likes it and I don't give it to him often."

Chandler ate a spoonful. Her eyes gleamed as she smiled. "Mr. Van Horn, this is the best. I mean the best."

"Thank you. The compliment coming from a chef, I believe you."

Chandler ate another and another spoonful. Then she said, "I'd love to take this recipe back to Cleveland with me and add it to my little black cookbook."

I let Chandler and Sam Van Horn do all the talking while I ate the richest, most flavorful vanilla ice cream I'd ever had. When my spoon disappointingly scraped the bottom of the bowl, I wanted to lick it.

"It's a long one," Sam Van Horn said.

"If you've got a pen and paper, I'll take the time to copy it. I don't want to leave here without it," Chandler insisted.

Sam Van Horn did as she asked. We sat at the table on the porch as she copied the ingredients and instructions. Mr. Van Horn wrote down the phone number of Ernest Lee Carter, the rocking chair maker, while we waited.

"Well," Chandler said, as she wrote the last word, "I've got it all down. I think Lorelei and I should help you clean up and then start our journey back to Little River."

"Buster and I will finish the dishes," Sam Van Horn said. "I may even share a piece of chicken with him."

"You sure about the dishes?" Chandler asked.

"I'm sure."

We all walked to the front yard and said our goodbyes. Sam Van Horn gave the both of us big hugs and Chandler looked at the bird-house one last time.

She and I were quiet on the trip back to Little River, but I felt we were thinking about the same things. We listened to the oldies but goodies station on the radio as we sang with the Carpenters and the Temptations.

* * * * *

On Monday, by the time I had gotten off work, attended to my children, and spent five minutes with myself, Chandler had written, in outline form, ideas for the restaurant. When I arrived at the hotel, she handed them to me.

"Call me sometime next week and let me know what you think," she said.

The next morning my girlfriend was leaving to go home. I convinced my boss that I had an early appointment and would be in by nine-thirty. I wanted to take Chandler, Topper and Three to the airport. Three was so excited that he was going to see his father, he threw up breakfast. My child displayed his emotions in the strangest ways. Topper helped pack their clothes and left instructions for me to relax while they were gone. She had my maternal instinct.

Chandler and I locked arms and walked through the airport, as our conversation was fragmented, in an attempt to cram it all in.

"You call my real estate agent," Chandler said. "Tell her what you're looking for so she can get started. I think she's fucking Wade, but I can't be petty, now can I?"

I said, "Yes you can, but we ain't got time for that now. Make sure Three don't get peanuts on the plane. He's allergic to'em."

Our gibberish went on, but we understood.

"I think I'll work for Creative Solutions another sixty days."

"Aunt Ruby said she's goin' to make yo' nectarine dessert for the church bake sale."

"The house has been sold, and I've got to find some place to live as soon as I get home."

"And see if you can't control yo'self from buyin' Topper all kinds of fancy things, Chandler."

"The piano is going to be the hardest to move."

"Tell Walter to call me as soon as he can."

"Flight one-fifty-eight to Cleveland is now boarding," the anonymous voice said on the loud speaker.

"Oh Lorelei, I guess this is it." Chandler pulled her purse up over her shoulder and called for my two children. She was in charge. Obediently, they came running.

I hugged the both of them tight and saved the tightest one for my best girlfriend. I whispered into her ear, "You right, Chandler. Our destinies have been chosen for us, and I think we should get on with-'em."

I watched three of the most important people in my life board the plane. As I turned to walk away, I thought that I had never been without at least one of my children. What was I going to do with all my free time?

Chapter 13

(Lorelei)

Tuesday, November 26, 1996   Midnight
Dear Chandler:

I got your message. Sorry I wasn't here when you called. I went to see Manny and his wife. We had a very interesting conversation, the three of us. I had no idea Manny was in so much pain about our mother abandoning us. He said that although Aunt Ruby was better than a mother to him, he still feels cheated and hates our mother. He told me that when he was twelve, he was going to hang himself. He blames her for that. And I thought he was the strongest of us all, but in reality he was the one living with the most hurt. Maybe it's because he's the oldest and remembers more. I don't know, Chandler, but I'm glad I now know how he feels.

I made the suggestion that maybe my brothers and I should get together one day and just talk about it—air our feelings out in the open. I didn't realize until I talked to Manny that I have suppressed many of mine. He agreed it would be a good idea.

Walter called as soon as he got home with Topper and Three. I was here, so I got a chance to talk with him. He sounded great. I was going to mention that I'm coming back to Cleveland, but I decided to wait, for a number of reasons. Besides, I'm sure Topper will say something, if you haven't already.

You're probably thinking, why am I writing a letter only hours after you've left? I'm bored already, Chandler. It is so quiet around here, I can hear the condo settling into its foundation. Tomorrow, I'm going to start reading over your notes for the restaurant. Since there are no distractions, I have time to think about what we're doing. It's right, girlfriend. It's as right as a summer rain.

I know Walter is capable, but check on Topper and Three for me, especially Topper, because she is a girl. And remember, Chandler, no expensive gifts. The both of them are spoiled enough.

Thanks for coming to visit. I got my Christmas present in November. My family is still talking about the meal you fixed. And thanks for sharing Sam Van Horn. He's the greatest.

Well, if I don't get to bed soon, there won't be a need. One more day of work before the holiday. I'm having dinner with Aunt Ruby and Uncle Simon. So is the rest of the family. Mike Ray is coming in from Atlanta, and Oceanna will be here, too. Then she's going to visit Walter for a few days. I hope your Thanksgiving with Kennedy is a nice one. I'm sure you'll be doing all the cooking. Tell her I said hello and call me the minute the baby is born.

Kisses, kisses,
Lorelei

It was difficult sleeping as I thought about the future. I kept hearing Walter's voice say, "Lorelei, it feels good to have my children here. I miss my family." I got out of bed to get the box from the closet that had the books that My Mother sent and the Disney World scrapbook in it.

Chapter 14

(Stevie Michelle)

An airport bombing in another part of the country had the mayor paranoid, so he had security tightened at the airport. I was unable to park at the pick-up/drop-off curb. The police pushed cars and people along like cattle. The parking garage was full as I drove the winding maze of concrete and steel to the roof.

Impatient, not wanting to wait for the elevator, I ran down seven or eight flights, across the parkway and through the airport. All I could think about was that I wanted to be there when Chandler walked off the plane. I used to hate when Carl wasn't at the gates when my flights arrived. It made me feel he had forgotten me.

Gasping to catch my breath, pulling change and keys out of my pockets, I dropped them into a tray. I walked through the metal detector. Chandler's plane was rolling to the gate when I got there. I noticed Walter leaning against the window, looking out at the plane. Chandler said that his kids were coming in on the same flight and he would be there to meet them. When I walked up to him, he said, "Stevie Michelle! What's goin' on?" I was surprised he recognized me.

"Hey, Walter. Nothin' much."

"I told Lorelei that I'd take Chandler home when I picked up Topper and Three," he said, "but Chandler insisted that you come get her."

"Well, Walter, I don't know if it was explained to you, but we have a project to do when we leave here. We made plans before she left for South Carolina. Other than that, I'm sure Chandler would've taken you up on your offer."

I never before had the opportunity to stare at him. I didn't want to be noticed staring at another woman's husband, but looking at Walter, I was able to admire how strikingly attractive he was. His skin, although in its forties, was smooth as a baby's cheek, and he appeared masculine and proud. The brushes of gray at his temples was art of noticeably good taste. How did Lorelei let him go?

"That's good to know," he said. "I thought it was something I said or did."

"No, Walter, I don't think so."

The gate attendant opened the door. Walter and I watched for our gang as a group of travelers rushed in. Topper and Three entered the waiting area. Walter was all smiles when he saw his children. They caressed and squeezed, and squealed and laughed. Three put a bear hug on Walter's leg that would have made any champion wrestler proud. Chandler soon filed in with a second group of people. Even she gave Walter an inconsequential clutch of affection. Then she walked over to me and said in a tired, breathless voice, "Good to be home and you should have been there."

After we all said our hellos and were leaving for baggage claim, Walter asked Chandler, "Did you enjoy your trip?"

"It was wonderful, Walter. I think I've fallen in love. With the south, that is."

Then in a quiet voice, almost at a whisper, he asked, "How's Lorelei?"

"She's great. But you should ask her yourself," Chandler said. Her tone was matter-of-fact, almost flippant. "That reminds me, Lorelei wants you to call as soon as you get home with the children."

"Okay," he said.

On the down escalator to the baggage claim area, I asked Chandler, "So, are you going to tell me all about it?"

"Yeah. But first I want to get my luggage and get out of here. I'll talk to you on the way to look at houses. I love Topper to death, but she never stopped talking and asking questions the whole trip. She's an inquisitive little thirteen-year-old. She asked, 'Since interracial couples can have babies, why don't animals like lions and tigers do the same thing?' She said, 'Then they could be called ligers.' The only answer I could give her was because they're from two different regions and they are smarter than humans."

With a chuckle, I said, "Well, we can see you haven't had much training with children."

"I haven't had any training with genetics or chromosomes, either. I'm a chef. Why couldn't she ask me about bananas Foster or demi-glace? And thanks for the confidence, Stevie Michelle. I know I screwed up, but now you've confirmed it."

"Oh, come on, Chandler. Lighten up. You're just tired. Don't be so hard on yourself. We'll look at the places and then get something to eat. Unless you want to cook?"

Chandler's stare was gouging as she said, "Stevie Michelle, I'm on the brink of losing it; don't push me. Today, I'm not cooking for myself, you, or anybody else. Now that that's settled, where are these places we're supposed to look at?"

"Two are in Cleveland Heights, one's in South Euclid, and one is on the border of Cleveland and Shaker."

"I don't know if I'm up to looking at all of them today."

"Come on, Chandler. Remember, we said we'd look together. We both need places and you've got only thirty or so more days before you're handed an eviction notice. You better get more enthusiastic than this."

"I'm just not in the mood, that's all. We probably should've waited until tomorrow."

"Don't put off until tomorrow what you can do today."

"Stevie Michelle, shut up. You're worse than Topper." Chandler looked behind her to make sure Topper wasn't listening.

Waiting at the baggage claim, the carousel began to move and luggage rolled out. Topper and Three ran to stand next to Chandler. They stood patiently as their bags appeared out from the shoot. Walter was instantly there to lift them off.

"Thanks," Chandler said.

"Sure. Thanks for coming back with my children. It eased a lot of stress when Lorelei told me you'd be traveling with them."

"I couldn't let my favorite little people travel alone. It was a pleasure."

Walter pulled the last of Topper and Three's bags off the track and picked them up with ease. "Do you need help with yours?" he asked Chandler.

"No, I've got my strong friend here," she said, slapping me on the back.

Walter's smile could have melted a glacier.

"You know, Chandler, you're just a bundle of joy today," I said. "Remind me when we get to the car to put you in the trunk with the luggage."

Walter laughed at us like we were doing an Abbott and Costello routine. "Nice seeing you girls again," he said. "Come on, kids."

Feeling absolutely ridiculous, I watched him as he and his children walked toward the bright red exit sign.

"She's coming home, Walter," Chandler yelled. "Lorelei's coming back to stay."

Walter stopped in his soulful stride as if he was going to turn around, but to my surprise he didn't. He was motionless for a few seconds and without making a comment, he picked up on his stride where he had left off. Chandler and I watched him walk out of the airport like a lone surviving outlaw after the biggest shootout of his life.

"Is Lorelei really coming back here to live, Chandler!?" I asked after Walter, Topper and Three disappeared from sight.

"Yeah, she is."

"When? Why?"

Chandler sighed. "I'll give you the details in the car."

She picked up one bag and I picked up the other. We took the same path leaving the airport as I used to get to the gate. We grunted as we tossed the bags into the trunk of my Saab.

Getting into the car, I said, "Okay, girlfrien', give me the 4-1-1."

"All right, Stevie Michelle. I'm going to be nice. I could make you wait, but I know that would be cruel and unusual punishment."

"Yes, it would, and you can be such a witch sometimes, Chandler."

"You better be nice or I'll keep it to myself."

"You love making me suffer, don't you?" I said, half joking and half serious.

"For some reason, today it doesn't feel as good as it usually does. Like I said, I'm tired and I've got a lot on my mind. The reason Lorelei is coming back is one of them."

I slammed the car door shut. "Come on, Chandler, spill it."

"Okay. Here it is. Lorelei's coming back because she's investing in the restaurant. I decided on my way down there that it's time for me to quit Creative Solutions and open Maroon. Lorelei said she wanted to help—against my better judgment—but she insisted. And I've got to admit that her accounting expertise would be an asset, no pun intended, not to mention a comfort. So, there you have it. All the details haven't been worked out, but the concept is definite."

I felt the blood crystallize in my veins. I didn't know how to describe the frosty feeling—envy, jealousy or just plain dismay.

"You two decided to start a business on a seven-day vacation?" I asked, a touch of intensity in my voice.

"No. We decided to follow through with an idea that I've been concentrating on for a long time. It's not as if the restaurant will open tomorrow, Stevie Michelle. Like I said, details have to be worked out."

"I see." I couldn't say more than that for fear of the inability to hide what I was feeling.

"So, tell me about the houses on this list," Chandler said, picking up the sheet from between the seats. "What do you know about them?"

"Not much more than what's written there. And what— What's her name?"

"Beverly."

"Yeah. What Beverly told me."

"You know she's fucking Wade," Chandler volunteered.

"No, she's not?" I said with sincere amazement.

"Yes, she is, girlfrien'. But I can't blame her. Right now I'd fuck him, too."

"Chandler, what's up with you? You're in rare form today, and I don't think it's just because you want to fuck Wade."

"I can't totally pinpoint it, Stevie Michelle. Maybe it's the anxiety of what I'm about to do with my life. I guess on a scale of one to ten, my bitchiness is running as high as number six today." Chandler rubbed her forehead with forcible pressure and sighed deeply.

"Let me know when you reach ten. I want to be the hell out of the way before you blow." I thought she'd laugh at my attempt at comic relief, but Chandler only sighed with deeper and heavier feeling. "Listen, if you really want to see the houses later, we'll just reschedule," I said.

"No, let's get it over with. The holiday is the day after tomorrow and then we'll be into next week. Like you said, don't put off until tomorrow what you can do today."

"Good girl," I said. "Which one do you want to see first?"

"It doesn't matter, Stevie Michelle. How about the one in South Euclid and then we'll make our way back through town?"

"Fine with me," I said, unable to stop thinking about Chandler and Lorelei's plans for the restaurant. The sigh I released was deeper and heavier than hers.

We saw the house in South Euclid. Then Chandler had the urge to talk to Kennedy. She picked up my car phone and dialed. Cornelius answered. He said Kennedy was having contractions that were approximately fifteen minutes apart. When Chandler spoke to Kennedy, Kennedy said she was all right and had talked to the doctor. She said they were on their way to the hospital and it wasn't necessary for Chandler to come, but that she'd have Cornelius call as soon as the baby was born. Chandler went home to wait. I waited with her.

"Are you excited about being an aunt?" I asked.

"Yeah, combined with alarm," Chandler said with an arid tone. "I've never been an aunt before and other than Kennedy, I'm the only other person the baby will have from our side of the family."

"Don't be silly, Chandler. You'll do fine. There's nothing to it. You'll listen to Kennedy complain about not having enough time to do things because of the baby taking up so much of it, and you'll come to the rescue, taking the bundle of joy as often as you can. And then you'll be an old pro at aunthood. The only thing you won't be able to do is breast feed."

"I hope it's that simple, Stevie Michelle."

"It is. Trust me. And Kennedy will appreciate it. The little help I got from my Grandma Shaky when Nelson was a newborn was really appreciated. She would have helped more, but we were living in two different states at the time."

Chandler got up from the sofa and headed for the kitchen. "You want a glass of wine?" she asked.

"Not on an empty stomach," I said.

She stopped. "You know, I haven't eaten either. Let's call Alonzo's and get buffalo wings and fries."

I threw up my hands. "Well, there goes my diet," I said. I picked up the phone and dialed the number to the restaurant. I knew it by heart. That was why I was on a diet. "A dirty dozen with two orders of fries," I said into the phone. "It's Stevie Michelle, Alonzo. And don't forget the blue cheese dressing. You did the last time. I'll be there in fifteen minutes. Thanks."

Chandler waited at the house just in case Cornelius called, and I did a myriad of thinking on my drive to Alonzo's. Although I was trying to convince myself that I was happy about Chandler and Lorelei's arrangement, I felt left out. Why didn't she ask me? I had money that I could contribute. I didn't have a college degree like them, but I wasn't stupid. Carl had taught me some things about law and if I wanted, I probably could have breezed through law school with what I already knew.

Or did Lorelei convince Chandler not to include me? She always did try to exclude me whenever she and Chandler had plans. Like the time they had talked about a long weekend in Toronto. It was a done deal, until Chandler suggested that I come along. Then, at the last minute, Lorelei said she had the flu. She was jealous of Chandler's and my relationship from the first day. Even though they were friends before I met Chandler, their rapport wasn't the same as Chandler's and mine. I believe that's why Lorelei always tried to exclude my participation in things. How could Chandler be so naive?

It was my day to encounter parking problems. Alonzo's was next to a grocery store and they shared the same lot. It was full. I had to wait for someone to pull out of a space. When I got inside the restaurant, Alonzo was standing behind the bar, where four men were sitting with a thick haze of smoke around their heads, mothering glasses of beer or nursing watered-down drinks.

"Ms. Stevie Michelle," Alonzo yelled across to me in an accent that always sounded generic. "It's so good to see you again."

"What's happenin', Alonzo?"

"The rent on this place and a heavy mortgage at home."

"So, you're doing fine?" I said.

"Absolutely. Absolutely. I've got your order right here." He placed it on the bar.

"How much?"

"Twelve fifty."

"The blue cheese dressing in there?" I asked as I counted out the money.

"I made sure of it myself," he said.

I handed Alonzo the money and took the bag. As he gave me change from the cash register, he asked, "How's Carl? You don't come in for pina coladas anymore. I miss that. You are good couple."

Fumbling with the bag, my head lowered, I said, "Oh, Carl's fine. He's had some heavy cases and hasn't had much time for anything. And his socializing has been cut back tremendously. I'll mention you asked about him."

"Do that." Alonzo handed me my change and I embarrassingly left.

Outside, I stood by the car for a minute wondering why I hadn't told Alonzo that Carl and I were divorced. I had been in the restaurant at least twenty times since then and each time I gave one excuse or another for Carl and me not coming in for pina coladas. It upset me that I was living a lie with certain people. To some I blurted it out and with others, I lived that lie. Maybe there was some underlying psychological problem brewing inside me.

I got into the car and put the wings on the seat next to me. I inhaled the aroma all the way back to Chandler's, thinking about the truth I kept from Alonzo and certain others, and Chandler leaving me out of the restaurant.

When I walked through the door of her house, Chandler was hanging up the phone. "She's pushing," she said.

"*Wut*!?"

"Kennedy. She's pushing. She's in delivery. When she got to the hospital, they took her straight into delivery. That was Cornelius. He's got his cell phone right in the delivery room. It's amazing that they let him do that. Now you can get a contraction by contraction description right over the phone. I could hear Kennedy in the background. Oh, Stevie Michelle, I should be there with her."

"She's fine, Chandler. We'll go as soon as Cornelius calls with, 'It's a boy—or girl!"

"Those wings smell awesome," Chandler said, distracted by the aroma, taking the bag from me. "It's been a long time since I've had Alonzo's wings." She pulled them out and we stood at the kitchen counter, eating out of Styrofoam and licking our fingers.

Chandler looked at me and said, "We really should sit down." Then she said, "I remember the first time you and Carl turned me and Wade on to these wings. I must have eaten two dozen all by myself."

"Two and a half," I informed her.

"I know I didn't want to see anymore for awhile."

Chandler got a bottle of white wine out of the refrigerator and poured two healthy glasses for us. Very primitively we ate chicken wings and fries, tossing the bones in the trash as we cleaned them. And we drank wine and laughed. We never did sit down.

"Then I turned Kennedy and Cornelius on to Alonzo's wings," Chandler said. "For the first couple months of her pregnancy, they were all Kennedy wanted and then after that, she craved nothing but garlic mashed potatoes. Once a week, I made a batch and took them over. I'm just glad it was something as simple as mashed potatoes. It could have been more complicated and expensive, like crab stuffed mushrooms or shrimp and lobster lasagna."

"Chandler, you sure know how to make these wings seem insignificant. You're real mean."

"What are you talking about, Stevie Michelle?"

"Which would you rather have, the shrimp and lobster lasagna or buffalo wings?" I asked.

"Right now, the wings."

"You would say that," I said.

"Well, it's the truth. I want the wings," Chandler insisted.

"Are you going to serve wings in the restaurant?"

Chandler's laughter emerged in a high-pitched cackle. "I don't think so, girlfrien'. I'll gladly give whoever wants wings Alonzo's phone number and address."

"What will you serve?" I asked.

"Shrimp and lobster lasagna, for one." Chandler paused and inhaled a deep breath. Letting it out long and steady, she said, "And then there will be a variety of cultural influences. French, Italian, American, African-American, even Asian. I don't want to put any limitations on my creativity. I've asked myself, what's wrong with collard greens and an egg roll? Nothing that I can see. So that's what I want to do, Stevie Michelle. I want to be one of the few who break traditions."

"Chandler, you've never been traditional, so that won't be anything new for you."

"Tradition is boring. That's how I see it."

"You're right. And—"

The phone rang. I could hear Chandler's heart skip a beat.

"That's Cornelius. I'll bet you," she said, quickly picking up the receiver. "Hello. . . Cornelius! . . . What is it?. . . She had a girl, Stevie Michelle!! I have a baby niece." Chandler's smile was broader than Texas, and her voice raised two octaves with each sentence. "I'm coming right down there. Is she pretty, Cornelius. . . she looks like me? I'll bet you're just saying that. . . Does she really? We're on our way. Stevie Michelle and I. . . Okay. I got it. They're taking her to room four-twenty. See you shortly."

Chandler banged the receiver in the cradle and hugged me. "I've got a niece, Stevie Michelle. We're starting another generation of Cawthornes with a girl. I can't wait to see her."

"Then why should we wait?" I said. "You want to drive or do you want me to?"

"Why don't I meet you there? That way, I won't hold you up when you're ready to go."

"Okay. That sounds good." I ate one last French fry and took a chicken wing for the road.

Chandler arrived at the hospital first, but waited for me in the lobby. We went to Kennedy's room where we saw the perfect family. Kennedy looked exhausted, but happy, and Cornelius was beaming, leaning over the bed, admiring his family.

Cornelius wasn't kidding. The baby did look like her Aunt Chandler in the same dark chocolate complexion with her small nose and vibrant eyes. It was too early to see a smile from baby Cawthorne, but if it was anything like Chandler's, it was going to be a knockout. Chandler said her niece was the baby that she never had. I had never asked her why she didn't have children, but I was curious.

Chandler apprehensively touched the baby's cheek. "What's her name?" she asked.

Together, Kennedy and Cornelius said, "Alexandria Nicole."

"That's pretty. How are you doing, Alexandria Nicole?" Chandler said quietly. She kissed her niece's forehead. "She's so tiny, Kennedy."

"She's only six pounds even, and twenty and a half inches long. She's a small baby like you were, Chandler," Kennedy confirmed.

"Is that the secret? You've got to be born small in order to stay that way?" I said. "I was an eight pounder and twenty-two inches."

"Well, the height is definitely there and you're not fat, Stevie Michelle. Five pounds would put you in there," Chandler said.

"More like ten," I confessed.

"Okay, ten. But nonetheless, we can still save you."

"Thanks a lot, Chandler."

"You're welcome."

The baby made sounds, bringing back our focus on the real reason we were there.

"She's talking already, Stevie Michelle. Did you hear her? She's probably telling us to shut up."

"She wouldn't be that rude, girlfrien'. She hasn't picked up any of your bad habits yet."

"You two act more like sisters than friends," Kennedy said. "And don't make me laugh. My bottom is still a little sore and laughter reminds me."

Chandler's arms were outstretched when she said, "Can I hold her?"

"Sure. I want you to. You are officially an aunt and babysitter." Kennedy handed the baby over.

Chandler was definitely more comfortable with a butcher's knife than with a baby. "I don't think I'll get used to this, Kennedy. I've handled chickens bigger than she is."

Kennedy held her belly as she laughed. Cornelius and I shook our heads.

"The difference between her and a chicken," Kennedy said, "is she'll grow much bigger. Just give her a little time."

"Well, ten more pounds would be good. I think I'll feel more confident that I won't break her."

"Just in case, she comes with a repair kit." Kennedy gave admiring looks at her sister and her baby.

Chandler stared down at her niece and said, "Alexandria Nicole, I'm going to give you the best life I possibly can. I may be poor as an alley rat, but I'll do the best I can."

"Planning on losing your job, big sister?"

"No, even worse. I'm going to quit to start Maroon."

Kennedy squealed. "You're kidding!? This is great. Do you know how long I've waited to hear you say that?"

"No. I don't. I didn't know it meant that much to you."

"It's not what it means to me, but what it means to you. Remember, I've lived with you and your dreams for a long time, Chandler. You've done what you've had to do, but now you're actually going to do something that you've wanted for years. I can't wait to point and say, that's my sister's restaurant."

"Hold it, little sister. You make it sound so easy."

"For me, it is easy. Like I said, all I have to do is point. You've got to make it happen. But you know I'll help as much as I can."

"You're not going to have time to do anything but raise my niece. I want her perfect. You hear me?"

"Yeah. Like you want everything else." Kennedy knew her sister well.

"Yes, Kennedy. The nutty perfectionist is what I call her," I said.

"Okay. You two can stop ganging up on me. I have no one to come to my defense. Cornelius always remains neutral in these discussions."

"I sure do. I know what's best." Cornelius reached for his baby daughter and Chandler politely handed her over. She started to cry. "Is this how it's going to be?" he asked.

"Because you are *so* neutral," Chandler said, "she can't sense if you're friend or foe."

As laughter filled the room, Cornelius gave Kennedy the baby. Kennedy gently separated her gown from herself and began breast feeding."

Chandler's eyes approvingly fixated on the sight. "I'm proud of you, little sister. That's the best food for her right now."

"I think so, too. And what better way to bond with her?" Kennedy said. Chandler stood close at the bed, next to her sister and niece.

"Hey, listen," I said, "I think it's time I get home. Nelson and a friend of his from school are here and I told them we'd catch a movie this evening. So, I'll see you guys later."

Once I made it home, I called through the house three times for Nelson before he and his friend, Lionel, came out of his room. "What are you guys up to?" I asked.

"Oh nothing. I was showing Lionel my baseball card collection."

"It's an awesome one, isn't it?" I said proudly. "Nelson's been collecting since around age eight. He's even been lucky to get a few autographed ones. I told him his collection is invaluable and to hold onto it for his kids."

Nelson was tall, but Lionel was a little taller at about six three or four. He had bedroom eyes and features that looked like they had been carved from a block of oatmeal-colored granite. He was of medium build with a perfect V-shape and a butt that I would have paid to see in Calvin Klein underwear ads. His muscles weren't large, but they were strong. And I couldn't keep my eyes off his lips. They were plump and prominently shaped, which made them appear perfectly outlined. He was very pretty.

"Where are your parents from, Lionel?" I asked.

"My dad's from Jamaica and my mother is from Indiana."

He looked Jamaican.

"Are they living in Indiana?"

"No. They live in Rhode Island."

"So you go to school significantly far from home?"

"Yeah. But I like Atlanta better than Rhode Island."

"Oh yeah? Why?"

"It's more black people there for one. And although I know prejudice is everywhere, I don't feel it as much down there. Rhode Island is for the bourgeois."

"And you don't consider yourself bourgeois?"

"Not at all."

"What do your parents do, Lionel?"

"My dad's a stockbroker and my mom's a nurse."

"And they don't care that you're not home for the holiday?"

"They're in Jamaica right now. They go every year and spend Thanksgiving through New Years, and then come back. My sister is with them. I said I didn't want to go this time. They didn't protest much. Maybe because I am twenty-three now, and it's time for me to make my own decisions."

"And deciding that you're not going to vacation with the family is a start?" I said.

"Mother . . ." Nelson signified.

"How old is your sister?" I asked.

"Nineteen. She's attending the School of Design in Rhode Island. She doesn't like to be away from my parents. Me. I get away as often and as far as I can. They can be smothering sometimes."

"They probably just love and think highly of their children."

"Mother!" Nelson, said again.

"Nelson, man, it's all right. Mrs. Wilkes is just expressing her opinion. I like that in a woman. I like that in any person."

Lionel's smile was honey-like. And his teeth were perfectly straight inside his beautiful mouth.

"You guys still want to make a movie tonight?" I asked.

They looked at one another and Lionel said, "Definitely. I hear Steven Seagal's new one is the bomb."

Nelson co-signed. "It starts in thirty-five minutes."

I was hoping for something less violent and a little more romantic, but the majority ruled and besides, Steven Seagal wasn't bad to look at, and I could always rent a video to see romance.

"Then Steven Seagal it is," I said. "You guys get ready."

* * * * *

I didn't remember much of the movie. One minute I was watching Steven Seagal kick the hell out of someone and then the next I was having a flashback. It had been a long, long time since the uncontrollable tremors, the heart palpitations and the beads of sweat popping out over my skin like a severe case of chicken pox. It had been at least ten years that I could remember going to la la land, and although I tried, I never made it. Uncle Lucius' clammy hands all over me and his sweaty body on top of mine pinned me to the seat, paralyzing my escape. I wanted to cry out for Nelson to help me, but I couldn't. Uncle Lucius had covered my mouth with his big, heavy hand.

What happened? What triggered the flashback? It frightened me to know.

At home again, I went straight to my room and sat on the bed with the lights out. Thinking of how Grandma Shaky had warned me that it exhausted too much energy to hate, I was hating. All over again, I hated the man that had molested me. After all the time, where did I have the hate buried? It unexpectedly surfaced and poured out like the molten and steam of a volcano that had been dormant for years, maybe decades. Just as I had thought I was safe—cured—in a movie theater the hot lava burned. Uncle Lucius had returned to my inner self, charring the essence of my soul. I never talked about him to anyone, not even Mama. And she hadn't spoke of Uncle Lucius either. It was as if we had an unspoken agreement. It was as if Uncle Lucius didn't exist. Was he dead? Certainly Mama would know if he was. Certainly she would say.

I picked up the phone. I thought I was going to call Mama, but I dialed Chandler instead.

Her voice was groggy.

"Are you sleeping?" I asked.

She groaned and I could hear the rustle of her covers. "What time is it, Stevie Michelle?"

"I don't know. I haven't looked at my watch for a long time." Her words intelligible, she asked, "Are you okay?"

"I don't know, Chandler."

I felt a frigid draft descend over my dank skin. First my cheeks, my armpits, and then my legs and feet. The urge to ask, "Why don't you want me to be a partner in Maroon?" emerged. "Is it because you don't think I have anything to contribute? I may not be a college graduate like you and Lorelei, but I'm far from stupid. I have something to offer."

"Hold it, Stevie Michelle. I've never thought you were stupid or anything like that. And I didn't *ask* Lorelei to be a partner. She included herself. I told you, I'm apprehensive. If I fail at this, I don't want anyone to fail with me. It's as simple as that. The restaurant business is risky. I'm only trying to protect the people I care about."

"Well, don't protect me. Allow me to feel a part of something. I haven't felt a part of anything for so long."

"What is it you want me to do?" Chandler's voice was sympathetic, but firm.

"Just what I said. Let me be a part of it? A part of Maroon. I'm not begging, Chandler. I'm just asking."

"Of course you're not *begging*. Beg is not in our vocabulary. And I think I understand where you're coming from."

"Then if you do, include me in."

Chandler's sigh was conclusive. I knew that. I had heard that definitive sigh many times.

"I have no problem with it, Stevie Michelle. The more the merrier, as long as everybody understands that I am the chef and no one interferes with the chef."

"I understand, and I agree with you. Lorelei is handling the accounting, and I've been thinking that I could handle the PR. What do you think?"

"At twelve-thirty in the morning, I think that's a great idea." There was a mutual silence before Chandler said, "Stevie Michelle, go to bed. Everything will be okay. I promise."

"Good night, Chandler."

"Good night, girlfrien'. I'll talk to you tomorrow."

My room and the phone acquired a dead silence simultaneously. I curled into the fetal position, pulled the blankets up over me, and sometime between twelve-thirty and sunrise I fell asleep.

Chapter 15

(Stevie Michelle)

The knock on my door startled me. "Mother, are you awake? Grandma's on the phone. She wants to talk to you."

It took me a few seconds to recognized the muffled voice as Nelson's.

"Mother, can you hear me?"

"Come in, Nelson."

The door creaked as he opened it. He started with, "Didn't you hear the phone ring? Grandma wants to talk to you."

I didn't remember, but when I checked, I must have turned the ringer off after I talked to Chandler. What was I thinking to do that?

"Thanks Nelson," I said, as I picked up the phone."

"Hi, Mama."

"You goin' to sleep all day, girl? It's nine-thirty and it's Thanksgivin'."

"I know what day it is, Mama, but thanks for the reminder."

"What, you went out drinkin' with one of your men last night? Is that why you can't get up this mornin'?

"For the record, I went to see a movie with Nelson and his friend last night. Then I came straight home and I've been here." I rolled over on my side, letting my head rest on the receiver. "Mama, did you call to interrogate me?"

"No. I called to see what time you plan to be here for dinner."

I asked, "What time is everybody else getting there?"

"About four or four-thirty."

"Then we'll be there about that time, too."

"Don't forget dessert, Stevie Michelle."

"Oh *shhhit*," I mumbled. I had forgotten that I was to bring a dessert. "Okay, Mama, I'll see you later." Hanging up the phone, I immediately picked it up again and called Chandler. She answered on the first ring. "Good morning, honey," I said.

"Good morning, Stevie Michelle."

"Whatcha doin'?"

"What most people do on Thanksgiving morning— I'm cooking. I just finished the cranberry relish and the stuffing for the turkey. I'm not going to asked what you're doing, because whatever it is, it ain't in the kitchen."

"Now, Chandler, there's no need to be cruel on this day of thanks."

"I'm not being cruel, just honest."

"Okay, then there's no need to be honest on this day of thanks."

"Stevie Michelle, some of us have things to do. What is it?"

"Look, I just wanted to say good morning and to *aahh* . . ."

"To what, Stevie Michelle?"

"To ask what you're making for dessert."

"Why?"

"Because I need a favor."

"No. No. No. I am not going to make dessert for you. Go to the store, Stevie Michelle, and get something."

"I don't want anything from the store, Chandler. Please. I'll pay you."

"You don't have enough money to pay me. You don't even have to cook dinner and you couldn't remember dessert? Sometimes I don't know about you."

"Chandler I don't need you to remind me of my forgetfulness. If you wanted to do something, you should have reminded me yesterday about dessert."

"Stevie Michelle, when are you going to grow up?"

"What does dessert have to do with me growing up?"

"It's called responsibility, girlfrien'."

"I am responsible."

"Yeah. To yourself. You don't forget to pick up your Clinique before you run out of it. You probably have a supply. But you can't remember dessert for one day."

"So what are you making?" I asked in an attempt to calm the subject.

"I'm making a chocolate raspberry cake and apple pie."

"Will you make an extra pie for me?"

"No."

"Please, Chandler? It won't happen again. Please?"

"*Stevie Michelle*!"

"Chandler, *pleeezz*." I knew I was wearing her down.

She sighed. "One pie. That's it."

"That's all I need. Thanks. I'll never forget this."

"Yes you will, but that's you."

"I still love you," I said, knowing that would raise the hairs on her back.

"Stevie Michelle, remind me not to pick up anymore friends like you, okay?"

"You're being cruel again," I said. "So, I guess I'll hang up now. Oh yeah, I'll need that pie about four o'clock. Bye!"

I put on my robe and went downstairs with Nelson and Lionel. They were at the kitchen table eating cereal and drinking coffee. I poured myself a cup.

"Nelson, what are your plans for today?"

"Well, Lionel and I are going with you to Grandma's and then I'm going over to Grandma Bean's. Dad and his wife are there. I talked to him last night. Oh, by the way, Lionel and I agreed that I should go alone, because I don't see them often and I need to talk to Dad."

"Okay. Then I'll bring Lionel back with me from Mama's."

"Thanks, Mother."

I picked the newspaper up off the table and took it and my coffee back to my room. I spent the rest of the morning reading about the world's turmoil and most of the early afternoon sorting through mine. Miles was in town and I was undecided if I should call to say hello. It had been over a year since I last talked to him and it was about Nelson. Oregon was a long way to come from for me not to ask him how he's doing. But in reality, I didn't think he cared if I called. And if I called, Mrs. Bean would deliberately drop the phone on the table and yell for Miles, not telling him who it was, because my name coming off her tongue, through her lips, would make her vomit her Thanksgiving turkey.

I thought about Carl. He was probably at his brother's. We used to alternate Thanksgiving and Christmas. I think it was Carl's year to go to St. Louis, or was it?

Bob Bragg. I couldn't call him. His wife wouldn't appreciate it, especially on Thanksgiving. Bob had convinced me to have an affair with him after multiple refusals on multiple occasions. But he caught me on a vulnerable day and there I was, at the Wyndham, my panties and self-respect on the floor, side by side. After the first time, it became easier and he started coming over regularly. Every Friday and Monday night. Now and then he'd give me a bonus of a Wednesday or Sunday.

Bob was my first married man and I had hoped my last. And, of course, he meant more to me than any of the single ones. He was the reason I had gained the extra fifteen pounds I was carrying on my butt. One of the thrills of seeing him, besides the intense sex we had, was he'd bring whatever I wanted to eat. Just as a test, I once asked for a margarita to go along with the Mexican food he brought. Somehow he had convinced the bartender to mix one and pack it to go. All I needed to add was ice.

I guessed Bob was as good to me as a married man with two teenagers could be. He used to say, "You are the best 'piecea' black ass I've ever had." Coming from a white man, I should have been offended, but I wasn't. After all, he was the best 'piecea' white ass, I'd ever had. We were fulfilling the voids and fantasies in our lives. I even met him in Chicago and Florida a few times when he went out of town on business. Our presence in Chicago was ignored, but the Floridians didn't care for our interracial involvement.

Eventually, for me, everything got boring—the food, the trips and the routine. I warned Bob of my tendency toward boredom. He called me everyday for a month after our breakup. So, on Thanksgiving day, there I was, in my room, thinking about past husbands, lovers and regrets.

Reluctantly lifting myself off the bed, I went into the bathroom, showered, patted myself dry and put on a pair of jeans that were too tight and a turtleneck sweater. I decided not to call anyone and instead went downstairs to ask Nelson what his father was up to. He and Lionel had moved to the den, listening to a CD with old Motown recordings.

"Nelson, when you talked to your father last night, how did he say he was doing?"

"He's great. Why?"

"I don't know. I was just contemplating if I should call to say hello."

"And what, Mother, make his day?" Nelson was the only one who laughed. "You know she's pregnant?" he said

"Who?" I said sharply.

"Dad's wife. Janice. He told me she's due in three months."

I wondered if I looked as crimson on the outside as I felt on the inside. "A baby!? What will that old goat do with a baby?"

"Be a father, Mother. A father to the baby like he's been a father to me."

"Well, you're finally getting the brother or sister you've always wanted."

"A half brother or sister. It's not the same, and it's a little late, Mother. I asked for a brother sixteen years ago. Unless he comes here in his twenties, I really have no use for him."

"I wonder where you get your attitude from, Nelson?"

"Like mother, like son," he said, embarrassing me in front of Lionel, who quietly observed our normal mother and son conversation.

To change the discussion, I announced, "Dinner is at four-thirty, Nelson. Try to be on time. You know how Mama can get."

"Only with you, Mother. She's always been a sweetheart and understanding with me."

"Nelson, just try to be on time. I'm going to stop by Chandler's first."

"What, to pick up your contribution to dinner?"

"You're nothing but a smart-alec, my dear son."

"I am not. I'm just factual. You can't fault me for that."

"Yes I can. See you at Mama's," I said, before I retreated to my room like a defeated animal. I shut the door behind me and sat on the bed. I didn't realize it while I was downstairs, but the announcement of Miles having a baby made me jealous. Not jealous in the sense of wanting him, but wanting him to be father to no one but Nelson. He was *my* only child. And after all this time, why start over? *"Foool!"* I said under my breath.

Looking at the clock, I had approximately three hours to be ready and out the door. I laid back on my pillow and took a mid-afternoon nap.

Chapter 16

(Stevie Michelle)

Nelson drove his car to Mama's and Lionel rode with him. I stopped at Chandler's to pick up the pie. When I walked in, the kitchen windows were steamed from the moisture with trickles of water chasing after one another. The warmth and the aroma of spices and herbs welcomed me. Chandler was putting the last touches on the cake she had baked.

"That is beautiful," I said. "Can I change my order?"

"No, you can't change your order, and be thankful you're getting the pie," she said, delicately spreading frosting.

"Oh, I'm thankful for the pie. Actually, I'm ecstatic. Just think, this morning I had nothing to bring to the table and all because of you, my dessert will be the bomb, as Nelson says."

Chandler had a glaze of perspiration over her entire face. She had been cooking all day and looked as if a lounge chair could easily become her best friend.

"What time are Cornelius and Kennedy coming?" I asked.

Chandler glanced at the clock on the wall. "In about an hour."

"Everything ready?"

"The cake was the last thing and here it is," she said, holding it out for her own admiration.

Looking around the kitchen, I asked, "So, while I'm here, what can I sample?"

Snickering, Chandler said, "Sample the pie I made you."

"I can't take a cut pie to dinner. That's tacky."

"Trying to eat *my* dinner before *my* guests arrive is tackier. I took it upon myself to look in the oven where there was a perfectly golden-brown turkey with bubbling hot stuffing. Closing the oven, I lifted the lids off the pots on the stove and there were greens, yams and a pan of homemade yeast dinner rolls, with melted butter spread over them.

"When did you make these?" I asked.

"Last night." Chandler was tossing used utensils in the sink into soapy dishwater.

"Aaah, that corner roll has my name on it. It's saying, 'I'm yours, baby.'"

"The only thing that has your name on it is the door, Stevie Michelle. It's calling you. Can't you hear it?"

"Oh, come on, Chandler, you know I'm dying to taste something. Just let me have a little of the greens, some yams and a roll. Nobody will ever know, except you and me."

She never looked in my direction, as she kept admiring the cake, when she said, "Okay, only a saucer."

I did not wait for her to change her mind. I quickly got a saucer and piled as much on as it could hold. Then I took the liberty of getting some cranberry relish out of the refrigerator. Her relish was the best. I could smell the orange zest and cranberries co-mingling while the chopped walnuts were an added complement. My girlfriend was the best cook in the world.

I didn't say much while I ate and Chandler went on with her preparations for dinner. After I scraped and ate the last bit of cranberry relish off the saucer, I lowered myself to her five-feet, six-inch frame and planted a kiss on Chandler's cheek. "Thanks." As I put the empty saucer into the sink and gathered my belongings, including the pie, I said, "It's no joke that you're the best friend I could have." Chandler ignored me. Show of affection wasn't one of her attributes, although she had the biggest heart in the world. It was touching to watch her at the hospital with Kennedy's baby. That was the most endearment and feeling I had ever seen her exhibit. I think it scared her as much as it astonished me. I knew Chandler had love and compassion in her, but buried how deep was the question.

"Have a good Thanksgiving and say hello to your family for me," she said in an exhausted tone.

"Okay, I'll try, but saying hello to everybody could take the whole night. We're a small platoon now. Mama's going to have to start having us come in shifts, with all the husbands, wives, grandchildren, etc., etc., etc. So, I'll talk to you later," I said.

Eight years after Carl and I were married we sold Mama's old rickety house on Eighty-third Street. I was surprised someone actually made an offer to buy it. That someone was a white man in his late fifties or early sixties. He said fixing old houses was a hobby. I think the old man had a vision or an inside scoop, because there is a new house where Mama's used to sit in a development called, The Milverton Estates. At one hundred to one hundred fifty thousand, they cost almost five times more than what Mama's house was purchased for.

Carl included the profit from Mama's old house to buy her a four-bedroom brick bungalow in the Lee-Harvard area. It was a foreclosure that Carl bought inexpensively and had renovated. He was innovative that way and Mama was happy with her new house. The apples and spices in the pie scented my car like burning incense in a Buddhist temple. By the time I got to Mama's, my mouth was watering to the point of almost drooling.

Festive was a benign description for the activity going on when I arrived. All my sisters and brothers were there. It felt like the old woman in the shoe. There was no formal dining. People sat and ate where they could, but that's how it was and no one complained, especially not Mama, and she was the one who mattered. When we weren't in St. Louis, Carl and I used to have Thanksgiving at our house, but after our separation, I just didn't feel like it anymore.

Barbara was at Mama's with her family of two teen boys and husband. I had seen her two days before the holiday at her hair salon. She was Chandler's and my hair stylist. Barbara never learned to cook worth a plugged nickel, but she was a damn impressive hair stylist. Roslyn, a secretary, showed with her current boyfriend, and Connie, unemployed by choice, and a newlywed, was clinging to her husband, kissing him every five seconds between spoon feedings from her plate. I wondered how long it would be before he bit the hand that fed him.

Faith and Faye, although twins, were on opposite ends of the spectrum. Faith, predictably unrealistic, swore never to marry, but was on her second husband and having her third baby, living in Michigan. Faye, astute and focused, wanted a husband and a large family. She was an elementary school teacher in Columbus and went home every night to cuddle with her two Persian cats.

Isaiah. There was everything to say about him. Master's degree in chemical engineering, studying for his Ph.D., he was cool. He had shed his naivety like a snake sheds dead skin. His wife, Terri, was the most adorable, petite girl. Although she was twenty-nine, she looked to be about eighteen. Married two years, they were doing wonderfully together. Little Lauren, as they called their daughter, was nine months old and attempting to take her first steps. When I walked in, she stared up at me with a big smile as she cruised the furniture on wobbly, unsure legs. She had the evidence of mashed potatoes over her face. Mama said she reminded her of me when I was a baby.

After they had some dinner, Nelson and Lionel went into the TV room to talk with Joseph.

"How did the three of you reserve this room?" I asked, breaking into their conversation.

Joseph responded, "I can't tolerate being packed like sardines. For me, it gets a little claustrophobic."

"Mother, Uncle Joe was just telling me he has a friend that's selling a Kawasaki motorcycle real cheap because he's buying another one. I'm going to look at it tomorrow."

I understood that Nelson was an adult, but my maternal instinct and authority kicked in immediately. "I don't think so, Nelson. You have no need for a motorcycle."

"Do you hear her, Uncle Joe?"

"Stevie Michelle, this man is grown. He can make is own decisions. Besides, he's only going to look at it."

I hated to do it, but I pulled rank in front of Nelson's uncle and his friend. "As long as Nelson is in college and on Miles' health insurance, he will have to sacrifice some things, and a motorcycle is one of them. They are dangerous, Joseph, and I don't want him on one."

The thought of Nelson on a motorcycle frightened me to death, especially with Joseph's past experience. At twenty-eight, Joseph broke his pelvis, loss vision in his left eye, and had to have a disc removed from his back as a result of a motorcycle accident. At thirty, his injuries had transformed him into a man on disability with little, if any, motivation. He was working at a dry cleaner.

"And have you forgotten what happened to you, Joseph?" I inquired. "How could you even condone Nelson buying a motorcycle?"

"No, I haven't forgotten what happened to me. I'm reminded everyday with the stiffness and not being able to see to my left without making a one-hundred-eighty-degree turn."

"So you have the same wish for my son?"

"Stevie Michelle, I'll ignore that you said that, because it was stupid. There are millions of people on motorcycles everyday who haven't had accidents. When are you going to let him be his own man, woman?"

"Joseph, I think that accident destroyed part of your brain."

"All I'm saying, Stevie Michelle, is you've sheltered Nelson all his life. Let him live and have some fun."

"He can live and have as much fun as he wants, but it won't be on a motorcycle." My temper was flailing. "And you're not much older than he is, so who the *hell* are you to judge how I raised my son? You're stepping out of bounds, Joseph."

I couldn't remember ever arguing with Joseph. We never had a reason, but the welfare of Nelson was a sure-fired way of getting one started.

"You can't—"

"Just shut up!" I said with a venomous tongue.

My steps were quick and direct as I stomped out of the room toward the kitchen. Stopping at the door's threshold, I breathed in deeply and slowly let it out. Her back was to me. Mama was standing at the stove, sniffing the aroma from a pot as she stirred. Not quite as plump, her hair pulled back into a bun and her apron tied snug around her waist, she displayed a semblance of Grandma Shaky in the kitchen. I gave thirty seconds or so to watching her with thoughtful eyes.

Finally, in the latter phases, Mama seemed relaxed with life. Considering her lunging start, she coasted to the finish line with contentment. Mama had mellowed. We didn't clash or argue like we used to. When I divorced Carl, she said, 'I'm proud of you. You stayed twenty years longer than I thought you would, Stevie Michelle. Regardless of what he had to offer and how he gave it to you, Carl's a good man, and I hope you either change yo' mind or the two of you get back together.' That was the greatest moment in our relationship. I wasn't reprimanded, ridiculed, shamed or blamed.

"Everything was good, Mama," I said, "especially the macaroni and cheese. You know how I love your mac and cheese."

She turned around and smiled. "I got started a little later this mornin' than I wanted to fixin' things, but everything came together at the last minute. Not havin' to bake was a blessin'." Mama looked over at the kitchen table and said, "And I know Chandler had somethin' to do with that pie. It's got her signature all over it with that fancy decoration of pastry leaves and apples on the top. She baked it to a perfect golden brown. It's almost too pretty to eat, but don't think I ain't goin' to."

"Yeah. She made it," I admitted.

"How is Chandler?"

"She's fine. She's getting ready to open a restaurant."

"You kiddin' me?"

"Nope. We're hoping that in the near future, Maroon will be a reality and not just a name."

"It sounds like you goin' to have somethin' to do with it?"

"I am, Mama. I'll be working with her. You remember Lorelei?"

"Sure I do."

"Well, she's the accountant and I'm going to handle the public relations and sales."

"I can picture you three as a team," Mama said.

"Really, Mama?"

"Sure I can. Why not? Just thinkin' about the time you girls were plannin' Nelson's surprise goin'-away-to college party. Between the three of y'all, everything was organized with a capital O! I was impressed, and so was his friends. And we ain't got to talk about the food. The table looked like somethin' from one of them fancy food magazines. Yep, I believe y'all will do good in business. I'll be yo' first customer. I just hope Chandler serves that tomato spread she makes. That stuff is good on French bread."

"As PR person, it's my job to tell her that."

"Well, make sure you do."

Mama turned off the eye on the stove and ladled gravy from the pot into a boat. Untying her apron she said, "This is it. I'm done in the kitchen for tonight. You girls can wash the dishes. I'm goin' to cut two pieces of Chandler's pie—one for now and one for later, before it's all gone—and then I'm goin' to sit on my a-s-s for the rest of the evenin'."

"Cut three pieces. I'll join you." Mama and I sat at the kitchen table talking and appreciating Chandler's apple pie. "She's a natural with food, Mama." I had never tasted an apple pie with lemon zest in the crust. It woke up the apples and spices. Mama said she was tempted to hide the rest of the pie. She commented, "They can eat that store-bought crap. This is too good to share."

"You're going to try to eat it all yourselves, aren't you?" Nelson had come into the kitchen. "You know I've got to have a piece of Chandler's pie," he said.

"Well, you better get it now, 'cause there ain't no guarantee," Mama said. "It's first come, first serve with this pie." She ate another bite. She licked her lips. "This is *fantabulous*, Stevie Michelle."

Nelson interrupted Mama's testimonial. "Mother, I'm headed over to Grandma Bean's house. Lionel is in the living room talking with Isaiah. I told him I'd be back at the house in a couple of hours."

"Okay, honey. I'll probably be here another half hour. Then we'll head home," I said. "See you later."

Nelson cut a slice of Chandler's pie, putting it in a napkin as he left the kitchen. Mama and I resumed our conversation.

"Stevie Michelle, do you remember me mentionin' Mr. Norton two doors down from here?"

"The white house?" I asked.

"That's him."

"I remember. Why?"

"He's supposed to stop over this evenin' and have a little dinner."

"Oh, really? Was he invited?"

She developed a smirk. "Of course he was invited, silly girl."

"And you're telling me this *becuzzz* . . ."

"Because in case he stops over while you still here, you'll know who he is. That's all."

"Is this serious, Mama?"

"Stevie Michelle, the only things serious at my age is findin' out there's no more Social Security to be had and not wakin' up the next mornin'. We're friends. He likes playin' bingo on Thursday nights and we been a few times together."

"So, I take it, he's single?"

"What would I look like at my age bein' with a married man? Of course he's single. His wife died and he has a daughter about yo' age. I ain't never met her, but I saw pictures. My girls are better lookin'."

"Mama!"

"I can only call it as I see it, Stevie Michelle. She must've taken after her mother, 'cause Al's got it goin' on. He's over sixty, but he's holdin'."

I couldn't contain the laughter. I said, "Mama, where did you learn to talk like that?"

"I don't remember, but you know what I'm talkin' about."

There was a knock at the back door.

"*Shhh*. That must be him," Mama said as she went to see. Pulling back the curtain, she smiled at the figure on the other side. She opened the door. "Come on in, Al. I'm glad you could make it."

To my surprise, he was sixty-something and holding. Mr. Norton was about six-feet and had shaved the rest of his head to match the part that was naturally bald. His mustache was thick and salt and peppered. His eyes were clear and bright, and he had a sexy smile. My eyes traveled to his mid-section where his shirt relaxed flat. The man must have worked out.

"Come on in and meet my oldest daughter," Mama said.

"Good evening. How are you?" His voice had an upward rhythm with a full single swing. His hazelnut complexion was smooth and healthy. He was neatly dressed in a light navy wool jacket and sharply creased slacks that the cuffs rested perfectly atop a pair of dark brown suede boots. He did have it going on.

"I'm holdin— I mean, I'm fine," I said, embarrassed.

"Edella has told me about you," Al said. "She said you are the articulate of the family."

I didn't think Mama used the word 'articulate'. It was probably more like, *She's the daughter who uses big words that I don't understand.*

"Come on, Al," Mama said, "I want you to meet the rest of the clan. I'll warn you now that it's a large one."

"I wish my family had been larger," he said.

That instant I experienced deja vu. What Al had said to Mama was similar to what Carl had told me when we met.

Al graciously allowed Mama to guide him through the house. I followed in a chaperone-like fashion. When Mama got around to introducing Isaiah, I excused myself and beckoned Lionel to come with me. Lionel and I said good-bye to the rest of the family. The late evening November air was refreshing. As we walked to the car, I engulfed the weightlessness into my lungs.

On the way home, Lionel and I talked about old movies and his plans after college. He seemed mature for his age, as I listened to his reference of the significance of being a positive figure for other black males and helping whenever he could. I was impressed with his philosophy.

I apologized for him having to witness the squabble between Joseph and myself.

He said, "Actually Mrs. Wilkes, I think you were appropriate about how you felt. Sometimes Nelson doesn't think. He's all for excitement and adventure, no matter what the price. He feels the need to do it all and be it all right now."

"He inherited that trait, Lionel. I used to be that way."

"But, Mrs. Wilkes, you seem so level-headed."

"Like I said, I *used* to be that way." Pulling into the drive, I quickly reflected on the old Stevie Michelle. In so many ways I was still her—passionate for excitement and remarkable experiences.

Once inside, Lionel headed straight for the den and the CDs. I followed.

"You know, this is an impressive collection," he mentioned.

"That's years of collecting, Lionel. My husband wasn't much for investing in music. He liked antiques and art. I do too, but music is. . . Well, it's. . ."

"It's universal," Lionel interjected.

With enthusiasm, I said, "Good term. Yeah. Universal."

We stared at one another.

"Would you like something to drink?" I asked. "Like a glass of wine or a beer."

"A beer, please."

In the kitchen, I noticed my heart. It was banging at my chest's door. It was the old Stevie Michelle. The Stevie Michelle that needed passionate experiences.

I poured myself a glass of wine and took Lionel a bottle of beer with a mug. He had put a Wes Montgomery CD into the player and was sitting in the leather chair that had been bought to replace the old worn one that fit my butt perfectly, whether it was fifteen pounds lighter or heavier. Wes's guitar was soft and seductive.

"You like Wes?" I asked.

"Oh, yeah. Just like Hendrix had a style of his own, Wes had his. Musicians have attempted to duplicate them, but none have excelled. Their music will live forever."

I swallowed a sip of wine. Lionel drank his beer out of the bottle.

He made a sound of approval as he drank. "I have a weakness for cold beer," he said.

"What are some of your other weaknesses, Lionel?"

"I believe they are fried pork chops, lemon meringue pie and the moon."

"The moon?"

Lionel's eyes widened when he said, "I believe the moon controls behavior and events. It forecasts the daily emotional weather, determining people's highs and lows, especially in its new and full states. I'm fascinated by it. I'll follow it anywhere."

I laughed. "You're not a werewolf, are you?"

"No. Just an avid believer of astrology."

I drank more wine and sat at the edge of the leather chair facing Lionel. "I have a weakness, too," I said.

"For what?"

"For pretty men. It's an admiration that I haven't been able to ignore."

"Don't you mean handsome men, Mrs. Wilkes?"

"No. I mean pretty men."

"How so? Explain."

My glass half empty, I swallowed another sip and began my explanation. "Handsome is having an impressive appearance, Lionel. The ugliest man can be handsome if he has class, style and charisma. But pretty, on the other hand, is having an exceptional appearance. It goes beyond personality and style. The man's dress appearance can be shabby and classless, but when you look into his face, you can see just how attractive he is."

"And how do you see me?" Lionel asked in a sensual tone that was his voice, but also someone else's manner. It was an expression he had practiced many times. I didn't know how I knew that, but I did.

"Pretty!" I answered.

"How so?" His eyes, with suspense, studied my eyes.

"Your lips, Lionel. They are perfect. Exceptional." I brushed them with my fingertip. He didn't move. Then I gracefully swept his cheek with the back of my hand. I felt the beginning of fine hair stubble. He leaned into my touch.

Then I think I heard him say something like, "Please, Mrs. Wilkes, this isn't right."

Then I think I said something like, "It'll be fine."

I kissed him. His lips were what I expected—firm, yet soft.

Then I think he said, "Oh, my God."

Then I think I asked, "Do you find me attractive, Lionel?"

I think he answered, "Yes, I do, but—"

I think I said, "But what?"

Then I think he said, "But not like th—"

I kissed him again. That time longer, with more passion.

Then I think I asked, "Then like what?"

Abruptly, Lionel turned away.

I gently grasped his chin in my hand and directed his face toward me. I'll never forget his facial expression. Then I think I said, "I don't mean to embarrass you, Lionel. I'm sorry. Can't we—"

"Mrs. Wilkes, you have nothing to do with me not being sexually attracted to women."

CHAPTER 17

(Chandler)

After Thanksgiving and before Christmas, my pace raced parallel with hectic. I went to see Kennedy and the baby at least four times out of a week, and Alex stayed with me overnight a few times. She brought out my maternal instincts. We cuddled at night, and while visions of the tasks I needed to do trotted across my mind, I listened to her soft, short baby breaths and heartbeat as she slept, eventually falling asleep myself. The only necessity for taking my niece home was more breast milk. I was grateful that Kennedy allowed me to be with Alex as often as she had, because within forty-five to sixty days I wouldn't have time for anything except contractors and the license departments at city hall.

Everything was happening at once. I moved from the house where Wade and I lived into a smaller one, near the restaurant on the border of Shaker Heights. The space I rented for the restaurant was ready for renovation and Lorelei was expected in town in two weeks. She and Stevie Michelle got separate condominiums in the same complex. Stevie Michelle didn't have to go through the hassle of selling her house, because Carl made her a generous offer, buying her share, paying one and a half times for the same property.

My new dwelling, a wonderful two-bedroom colonial, was just enough for me and Alex when she visited. I imagined her in the backyard on the tricycle I would buy on her second birthday. I genuinely liked the coziness of the house with its two fireplaces, one in the living room and the other in the master bedroom, but realistically, the house was no place for my piano. I stored the living room furniture, except for two chairs and a table and lamp, in the basement. The piano claimed three of the four walls. As soon as the restaurant was finished, I would have it moved there. The kitchen in the house was small, but I didn't need a large kitchen when I would have a more than adequate one in the restaurant.

Making reservations for vacation to the Bahamas for Stevie Michelle, Lorelei and myself wasn't easy, either. Every hotel was booked, but luckily I knew a couple who had the same type of time-share as the one Wade and I had, and asked if I could purchase theirs. I didn't want to ask Wade for his, but I probably would have if I couldn't arrange for anything else. My inquiry paid off. I got us a two-bedroom condo with a sleep sofa for six full days in Freeport from Thursday to Wednesday, January 1st. It wasn't oceanfront, but that was okay.

The three of us were excited. Lorelei had made the necessary provisions for the children with Walter, and Stevie Michelle and I requested time away from work. The three of us hadn't traveled together in years. I held the tickets in my hand while on the phone with Stevie Michelle.

"They're right here," I said. "They came today. We fly out of Hopkins to Miami and from there to Freeport. We've got to be at the airport at six-thirty a.m."

"We have to be there at six-thirty?" Stevie Michelle whined.

"Yep. There."

"Make sure you call and wake me," she requested.

I said, "Set a damn alarm clock, woman."

"I'm going to nickname you 'snapping turtle', Chandler, if your attitude doesn't change."

"I don't care what you call me. I'm not going to be your alarm clock, so get over it."

"Have you talked to Lorelei?" she asked.

"No. I'll call her as soon as I get off the phone with you. She's been so busy, transferring records and funds, and getting things packed for the move. She said it's almost costing her double to move from South Carolina than it did to move down there."

"Did she say how Walter was taking it?"

"She says he's ecstatic about having his children back within driving distance. She told me he's called every day this week to see if there's anything he can do. Lorelei said he even offered to pay the children's flight."

"But he didn't offer to pay hers?"

"No. Why should he? The offer to help was a bonus."

"I guess."

"There's no guessing about it, Stevie Michelle. Walter could leave his responsibility at paying child support. According to the courts, that's where his responsibility ends. They don't even give a damn about visitation. And, instead of telling Lorelei to get a babysitter while she's in the Bahamas, he's agreed to keep the children. I admire him for that. He could be off having fun."

"You're right."

"I know I am. But anyway, enough about that. I'm going to call Lorelei and then fill out these vendor and liquor license applications that are staring back at me. The questions are so in depth. They practically want to know your life history and who your great grandparents were."

"Is everything falling into place?" Stevie Michelle asked.

"I don't know yet. I'm sure the bureaucracy will begin as soon as I submit the paperwork. I anticipate anxieties and frustrations galore before all this is over. I'm so nervous, I dreamed last night that there was a fake food license on the wall in the restaurant, and the inspector, and three men with guns, rushed in while it was filled with customers, ripped the framed paper off the wall and closed the restaurant right on the spot. Then they said that the customers were under arrest for patronizing an illegal establishment."

"What do you think that means, Chandler?"

"I think it means I shouldn't have eaten a hamburger and onion rings at nine-thirty before going to bed. And it doesn't help that I'm not sleeping at night."

"Why not?"

"Nervous, Stevie Michelle. I'm so nervous about what we're doing that today I literally started shaking at my desk. Julie walked into my office to give me some information and when I tried to write it down, my hand trembled uncontrollably. She asked if I was all right."

"She'll probably start a rumor that you're on drugs or something, like she did when Sandy Tate passed out at her desk. Julie said she saw Sandy swallow some pills before she collapsed."

"I don't care what she says. I've got approximately a month and a half before I make the big announcement."

"Is Lorelei going to get a job before the restaurant opens?"

"She says she's not. She said that she'll watch her pennies and help as much as she can to get everything for Maroon set up. While we're in the Bahamas, the three of us should do some brainstorming."

"Do you really think we'll do that, Chandler?"

"Yes, I do. This endeavor is very important. Our livelihoods depend on this restaurant."

"You've got to calm down," Stevie Michelle demanded. "You're going to have a nervous breakdown before you can prepare the first appetizer. We'll be in the Bahamas to chill. Rest. Relax. Play with the men. Soak up some sun. Do you remember how to do that stuff?"

"I'm sorry. I'm just a bundle of nerves. Maybe I need to call my doctor so he can prescribe something."

"And make Julie's accusation true? No way, Chandler. Just keep reminding yourself that you can do anything you want, and throw that I-can't-do-it shit out of your mind. I'm supposed to be a partner, in case you've forgotten. Give me some things to do."

"I haven't forgotten that you're a partner, but I need to know what I'm doing before I can delegate."

"When are the contractors coming?" Stevie Michelle asked.

"The next Monday after we get back. The plans should be approved and ready for me to look over."

"Ready for *us* to look over, Chandler. It would be wise for the three of us to be there so that *all* three will know what's going on."

"You're right," I said. "It's just that I'm so used to doing everything myself."

"I know. But you don't have to anymore. You've got a partnership now, honey, and you've got to get used to that or I'm going to feel worthless."

"Stevie Michelle, I'll get better, I promise. As a matter of fact, I'll make a list in the next couple of days of things that need to be done and split it in half with you. Okay?"

"Okay."

I glanced at my watch. "I'm calling, Lorelei," I said. "I'll talk to you later."

"See ya, Chandler."

Stevie Michelle was gone and I immediately dialed Little River, South Carolina. Topper answered the phone.

"Topper, honey, how are you doing?"

"I'm fine, Miss Chandler. How about you? We're packing to come home. And Mommy's enrolling me in parochial school, and Three says he likes the school here and he's not going. I told him to stop being stupid."

"Topper, is—"

"Mommy said I could go to drama school when we move back home. She said there was one in Cleveland called Karamu."

"Topper—"

"She said Halle Berry is from Cleveland. And I like Halle Berry. She's really pretty. And I want to be an actress like her."

"Topper, honey," I said in a persistent tone.

"Yes, Miss Chandler?"

"All that sounds wonderful and I think we should talk about it when you get here, but right now I need to know, is Lorelei there?"

"Yes, ma'am."

"May I speak with her?"

"Yes, ma'am. Hold on."

It sounded like a firecracker popping in my ear when Topper put the phone down. I jumped. *I must really be on the edge*, I thought.

"You must have ESP," I heard my girlfriend say. Her accent had stretched since her sojourn to Little River.

"No. The jitters. I'm so uptight, Lorelei. I was just on the phone with Stevie Michelle and I thought I would jump out of my skin. I'm making a mistake. The restaurant is a stupid idea and having the both of you go in with me is even more stupid."

"Chandler."

"I can't believe I talked myself into this. I mean, do you know how many restaurants fail in a year? You can get equipment at auctions with the warranties still on them."

"Chandler—"

"I can't believe I talked myself into this, Lorelei."

"Chandler!" Lorelei yelled.

"I can't bel— What, Lorelei?"

"I want you to take three deep breaths and let them out slowly."

"I don't have ti—"

"Go ahead, Chandler. Do it, now!"

I did as my compadre demanded.

"Now," she said. "Let's start again. How you doin', other than goin' crazy?"

"That's it. I'm just going crazy."

"But there ain't no need to *spazz*, Chandler. If worse comes to worse, we do like the white folks. We run the restaurant up until they put the padlock on the door and then we walk away, file bankruptcy, get jobs and all live in a two-bedroom apartment in East Cleveland."

"Oh, that makes me feel a hundred percent better, Lorelei. Thanks. Besides, your scenario was accurate until you mentioned East Cleveland. White people don't move to East Cleveland."

"Well, we'll be too poor to move anywhere else other than across the bridge to West 25th Street and I don't want to live on the west side."

"Keep talking, Lorelei. I'm feeling more confident by the second."

"I'm glad I can help."

It was the first time I had laughed all day.

Lorelei's southern slur was soothing. Her tone was relaxed and laid back like a soft breeze tickling the weeping branches of a willow tree.

"We'll be all right, Chandler. You got a talent that my family is still talkin' about. Aussie told me that he was bringin' his wife to the restaurant for their weddin' anniversary."

"Oh, come on, Lorelei. You sure know how to make up stories. He's not talking about driving to Calabash."

"This ain't no story. That's what he said and I believe'im. He was just that impressed with yo' food. I ain't sayin' that would be his only reason for comin', but for him to think about it, should tell you somethin'."

"It does. Your family is as nuts as you are."

"You can downplay what I say if you want, but it's the truth."

The truth was, I wanted Lorelei to keep complimenting me—my cooking. It was the only way I would be convinced that Maroon could survive. I had to be one of the best and most creative chefs there was, and the only way I could do that was with a clear head and an abundance of confidence. I was deficient in both.

"Chandler, tell me somethin'?"

"Yeah?"

"What you so scared about? Exactly."

"The big "F" word."

"And what's that, fondue?"

"Failure, Lorelei. Failure."

"Then don't think about the big "F" word. Think about the big "S" word.

"What, success?"

"Yeah. Success. It's easier and a lot less stressful. It's as simple as that. We ain't goin' to lose, girl. We can't. Not with yo' talent and my creativity with figures. And we ain't got to mention Stevie Michelle's lurin' abilities. We can count on her to bring somebody in at least twice a week."

My giggles lifted the load.

"Now that's enough about you, Ms. Cawthorne," Lorelei said. "I'm the one movin' in two weeks with two excited, out-of-control children. I can't convince Three that we ain't movin' back with Walter. It seems so logical to him that's what should happen."

I said, "Topper told me he doesn't want to leave the school he's in."

"Chandler, Three don't know what he wants. He's my savage son and Topper's the chatterbox."

I chuckled. "Ain't that the truth."

"And I got this feelin' that I ain't goin' to recognize Oceanna when I see her. Talkin' to her on the phone, I'm expectin' this preppie, obnoxious white girl in a black girl's body."

"Why do you say that, Lorelei?"

"Do you know what she said to me the other day when she called?"

"No. What?"

"I asked her if she wanted a room at Walter's or to share Topper's bedroom 'cause there's only three in the condo? I said, 'Walter said it ain't no problem you stayin' with him when you come home from school for the holidays and vacations.'"

"So, what did she say?"

"She told me, the little smart mouth, 'Mom, I don't see how it could be any other way. All of us in a small condo won't work. I'm used to my space and independence now.' She's been gone how long? Does she know who arranged for her new-found space and independence? I think I'll remind her when she gets home."

I felt Lorelei was more disappointed than angry with Oceanna. I was certain my girlfriend had visions of losing her first born to her friends' influences and Walter's affluence.

"Lorelei, she's young. She knows not what she says. And you always said her arrogance runs from the same trough as Walter's. Don't blame her."

"Does she think all this is easy, Chandler?"

"That's just it, she's not thinking. She's operating on raging hormones and cocky confidence, Lorelei, that she hasn't learned to channel properly. Don't take what she says personally."

"I can't help it. She hurt my feelin's."

"You're not going to cry, are you?" She sounded tearful.

"No. But I do want to scream. This move ain't never goin' to come together."

"Yes it will, and I'm surprised at you. You are the most organized person I know, and a little move is not what I expected would turn you into a jellyfish."

"Oh, you sayin' I ain't got no backbone, hunh?"

"Would I say that?"

"Directly, no."

"Then do what you got to do, girlfrien', because when you get here, the real screaming will begin. Stevie Michelle suggested that I stop trying to do everything myself and delegate. And delegate is what I'm going to do—starting with having you handle the bank accounts that need to be set up right away. Once the attorneys draw up the partnership, and the plans are approved, the contractors will want money. Lots of it. It's time to put the kitty together. May the screaming begin. Now is the time for everybody to put up or shut up."

"Chandler, I already started workin' on a bookkeepin' system, so cool yo' jets."

"Have you really?"

"Yes, I have, and we'll talk about it when I get there."

"Lorelei, listen, I'm going to be unbearable at times. I know it. Please hang in there."

"Don't worry about me. I know I got my work cut out dealin' with you and Oceanna. I'm ready."

Lorelei's patience was a blessing. I needed her more than ever. She gave my unbalanced personality balance. She evened the load.

"Hey, I better be going," I said. "Work tomorrow and I've got to get some things done tonight. I'll call you tomorrow to see how you're coming along."

"It will be the same as today, Chandler, but call anyway."

"Okay, bye."

"Bye."

I went straight for the freezer when I hung up the phone. A pint of Haagen Dazs butter pecan ice cream was my companion while I sat at the table listing restaurant equipment, drawing a line after each piece to later insert prices. I wasn't going to tell Lorelei or Stevie Michelle, and not that I was skeptical or pessimistic, but I had to constantly pinch myself to the fact that I was participating in the fulfillment of a dream—my dream. For me, dreams didn't come true and if they did, they didn't come without painstaking sacrifice. Sitting there, licking ice cream off the spoon, recollecting the past, I knew my dreams were crystal clear, but had not crystalized. All the top self-help and motivational books I had read stated that, "you must believe and then implement", but they weren't written for me—a black woman in white America. I had all the right stuff—the motivation, vision, and all the selves—self-confidence, self-esteem, self-worth—but I also had black skin. I believed that there were three types of people: The ones who lived their dreams with ease; those who didn't believe they had destinies; and me, who believed my destiny had already been constructed and I had no clue if I was living a dream or following my destiny.

Chapter 18

(Chandler)

How we got from point "A", loading Stevie Michelle and Lorelei's luggage in the trunk of my car, to point "B", trying to unlock the door of the condominium on the Grand Bahama Island of Freeport, I don't quite remember.

What happened the weeks before was also a blur. Lorelei safely made the move to Cleveland with most of her sanity. There was shopping, planning and preparing for the holiday. Meeting with attorneys and contractors. Christmas came and went before I could finish cooking the fantastic feast we had. Christmas Eve dinner was at my house and my two girlfriends, their children, and my sister and her husband and beautiful baby shared their Christmas Eve with me. That night, I knew Christmas Eve dinner at my house would be a tradition. I roasted a turkey and a standing prime rib. I baked butternut squash, rolls, corn bread, chocolate pound cake and apple and sweet potato pies. The greens, string beans, and fried corn with chopped red and green peppers were the talk of the table.

We had pulled names and exchanged gifts after dinner. Stevie Michelle had my name and I had hers. She bought my favorite perfume and I got her a new wallet. Cornelius was the photographer, but I didn't need pictures to remind me that Christmas 1996 was the best Christmas of my life.

"Chandler, you tried all three keys?" Lorelei asked, breathing down my neck as I attempted to turn the key in the lock.

"Yes."

"Then try puttin' it in the other way."

"Lorelei, I've *tried* it every way, except head first."

"Here, let me do it," she said, taking the key from me. "I used to be in this business, you know."

"Well, I don't think it takes a neurosurgeon, a locksmith or an accountant to open a door, if you've got the right key," I said.

"I hope you two figure this out soon. I've got to pee," Stevie Michelle said with urgency.

"I think we all have a need to relieve ourselves, Stevie Michelle. See if you can be a big girl and hold it for a little longer," I quipped.

"I'm holding it. I'm just tired of holding it."

"If you hadn't drunk those three beers on the plane, you wouldn't be having this problem."

"Am I going to have you monitoring my alcohol consumption while I'm here?"

"I don't care what you consume, Stevie Michelle, and further—"

"*Shuddup*. The both of you," Lorelei yelled as if she was talking to Topper and Three. "We all tired and got to pee, but that ain't getting' this door open." She turned and looked at me. "Chandler, this is the wrong key."

"You sure?"

"I'm as sure as I was the night Three was conceived and he's eight now."

"Shit!"

"Shit is right," Stevie Michelle confirmed.

I looked around the resort complex and then down the road. "The management office is about a half-mile from here. We don't have a car or a phone to call," I said.

"Chandler, in order to get inside, we've got to have the right key."

"That's true, Stevie Michelle, so what do you suggest?"

"I'm going over there where that guy is sitting on his balcony and ask if I can use his toilet and phone. What's the number to the office?"

I scrambled in my purse for the sheet of paper that I had written all the instructions and numbers I needed. I handed it to Stevie Michelle.

"I'll be back soon," she said, waving at the man as she walked toward him. Lorelei and I sat on our luggage and watched. Stevie Michelle, our girlfriend, was all woman. Regardless of the food and festivities of the holidays, she had shed the fifteen pounds she had sworn to. Watching her shoulder-length hair stylishly blow in the mellow tropical breeze, and her hips move like the swaying branches of the palm trees, she didn't look a day over thirty-two.

I leaned over Stevie Michelle's suitcases that were between Lorelei and myself, and asked, "How long do you think she'll keep us waiting here?"

"The way he looks from where I sit we could be left here for the next three days—no key, no bathroom, no Stevie Michelle."

I slapped my thigh and gave an "Amen."

We waited, staring at the balcony for twenty minutes, before Stevie Michelle and the mystery man walked out on it. The both of them were holding glasses in their hands and talking.

"When she gets back over here, I'm going to kill her," I said.

"No, not before I pull every stran' of that fine hair out of her head," Lorelei said with a diabolical smile.

The sound of a car coming up the road stopped our demonic plans. I recognized it. The red Chrysler was the same one that we rode in from the airport. One of the courtesies of staying at the condominium was a ride to the complex. I didn't recognize the driver. He was not the one who picked us up from the airport. He got out of the car wearing a huge smile, an orange shirt printed with fruit, and a pair of tan shorts, apologetically saying in a thick Bahamian accent, "Oh, ladies, we're very sorry for the mix-up. I have the proper keys right here in my hand." He dangled them in front of us. "Which one of you called?" he asked.

Lorelei and I looked at one another and smiling, I said, "Neither." Then pointing, I proclaimed, "The floozy on the balcony over there did." Lorelei chuckled. The man looked confused. I waved my hand at him and said, "It's a private joke. Don't worry. We're just happy you're here." He walked past us and magically opened the door. I looked across to the balcony at Stevie Michelle. She waved for me to go inside. Waving back, I thought, *I hope the man is married and his wife comes in and plucks out those beautiful brown eyes of yours*. The man from the office picked up Stevie Michelle's two cases and insisted that Lorelei and I wait for him to take ours in. Once inside, we stood in a beautifully blue-hued living room. There were shades of the cool color throughout the condo—from royal to a pale iced blue in the master bathroom. I liked it.

"Can I be of any further help to you?" the man asked as he set the last of our suitcases inside the door, handing the correct keys to me.

"What is your name?" I inquired.

"I'm called Adam."

"Adam, thank you. I think we're fine now. Thanks a lot." I didn't tip him. After all, it was the office's fault that someone had to come back. Adam didn't seem to mind, though. He kept smiling as he backed out the door, apologizing again for the confusion. When he shut the door, I plopped onto the sofa and rested my head. In the silence of the condo, I could hear Lorelei in the bathroom relieving her full bladder. The walls were obviously thin. Closing my eyes, I smiled. At forty, I didn't think that being on a romantic tropical island with two women was the way it was supposed to be. I whispered to myself, "I'm forty, lonely and horny." Among the move to the new house, the workload at the office, the time spent with my niece, the holidays and the plans for the restaurant, I hadn't given my sexuality much thought, but it had inconspicuously landed on the island with me.

I didn't notice Lorelei until she sat on the sofa. "You know, girl-frien'," I said to her, "I'm forty years old and fucking in the mood for love."

"Chandler, I know what you mean. I think the only one getting some these days is Stevie Michelle." Lorelei leaned back on the sofa to keep me company. We sat in the silence until Stevie Michelle walked in. She was smiling from ear to ear.

"I was waving for you guys to come on over."

"Looked more like you were waving for us to go inside," I said. "I know how we embarrass you."

"So, what's his name?" Lorelei asked.

"Banning."

"Banning? What a strange name," I said.

"Yeah. Banning Morris is his name and he's English. Damn, I could have listened to his accent all afternoon."

I looked at my watch. "You just about did."

"Oh, be quiet, Chandler. I can still hear his voice. Such a nice voice." Stevie Michelle had the dreamy look of a sixteen-year-old that had been kissed for the first time.

"So, what time is he pickin' you up tonight?" Lorelei asked.

"Seven-thirty, but only if we don't have plans."

Looking at Lorelei, I said, "Do we have plans tonight?"

"Oh, I forgot to tell you about the two messages in the kitchen from Denzel and Wesley, sayin' they pleased that we made it to the island safely and they will send a limo for us at six-thirty for cocktails and we'd have dinner at eight. So see, Stevie Michelle, there's the two of us and the two of them. You go ahead and have a good'ol time with the Englishman tonight."

"I think the both of you need a nap. You're cranky," Stevie Michelle snarled.

"Lorelei may be cranky, but I've just confessed to being horny."

"Sea air will do that to you. I stayed that way when I was in South Carolina," Lorelei said. She got up from the sofa and opened the balcony doors. The wind sailed in. I inhaled.

"All I want to do while we're here is relax," I said.

"You mean you've changed your mind about working on the plans for the restaurant?"

"Stevie Michelle, all I said was we might talk about them. We're not on retreat, we're on vacation—the last vacation we may get for a long, long time."

"*Oooh*, don't scare me," she said, shuddering.

"I've had enough of this," I said. "The first thing we've got to do is decide who sleeps on this sofa bed."

"And how do you propose we do that?" Stevie Michelle asked.

"I suggest we draw numbers out of a hat. Number one representing the master bedroom, two the second bedroom, and three being the infamous sofa bed." I looked at the both of them and said, "Okay?"

"That sounds fair enough to me," Stevie Michelle said.

"Then let's do it," Lorelei confirmed.

I went into the kitchen and saw the notepad on the counter. I wrote the numbers on three sheets and folded them. None of us brought a hat, so I pulled a pot from the cabinet and dropped the numbers in. Back in the room with Lorelei and Stevie Michelle, I held out the pot, shaking it a little, and said, "Okay, pick one." The three of us stuck our hands in and fumbled for the pieces of paper. When each of us had one, I said, "Okay, let's open them together." We did.

Stevie Michelle squealed when she saw that she had number one—the master bedroom. Lorelei exhaled reading the number two. That left me with number three. I looked at the both of them and said, "Get out of my bedroom."

Lorelei had the stare of guilt, as if she didn't deserve the bedroom. Stevie Michelle picked up her luggage and headed straight for the comfort of the master bed and bath.

"Aw, Chandler, look. Why don't we take turns sharin' the bedroom," Lorelei said.

"No. You won it fair and square. I don't mind sleeping out here. There's a wonderful view from the balcony and I'm comfortable with that. So take your things into *your* room."

Lorelei took a suitcase in each hand and rounded the corner to the second bedroom. The two tan pieces of Hartmann luggage that I had taken many trips with over the ten years that I had it, stood unknowingly by the door. I looked around the room. There was no place to store it in the living room. I picked it up and headed into Stevie Michelle's room. She was neatly placing her underwear in the drawer. I gave her a hard stare. "You may have the room, but you've got to share the closet and the bathroom with me."

* * * * *

Stevie Michelle was right. We did need naps and all three of us took one, them in their bedrooms and me on the sofa. I got a pillow and blanket out of the closet and with the tranquilizing tropical air, I slept like a nursing baby. When I awoke, the sun was setting in a hot pumpkin hue. It was the most beautiful act of nature I'd seen in a long time, with many, many trees and richly green vegetation covered with exotic flowers in the forefront. Lorelei came out of her room. "At least you got a view," she said, standing next to me.

"Isn't it gorgeous?"

"Only the naked eye can do it justice. Not even a picture could tell the story right," she added.

"Lorelei, if the sun is setting, I think we should talk about what we're going to eat. I'm hungry."

"Me too."

It was seven o'clock. I could hear Stevie Michelle in her room, opening and closing drawers and dragging the wire hangers across the metal bar in the closet. Laughing, I said, "Our diva is getting ready for her performance tonight."

"Chandler, why you so hard on Stevie Michelle?"

"Am I? I hadn't noticed. I don't treat her any different than I treat you."

"Yes you do, 'cause we two different people."

"Okay, so you are. But I'm not cruel or anything like that, am I?"

"No. But sometimes you are impatient."

"Because sometimes she's— Oh, let's not talk about Stevie Michelle. All I can say is I love her—the both of you—like sisters. And I know she knows that. So, what are we going to eat? There's a couple of restaurants within walking distance. The office recommended Fisherman's Cove for good grouper. I like grouper. How about you?'

"I ain't never had it, I don't think."

"Well, girlfrien', I think you should try it with me tonight."

"Okay."

"I'm going to freshen up as soon as Ms. Thang comes out of her boudoir," I said. "Then we can go."

"See, you doin' it again, Chandler."

"Lorelei, I'm only teasing."

The bedroom door opened and Stevie Michelle came out wearing a striking yellow dress that was buttoned in shiny black buttons down the back, with a sweetheart neckline that tastefully displayed her cleavage, which was smooth and plump. She had added a few curls to her hair and eliminated some make-up, allowing her natural beauty to radiate. The black patent leather purse that hung from her shoulder matched her sandals. She looked elegant.

"You go, girl," Lorelei said.

I smiled with approval and said, "Young lady, I want to know a little more about this date of yours before you walk out of here tonight."

"Chandler, I'm a big girl."

"Yes, I know that, but we're responsible for one another while we're on this island and for all I know he could be Hannibal Lector, and you sure look good enough to eat."

Gales of laughter filled the room.

"His name is Banning," Stevie Michelle said.

"We know that," I said.

"He's English."

"We know that, too."

"He's a journalist."

"We didn't know that."

"And he's here on vacation. His brother was with him, but left to spend a few days in Florida."

With a hint of suspicion, Lorelei asked, "Is he married?"

"No, he's single."

"It's still not enough."

Stevie Michelle protested, "Chandler, what is it that you want to know?"

"Where is he taking you?"

"I don't know. And if he told me, I still wouldn't know. He said we'd go out to dinner. That's all."

"I'm going to have a talk with boyfriend when he gets here," I said. "If he thinks . . ."

There was a knock at the door.

Stevie Michelle pushed back a curl from her face. "Oh my God, it's him. I can't let him see me."

"Why not? If he can't see you, then it's impossible for you to go on a date with him," I said.

"Chandler, you get the door. I've got to make an entrance."

"Make a what!?"

"Just get the door, damn it!"

I chuckled. Lorelei stood by the sliding doors to the balcony, smiling and shaking her head. Stevie Michelle's behavior was a side of her that I mused at. She disappeared into the bedroom.

The knock came again. I cleared my throat and looking through the peephole, I saw an eye staring back. The sight startled me and I softly squealed and jerked my head. When I opened the door, the man on the other side said, "Hello, my name is Banning Morris and I'm here for Stevie Michelle."

I stood there, staring, thinking how interesting it would be to meet his parents, the two people who had created such an intriguingly handsome human being. His skin was a deep rich bark brown and his hair was cut close in tight, almost Persian lamb-like curls. Coal black, his eyebrows were thick, as were his eyelashes. His teeth were so white they looked false, but they weren't because he had slight gaps in them.

"You must be Chandler, the great chef?"

I looked down at myself, wondering where my identify had been pasted. "Yes. Yes I am," I said. "How did you know?"

"Stevie Michelle, of course. She told me all about you this afternoon."

As Banning Morris talked, I realized how awkward it sounded to hear a black man with a British accent. It seemed like his voice was being dubbed, and the way he said, "Stevie Michelle," I knew my girlfriend was going to leave a specimen in her panties each time she heard it.

"I'm sorry, Banning. Please come in. Stevie Michelle will be ready in a minute." I estimated that he was thirty-five, thirty-six at the most.

He entered and walked past me into the living room. His rear was as impressive as his front. The white polo shirt was fitted to his shoulders and back, and his butt, protruding ever so modestly underneath his khakis, was tight with prominent hamstrings that enhanced his thighs. *Definitely athletic*, I thought.

Gingerly smiling, he said, "And how are you this evening, Lorelei?"

All I could think at the time was no matter what name he pronounced, he said it with a seductive, sultry and alluring tone.

Lorelei's large brown eyes said everything. They said she was impressed, intrigued, beguiled and in a trance. "Please have a seat," she said, never taking her eyes away from his presence.

"Banning, Stevie Michelle says you're going out for cocktails and dinner tonight?" I said.

"Yes. I thought we'd drive to the Princess Resort, have drinks poolside and dine at the Crown Room. They prepare excellent food. And then if she's agreeable, I'm hoping afterward we can do some dancing. She does like to dance, doesn't she?"

"Oh, yeah, she's—"

Stevie Michelle entered the living room like a professional model.

"Stevie Michelle," Banning said in a low, polished voice as he stood, "you look wonderful. I will be envied the entire evening."

I thought I would evaporate. Lorelei hadn't closed her mouth from the awe of seeing or hearing him. And if he said any one of our names again, I was going to run out of the condominium, crazed by his sultry song.

I watched Stevie Michelle blush. The three of us were blushing. That's when I took it upon myself to push the storybook couple out the door. "Well, Stevie Michelle and Banning, you two have a nice time tonight. And have her back by midnight, young man." We all chuckled.

Banning took Stevie Michelle's hand as they walked to the door. "It was nice meeting the both of you." Lorelei and I acknowledged his departing comment.

When the door closed, Lorelei and I exhaled simultaneously, and then I yelped, "Did you see that? He's no one I've ever seen before. Oh, I feel sorry for Stevie Michelle tonight. She's going to get hooked. Did you hear how charming he was? That man's got it goin' on."

Lorelei excitedly added, "And did you hear the way he said our names!?"

I turned in a circle, once again facing Lorelei when I stopped, and said, "Did I ever! I thought I would pass out right here from the euphoria of his voice. All I got to say is, charisma, charisma, charisma!"

"And they looked so good together," Lorelei added. "Damn, they looked good together."

"Well, if things go right, we won't see much of her on this vacation," I predicted.

The excitement of meeting a gorgeous, charming Englishman subsiding, I calmly said, "I'll be right back and then we can go to dinner. When I walked into Stevie Michelle's bedroom, I saw it had taken her a little while to decide which dress to wear. There were four of them heaped over the bed and a pair of shoes on the floor for each dress. Her make-up was left on the sink in the bathroom, opened. I pushed it all to one side and turned the faucet on. Alone, washing my hands, I stared at my reflection in the mirror. I removed a cloth from the rack and dampened it. Enjoying the coolness on my skin, I patted my face and neck, repeating the process. I looked in the mirror at myself. The Chandler I saw was the Chandler I sometimes didn't recognize. It was the reflection that had an alienation from emotion and attachment. I didn't like that image, because it meant there was an unfulfilled, frightened and lonely woman staring back.

I heard Lorelei say, "Chandler, you ready yet? I'm starvin'. C'mon."

"I'm coming." Taking one last look at myself, I said, "You'll be okay. All the self-doubt and loneliness you feel is only a phase."

* * * * *

The food at Fisherman's Cove was delicious. Lorelei and I ate everything. She liked the grouper. After dinner, we went to the outside bar and had a couple of Bahama Mamas each, listening to the locals play their island instruments and sing their native songs.

Back at the condo, standing over the sofa bed, making it up, I felt lighthearted and giddy as I hummed the tunes I'd heard at the bar. Throwing the pillows on, I went into Lorelei's room. She was sitting on the bed, filing her nails.

"Stevie Michelle's not back yet," I said.

"You expected her to be?"

"She must be having a good time."

"Must be."

Suddenly, the lightheartedness was gone and I felt the encumbrance against my chest. "Lorelei, can I ask you something?"

"Shoot." She put the file down and picked up her brush. She went through her hair with long, firm strokes.

I fluffed the curls in my hair and began. "Just tell me that you believe we'll make it. I mean, do you think we'll be successful?"

"Sure we will." She kept brushing.

"No. I mean it, Lorelei. We're pouring a lot of money into this venture. Not only do I have to be worried about my money, but yours and Stevie Michelle's, too. Sometimes I think it's more than I can endure. I'd want to die if we don't get a return on our investment."

"Chandler—"

"Lorelei, I know you've told me to think about success and not failure. I'm trying. Really I am. But the fact still remains that I've got two other people believing in my product. Believing in that widget that I have to create in order for it all to work."

"It will work, Chandler, 'cause that 'widget' you talkin' about is yo' ability to cook. You underestimate yo'self. You always do." Lorelei put the brush on the nightstand. "Come here and sit down," she said. I felt like a child, one of her children, as I did as she asked. "Chandler, I thought about failin', too. But only in the sense of keepin' it—meanin' ourselves—together, so that we can handle any adversity that comes for us. We have to keep our wit and cunnin' about us. And one thing the virtuoso trio have is wit and cunnin'.

"What did you call us?" I asked.

"The virtuoso trio."

"Where did you come up with that one, Lorelei?"

"I don't remember, but it's the first time I let anybody hear it."

I chuckled and then laughed. "The virtuoso trio," I repeated.

"Chandler, it's like this. It's just how Walter and I started our lives together. You remember how I told you we got together?"

"Yeah."

"Well, our relationship started as a risk. I could have let things be status quo, but he was who I wanted. I was riskin' my reputation and the love and respect of my family. But if I hadn't followed my heart—taken that risk—I could have been unhappy for the rest of my life. The return on my investment was bein' with the one I loved and three beautiful children—all by the same man. Now, some people could say that I failed, bein' divorced, but we'll just say I knew when to get out. And after twenty years in the restaurant business, we could be ready to get out of that, too." Lorelei's smile was a reassured one. She put her arm over my shoulders. "I know usin' my marriage as an example ain't quite the same thing, but I hope you get my drift."

"I think I do," I said.

"Remember, Chandler, no matter what happens, let's not forget to maintain our sense of humor. Those evil forces will be tryin' to get at us. Humor and kind words for one another is what will keep'em away. You got it goin' on and now it's time to let the world experience it. You keep cookin' the way you do and Julia Child will be comin' to yo' kitchen to see what the real deal is."

"Lorelei, I feel ridiculous coming to you like this, but until I take the plunge—dive—I—I won't know how deep the water is."

"Wasn't it you who told me that it's a fool who ain't scared of the unknown? And, even if it wasn't you who told me, it still applies. We go forward with caution when we scared, Chandler, and that ain't a bad thing. And I want to tell you," Lorelei said pointing a finger at me, "that good things come to those who wait, but not to those who wait too late. Yo' time is now, girlfrien'. Right now! And I'm here to help, and I want to share in the beauty and glory of it. I want to be part of the phenomenon, 'cause when you take that dive, whether you know how deep the water is or not, you goin' to swim. We all are."

The love and admiration of my girlfriend would carry me through. I had talent. I had perseverance. I had gumption. "Yeah!" I shouted. Then looking at her, I said, "I'll be calling you every three or four days for this kind of pep talk."

Lorelei laughed. "Gone girl. You crazy."

"Thanks for being here," I said.

"I feel the same way."

"I think it's time for me to get to bed." Looking at my watch, it was twelve-thirty. "Well, I guess Diva Stevie Michelle and Prince Charisma have ignored their curfew," I joked.

"They probably rode off into the moonlight."

Chapter 19

(Chandler)

Friday, Dec. 27

Although I slept in the living room, I didn't hear Stevie Michelle come in. I wondered if she came in at all. I sat up in the bed and looked out the balcony doors into a magnificent sunrise. Regardless of the time I went to bed, I would always wake by seven-thirty. The sun was rising over the foliage and the mango-colored flowers stretched to receive it. I got out of bed and walked onto the balcony. Not all the balconies were screened, but ours was. Maybe it was because I was on an island, but it felt natural standing there in nothing but my white cotton nightgown. It was transparent in the bright light, but I wasn't self-conscious, and if the flowers didn't blush, I wouldn't either. The air, gently entering my gown, changed my skin to gooseflesh. Folding my arms, hugging myself, I felt my gown faintly ruffle against my legs. I hugged myself tighter, hoping to abolish the millions of tiny pimples over my body.

I looked at the sunrise and the flowers for another minute or so before I went back inside. Going into the kitchen, I got the coffee from the cupboard that I had brought with me and started a pot. It was my favorite. Chocolate raspberry. The aroma was beginning to permeate the condo as I walked from the kitchen to Stevie Michelle's bedroom. I didn't knock, because if she was asleep I didn't want to wake her, and if she wasn't there, there was no need to knock. I cautiously opened the door. She was under the blankets, facing the window, still sleeping. I thought, *I must have been tired not to hear her come in.* I tiptoed to the dresser, searching in my designated drawers for underwear and clothes. I picked up my toiletry bag and took them in the bathroom, closing the door. Brushing my teeth as quietly as I could, I then turned on the shower and got in.

After my shower, I put on a pink tank top, navy shorts and a pair of brown sandals. I gently opened the door. Up on her elbow, staring, Stevie Michelle said, "Good morning." She startled me.

"*Wooo*, good morning. I didn't expect for you to be awake."

"Well, when I heard the water running it reminded me that I've got to pee, so I'm awake." Stevie Michelle slid out of bed and walked past me into the bathroom.

I put my night clothes away and dropped my toiletry bag in the corner. Stevie Michelle came out of the bathroom.

"You want a cup of coffee?" I asked.

"I thought I smelled coffee," she said.

"Yeah. Our favorite. Chocolate raspberry."

"Where'd you get that?" she asked.

"I brought it with me. You know, it was on the necessity list with credit card, underwear and curling iron."

"As soon as I get dressed, I'll meet you in the kitchen."

"Okay. See you in a minute," I said, walking out.

Back in the kitchen, I washed two cups and set them on the counter. Looking through the drawers, I found the spoons. I searched in the cabinets and found utensils that would come in handy if I decided to cook. The thing was to find a grocery store close. We didn't have a car and I wasn't eager to rent one. Stevie Michelle and Lorelei agreed with me. We wanted to walk the island, like the natives. The office had told us that a bus came every two hours that went to the beach, starting at nine o'clock. I thought I might take on a little sand and sun in the afternoon. While relaxing, I would make notes for the restaurant. I had to start creating a checklist.

"Boy, that smells so good, Chandler." Stevie Michelle had put on a pair of drawstring baggy pants and a t-shirt. She looked ready for the gym, although I knew she wasn't going.

"It does, doesn't it."

"But you forgot one thing."

"What's that?"

"Cream. You know I like cream in my coffee."

"Whala!" I said as I pulled the jar of Coffee-mate out of the cabinet. "I know it's not the real thing, but it's the safest. Non-perishable stuff."

"Something is better than nothing. Start pouring, honey."

I poured two mugs of coffee and Stevie Michelle and I both lightened our java to a toasted almond beige. I sniffed the aroma before I took a deep, long sip. "*Mmmm*, just what Chef Boyardee ordered," I said.

"Chandler, do we have sugar?"

'No. But when did you start taking sugar in your coffee?"

"*Ummm*, it's not for me. It's for our sugar cookie in the bedroom."

"Oh, shit," I said. "I forgot about Lorelei." I started opening draws, hoping to find packets of sugar that the last tenants left from carry-out orders. There were five in a drawer with plastic forks and napkins from a restaurant called the Lemon Peel. I pulled the sugar packets out and laid them on the counter. Then I said, "Okay, girlfrien', I know you couldn't just start in on it without me asking first, so how was last night?"

Stevie Michelle was grinning. Her face said that it was nice, but I wanted the details.

The voice was that of a southerner's, a woman southerner. It came from around the corner of the living room. "Don't start tellin' nothin' before I get in there," Lorelei said. "And there better be some coffee left, 'cause I smell chocolate raspberry." She came into the kitchen wearing her nightgown with a light pink cotton robe on top.

I got another mug from the cupboard, rinsed it and poured my girlfriend a cup of coffee.

"Thanks, Chandler." Lorelei spooned in the creamer and used all five packs of sugar. Stirring, she sipped and grimaced. "Not sweet enough," she said. "There ain't no more sugar?"

"I found those in the drawer over there," I said.

Lorelei opened the drawer and rummaged inside. Blindly searching, she pulled out one more packet of sugar. Stevie Michelle and I watched with amazement as she stirred it in.

"So, Stevie Michelle," she said, testing her coffee with a cautious sip, "tell us about yo' date."

"And there is something to tell," Stevie Michelle said, giving the both of us a naughty gaze.

"Then spill it," I said.

We stood about the small kitchen like three middle-aged teenagers.

Stevie Michelle dithered with the facts when she said, "You know, I hadn't given it any thought, but there aren't seasons down here. The weather is pretty consistent, between seventy-two to eighty. I could get used to this."

"Stevie Michelle, the hell with the weather report, honey, give us the facts, the facts," I wheedled.

"Okay, the facts. Well, let me see. He's one of the most appealing men I've been with in a long time. He reminds me of Carl. I was engrossed the whole night. We went to the Princess Casino and he taught me how to play blackjack. I won twenty-five dollars on the slot machine. Then we went to a restaurant in the resort called the Crown Room. He buttered my bread."

"*Oooo* girl!" I said, teasing her.

"Then after dinner—"

I stopped her. "What did you have for dinner?"

"Oh, yeah. You would want to know that. Banning had sautéed prawns in a garlic wine sauce that came to the table still sizzling, and I had the roasted herb chicken breast."

"Of all the things I know were on the menu, Stevie Michelle, you had chicken? I—"

"Yeah. And it was good, too," she said, her voice protesting my challenge.

"Go ahead," Lorelei said. "Finish tellin' us."

"Then we walked out of the restaurant through an atrium into a courtyard where there was a patio bar and music. We sat at one of the tables and had rum runners. After that, Banning took me to a fabulous night club. From what I understand, it's brand new. It's called Club 2001. The music was great and the company even better. That boy can dance. Banning is fantastic. Smart. Intellectual and funny. Then after dancing, we drove to a shopping plaza that had a pier and we walked, looking into the stores, window shopping. There were so many couples walking and kissing."

"Did you kiss him?" I asked.

"No."

"What?"

"He kissed me."

"You know what I mean, miss smarty," I said.

"How was it?" Lorelei asked.

"Polite."

"Polite?"

"Yeah, polite. He didn't try sticking his tongue down my throat or sucking my face off."

"I know just what you mean," Lorelei said. "You don't know if you kissin' a snake or a Kirby vacuum cleaner sometimes. My first husband was a lousy kisser, but Walter put the I-S-S in the word kiss."

Reminiscing, I said, "Wade was pretty good, too. The way he used to kiss me on the back of my neck, just above my shoulder, drove me crazy. I'd melt like chocolate over a double boiler. He knew he was guaranteed some pussy whenever he did that."

"Chandler, it's been too long for you. I can tell," Stevie Michelle said. "You better get out more, darling."

"If there was someone worthwhile dating, I would."

Stevie Michelle put her cup on the counter and pointed a finger at me. "If I've told you once, I've told you a thousand times, your standards are too high. It's a date, Chandler, not a walk to the altar. Relax a little. Take it for what it's worth—a little fun and maybe some safe sex. But your problem is, you're looking for the relationship first. It's the nineties and we're in our forties, and I know that our past good lives have spoiled us, but we've got to be a little more tolerating of the bullshit that's presented these days. Not letting men off the hook, though," Stevie Michelle said with a neck roll and hand gesture. "Because I know the three women standing here have been given the experience of what is called the good life. Anything less than that can be—well—a waste of our precious time. We've still got it goin' on, and the fact is our time is becoming more precious by the day."

"You could be right, Stevie Michelle," I said, "but if we let men get away with being mediocre, then that's all we're going to get."

"You both right," Lorelei said. "Chandler, we got to set the standards, but also, Stevie Michelle, we ain't got a leg to stand on with all these hoochie mamas out here lettin' men treat'em any ol'kinda way, along with havin' their way. And it don't make no difference how much money the man makes, he can still treat a woman like a lady. Now don't misunderstan' me, I still believe finance without romance is a nuisance, but that don't stop a man from treatin' a woman with respect."

"That's true. So, all I'm saying to you, Chandler," Stevie Michelle said, "is try letting your guard down a little. You're too stiff. Loosen up, girlfrien'."

"What I am is not up for the nonsense. I expect certain things and—"

"We all do," Stevie Michelle argued.

"Listen," Lorelei said, "we can debate the man and woman issue, especially the black man and black woman issue, all day long. But the issue here is we in the Bahamas. The sun is shinin' and the beach is only a bus ride away. I say we go get some breakfast and then go to the beach. I ain't been near an ocean since I left South Carolina and I'm about due."

"We can't go anywhere until you get dressed," I said.

Lorelei walked out of the kitchen with her coffee cup into her bedroom. "Give me a half hour," she yelled as the door closed.

"Stevie Michelle," I said, "I'll see if I can't be a little less *stiff*."

"It would do you good," she said in a confirming tone.

I poured myself another cup of coffee. Stevie Michelle declined a second cup.

"Chandler, this was a wonderful idea. I can't think of a better way to bring in the New Year," she said.

"Well, you know what they say, 'It's better in the Bahamas'."

"And so far, so good."

"I just wi—" The phone rang. I realized that it had been almost twenty-four hours since I had heard a phone. The ring sounded the same as it did in the States. I answered. "Hello?"

"Hello, this is Banning. How are you this morning?"

"I'm fine, and you?"

"I'm great. I hope I didn't wake you?"

"No. As a matter of fact, I'm on my second cup of coffee."

"Good. I wanted to speak with Stevie Michelle before she got away today. Is she awake?"

"Oh yes. She's awake. Wide awake. She's had a lot to say already this morning and it's not even ten o'clock yet. Hold on," I said. I handed the phone to Stevie Michelle. I whispered, "Banning. But I'll bet you already knew that."

She held the receiver to her ear like a mother cuddling her soft, precious baby. "Good morning," she said.

I felt uncomfortable standing there, so I went onto the balcony and finished my coffee.

Stevie Michelle was still on the phone when Lorelei came out of the bedroom in a bright red and yellow striped shorts set.

"Girlfrien'!" I said. "It'll be hard to lose you in a crowd. I'm going to have to keep my sunglasses on while you're around."

"Too bright?" she asked.

"No. I love it. I was just harassing you. I like it a lot."

"Good. You might as well, 'cause I ain't goin' to change. Now, let's go; I'm starvin'."

"You were starving last night. You ate everything except the lilies on the table. Either you're P-M-S-ing, Lorelei, or you're pregnant."

"Neither, Chandler. Eatin' is part of a good vacation, and I think I saw you eat the lilies last night, so let's go."

"Excuse me, but we're waiting for the love goddess to get off the phone."

"Don't tell me, Banning?"

"You've got it."

"We might as well go. From the way she's hooked to that phone, she ain't havin' breakfast with us."

Stevie Michelle hung up and came onto the balcony. It was crowded with the three of us out there.

"He is such a breath of fresh air," she said.

"So, you ready for breakfast?" I asked.

"Aaah, I told Banning I'd have breakfast with him."

The grin on Lorelei's face said, I told you so.

"Stevie Michelle, in case you weren't aware, the only reason we're waiting out here is for you. We could have been gone ten minutes ago," I said.

"Chandler," Lorelei said," calm down. We got nothin' but time while we here. As a matter of fact, there ain't no need to even worry about time."

"Yeah, chill," Stevie Michelle said.

The smile on my face was as plastic as a set of Tupperware when I said, "You're right. Let's go, Lorelei." When I reached the door, I asked Stevie Michelle, "Are you planning to go to the beach with us, or does Banning have that covered, too?"

"I'll be going to the beach with you. Banning has to pick his brother up from the airport. He's coming in from Florida today. So, when you two finish breakfast, I'll meet you back here."

I looked at my watch, although I wasn't supposed to be concerned with time, and said, "We'll meet you back here at high noon."

"Okay," Stevie Michelle said.

Lorelei and I walked out of the condo into the bright sun and green palm trees. If we weren't in heaven, I felt it was as close as we were going to get before we died. Into the parking lot, down the drive, we moseyed onto the unpaved road and headed to the restaurant to have breakfast.

The afternoon went as planned. The three of us were back at the condominium at noon. We were changing into our beachwear and gabbing like three old hens, laughing and making fun of the waiter at the restaurant that tried to feed Lorelei her fruit.

"Well, they say it's paradise," I said.

It was so funny to see the three of us scrambling to be ready by the time the bus arrived. Stevie Michelle looked like she had packed for a safari, Lorelei couldn't decide whether to wear her yellow or teal flip-flops, and I had to make up my mind which one of my Calvin

Klein swimsuits looked best, the black or red. I must have tried them each three or four times.

"Come on!" I yelled through the condo. "We've got five minutes to get down to the stop to catch the one o'clock bus."

"I'm ready," Lorelei yelled back.

"Give me one minute," Stevie Michelle said. "I've got to get my hair in a ponytail."

"Hurry up, Stevie Michelle."

Lorelei, wearing her teal flip-flops, and me, sporting my black Calvin Klein, were standing by the door when Stevie Michelle came running out of her room with two canvas bags.

"What the hell is all that?" I asked.

"Sunscreen, sun oil, towels, my comb and brush, make-up, nail polish remover and nail polish."

I shook my head and said, "Let's go, girls."

We made it to the bus stop as the bus was coming up the road. The seats we're filled and we had to stand, but it was worth it, as we walked from the drop-off to the top of the hill that led to the sandy beach of Freeport. There was water as far as I could see. People's heads, black and white, bobbed up and down in the salted sea as they splashed and played. The colorful umbrellas and chairs lined the sand.

"Oh God, this is great," Lorelei said.

"It sure is," I agreed.

"So, what are we waiting for? Let's claim our spot," Stevie Michelle said.

We slipped and stumbled down the steep hill that was covered in sparse, desiccate vegetation. We walked approximately fifty feet before we found the right umbrella and chairs. We set up camp not far from a conch and soda stand.

"That's one thing I'm not crazy about," I said to Lorelei and Stevie Michelle.

"What's that?" Lorelei asked.

"Conch. It's too rubbery."

"I ain't never had it," Lorelei said.

"Well, if you want to try it, just walk right over there. They'll make you a conch salad, a conch sandwich, a conch shish-ka-bob, a conch cocktail. You just tell'em what kind of conch you want and they'll make it."

"Chandler," Stevie Michelle giggled, "thanks for your translation. I'm going over for a soda. Want anything?"

"I'll take an uncola," I said.

"I'll go with you," Lorelei said. "I think I want to try some of that conch."

Brushing out the lounge chair and spreading my towel over it, I then stood tall with my hands on my hips and inhaled deeply. Looking out over the water, I could smell and taste the salted air. I don't know what made me say it, but standing there, alone and tranquil, I thanked God for the strength and assistance that I had been provided. And most of all for the two women that had in some kind of way become the best friends I could have.

I hadn't noticed Stevie Michelle standing next to me, drinking a Coke. Handing me my soda, she said, "It is beautiful, isn't it?"

"It's more than that. It's phenomenal," I said. "Thousands of writers and artists have tried to explain and recreate what goes on with the water, sand and sun, but as far as I'm concerned, you've got to be here in order to smell it, taste it, feel it and see it."

"I hope this stuff tastes good," Lorelei said as she sat on the chair under the umbrella. "It looks like chopped lobster."

I laughed. "You wish."

Stevie Michelle and I stripped off our pants and joined Lorelei in the chairs. I got up and pulled mine out from under the umbrella into the sun.

"Girl, it's too hot out there," Stevie Michelle said.

"It's never too hot," I protested. "I wish I could bottle all this sun and heat and take it with me. I know what's waiting for us back home."

"This is good," Lorelei said. "Chandler, I don't know what you don't like about it. It's a little chewy, but the flavor is mild and sweet."

"Taste is in the mouth of the beholder," I said.

Stevie Michelle interrupted our discussion. "Look at that coming up the beach!"

Our gazes followed her stare and not to my surprise, she had chosen the finest specimen of a man I'd seen in a long time, especially a man with as little as he had on. Wearing red trunks, and a pair of jogging shoes, he had muscles—Olympic style muscles. As he came running toward us, just as it would over the black shiny coat of a seal, the sun glistened on his skin. He was oiled and moist. He stopped at the foot of the ocean in our view.

"Jesus!" Stevie Michelle shrieked.

"Amen!" I squealed. "I knew I should have worn my red suit."

"He is a god," Lorelei said.

"I'll bet he's not from here," Stevie Michelle said.

"Bet he is," I said.

Lorelei said, "Who cares? The fact is, he's here."

I took my eyes off the specimen long enough to look at Lorelei to say, "Girlfrien', you are so right, again."

We were very obvious with our stares and weren't ashamed. He knew we were watching and he put on an unassuming show for us, flexing his muscles.

"Lorelei, what would you do with a man like that?" Stevie Michelle inquired.

"Oh girl, I'd chain'im to my bedpost for starters."

"And you, Chandler?"

"I'd grill two salmon fillets with a honey-ginger glaze, herb potatoes and green beans, and choose the finest young bottle of Cabernet Sauvignon I could find. I'd give the salmon entrees to the two of you, tell you to get lost, and then I'd pour the wine all over him and start licking."

Our cackles floated out to sea.

"Chandler, you never cease to amaze me." Lorelei continued to laugh, holding her stomach.

Stevie Michelle boasted, "I'm not going anywhere. I want to watch."

"You have always been kinky," I said.

"You're calling me kinky?"

Our black god started running down the beach in the direction of some kite flyers.

"Well, there he goes," I said. "The show is over."

"Yeah. So what do we do now?" Lorelei asked.

Stevie Michelle said, "Let's go after him."

I said, "I've got a better idea. Let's jot down some plans for the restaurant."

"Oh, Chandler, now!?" Stevie Michelle's face was disapprovingly twisted.

"Yeah. Now. Now is as good a time as any.'

"Come on," Lorelei encouraged Stevie Michelle. "It ain't goin' to hurt to spend a little time talkin' about it."

"All right." Stevie Michelle's tone was sharp.

"Okay girls," I said, ignoring her uncooperative manner, and conveniently pulling a legal pad and pen out my bag. "We're opening a restaurant the beginning of next year. I estimate it'll happen around April or May. Now that we've got the location, we've got to make a business plan, plan the layout, buy equipment and inventory, design a logo and business cards, make projections and work out operations. And believe it or not, that's the easy stuff. So, I thought we'd . . .

Stevie Michelle and Lorelei tolerated discussing the restaurant for an hour or so. After that, they protested. Stevie Michelle got up and bought another Coke. Lorelei went to the ocean and waded in the water. I sat under the umbrella and mentally went through the things that had to be done for the restaurant. Then we caught the three o'clock bus back to the condo, showered and had an early dinner at one of the small eateries on the strip.

Once again, at the condo, sitting on the balcony watching the sun set, the three of us were content and lazy like three beached walruses. We babbled about nothing of significance and laughed at everything. The phone rang.

"Get that, Stevie Michelle," I said. "I know it's for you." My intuition was one more thing for us to laugh about.

Banning Morris was checking in with his newest interest. We couldn't hear her conversation from the balcony, but it was brief and Stevie Michelle was outside again, telling us about her plans for the evening.

"Banning and I are going out tonight," she said.

I implied, "Again? Stevie Michelle, you're making this guy a habit."

"Only for the week I'm here. I know it won't go any further than this. But that's okay."

"Well, you can never say," Lorelei said. "You could be needin' yo' passport for a little overseas travelin'."

Stevie Michelle ignored Lorelei's statement. "I've got to get ready. He'll be here in about an hour."

Glancing at Lorelei, I said, "Well, I guess it's you and me again, doll. Anything on television you want to see?"

Lorelei sat up in her chair. "Let's go out too, Chandler."

"What?"

"Let's go to the casinos and pull on the slot machines for awhile."

"Did you get sun-stroked today, girl?"

"No, but I am gettin' bored. I don't want to sit in here with you tonight. We on vacation. Come on, Chandler. We can get a cab to the casino and maybe catch one of them shows we been seein' advertised."

I looked at Lorelei squarely. She was serious. I stared a few seconds longer and then said, "Okay. We'll go out."

Lorelei went to her bedroom to get dressed and I informed Ms. Parks that she had to share her room and bath with me while the both of us got ready. It wasn't easy. She methodically confined me to a three by five area in the bedroom, and the bathroom was a disaster once she came out. She couldn't possibly wear all the makeup she had on the sink. Again, I pushed it to one side and put on my lipstick and eyeliner. Looking at my face in the mirror, it had a glow. I had developed a nice color from the sun. I could've gone without makeup.

I put on a cream colored halter dress and brown sandals, sprayed perfume lightly over my skin, and I then took one last look in the full-length mirror. "I'm ready."

Lorelei let Banning in to pick up Stevie Michelle. Our cab was waiting. We all left out of the door together. Lorelei and I, in our cab, went in one direction, and Banning and Stevie Michelle in his rented Escort went in another.

Chapter 20

(Chandler)

Saturday, Dec 28

I woke before Stevie Michelle and Lorelei. Although the night had been exciting and long, the next morning my feet hit the floor around seven fifteen. Sleep hadn't been my priority for a long time, even before I went to the Bahamas. It was our third day in Freeport and I was relaxing—at least to the degree that I knew to relax. When I went into Stevie Michelle's room, she was on her stomach, asleep, her face flat in the pillow. I assessed she'd had a lot of fun, probably more than her share to drink, and slept in the I-partied-too-hard-and-too-long-last-night position. I assumed Lorelei was still sleeping, too. She'd probably be suffering from slot-machine elbow when she woke. I played most of the night on the machines that had push-button action. I won fifty-dollars and I think Lorelei broke even.

Dressed, I went into the kitchen to start coffee when suddenly I decided not to. Instead, in the serenity of the condo, I took the pad and pencil on the counter and wrote out a grocery list. I was going to cook. I had the urge to touch and smell fresh vegetables, fruits, herbs and spices. I was going to take my casino winnings, buy groceries, and then prepare breakfast and dinner for my girlfriends. I saw a store the night before as the cab driver passed it. I estimated it to be approximately two miles from the condo. Completing my grocery list, I went into the living room, slid the money and my key off the coffee table, and pushed them in my pocket. I slipped out of my house shoes into a pair of socks and my walkers.

Stepping outside, I quietly closed the door behind me and became part of the surrounding scenery. I walked toward the road and let my mind drift. Listening to the island creatures make their early morning wake-up calls, I walked slowly, gradually reaching a power-walk speed. Not until I was almost at my destination did I think that I should have left a note for Stevie Michelle and Lorelei. I could see the store and across the road was an open market. The women and men stood in thatch and wood huts, attracting my attention in Bahamian accents. Their voices were melodic. They waved and wished me a good morning, calling out to me, "I got every'ting you need right here, honey," and, "Baby, my fruits and vegetables are the freshest," and, "Darling, make sure you come over to see my tings."

I waved at them and yelled, "I'll be back." I needed staples like flour and sugar, eggs and milk. Going into the grocery, I was transferred from the Bahamas back into the commercial atmosphere of home. The store was a chain with the laminated signs, shelves, coolers, and frozen food cases. The air was chilling, preserving the perishables and the employees, who were in uniform, appearing as if they wanted to be set free to go work at the open market across the road where the voices and air were natural.

I quickly went through the aisles looking for what I needed. I didn't want to serve fish or beef for dinner, so I leaned toward preparing chicken. As I pushed the grocery cart, I picked up salt, pepper, paprika, flour, sugar, butter, eggs, oil, bacon, six chicken breasts, etc. I thought I'd try my version of chicken paprikash with rice and peas. *Lorelei and Stevie Michelle will like that*, I thought.

After I paid for my groceries, I rushed out of the store and crossed the road to the merchants who anticipated my visit. Their voices were lulling and persuasive. I visited each, buying something from all. One lady sold me exotic fruit and onions. Another gave me an herb that she said would be wonderful in the rice that I was making. An old man, whose flesh had been darkened by the tropical sun to a well-done hue, sat in his hut wearing a tattered straw hat, saying nothing while I bought things from the other merchants. As I was about to walk away, in a dusty weathered voice, he said, "You and your lady friends will like these." He held up three strands of shell and bead necklaces. The colors were brilliant in shades of brown, green and blue. I asked, "How much?" I thought it would be fun to wear them while on the island.

"Ten dollars," he said.

"Each?"

"Yes."

"That's thirty dollars. Will you take twenty-five for the three?" I asked.

The old man smiled a wide grin. "Twenty-five is good," he said. He wrapped each strand in crumbled tissue paper that had obviously been used before. I handed him the money and I put the necklaces in my purse. Leaving his hut, I stopped, turned and asked, "How did you know I have 'lady friends'?"

Although it seemed impossible, his grin grew and he said, "Because you are the three angels who have graced our island."

His answer did not satisfy my question, but I assumed that was his way, so I did not inquire any further. I lifted my grocery bags off the sandy soil and walked in the direction of the condominium. During my journey back to the condo, I allowed myself to pretend that I was someone other than me—a native of Freeport. I thought, *Born an island girl, I have a beautiful brown husband and two mocha-colored children who are so happy they never have reason to cry. We live on the ocean and each morning I go to the market to buy fresh produce to cook for them. My family is loving and adore me, as I adore them. We never argue, because with life on the island there is nothing to argue about. My husband is an import/export broker and we travel discovering new products and concepts.*

The honk of a horn stopped my fantasizing. Two men in a small, rusted white hatchback slowed and asked if I wanted a ride. I politely declined and they sped off. Not until I emerged from my fantasy did I realize how burdening the bags were. I put them down, stretched my arms and hands, attempting to generate some circulation. I lifted the bags again and returned to my imagined life. *Our children travel with us, learning other cultures and speaking the languages, while I'm taught different culinary principles. When we aren't traveling, our days are slow and easy. I spend much time in the garden watching the hummingbirds sip nectar from my flowers. In the evenings, my husband and I play games with the children before they go to bed and then my beloved and I sit in the cool breeze of the ocean, sampling a glass or two of the wines we have brought back from our journeys, reminiscing as we drink.*

Travel time to the condo seemed less than going to the store. Lorelei was standing outside when I walked up the driveway. She rushed toward me and grabbed a bag. "I didn't know what to think," she said. "Couldn't you wait for somebody to go with you or left a note?"

"I didn't want anyone to go with me and I thought about the note after I was too far to come back."

"Well, excuse me."

"You're excused. Is Stevie Michelle up?" I asked.

"I think I heard her in her room."

"Lorelei, we're having breakfast here today. I don't want to eat out. And I'm cooking dinner, too."

"You think I'm goin' to argue about that?"

"No, but I thought I'd tell you, anyway."

"I made coffee," Lorelei said.

"What I want is a tall glass of cold water. International travel can be dehydrating."

"What, Chandler?"

"Nothing, Lorelei. Nothing."

"So, what we havin' for breakfast?"

"It's a surprise," I said, though what I had to work with wasn't anything exotic. In the kitchen, I started pulling groceries out of the bags and organizing them in the cabinets, refrigerator and on the counter. With the ingredients I had, I decided on bacon, eggs and biscuits.

"You want me to help?" Lorelei asked as she put ice in a glass for me.

"No. This won't take long. But you can see how much time sleeping beauty will need before she's dressed. I want everything to be hot when we sit down."

Lorelei filled the glass with water and set it on the counter. I immediately picked it up and drank half before I took a breath. Gasping, I said, "Thanks, I needed that."

"You welcome. I'll go see how much longer Stevie Michelle will be."

The three of us had a hearty breakfast and talked about the night before. I reminded them that we were having dinner together and not to make any other plans. I said it more for Stevie Michelle's sake than Lorelei's. Stevie Michelle said she wanted to invite Banning and his brother for dinner. She softened my adversity by saying that she had bragged to Banning about my cooking and that he was dying to try it. I couldn't deny him. I had purchased six whole breasts. I was sure it would be enough, but there was no dessert. With flour, sugar, eggs and butter, I had the basics. I only had to be creative and let my culinary expertise work for me.

I told Stevie Michelle to let Banning and his brother know that dinner would be at six o'clock sharp. She didn't finish her breakfast before she was in the kitchen on the phone with the Englishman.

She was hanging up when I walked in. "You like him a lot, don't you?" I asked, running water to wash the breakfast dishes.

"He's fun to be with, Chandler. That's all."

"No, Stevie Michelle. I've seen you with other men. They're fun to be with. I think Banning is more than that. Quite a bit more. He's like an amusement park with roller coasters and water slides wrapped up in one man. The others are only on carnival level."

"Chandler, I'm having a good time. Don't make more of it than it is. Okay?"

"Okay. But remember I know you, and I know you're captivated."

"Didn't you say this may be our last vacation for a long time?"

"Yes. That was me," I said.

"Well, I'm making the best of it. I've found a companion on this beautiful island and I'm going to spend as much time with him while we're here as he wants to spend with me. I like Banning and I do enjoy being with him. Simple as that."

"Okay, girlfrien'. You won't get an argument from me. I'm sorry I brought it up."

"Thanks for being concerned, Chandler, but I have control of this one."

"Good," I said, sliding our breakfast plates into the soapy dish water. "Have you met Banning's brother?"

"No. Tonight will be the first for me, too."

"So what plans do you have with Banning for today?"

"None. I'm going to spend the day with you and Lorelei."

"You are?"

"Yeah. I thought we'd do some shopping. I want to go to the International Bazaar."

"Sounds good to me. Tell Lorelei," I said. "And call a taxi."

We were ready to go out the door by eleven o'clock. Standing outside, waiting for the cab, I remembered the necklaces I had bought. I took them out of my purse and handed Lorelei and Stevie Michelle one.

"What's this?" Lorelei asked.

"Open it," I said.

They unwrapped the worn tissue paper and pulled out the necklaces. They both held the strands up into the daylight.

"Look how colorful," Stevie Michelle said.

I unwrapped mine and put it on. Stevie Michelle and Lorelei did the same.

"Thanks," Lorelei said.

"It's very pretty," Stevie Michelle added. "I'll keep it forever."

"At least until it breaks," I said. "They weren't the most expensive, but I thought they'd be nice souvenirs."

The cab pulled into the drive. I sat in the front with the driver. Stevie Michelle explained where we wanted to go and the driver took off down the road headed in the direction. On the way, he asked typical taxi driver questions and I gave him typical tourist answers. When we arrived at the bazaar, I led Lorelei and Stevie Michelle to a beautiful pink stucco building. The structure reminded me of a house I had seen in South Carolina. The steep steps went up to a large gray porch with big double doors. The sign outside the building read Freeport Perfume Factory. The three of us went inside. The interior of the house had glass and wood tables that were filled with gift boxes of soaps, oils, perfumes and crystal.

A young woman immediately walked up to us, introduced herself and asked if we had ever been in the perfume factory before. We said no. She began explaining the operation of the factory and how we could create our own fragrances. She directed us into a room where the walls were lined with shelves holding curved long-neck bottles with tubes leading from them to spigots. The spigots were labeled with names like honeysuckle, lilac, rose, spice, citrus, peach blossom and strawberry. On the lower shelves were small cosmetic bottles and funnels. Measuring was done in the metric system.

Stevie Michelle, Lorelei and I looked like intense female chemists standing in front of the spigots measuring the extracts and oils to mix our own special fragrances. Lorelei and I liked floral fragrances, while Stevie Michelle wanted more of a spicy, citrus scent to her perfume.

When we were done mixing, we chose names for our fragrances. Lorelei named hers *Pretty Woman*. Stevie Michelle called hers *After the Rain* and I named mine, *Maroon,* simply because I wanted to see the word in print. It seemed authentic. Labels with the names of our fragrances were adhered to the bottles.

The sun was high and hot when we left the fragrance store. We walked around the bazaar for a couple more hours. We bought postcards to send home. Stevie Michelle purchased a pair of earrings for herself and a t-shirt for Nelson. Lorelei got souvenirs for Topper and Three, and a crystal bud vase for herself. I bought three pieces of blown glass for Kennedy, Alex and myself, and a t-shirt for Cornelius.

I looked at my watch and said to my girlfriends, "I know time is not a subject while we're in the Bahamas, but if I'm to have dinner ready on time, I think we should be getting back to the condo." Stevie Michelle and Lorelei did not hesitate in agreeing with me. We didn't stop for lunch while we shopped. They were both hungry and exhausted. There was a taxi waiting for a fare where we were dropped off. We poured ourselves into the seats and were silent going to the condo. We set our packages inside the door and went in different directions. Lorelei to her room, Stevie Michelle to hers, and I went into the kitchen. Washing my hands, I had approximately an hour and a half to have everything ready. Forty-five minutes was all I needed.

My girlfriends appeared in the kitchen, ready to help. Before they said anything, I said, "Lorelei, chop some onions and Stevie Michelle, I need you to rinse two cups of rice. Do you know how to do that?"

She looked at me quizzically and said, "Not really."

I looked in the cupboards. There wasn't a colander or strainer, so I had her put the rice in a pot with cold water, swish it around and drain it five times.

"What am I doing this for, Chandler?"

"You're washing off the starch. It keeps the rice from becoming sticky."

She chuckled and said, "I guess that's why you're the chef."

Lorelei announced, "Onions chopped, chef."

"Okay. Good. Now put about a tablespoon of butter and two tablespoons of oil in that pan and turn it on medium heat." I continued seasoning the chicken, prepping it to cook in the hot butter and oil.

"You need anything else?" Lorelei asked.

"No. Thanks." I was ready to be alone in the place I loved the most. I lightly floured the breasts and placed them in the pan, listening to the oil sizzle. I sautéed each on both sides, placed the rice in boiling water, covered it and turned the heat to a low simmer. I placed the lentils and herbs into another pot and cooked them.

The whole time I cooked, I thought, *Dessert . . . dessert . . . dessert.* I snapped my fingers. "Butter cookies. I think I can remember that simple recipe." At that moment, I swore to never leave home without my little black book of recipes again—no matter where I went. Lorelei," I yelled into the condo.

She came running like an obedient child. "Yeah, Chandler?"

"I want you to write this down as I recite it. I'm trying to remember a butter cookie recipe. That's going to be our dessert. It's a basic recipe that can be used as is or flavored with just about anything—cocoa to make macaroons, almond or lemon extract."

She leaned over the counter with the pen in her hand and said, "Shoot."

I began with the butter. "Three sticks of salted butter and one cup of firmly-packed dark brown sugar creamed together, gradually adding three and a half cups of flour until blended. Then roll the dough into two logs and chill until firm." When I was done, I asked Lorelei to read it back to me. She did, and I said, "I think that's it. After the dough chills, we'll cut cookies from the logs and bake at 350 for about 12 to 15 minutes."

"You want me to help?" she asked.

"Sure. It's going to take a little longer without a mixer, but it can be done. Cream the sugar and butter first." I realized there was no cookie sheet. I improvised with a baking pan.

Lorelei looked at me and said, "Chandler, you a genius in the kitchen. Sometimes I can't remember what day it is and you standin' here givin' me a recipe off the top of yo' head."

"Only because it's a real simple one. A simple cookie dough is easy to repair if you make a mistake. You'll either need more wet or dry ingredients. We'll make a couple test cookies before I commit the whole batch."

Lorelei followed the recipe as I gave it to her. She quickly chilled the dough in the freezer and baked three test cookies while I finished preparing dinner. Before they cooled, Lorelei and I ate two. "Stevie Michelle," she called.

"Yeah."

"Come here. I want you to taste somethin'."

As soon as she entered the kitchen, Lorelei popped a piece of cookie into Stevie Michelle's mouth.

"What do you think?" she asked.

"Butter. I taste lots of rich, delicious butter."

"That's good," I said, "but what about the texture? What do you think about the cookie as a cookie?"

"I think you should bag'em up and put them on the shelves next to Famous Amos's chocolate chips."

"Stevie Michelle," I said, chuckling, "one of these days you're going to give simple answers to simple questions."

"You want a simple answer? Okay. Delicious! Where are the rest?"

"My assistant has to complete the baking. They're for our dessert. I know cookies aren't fancy, but I hate to have company and have nothing to present for dessert. Artless, but pertinent," I said.

"I think it's different, Chandler," Stevie Michelle said. "I'll call Banning and tell him to bring some tea bags with him. He likes tea instead of coffee. We can all have cookies and tea after dinner."

I listened to my girlfriend talk about the Englishman. I thought, *She's in love. It is definite love.* "You do that," I said, "but don't you tell him what's for dinner or dessert."

"All right." Stevie Michelle picked up the phone doing as I requested.

Staring at the watch on my wrist, the chicken paprikash and the cookies had been prepared in sixty-five minutes. I was twenty minutes over my estimated time. Excusing myself, I went into the bedroom. I thought, *I have twenty-five minutes to inject life back into my limp, exhausted body*. Turning on the shower, I peeled off my clothes. There was instant gratification from the relaxing power of warm water. I couldn't stay long, but I was appreciative for the time I had. Getting out of the shower, I dried and dressed myself quickly.

Stevie Michelle came into the bedroom to refresh her makeup.

Before we left the room, she hugged me and said, "Thanks Chandler. You've come through again. I want you to get to know Banning."

I stepped back to look at her. I thought, *This is love*. But I said, "It's nothing, Stevie Michelle. We're here to relax and have fun, remember? And that's what we're doing."

"Yeah. I know. And like you said, it's better in the Bahamas."

We could hear voices.

"That's Banning," Stevie Michelle said, excited.

Lorelei was standing in the narrow hall with Banning and another man who had to be his brother. Approximately the same height, they almost looked like twins.

When Banning caught a glimpse of Stevie Michelle, he came to meet her. Holding both her hands, easily guiding her toward him and kissing her cheek, he said, "How are you this evening, my love?"

I stood envious and embarrassed. *How could she not be in love*? I thought.

"PJ," he said, "please come meet Stevie Michelle and Chandler."

The man that walked into the room was as fine as his brother. I didn't know why, but Lorelei remained standing in the hall. Banning introduced us. "PJ, here in my hands is Stevie Michelle Parks, the lady I haven't stopped talking about. And next to her is her best friend, Chandler Elizabeth Cawthorne."

I was impressed that he knew my whole name.

"And you've already met Lorelei," he said, turning, looking around the room to find her.

She was still in the shadow of the hallway when I called to her. "Lorelei?"

"I'm comin'," she said. When Lorelei became visible, she had a bottle of wine in each hand and the strangest look on her face. I didn't know what was wrong. She said to me, "I think I should put these in the refrigerator. Banning and PJ brought'em."

I wondered if she was having a bad reaction to the cookies she ate. I thought I had better check before I served them to our guests. I excused myself and followed Lorelei into the kitchen. She fumbled in the refrigerator.

"Lorelei, what's gotten into you?"

She turned and looked at me wide-eyed. In a desperate whisper, she asked, "Don't he look familiar to you?"

I looked in the direction of the living room, although I couldn't see PJ, and said, "No. Should he?"

"Think, Chandler. The beach today. The red trunks."

My mouth dropped open. "Are you sure, Lorelei?"

"I thought about it. I been back to the beach in my mind about six times since he's been here and if I was asked to make a line-up identification, it would be him."

Lorelei had me thinking. It was hard to tell with his clothes on, but she could have been right. Then I wondered if Stevie Michelle recognized him. She seemed unaware at the time we were introduced. I strolled back into the living room, staring at PJ's backside as I went in. It was difficult to tell with his clothes on. He was certainly black enough, but I needed more proof. I needed to see some naked hamstrings.

"Excuse me," I said to our guests. "Stevie Michelle, can I steal you for a minute? I need help in the kitchen." We politely excused ourselves and Stevie Michelle completed the threesome necessary to confirm what Lorelei suspected.

Before I could say anything, Lorelei belted in that same desperate whisper, "Stevie Michelle, don't he look familiar to you?"

"Who, Banning?" she said.

That was confirmation enough for me. She was stupid, too. I didn't feel so bad. I got goose pimples thinking that my fantasy had walked into a condo that I was staying in. It was better than bumping into a celebrity on the streets of New York.

"No, Stevie Michelle, PJ."

Stevie Michelle looked at me and Lorelei, and started giggling uncontrollably. Then she said, "The beach. Today. Red trunks. That's him?"

Our voices collided in laughter. After we gained control, Stevie Michelle opened the refrigerator and took out a bottle of the wine. She held it up to the light and read the label to us. "Voss, Chardonnay, nineteen-ninety-three. *Mmmm*, that's too bad, Chandler." She handed the bottle to me and said, "You pour."

Stevie Michelle waited while I opened the bottle and filled the wine glasses. She picked up two by the stem, just the way I had taught her, and left the kitchen with Lorelei following, carrying two more glasses. They were quietly giggling as they entered the living room. I remained in the kitchen and inhaled a couple long sips of wine before I joined them.

"I hope you like it," I heard PJ say as I entered the living room. "The wine merchant assured me it's one of the best." Everyone agreed that it was nice.

Lorelei said, "PJ, I didn't know California wines were sold in the Bahamas."

"I didn't get it here. I picked it up in Florida."

"Do you have friends in Florida?" she asked.

"No. I have, hopefully, a job. I'll know before I leave on Monday."

"Oh, what kind of job?"

I thought, *She's an inquisitive little thing tonight*.

"With the government. I don't know if Banning told you, but I'm a forensic specialist and I've applied for a job with the FBI. I'm also studying to become a profiler."

Lorelei giggled. "A what?"

"A profiler. He— or she, is someone who helps the district attorney's office or the police profile a person. For example, a serial killer. A profiler takes evidence like a murder weapon, location of the body, notes or phone calls from the killer and lifestyle. He then makes as precise a profile of the killer as possible, including a physical appearance."

"The closest I thought I would get to somebody like you, PJ, is watchin' television," Lorelei said.

I had never really seen her flirt. All the years I'd known Lorelei, she was loving and devoted to Walter.

"Please believe me, Lorelei, when I say, it's not like on television. The case isn't solved in one episode and sometimes it's never solved."

"But do you like yo' work?" she asked.

"Very much. The rush I get when that last piece to the puzzle is put into place is inexpressible."

"Are you planning to leave England for good?" I asked.

"If I get the job and the FBI likes my work, and I like the United States, yes. I'll miss my family, but—"

"And your family is?"

PJ smiled. He understood where I was headed with my question. After all, he was a forensic specialist.

"Banning. My mom and dad. I know Banning will visit whenever he gets the opportunity, but my parents are a different story. I'll have to go home to see them."

"Have you two ever worked together?" I asked. "Banning being in journalism and you an investigator." I drank more wine. I was beginning to relax.

Banning laughed. "I write uneventful columns, Chandler. There's no investigating necessary, except maybe at the library. That's as far as my research stretches. Although I did do some freelance work for a magazine regarding the details required for a forensic investigator. I followed PJ around about two weeks for that story."

"He did. And believe it or not, he pointed something out on the case that I had overlooked," PJ added.

"My sister-in-law in Little River, South Carolina, used to want to be a writer, but she stopped talkin' about it when she married my brother, Manny," Lorelei said.

"I think we should continue this conversation during dinner," I said. "Everything is ready."

"I've been looking forward to this," Banning said, ogling at Stevie Michelle. Surprisingly, she had not said much since Banning and his brother arrived.

"Well, thank you," I said. "I've managed to find plates, glasses and silverware. They don't match, but everyone has a setting of their own. Have a seat at the table and if one of my girlfriends will help me in the kitchen, we'll be eating in about ten minutes." Stevie Michelle volunteered.

"He's great, isn't he?" she asked once we were in the kitchen.

"You've been awfully quiet since they got here, Stevie Michelle. What's wrong?"

"Nothing. What could be wrong?"

"I don't know. That's why I'm asking."

We were silent as we "plated up" the chicken paprikash and rice. Before we went to put dinner on the table, Stevie Michelle said, "He's leaving Monday. It's coming so quickly. The day after tomorrow he's going home."

I wouldn't look at her. I didn't comment. My feeling was that her thinking out loud didn't need a comment. Stevie Michelle's candidness was private. She would let me know when she wanted to talk about it. I just hoped that Banning had some semblance of the feelings she did. I conceived that while we were in the kitchen, Lorelei was being entertained by two of the most charming Englishmen in the world. They were certainly two of the most handsome. Stevie Michelle carried two plates to the table and I carried the other three, one balanced on my arm. We set them down and Banning, PJ and Lorelei made multiple sounds of approval. Stevie Michelle and I took our places at the table. Banning offered grace, and we talked and laughed while we ate and drank more wine. Things seemed to be perfect.

"Before Banning and I came over," PJ said, "we discussed going out tonight, having the three of you join us."

Lorelei, Stevie Michelle and I looked at one another. For the first time, I was ready to do something. We smiled at one another and I said, "Why not? It sounds like fun. What did you have in mind?"

"How about a show and then some dancing?" Banning suggested.

"That's great," Lorelei said. "I been wantin' to see the casino show since we got here."

"We'll see the show first and then go dancing," PJ said.

We all agreed. Staring at the table, I noticed that there were only chicken bones left on the plates. I felt good about that and immediately stood, clearing them away. I was graciously praised for my culinary endeavor by my girlfriends and our guests. I offered dessert and everyone accepted.

"You need help?" Lorelei asked.

"No, I can handle this alone. Does anyone want coffee or tea?"

I heard two coffees and two teas. At the last minute, I sliced starfruit, a couple Asian pears, and added some strawberries for color, putting them on the plate with the cookies. The combination was beautiful on the plate.

We had our dessert in the living room, sitting around the small coffee table.

"Chandler, this is wonderful," PJ said. "This is how we have dessert in England."

"It is?"

"Certainly. The desserts in America are too presumptuously sweet. I like simple pastries."

"Well, PJ, this is as simple as it gets and I'm glad you like it," I said, proud that I had impressed our guests.

After dessert and a little more conversation, Banning and PJ offered to pick us up at nine-thirty. The show at the casino began at ten.

Chapter 21

(Chandler)

Sunday, Dec. 29

I sat on the side of the sofabed, my body feeling like it was still doing the bounce and the butterfly. I couldn't remember the last time I had danced and had so much fun. It helped that Banning and PJ were great escorts. It was after two when PJ dropped me and Lorelei at the condo. Banning and Stevie Michelle left the club before the three of us. All evening they looked as if they wanted to be alone.

At the bottom of the sofabed, the clothes I wore dancing were neatly spread out. I hadn't changed into my gown, but left on my purple panty and bra set. I lightly touched my face. It was oily. I hadn't cleaned it before I went to bed. "Disgusting," I mumbled.

Standing, off-balance, I was reminded of the Bahama Mamas I had consumed. Those things were fruity and silent killers. You don't feel them until after you've had too many. My legs felt atrophic. Like doing the hoky-poky, I put my left leg out, shook it, and then followed with my right leg. They were wobbly. With a wide gait, I made it to Stevie Michelle's door and without knocking, I entered. I recognized her lump under the covers. *She made it in*, I thought.

The blinds were closed and other than the light that I turned on when I went into the bathroom, her room was dark. Closing the door behind me, I stared in the mirror at the woman that I didn't like to see. Remembering what happened the night before, the jealousy reappeared. I recalled PJ and Lorelei dancing almost every dance, and how he pushed her hair away from her face every chance he got. Standing there, I thought, *Why wasn't it me? Do I look too old? Am I not pretty? Was I too aggressive or too shy last night?* I pushed the skin back on my face and held it. *I am looking tired these days and maybe I should try a little more makeup than I'm used to wearing.* Looking at the makeup Stevie Michelle had on the sink, I picked up her foundation and read "toasted tan." The color was too light for me, but when I returned home I would find the right shade for myself and some brighter lipsticks. *Who am I fooling*? I thought. PJ preferred Lorelei over me. That was the bottom line. There was no more or less to it. I placed Stevie Michelle's makeup back on the counter. Somehow, something in the toilet caught my attention. When I recognized it, I gasped. It was a condom. Then I thought, *Is he still in bed with her*? I reached to flush the toilet, but promptly withdrew. They would hear me. I looked down at myself. There was no covering up the fact that I was in my underwear. I pulled a towel off the rack and wrapped it around my torso.

As quietly as I could, I opened the door and stuck my head out. Whoever was in the bed, was still there. Tiptoeing, I left the bedroom. When I was in the hallway I inhaled deeply, letting it out with exasperation. I went back into the living room. Dropping to the sofabed, I instantly jumped up. I thought, *What if they come out? I can't be here.* I made my way down the short hall to Lorelei's room. I knocked and she answered.

"Lorelei, can I come in?"

"Come on."

She was propped on her pillows writing something on a pad. "I was just makin' some notes for the restaurant," she said. "PJ had a couple great ideas last night and I didn't want to forget'em."

I wasn't listening to her. "Lorelei, do you know what I just saw?"

"One of Three's boogeymen? He usually has the same look on his face as you do right now when he's seen one of'em."

"Funny, Lorelei."

"Well, if it ain't the boogeyman, then what is it?"

I stuttered and stammered before I could get it out. "A condom. In the toilet. In the bathroom, there's a condom. A *used* condom."

"So I take it Banning came back with Stevie Michelle last night?"

"I would assume so," I said, my voice irritated.

Lorelei puffed the pillows and propped herself higher. She asked, "Chandler, why you got a towel wrapped aroun' you?"

In frustration, I said, "Because I think there's a man in the house and my robe is in the room with him."

Lorelei got out of bed and handed me her robe. The towel fell to the floor as I put it on.

"Nice undies," she commented. 'Purple is yo' color."

"How can you think this is so funny, Lorelei? There is a strange man in here."

"Chandler, he ain't strange. His name is Banning Morris and he's in bed with Stevie Michelle. And—"

"But the—"

"And all I can say is I'm happy she's practicin' safe sex."

"It's just inconsiderate, Lorelei."

"Maybe. But you pretendin' we don't know the Stevie Michelle who's in that bedroom. She's got her inconsiderate side. Her selfish moments. So what?"

I stormed out of Lorelei's room into the living room and sat on the sofabed, only to stand again and go back into her room. "You're always defending her," I said. "I can't wait in there. He may come out and see me."

As I was speaking, I heard voices. The one voice was definitely with an accent and it was Banning's.

"You hear that, Lorelei? It's Banning. He *is* here. And what do we do now?"

"We wait. From the way it sounds, he's leavin'."

Lorelei and I didn't speak while we waited. Stevie Michelle and Banning stopped talking and we heard the door close.

"I think he's gone," I said.

I waited another half minute or so before I went out. Just as I reached Stevie Michelle's door, it was closing. I pushed it open. Looking at her, she seemed relaxed and thoughtful. Her appearance made my mindset seem inappropriate. I stopped for a second, but then plowed full speed verbalizing my discomfort. "Stevie Michelle, how can you be so disconcerting, disrespecting Lorelei's and my privacy like this?"

"Well, good morning to you, too," she said.

"Don't good morning me."

"Chandler, don't start with your shit this—"

"Don't you tell me what to do," I sputtered back. "Obviously, you don't know what to do yourself."

Stevie Michelle made one step backward into the room and I matched her one step with one forward.

"I'm not a child, Chandler, so find someone else to yell at. I'm not the one."

"You deserve this, Stevie Michelle. This is the last straw. You go ar—"

"You two stop it!" Lorelei loudly demanded.

Stevie Michelle and I heard her, but ignored the order for peace.

"Chandler I don't think I've done anything wrong," Stevie Michelle said. "So not you or anybody else can make me feel guilty. I feel too good. You hear me? Too good."

"Hey!" Lorelei yelled. "This is crazy."

"Make you feel guilty?" I said. "The guilt fairy is beyond making you feel guilty. You don't think about weighing the consequences before you do the things you do."

"Who the *hell* are you, Chandler, God?"

I heard the door close. Looking behind me, Lorelei had disappeared. I was alone on my conquest.

Turning around to face Stevie Michelle again, I said, "Being God has nothing to do with this. I walked in here this morning with nothing on but my underwear to find a man sleeping in your bed."

"Well, I can't think of a better bed for him to sleep in or a better man for me to sleep with."

"That was a great comeback, Stevie Michelle. You're not serious about a damn thing."

"And you're too damn serious about everything. You're beginning to be the ant at the picnic, the rain on the parade, the—"

"Shuddup, Stevie Michelle!" Glaring at her, I turned and stormed out of the room.

In the living room I changed from Lorelei's robe into the same clothes I had on the night before and walked out of the condo. There were tears of frustration and anger floating in my eyes.

I must have walked for about an hour before I returned to find Lorelei in the kitchen, making breakfast.

Continuing, without looking at me, she said, "Ready for some coffee and breakfast?"

I didn't answer, but got a cup and poured coffee. "Is Stevie Michelle still here?" I asked, my voice teetering on heavy.

"Yeah. She's been in there ever since you left. Personally, I think you two need to apologize to one another."

"What!?"

"Chandler, I thought you walked off all that anger?"

I exhaled with a huff. "Lorelei?"

"Yeah?"

"Why did you close the door on us?"

"It was time, Chandler. That's all. It's like with Topper and Three. I can try to keep a fight from brewin' for hours, sometimes even days, but eventually it has to happen. The only thing I try to make sure of is everybody fights fair. No kickin', bitin', scratchin' or name callin'. Them the rules. Other than that, I don't interfere. They exhaust themselves and the whole household develops a calm about it. It's like the hurricane that hits. After it's gone, the sun shines and the wind is soft. The only thing that reminds you it's been there is the damage it leaves behind. That's what I try to make sure don't happen—the damage."

"I don't know how much damage was done in there, Lorelei."

"Nothin' that can't be repaired. These walls are thin. I heard everything." Lorelei giggled. "You two fought fair."

I hugged my girlfriend from behind and went to Stevie Michelle's room. I knocked.

"Come in." My girlfriend was sitting on the bed, folding her clothes.

"Going somewhere?" I asked.

"No. I was just putting away some things that I decided not to wear." Stevie Michelle didn't look at me when she spoke.

"Oh," I said. I looked past her out of the open blinds onto the garden. Over the days we had been there, the flowers seemed to have changed from a mango color to a richer persimmon. Within the silence between us, I finally said, "I'm sorry."

"Me too," she replied. "I didn't expect for Banning to come in at all last night. I was tired and that's why I left the club when I did. I guess going out every night caught up with me. But he walked me to the door and kissed me, and the next thing I knew we were in here, seducing one another. He was supposed to be gone before you got home, but we fell asleep. Into a deep sleep, Chandler. It was like I had slept with him all my life. It felt right and easy. Our bodies molded perfectly and so we slept that way."

"Everything's okay, Stevie Michelle. I understand."

"I don't think you do. You see, Chandler, this morning from this very bed I looked up, right where you're standing now, into the black of his eyes and saw and felt something that I've never felt before with anyone, not even Carl."

"You think it may be called love?"

"How can I say I'm in love with someone I've known all of seventy-two hours?"

"Well, I can only explain it as sometimes when you talk to a person for the first time, you know there is a chemistry. And then as you keep talking and spending time with one another, the time spent confirms it." I sat next to Stevie Michelle. I laughed. "Did you get what I just said? Because if you did, then you are good, girlfrien'."

Stevie Michelle chuckled. "Yeah, I got it."

I asked, "Do you think Banning feels the same way?"

"I don't know, Chandler, and it's really not important. There are some facts and some assumptions that make how Banning feels, or how I feel for that matter, insignificant—irrelevant."

"What facts? What assumptions?"

"The fact that he lives thousands of miles away. The fact that he has no plans of relocating and neither do I. Then I have to assume that there is a woman, Chandler. Someone he's connected with. He's too handsome, too brilliant, and too good a catch not to have somebody."

"Okay, what if he doesn't have a relationship? Are you going to let him leave without at least confirming it?"

"Chandler, this is not a love story in a movie. Boy doesn't meet girl and they fall in love, and he takes her to his faraway castle and they live happily ever after. We've had fun for a few days and then he'll go back to reality tomorrow and I'll return to my life a few days after that. So, let's drop it."

"Okay. But I still think you're making a mistake not to inquire."

Stevie Michelle boycotted my statement by saying, "Chandler, I didn't mean those things I said. It's just that sometimes you make me feel guilty. I know I could be more serious, even more responsible, but the fact is, I don't want to. Being like I am keeps me from losing the little sanity I have. It keeps me from falling into the raw sewage of what can be presented in a lifetime."

I displayed a loving smile at my girlfriend. "Look, Stevie Michelle, I have no right to judge you. Along with Lorelei, you are one of the best people I know. I just lost it this morning. I told you I'd get a little cranky before all this restaurant stuff is taken care of. And maybe underneath it all, I might be a little jealous. Regardless of how I pour myself into other things, I miss having someone in my life. There hasn't been anyone since Wade and the way it looks, I don't think there will be."

"There could be, if you'd just loosen up. Let that beautiful feminine side of yours come to the forefront. I think you've forgotten how sexy you are."

"I haven't felt sexy in a long time," I said.

"Then I want you to start thinking about it. We both know sexy begins in the mind and then flows to the body. Have you forgotten that you're the one who drilled in me that for a woman to be effective, she has to tap into her feminine, sexy side first?"

"I did say that, didn't I? Thanks for reminding me."

Our conversation brightened. We talked about how we would bring in the new year in the Bahamas. We called Lorelei in and she suggested we have a fabulous dinner in a fantastic restaurant and then sip champagne at Club 2001.

Chapter 22

(Chandler)

Monday, Dec. 30

Lorelei and I lounged around the condo like two fat house cats. We watched a little television, listened to music, sat on the balcony and read, and ate and drank iced tea most of the afternoon. We had planned to go to the beach, but agreed that it would take more effort to get there than we were willing to exert.

It was Monday, and Banning and PJ had an evening flight to London. Stevie Michelle got up early, dressed and shut the condo door behind her when she left with Banning. They had been together the whole day and a couple times, while we were on the balcony, Lorelei and I saw them walking in the garden. We conceded that they were something from a romance novel, or a movie, or both.

PJ had called Lorelei and offered her a seat next to him at his condominium while he waited for a phone call from the Federal Bureau of Investigation. She declined. We laughed when she said, "Go over there for what, so I can end up like Stevie Michelle? No thanks. I told'im to call me if and when the news came and I would be the first to congratulate'im."

"It's a damn shame, Lorelei."

"What is?" she said, laying the book she was reading on her lap.

"That we can't do this for the rest of our lives."

"What? Sit aroun' baskin' in the sunshine, breathin' fresh air, flirtin' with gorgeous men, fantasizin'? No way, Chandler, not me. All this luxury could keep me youthful and vibrant. How would I explain that to Walter, especially after I vowed that's what Oceanna, Topper and Three do for me. He'll think I been lyin' all this time. No way, Chandler, not me. I love the snow, the cold, the pollution, rude Americans and most of all the unlimited access to any type and style of prejudice you can imagine."

Laughing, I said, "Sorry I said anything."

"Chandler, have you noticed how few of'em there are here, compared to us?"

"You mean white people?"

"Yeah. It's so refreshin' to see the deep color of our people everywhere and doin' fine. Workin' in their own businesses, even if it's a business sellin' t-shirts from a small hut in an open-air market. Most of the white people I see are on vacation. PJ explained it to me last night. He said white people ain't given incentive to come here other than to visit. They ain't invited to have businesses here. And if they feel they gotta have a business in the Bahamas, the government takes more than half of the gross profits." Lorelei banged her hand hard on the chrome and glass table next to her chair. The impact should have broken the glass. "They gettin' a taste of their own medicine," she said with conviction.

I had always wanted to ask her, but never had the nerve. Maybe it was the caffeine stimulation that gave me the courage. Staring into her beautifully clear bright eyes, I said, "Lorelei, do you teach your children to dislike white people?"

In gist, she answered, "No, I don't. I teach my children to look white folks in their eyes when they are talkin' to'em, and to know what they talkin' about when they speak, which in short means I teach my children to have confidence and knowledge, and not fear or feel inferior to anyone, especially white people."

Right at that moment, I didn't see my girlfriend, Lorelei, as a prejudice radical, but a woman who understood the intimidations of the white race, and who taught her children how to cope and deal with the adversities. I admired her. She had no part in the problem of ongoing hatred, but was the solution to her family's understanding of the dislike from both sides.

Lorelei stared back. "Chandler," she said, "why you lookin' at me like that?"

"Because you are a complex woman and every time I think I know you, you reveal another dimension of your cognizance."

"I hope that's good, 'cause I don't know what the hell you just said to me."

"It's very good, Lorelei. Very good."

"If you think I'm—"

All of a sudden our tranquil conversation and afternoon on the balcony was interrupted with Stevie Michelle coming through the door and the phone ringing. "I'll get it," she yelled, her voice cheerful. A few seconds later she bellowed, "Lorelei, it's for you."

Lorelei and I scowled at one another thinking of who it could be. My first thought was Walter. She had talked to him twice since we had been in the Bahamas. She called when we got there and he called when Three wanted to talk to her. Nimbly, Lorelei rose from the chair and made her way to the phone.

Stevie Michelle passed her through the living room and came out onto the balcony. She took Lorelei's seat. "Chandler, I think this has been the most beautiful day our entire stay here."

Grinning at her, I said, "Oh yeah? How so?"

"I've been talking to Banning."

"*Noooo*!"

"Chandler, are you going to make fun of me? Because if you are, I'll just stop the conversation right now."

"Stevie Michelle, listen to yourself. I've seen you in the garden walking with him at least three times since this morning. You two have been inseparable. So, I know you've been talking to him. But if I'm upsetting you, then no more teasing. I promise." I held up my right hand. "So tell me, what did you talk about?"

"You were right. Some things need to be said to get an understanding. Chandler, he told me that his last girlfriend, who he was planning to marry, dumped him. Can you imagine that? Somebody dumping Banning Morris? I can't." Stevie Michelle was talking a mile a minute. It was amusing to listen and watch her. "He wants to visit me in Cleveland. I can't imagine somebody coming to Cleveland from overseas just to visit, but he swears that's what he wants to do. And you know what else? His father is a corporate executive and his mother is some kind of diplomat in the embassy." She stopped to take a breath. "He also invited me to London. I've never been out of the country before, Chandler. I mean, I don't consider this out of the country because it's so Americanized and everybody speaks English, although English is the language there, too. But you know what's—"

"Stevie Michelle. Slow down," I said. She was giddy to the point of overdosing. I was happy for her. She had found someone who was intriguing. Usually, it took more than most men possessed to keep Stevie Michelle entertained. For once, I felt she had met her match.

Too bad her match lived bodies of water away. "So, do you think you're in love?"

"Truthfully, no, but I feel that if we spend anymore time together, I could be."

"Well, welcome home," Lorelei said as she stepped through the threshold of the balcony. "Long time no see. I know you been givin' Chandler the juicy details of yo' day. And now you got to start all over."

"Who was that on the phone?" I asked.

In unison, Lorelei and Stevie Michelle said, "PJ."

"Did he get the job?" I asked.

"Yep," Lorelei said. "And when he gets settled in Florida he wants me to come see'im."

My girlfriends were scoring big in the man arena and I was left wondering how I'd missed out. I didn't express that to them, though.

"What time are the Morris brothers leaving today?" I asked.

"In about fifteen minutes," Lorelei said. "Stevie Michelle, Banning and PJ want us to come over to their condo to say goodbye."

They both looked at me. "What the hell are you looking at me for? Go!"

They raced out the door. I wasn't feeling sorry for myself, but I sure was feeling alone. I went inside and poured another glass of tea. Back on the balcony, I began making notes and projections for Maroon. *At least I have Maroon to look forward to*, I thought.

Chapter 23

(Chandler)

Tuesday, Dec. 31

We were lightheartedly silly all morning. Stevie Michelle, Lorelei and I cooked breakfast dressed in our underwear, and the three of us sat at the table that way. I assessed that we based our purchases of undergarments on the amount of lace and color. Stevie Michelle was wearing a coral combination, Lorelei was in a lavender ensemble and I wore turquoise. Pretty, lacy, sexy underwear was another thing we had in common.

It was New Year's Eve and I selfishly knew that I had my girlfriends to myself. There would be no Banning or PJ to compete with. They were going to spend the whole day and all night with me. I suggested that we start an early celebration of the new year by having lunch in one of the fancier restaurants and ordering a bottle of champagne, exposing our most private resolutions and goals. But before we did that, Lorelei, Stevie Michelle and I got dressed, left the condo and walked along the unpaved road, kicking rocks and sand, smelling flowers, waving at passersby and telling jokes. Looking at my girlfriends and myself, the sun had roasted our skin into richer shades of browns. We glistened from the rays and our complexions were healthy.

Stevie Michelle giggled through, "Okay, I've got a good one. What do you call a man with a small penis?"

I said, "I don't know. What do you call a man with a small penis?"

"Penislized."

Lorelei and I booed and hissed.

"Come on, girls, don't you get it? Penalized. *Penislized.*"

"We got it, but it's still a corny joke," I said.

"I got a better one," Lorelei said. "What do you call a car on fire?"

"I don't know," I said. "What do you call a car on fire?"

"A carbeque."

Comedians we were not, and the jokes got worse before we made it back to the condo. We kicked off our shoes and sat on the balcony before we changed for lunch. Stevie Michelle and Lorelei insisted that I choose the restaurant. I chose Guanahani's. Inside, there was a wonderful tropical setting with palm plants, salt water fish tanks, lively reggae music piped throughout, and handsome waiters in bright Hawaiian shirts. Lorelei, Stevie Michelle and I danced to our seats. We ate delectably rich cuisine and drank two bottles of champagne. Our waiter loved us so much, he brought dessert and said it was his treat.

"Okay, girls, I'll start with a resolution and goal," I said as we ate our coconut, pineapple torte. "My New Year's resolution is to be less stiff and my goal is to be loose like Stevie Michelle, because obviously that works and definitely appears to be more fun. She's developed an international relationship and is my idol." I held my champagne flute in the air for my girlfriends to join me in a toast. They were laughing too hard to respond. "What's so damn funny? I'm being serious here."

Stevie Michelle said, "Chandler, am I supposed to be flattered or insulted?"

"You should be too intoxicated by now to know the difference."

We raised our glasses to a toast. Then Steve Michelle said, "My turn." Clearing her throat, her words materialized slowly. "My resolution is to stop evading the issues I don't want to deal with. I have to stop going to la la land, open up more and not keep so much locked inside."

"Where do you go?" Lorelei asked, chuckling.

"When I open up one day, I'll tell you all about it."

I responded, "You just said that's what you're going to start doing, Stevie Michelle."

Her voice became direct. "Look, I told you I'd talk about it some other time. Now, do you want to hear my goal or not?"

I raised my brow and said, "Okay. Sure. Go ahead."

Her voice and stare became less rigid when she said, "Goal wise, I'm going to pursue some of the things that I've wanted to do most of my life."

"No fair," Lorelei said. "You doin' it again. Stevie Michelle, you gotta be more specific than that."

"I don't have to."

"Oh, yes you do," I insisted.

"Okay. But don't you laugh." Neither Lorelei or I agreed to that, but Stevie Michelle proceeded anyway. "One of the things is getting a college degree. I've convinced myself that it's never too late."

It was definitely the first I had heard that Stevie Michelle wanted to go to school, but I wasn't knocking it. I said, "Why would we laugh about that?"

"What you goin' for?" Lorelei asked.

"What else? Public relations, maybe even communications. Chandler says I'm good at it and I haven't even been formally trained. Just think how good I'd be if I was educated to do what I do."

I said, "You definitely are a natural, girlfrien'. You could charm a scorpion out of its stinger, knowing that's the only defense it has."

"That's not all," she said shyly. "I also want to go to modeling school."

The music pervaded my thoughts. I was silent, but Lorelei said, "Stevie Michelle, how well have you thought this out?"

"I know what you're thinking, Lorelei, but I've investigated this thing. Department stores are looking for the mature woman to model more of the mature clothing. I know it's not going to be a career, but I think I'll enjoy it as a hobby. I feel it's no different than taking up golf or any other hobby, only I chose modeling."

"Okay, if you look at it that way," I said. Changing the direction, but not the subject, I said, "Lorelei, it's your turn, girl."

"Well," she said, her eyes revealing her champagne consumption, "I been thinkin' and I ain't got no resolutions, bein' perfect and all, but I do have a goal. I've had it for some time now, and I think I can handle the outcome, whatever it is. I don't know—"

"For Pete's sake, Lorelei, what is it? At the rate you're going, New Year's'll be here and gone before you get it out."

"Chandler, yo' resolution should be to limit yo' pushy persuasion. But anyway, as I was sayin', I can't remember right now how much of my backgroun' I told you, but I know I said some things about My Mother—*annd— welll* I think it's time I find her. Dead or alive, I want to know where she is." Lorelei inhaled. Letting it out slowly, she lifted her glass and drank as if washing down the bitter words she had spoken. She swallowed with effort, as though the words had gotten stuck in her throat.

"Lorelei, that could take a long time," Stevie Michelle informed her.

"I know. I got time. I'll start with a missin' persons agency and ask how's best to go about it, but I'm determined."

I said, "If you need help, Stevie Michelle and I are here."

"Wait a minute, Chandler," Stevie Michelle protested. "I didn't tell you about my third goal and it'll have me pretty tied up. I mean, I've gotta work some mojo in the coming months."

"Stevie Michelle, what are you talking about?" I asked.

"Sitting here sipping on champagne, I've decided that I'm not going to let Mr. Banning Morris off the hook just yet. I think I want to see more of him and I've got to see to it that he feels like seeing more of me, too. And that ain't going to be easy long distance. He hasn't been gone twelve hours and all my senses are missing him. That's a sure sign. I mean, I'm not one to go around missing people."

Stevie Michelle was good. She knew how to lighten things when they were on the curve of becoming too heavy or serious. She was deeply interested in Banning, but her reason for talking about him then was to lift the downswing of our conversation. Public relations was definitely her purpose in life.

I said, "Girl, that's the champagne your senses are responding to. You'll know it in the morning when you wake up with a colossal headache to remind you. So, I say we pour the rest in our glasses, make a toast and go back to the condo to continue our party tonight." I evenly distributed the champagne between the three of us, raising my glass. "Here's to my best friends," I said. "The bestest of friends, through thick and thin, until the end."

Our delicate flutes made crystal music when we put them together.

CHAPTER 24

(Chandler)

Wednesday, Jan. 1

We, Stevie Michelle, Lorelei and I, rang in the New Year with iced tea. We decided that the two bottles of champagne we had at lunch was enough and we also agreed that we didn't want to go to Club 2001 to celebrate. I made crepes, stuffed with cheese and whatever leftovers I found in the refrigerator, and we snacked on those. Lorelei and Stevie Michelle said that they were not the best, but considering what was there to cook with, my feelings weren't bruised. It was an unsuccessful experiment.

The highlight of the evening, though, was when Banning phoned Stevie Michelle to wish her a happy new year. Stevie Michelle called Nelson. Lorelei talked to Walter and the children, and I called Kennedy, Cornelius and my niece, Alex, wishing them a happy new year. Kennedy actually put the phone to Alex's ear. She said she smiled when she heard my voice.

Lorelei, Stevie Michelle and I went to bed around three o'clock. At approximately seven-thirty we were up scrambling to get things together for our return to Cleveland. We were to be picked up for the airport at nine-thirty, and while we packed, we admitted to one another that our trip to paradise was enjoyable, but we were ready to go home to grey skies, the snow, the cold, the pollution and most of all, our families and new careers.

Adam, in the red Chrysler, was waiting for us at nine-twenty-five. I was the last one out of the condominium, shutting the door behind me. I thought, *There's no turning back now or ever.*

BOOK II

Chapter 25

(Chandler)

I asked Stevie Michelle and Lorelei to meet me at two-thirty. I was there to open the door at one-thirty. It had rained and water droplets still clung to the bare branches of, what I guessed, to be a weeping cherry tree. I thought, *It will be beautiful when it blooms in the spring.* Back inside, in the dampness of the room, bundled in my old navy pea coat and black rubber ankle boots, I walked the dimensions for the dining room, the kitchen, and even the restrooms. I counted the number of ceiling fans I thought should slowly rotate above our guests. I visualized many wall and accessory color combinations. Flowers. I mentally placed vases of fresh-cut Casablanca lilies, lilacs, roses and Irises on the dinner tables and in the reception area.

Looking through the dirt and water-stained window, I saw my girlfriends pull to the curb in Stevie Michelle's Saab. I waited until they reached the door before I opened it. "Welcome to Maroon, ladies," I said in my most celebrated voice. "Thank you for coming."

They walked past me, gawking.

"It's just one big shell of a room," Lorelei said.

"It's supposed to be ready when?" Stevie Michelle asked.

"Come on, guys," I said. "Don't start with the cold feet already."

"We're not, Chandler, but this place doesn't begin to resemble a restaurant."

"I know that. That's why I had you meet me here today. I want you to see what we have to work with and how much work we've got ahead of us."

Our voices echoed as we talked. I began explaining to my partners how I saw Maroon and as they began to understand my concept, my madness, they began to collaborate with me.

"What do you think about hanging shutters at the windows?" Stevie Michelle asked.

Lorelei said, "I think shutters would be a good idea, and I think we should stain'em the same color as the floor. "We keepin' the hardwood floor, ain't we, Chandler?"

"Yes. They're too beautiful, even in the condition they're in now, to cover. Carpeting would be a waste." Walking away from Lorelei and Stevie Michelle, I stepped up into the bay window, extended my arms and said, "Stevie Michelle and Lorelei, this will be it! This will be our business in the coming six months. I don't know about you, but I'm scared and excited at the same time. But, I know I don't want to do anything else. I don't want to turn back. My name is Chandler Elizabeth Cawthorne and *I am* Chef de Cuisine for Maroon, the most fantastic new age restaurant in the world. And by fall we will be the talk of this town."

Lorelei clapped her hands and Stevie Michelle joined in. I started clapping, too. The echoes sang a song. I jumped from the window and ran to hug my girlfriends. Kissing them on their cheeks, I whispered, "Without the two of you, this wouldn't be possible. I love you both, because dreams coming true are phenomenal."

We locked arms and Lorelei yelled, "To the virtuoso trio!"

Then I said, "The bestest of friends, through thick and thin, until the end!"

Stevie Michelle added, "No bout a doubt it!"

Reaching into my pocket, I pulled out two brass key rings with a key attached to each. Handing one to Stevie Michelle and the other to Lorelei, I said, "These make it official." Engraved on one side of the rings were their names and on the other: Maroon. "You now possess the keys to our future," I said.

Lorelei, with the amazement of a child, asked, "Chandler, when did you do this?"

"Well, I had the rings engraved before we went to the Bahamas, but I put the keys on them this morning."

Stevie Michelle choked through, "I guess this does make it official. My own key."

I said, "Now that the important business is taken care of, I think we should go have dinner and critique somebody else's restaurant."

Stevie Michelle said, "That sounds like a good idea."

"I'm glad you think so. You can drive." I listened to our footsteps as we walked out. I thought, *Ordinary, we ain't. I can hear it when we walk.*

Lorelei used her key to lock the door of Maroon.

Chapter 26

(Chandler)

In my forty-two years, I believed it to be the coolest June in history. It was the middle and Mother Nature was still threatening night-time frost. During the month of February, I bought ornate terra cotta pots that weighed at least sixty pounds each. The delivery man placed them on each side of the walk at the entrance of the restaurant, like I had asked him. I purchased potting soil and decided that no matter what Mother Nature had planned, it was time to plant flowers.

It was eight o'clock, Sunday morning, and I was the first to arrive at the restaurant. Most times I would be in the kitchen testing recipes, but that morning I poured dirt, planting purple petunias, pink new guinea impatiens, salvia, nasturtium, marigolds and some herbs—lemon thyme, basil and lavender. Untangling the variegated vines, stretching them out over the small patch of grass, I heard Stevie Michelle's car. Her Saab drove with a distinctive low hum in the engine. She pulled in front of the restaurant instead of into the lot. Getting out, she said, "I tried to call you. When I got your voice mail at home and no answer here, I got worried."

"I could have been in the shower."

"Chandler, the world knows you shower at night, no matter what."

I chuckled from the thought that my girlfriends knew me better than any man I had known, even Wade—sometimes better than I knew myself. "What's so urgent?"

"Oh, nothing. I just wanted to bounce an idea off you."

"Okay. And it couldn't wait? It must be a compelling idea."

"Chandler, just shut up and listen."

"Okay, but—"

"Shuddup!"

I often was tempted to frazzle Stevie Michelle. It was just my kind of love for her. I couldn't explain it and I didn't feel I had to—not to her, Lorelei or anyone else.

"Now, here's the idea," she started. "I think we should serve breakfast and lunch."

"Woman, are you crazy!?" I yelped. "*Oh no, no, no, no, no.*"

"Chandler, let me finish," she said in a rapid, blunt tone, "We both know that the 'other restaurant' across the tracks does a hell of a business for breakfast and lunch, and they do it with the traditional bacon, sausage, eggs, toast and pancakes. But I thought we could do things like crepes, fancy omelets and fancy pastries."

"Stevie Michelle, the 'other restaurant' is only one and a half steps above fast food. I don't believe people, on a daily basis, will support your concept. It would cost too much. Now, regarding lunch, maybe we should give that some thought."

Speaking of the "other restaurant", Stevie Michelle, Lorelei and I named it that after the owners, a sun-colored balding little man, and a large mass of a blonde-haired woman, walked through the door of Maroon and demanded that the name of their establishment never be mentioned by us again. We agreed because we held no animosity toward them or their business. What occurred was we—I—hired a dishwasher who worked for them, not knowing he came to work for Maroon to spy on us. Working three weeks, he quit and went back across the tracks to the "other restaurant" even after he made twenty cents an hour more with Maroon. The dishwasher had heard us mention things like, "heart attack on a plate" and "back stroking in grease" and "hardening of the arteries waiting to happen". The things we said were all in fun and we never bashed the "other restaurant" to our customers.

"Stevie Michelle, I don't mean to insinuate that your idea isn't good, but realistically, it would mean many more hours for me."

"It wouldn't, Chandler, if you'd just stop being so stubborn about hiring someone to work with you."

"I don't need anyone else to work with me. Jorge is enough." Pointing in the direction, I said, "That kitchen in there belongs to me. Too many people in it means I lose control. Jorge and I work well together. I don't think anybody else will work with either one of us as well."

"That's because he's as finicky as you are."

"Now, now, now. Did I call you names this morning?"

At that moment, Lorelei stopped her car behind Stevie Michelle's. I threw my hands in the air. Dirt on the spade I held flew off into the grass. "What is this?" I said.

Lorelei trotted up the walkway. I looked at my watch. It was eight-forty-five.

"Is somethin' wrong?" she asked, her brilliant eyes anticipating an answer.

Stevie Michelle, with a furrowed stare, said, "No. Should there be?"

"Well, when I didn't get an answer at Chandler's, then when I called you and there was no answer, I called here, but there was no answer either, so I thought somethin' happened after we left last night, and—"

"All this because I couldn't sleep," I interjected. "If I had suggested a meeting this time of the morning, you two would have instantly protested." I pushed one of the delicate petunias out of its plastic container and firmly planted it in the pot. Stevie Michelle and Lorelei were staring at me. "You know, this could get done faster if the two of you helped."

Lorelei immediately dropped her keys on the ground and began pouring soil in the pot on the other side of the walk.

Stevie Michelle said, "Chandler, I'm not dressed for hard labor."

"This ain't hard labor, girlfrien'. I like to think of it as therapy."

"Anything where I get my hands and clothes dirty, I call hard labor. I don't like dirt under my nails."

"Okay then, I'll tell you this. In the restaurant there's an apron to keep your clothes clean and a pair of rubber gloves for your hands. I suggest you retrieve both and get back out here."

Stevie Michelle stomped her foot like a spoiled six-year-old and asked, "Why do I have to do this? My job is public relations, not garden and landscape."

"Okay, I didn't know we had to go here, but let me explain it to you this way." I inhaled. "You see that Saab at the curb? I've got a feeling that one day you'll want to replace it—not with a Pinto or Pacer—but another Saab, and Carl's not around to get it for you because you divorced your cash cow. Therefore, your next automobile is on you, my dear, which means you have an obligation to your style of living and the partnership of this business to do whatever's necessary to maintain both. So, go get the apron and gloves, and start plantin', honey." I exhaled.

Before Stevie Michelle went into the restaurant, Lorelei said, "Chandler, we should do window boxes, too." Then she giggled.

When Stevie Michelle returned with an apron on and gloves in hand, I asked her to tell Lorelei her idea about breakfast and lunch. Lorelei had another suggestion.

"I don't think breakfast and lunch every day is a good idea for two reasons," she said. "One is, financial. We just beginnin' to build capital and more hours would dilute the growth. Two, with the 'other restaurant' servin' breakfast, the customers will be divided. But, if Chandler thought she could handle it, Sunday brunch would be an excellent addition to our services."

"Brunch! Why didn't I think of that?" I said. "Stevie Michelle, that's the answer to your breakfast and lunch. Brunch."

The three of us smiled at the idea. We had found a happy medium. We finished planting and the pots were stuffed with color and fragrance. The purples and pinks were cool colors, while the yellows and oranges were blasts of sunshine.

Stevie Michelle brushed the dirt from the apron and pulled off the rubber gloves. "I'm going home for awhile," she said. "Is there anything else that needs to be done before I leave?"

"No. But how do the reservations look for tonight?" I asked.

"If I'm not mistaken, I think the president of the Pee Dee is coming."

"Oh, that's nice. He's becoming a regular. I think the wild mushrooms in puffed pastry will be a winner with him."

"Is that the special?" Lorelei asked.

"Yeah. The supplier had a good price on mushrooms—shitake, cremini and portabella."

Lorelei got her keys off the ground and announced that she was also going home.

"I'll be here a little longer," I said. I knew I would regret not leaving then. It made for an unbearably late night, but I wanted to prepare the sauce for the mushrooms, and also design the Sunday brunch menu. While planting flowers, Lorelei, Stevie Michelle and I set a date of July thirteenth for our first brunch. I was excited.

Walking through the restaurant into the kitchen, I opened the back door and invited in the summer breeze. I went over to the small table where I had a portable CD player and looked through the stack of CD's that consisted of Marvin Gaye, Peabo Bryson, and Isaac Hayes' *Hot Buttered Soul*. I chose that one. I slipped it into the player and skipped the first selection to the second—*Hyperbolicsyllabicsesquedalymistic*. Isaac's voice, deep and sexy, and the rhythm of the music rocking with a heavy beat, made me dance. I danced from the refrigerator to the stove, carrying a container of veal stock, pouring half the content into a saucepan. I turned on the flame. I sang with Isaac while I continued to dance, feeling the beat. I boogied over to the CD and cranked the volume higher. Dancing over to the stove again, I stirred the stock, lowering the heat. The kitchen filled with the aroma of consommé and the pulse of *Hyperbolicsyllabicsesquedalymistic*. My feet glided over the glossed linoleum floor. I stopped to jam on my imaginary piano. I started to dance again. The movement of the music took me from one end of the kitchen to the other. Pretending to play the guitar, my fingers performed with dexterity. Grabbing the freezer handle, I performed some fancy Paula Abdul footwork with a charismatic spin. I stopped at one-hundred-eighty degrees and screamed in surprise. I shouted, "Marcus Anthony Taylor, Jr., what are you doing?!" My heart pounded as I turned the volume down on the music.

"I didn't know you could move like that, Ms. C."

"It's not nice to sneak up on people, Marcus."

"The door was open, the music was jammin', so I just came right on in. Are you embarrassed, Ms. C?"

"Why should I be embarrassed? I was dancing in my own kitchen."

"You are embarrassed," he said, a smile reconstructing his face. His eyes squinted until they looked like small slits. Marcus had one of the most beautiful smiles in the world. His expression ignited a room. Then, sometimes developing all the way from the gut, he would let out a jolly man's laugh.

"I'm not embarrassed, Marcus," I said, realizing that I was allowing a thirteen-year-old to intimidate me.

"You by yourself today, Ms. C. Why?" he asked.

"Stevie Michelle and Lorelei were here earlier, but they left. I decided to stay and prepare the sauce for tonight's special."

"What's the special?"

"Wild mushrooms in puffed pastry with a veal stock sauce."

"One of these days, I'm goin' to convince you to have barbequed baby back ribs, French fries and cole slaw for the special."

"Oh, really now?" I said, laughing.

"Yeah. It ain't like I'm watchin' my diet." At that moment Marcus reminded me of a smiling chocolate Buddha. On anyone's scale, he would have been five-feet, four inches of obesity. I didn't see him that way because as large as he was, he moved with agility and grace. He carried his weight with comfort, although I knew the weight he carried was unhealthy.

The first time Marcus appeared at the restaurant, he was on a hustle. He walked through the front door during renovations and introduced himself. His voice tenor-like and airy, he said, *"My name is Marcus Anthony Taylor, Jr. and I've heard that you need some help with this place."* I listened to him and instantly I was pulled by his lulling voice. It was musical. *"And who told you that?" I asked, leaning against the wall the broom I'd used to sweep the sawdust. "The word down the hill is there's three women up the hill startin' a restaurant." "That's correct. We'll be open in a week, so when you go back down the hill, tell'em our doors will open next Saturday night." "So that means you'll need somebody to empty the garbage, scrub the floor, clean the crumbs out of the chairs. You know." "And you're willing to do all that?" "For a fee, I am. I ain't into charity or nothin' like that." "But we already have clean-up staff." "So where are they?" "They haven't started yet." "But it looks like you need'em now." I found myself looking through the restaurant, following his gaze. Then I found myself asking, "How much do you charge?" "Five dollars an hour, minimum three hours and no taxes." "You've done this before. How old are you?" I asked. "Fifteen."* I knew he was lying, but I still liked him and his ambition. From that day forward, Marcus Anthony Taylor, Jr. helped at the restaurant.

"Have you had breakfast, Marcus?"

"Naw, Ms. C."

"How about I fix you something?"

"That sounds sweet," Marcus said in anticipation, staring into my eyes.

"I don't know why I'm so nice to you?" I said playfully. "I guess I'm just a sucker, that's all."

"Yeah. Why do you do things for me, Ms. C, when you don't have to?"

"Because I'm crazy about you." Marcus wore a gentle gaze. His blush warmed me. "You help keep the restaurant spic and span, and you watch out for things around here," I said. "So, you see, just the way you don't think about the things you do for me, I don't give helping you a thought, either. I guess it all comes natural because we care for one another. When you had a cold, I made chicken noodle soup and honey-lemon tea for you, hoping it would help you feel better."

"Yeah, you did. That soup was the bomb. I could eat that anytime, sick or not. So, when you say it's natural, Ms. C, you mean that you don't force yourself to do it?"

"That's right. I love doing things for you."

"Ms. C, are you going to marry Doc Stohn?"

"What makes you ask, Marcus?"

"I don't know. Maybe because you look so happy when he's around. You look the same when flowers are delivered." Shrugging his shoulders, he stated, "All happy and stuff."

"Marcus, I want to explain that Dr. Stohn—Dr. Bradford, that is—is a good friend of mine, and I am grateful for his friendship, so I try to make him feel welcome when he comes into the restaurant. And I don't do any more for him than I do for the other customers." Marcus looked at me suspiciously. "Okay, maybe I do a little more for him, but he does deserve it. Like I mentioned before, he's a good friend. And you're a good friend, too," I said, grabbing Marcus around the neck, tugging playfully. He enjoyed the attention. "Let me finish this sauce and I'll fix you pancakes and . . ." Looking into the refrigerator, I said, "And something. But don't worry, I'll figure it out. There isn't much breakfast food here, but that's going to change. We're starting a brunch menu in July."

"I got faith you'll cook me somethin' good, Ms. C. You always do. I'll go get the fingerprints off the piano." Part of Marcus' job was to polish the cabinet of the piano, removing the prints that accumulated during the week.

"Thanks, Marcus. You know how they make me crazy."

"Don't worry, Ms. C, I gotcha covered. Oh, by the way," he said, "cool pots out front." Marcus and I had an unspoken bond. He respected my feelings and I tried to understand his.

"Thanks." Turning to face the stove, out the corner of my eye I saw a shoe box on the edge of the counter by the door. I yelled, "Freeze, Marcus." He stopped. "What's in the box?"

"Aw, Ms. C, it ain't nothin' but my mouse, Horace."

"Marcus Anthony Taylor, Jr., what have I told you? No pets in the restaurant. No turtles, no snakes, no birds, no mice, no insects. No animals of any kind. Now get *Horace* outside and keep him there until you leave."

Marcus hung his head and did as I requested. He was a most unusual kid. Although streetwise, Marcus was the smartest boy I'd ever encountered. He loved animals and said he wanted to be a zoologist or veterinarian. With the right guidance, he could be. I had never met his parents and he never talked about his life. He seemed to just enjoy being "up the hill", as he called it, working for five dollars an hour, three hours minimum, no taxes, and then he'd disappear down the hill again. He said he didn't use drugs and he didn't "gang bang", but his life was still a mystery. And if I asked questions, he would change the subject. I swore to myself that one day I would follow him down the hill to see what his private life was like.

I poured red wine into the boiling stock and added fresh chopped rosemary, butter and a bay leaf. While the liquid reduced, I mixed pancakes for Marcus from my own recipe. Then, frying apple slices in butter, I added sugar, cinnamon, nutmeg, more butter and lemon zest, creating a hot apple and syrup topping for his pancakes. I broiled a steak and scrambled eggs for him. I had prepared my first brunch for Maroon and for Marcus.

"Breakfast is served," I shouted into the dining room.

Marcus ate in the kitchen with me and devoured everything on his plate. "Thanks, Ms. C. You've done it again," he said, tossing the napkin as a finale.

"I'm glad you liked it."

"Those apples were the bomb. You should definitely serve them at your brunch."

"I think I will, Marcus."

Chapter 27

(Chandler)

For the first time, I thought we would run out of ice, dishes and energy. The restaurant was booming. Every table was occupied and there were at least a dozen people at the bar and another dozen waiting to be seated. It was the best Sunday night at Maroon, ever. By the time nine o'clock ticked in, my brain was broiled and my fingers fried. Stevie Michelle was clearing tables with the busboy, in between seating "company", and Lorelei was in the kitchen with me and Jorge, doing whatever she could to help. We had run out of the wild mushroom puffed pastry special, which was "the bomb," as Marcus would explain it.

The president of the newspaper came with three others and the regular "company", like Mr. Cooley and Mrs. Wilcox were in the dining room. Stohn called and left a request for a late-night snack, a slice of my chocolate raspberry cake, a snifter of Gabriel & Andrieu, and my presence at his table. I put aside a special for him.

Looking out of the kitchen into the restaurant, I could see Mrs. Wilcox at her usual table, eating her favorite meal—crab and shrimp cakes with vegetable cous cous. Mrs. Wilcox had been given special attention after the death of her husband. Mr. Wilcox, when he retired from his full-time job, worked at the restaurant fixing things and running errands for us. He said it was a legitimate excuse to get out of the house. He had purchased real estate and invested in stocks with the company he worked for, so Mr. Wilcox left Mrs. Wilcox financially confident. He was no saint, though. He was a ladies' man, probably up until he took his last breath. He used to say the three of us, Stevie Michelle, Lorelei and myself, were the closest he would get to heaven, "considering everything I've done in my life," he said.

Mrs. Wilcox once confided in Lorelei that she was very well aware of Mr. Wilcox's infidelities, but she said all she ever asked of him was that he take care of her and never bring his outside activities into their home. He complied and they were married forty-eight years. They were childless, although there was rumor that he, after his marriage to Mrs. Wilcox, had two sons from a woman on the far eastside of town. It was also rumored that his illegitimate family lived in property he owned. Regularly inviting Mrs. Wilcox to the restaurant was our way of checking on her to make sure she was well. She didn't suspect a thing. We felt it was the least we could do for her. Pulling up the sleeve of my chef's jacket, I looked at my watch. The time was ten o'clock. It was an hour before we officially closed. The orders had stopped coming into the kitchen and I could see the three waiters catching their breaths, clustered in the coffee and set-up cubbyhole. I was sure they had a good night in tips. I unbuttoned my jacket just above my breastbone to expose my perspiring chest. Gently massaging it with the tips of my fingers, inhaling and exhaling, I said to Jorge as he was plating-up an order, "It's all yours. I didn't get an opportunity to talk to any of the company tonight." When I worked, I liked to leave the kitchen and go out among the "company" and get a sense of how they enjoyed the food, and to let them know we appreciated their patronage.

"Okay, Chandler. I think I can handle it from here. Besides, there isn't much left to serve. They've eaten everything except some chopped tomato and the sauce from the mushrooms, and I don't think even you can create an entree from that." Jorge was Puerto Rican, but he didn't have an accent, although he spoke fluent Spanish. Born and raised in the U.S., his parents were from the Dominican Republic. He was a damned good chef and I anticipated a day when I would lose him to a better offer or his own restaurant.

Laughing at his statement, I said, "You've got me stumped there," as I took off my apron and threw it on the table. As I walked out of the kitchen, I could hear piping through the restaurant the smooth, melodic piano of Joe Sample from his *Invitation* CD. Stohn came in when I entered the dining room. I called into the kitchen, "Jorge, Dr. Bradford's here. Would you prepare the pastry entree for him, please?"

"Got it," he said, knowing that Stohn's timing couldn't have been better.

The perfume I generously sprayed over my body that morning had been camouflaged by the scents of herbs, spices and grilled meats. It bothered me only when Stohn wanted to hug me. "How's the greatest chef in the world, tonight?" he asked as he pulled me in.

I inconspicuously sniffed his cologne and said, "Sweaty, tired and ready for a tall 10 o'clocktail. He kissed me on the cheek. "Please, let me buy you one."

"Jorge's preparing your dinner," I said as we walked to the bar.

With a gorgeous grin, Stohn stated, "I'm not going to ask what it is."

I assessed his smile. Stohn had taken care of himself. His gray temples were sexy and distinguished. He had aged in a vogue kind of way. I thought, *He must be fifty or fifty-one now. Fifty-something and fine*. I ordered from the bartender, "A Gabriel and Andrieu for Dr. Bradford, and a champagne split with a Grand Marnier sugar cube for me, please."

Stohn sat on the stool next to mine. "Chandler, I love it when you look like this."

"Like what? Fossilized?"

"No. Satisfied that you've had a good day."

"Stohn, you can't tell when I've had a good day. I mean, after all, we don't spend that much time together, and we definitely didn't have much time before . . . Well, you know."

"Whatever time we have or haven't spent, Chandler, I've observed as much about you as I can. I know that if you hadn't become a chef, you would have been unfulfilled for a long time, if not forever. Not to mention that a great talent would have been wasted."

I blushed. What he described was definitely the way I needed Stohn Bradford to see me. We didn't have much of a past, but for the first time I understood why. We were meant to have the present.

"Since I've found you again," Stohn continued, "I've wanted to ask you to fix fried chicken and baked beans with pineapple. But, I know your culinary tastes have graduated."

"I still know how to fry chicken and make baked beans with pineapple."

"Can I get a couple of those butter cookies to go, too?"

"Just tell the chef what you want," I said.

"I want the chef . . . *tooo, well, ahhh* . . . How should I put it? Allow me to have some quality time with her."

The bartender placed our drinks in front of us.

Before I could comment on his request, our waiter announced that Stohn's meal was almost ready. He informed us that the "conference room" table, set with silverware and napkins, was available. The waiter picked up both our drinks and took them to the table. I whispered to Stohn, "I'm impressed with the service."

Resuming our conversation when we sat down, Stohn said, "Chandler, how can you so conveniently ignore me?"

"Why would you say that?" I asked. "I don't ignore you."

"Then would disregard be a better word?"

"I don't disregard you, either."

"Then what would you call it?"

"I'd call it I hadn't seen you in over twenty years when one day you come in here and crash my restaurant, giving me heart palpitations."

"And it's taken you almost two years to get over that? C'mon Chandler, you're not that fragile."

"Believe it or not, I'm still in shock, Stohn. Sometimes I touch you in disbelief."

"Well, believe it. I'm here. And for the record, I did not crash your restaurant. In case you haven't realized it, Maroon's a public place, Chandler. My intentions were to have dinner and let everybody know that I had waited over two decades to see you again."

I shrank in my chair. "I'm sorry," I said. "I didn't mean to sound arrogant."

"That night, my hands perspired and my heart pounded all the way here," he said. "I wanted our reunion to be something out of a storybook. I played the scenario in my mind over and over." Stohn's eyes were honest. I remembered the night he came in and how he explained he had read an article in the paper on the restaurants to frequent in the city. Maroon and my name were mentioned. He said, "*There's only one Chandler Cawthorne in the world. I know because I've checked, and when I saw your name in the paper, I couldn't get here fast enough.*" Then Stohn told me he was divorced and his daughter's name is Casey Elizabeth Bradford.

As promised, the waiter brought Stohn's dinner. I witnessed Jorge's creative ability. The mushrooms in puffed pastry was surrounded with sautéed string beans, red and yellow bell pepper strips and onion that were aromatic with herbs and spices. The one thing Jorge and I had in common was our respect for the herbs and spices of the earth. We liked to work with them. The large off-white ceramic plate had been sprinkled with chopped chives.

"Wow, I didn't expect this," Stohn said. "A ham sandwich with chips would've been fine." I loved his humor.

"We're out of ham and the chips are stale," I joked.

"Good thing." He looked over at my empty place at the table. "You're not having anything?"

"No. For one, it's a little late for me to eat and two, I get my nourishment by inhalation. I smell the food all day. I don't want to eat it, too."

It was ten-thirty and everybody was going through their rituals to close. The busboy and waiters were breaking down the tables and Jorge emerged from the kitchen to have his last tall glass of Coke. The bartender was cashing out the bar, and Stevie Michelle and Lorelei were talking with the last of the "company".

I watched Stohn as he ate a bite of mushroom pastry. He closed his eyes and moaned. Chewing slowly, he said, "Chandler, this is indescribable."

"Come on. You have an extensive vocabulary. Try," I said.

"Okay. Mmm, Mmm good!"

"Oh, that was vocalized with expressive, poetic eloquence, Dr. Bradford," I said, laughing.

"Chandler, I don't care about being poetic. I want to eat."

And eat, he did. I didn't disturb him until I heard the fork hit the plate with finalization. The waiter must have been watching, because he immediately came and cleared away the plate. He then returned with dessert. Stohn said, "You remembered everything, Chandler."

"Of course, I did." Marcus was right. I enjoyed accommodating Dr. Stohn Bradford.

Stohn finished his dessert, drank a cup of decaf, had one more cognac and then leaned back in his chair, rubbing his flat abdomen. "I can only commend the chef," he said.

"Thank you, Dr. Bradford. Is there anything else we can do for you at Maroon?"

"Ahh, maybe pull in a cot for a nap." Stohn looked at his watch. He said, "Eleven-fifteen, already. I hate to eat and run, Chandler, but my mornings start early."

"I know, Stohn."

"However, I'm not ready to leave you just yet, so the morning will have to wait."

I giggled. His attention made me feel rich. I understood how Marcus felt when I was attentive to him. The waiter brought the check to the table and he was paid with a generous tip attached. Stohn insisted on paying, always.

I waited until what I thought was an adequate time before I said, "Stohn, I want to talk to you about something that's been on my mind for a couple weeks. Actually, I want to ask your opinion that may lead to me asking for a favor."

"Yes, Chandler, I do think that you should marry and, yes, I'd be happy to, and I wouldn't consider it a favor."

"What are you talking about?" I asked.

"I thought you were going to ask me to marry you."

"No, I was not. Although, today Marcus asked about my marital plans."

"Marcus is the kid that comes in here who has a crush on you, right?"

"He doesn't have a crush on me," I said, slightly blushing.

"As big of one as I have and the sad thing is, I'm jealous of a thirteen-year-old."

"Stohn, stop joking. I'm being serious."

"I am, too. I'm really jealous."

"Then what I want is out of the question?"

"Nothing you want is out of the question. I just hope I can fulfill what it is you need."

"I know you can. It's about Marcus. I want to help him, Stohn, and I thought maybe you could also help."

"How?"

"Marcus is very smart. I notice how he does things around here. He's very attentive and does them with precision. One day he was in the kitchen with me while I was doubling a recipe. I said something like, two-thirds and two-thirds equals, and he said one and a third cups. Just like that, Stohn, he knew the answer. I know that doesn't make him a genius, but he was quick and to tell the truth, I had to think about the answer."

"So, he's good at math," Stohn commented, pretending not to be impressed.

"I'm going to cut to the chase," I said. "Marcus says he wants to be a zoologist or veterinarian, but it will take more than his desire. He needs guidance, incentive. He needs an avenue."

"You still haven't told me what I can do, Chandler."

"What I think would help is if Marcus had contact with those types of people. You're a doctor. I thought you could get him in touch with a veterinarian or someone at the zoo. You know, he could do some . . ." Lost for the word, I became slightly frustrated. Stohn helped me.

"Shadowing?"

"That's it! He could shadow someone in the profession."

"Truthfully, Chandler, I don't know any veterinarians or zoologists, but I know that when you set your mind on something, there's nothing for a person to do but follow your lead or get out of the way. I don't want to get out of the way, so I'll see what I can do. I may know someone, who knows someone else. And you think he's that sincere?"

"Yes."

"Then we'll give it a shot. I'd like to talk to him more."

"He's usually here after school until I send him home to do his homework. I don't know if he goes, but I send him anyway."

"All right, pretty girl. Your wish is my command."

"Stohn, you should walk off some of that food you ate. I need to say goodnight to a few people. Come with me."

"Sure. You can introduce me as your not-so-secret admirer."

"Oh, come on, and shut up," I said. I took his hand and gently pulled him along with me.

Mrs. Wilcox was searching in her purse as Stohn and I walked toward her. She was a short woman with shoulders as wide and she was stout. When we approached, she looked at us and said, "Chandler, how you doing, sweetie? My dinner was excellent tonight, as usual." Looking at Stohn, she said, "Hey, I've noticed you. I asked Lorelei if you were attached." Holding out her hand, she stated, "Gertrude Wilcox, and you are?"

"Stohn Bradford."

"Well, how do you do, Mr. Stohn Bradford?"

"*Dr.* Stohn Bradford,"I corrected.

Raising a brow, Mrs. Wilcox said, "Doctor, hunh? What kind?"

"Orthopedics, ma'am." At that moment, Stohn was one-hundred-ninety pounds of shyness.

"I've needed all kinds of doctors in my lifetime," but never an orthopedic doctor." She seemingly dismissed Stohn as someone to put on her important contact list and went back to her purse.

I said, "I'm glad you enjoyed your dinner."

Mrs. Wilcox looked up again. "You know, Dr. Bradford, Chandler is one of the best chefs in this city. My husband, Henry—bless his soul—said there was no way this place wasn't going to be a success. It's so wonderful to see our own make it. And these girls are smart, too. They run a good business. A no-nonsense business. They're here every day and still take the time to give me a call to check on me. They don't think I know that's what they're doing. They are level-headed business women who work hard. That's why I'm happy to see Chandler with someone. I was beginning to worry about her. And you look like her type, too—sophisticated, handsome and rich."

Embarrassed, I whispered, "Stohn and I are good friends. That's all, Mrs. Wilcox."

Through her search in her purse, Mrs. Wilcox raised an eye without lifting her head and said, "And I don't know what he says to you while you two sit over there in that corner, but I can see what his eyes say when he looks at you."

I decided to stop her fueled fire and let her have her opinion about Stohn's and my relationship. Stevie Michelle heard the conversation from where she stood. Removing empty wine glasses from a table, Lorelei couldn't contain her laughter. Mrs. Wilcox didn't seem as cute to Stevie Michelle and Lorelei when she said, "As a matter of fact, the three of you girls should start thinking more about your personal lives. You're not getting any younger." I chuckled. Then within the same breath, Mrs. Wilcox said, "Here they are!" as she pulled a Walt Disney Snow White key ring out her purse. Three keys dangled from it. She looked around the room as she asked, "Is Mr. Cooley still here? Maybe he can escort me to my car?"

"If he isn't, I will," said Stohn.

"You see, Chandler, this is how it happens. He walks me to my car and I make a move on him, like one of those strumpets." Mrs. Wilcox let out a diabolical laugh. At that moment I wondered how many black Russians she'd had with dinner.

Sitting the glasses behind the bar, Lorelei walked over to join the conversation. She asked, "What's a strumpet, Mrs. Wilcox?"

"Your competition."

I cut in to say, "If I remember correctly, I first heard the term in Shakespeare's writings. I think it was *Othello*. I think that's what Othello called Desdemona after he suspected her unfaithfulness with—"

"Othello was a fool," Mrs. Wilcox blurted. "He was a foolish black man with power, with an army and with a white woman. Tell me, what made him think he could trust a white man's word?"

"Amen to that," Lorelei co-signed.

I didn't have the courage to remind Mrs. Wilcox—the both of them—that Othello was a writing of fiction. Mrs. Wilcox continued with her definition of a strumpet. "Now Lorelei, a strumpet would see a fine man like Dr. Bradford, and before you know it she'd have him hypnotized with her cheap perfume and her tight revealing clothes. That's the modern version of a strumpet," she said as she regarded me with a smile. "Keep in perspective," Mrs. Wilcox informed us, sounding like a lecturing college professor, "that she is not a whore, but a woman looking for a man. Also, understand the attraction would be short lived and strictly physical from the man, but that girl would never stop trying to entice him. Her slinky ways would be just enough to make him confused and temporarily pussywhipped."

The drop of a pin could have been heard. Slightly astonished, I stood stiff. Only my eyes moved. My wandering gaze settled upon Stohn's face. I asked him to walk with Mrs. Wilcox to her car, thinking Maroon served all kinds of "company".

While Stohn was out with Mrs. Wilcox, I went into the kitchen to check that everything was turned off. The kitchen was spotless, and Jorge and the other staff had slipped out unnoticed. When I returned to the reception area, Mr. Cooley was standing there. I asked him where he had been, and in a coarse broken voice, he said, "I knew Gertrude would try to get me to walk her to her car, and I didn't want to have to stand out there twenty minutes listening to how well-off Henry left her and how she doesn't think she'll live long enough to enjoy it all by herself. Then she'll tell me how she wants to spend some time on one of those exotic islands and maybe take a friend with her. So, I made my way into the men's room until she left. Don't misunderstand me, Chandler, I don't have anything against Gertrude, but I get this feeling that Henry's looking down on us and I don't want to offend the man's spirit."

Robert Cooley, as much as we knew of him, was tormented with paranoia and hypochondria. When he was introduced to Stohn, he explained and complained of symptoms, asking Stohn for his diagnoses and prognoses. It didn't matter to Mr. Cooley that Stohn was an orthopedist; he still wanted his opinion. He asked, "He's a doctor, isn't he? He knows the human body, doesn't he? Then he can answer this simple question for me." Mr. Cooley had questions about urology, cardiology and even pediatrics. He iterated that many of his illnesses stemmed from his sickly childhood. His skin was ashen with a hint of a muddy-water color.

Mr. Cooley was a retired history professor. His eyeglasses sat low on his nose, pinching his nostrils. The thickness of his graying mustache covered his upper lip, almost hiding it. His height was average, and he was a wiry man who wore his clothes too large. The white shirt he had on encompassed his throat like a plow horse's collar, revealing his chicken neck with a big Adam's apple. A man-made blend, his navy suit coat hung below the normal targeted areas of his torso. His pants, a drawstring bag on his small frame, were held on by a belt that had multiple extra holes haphazardly punched into the leather.

Never married, Robert Cooley had no family to speak of. He lived in a small bungalow around the corner from the restaurant. The house was rumored to have over two thousand books inside, from the attic to the basement. He was known in the neighborhood as, "the book man of Algonac Street". He ate at the restaurant two to three times a week and had sampled every beer we served. He did it in alphabetical order. We stocked twenty-three brands.

Lorelei watched me peruse Mr. Cooley's apparel from head to toe when she said in her southern drawl, "Would you mind walkin' Stevie Michelle and me to our cars, Mr. Cooley?"

"Two beautiful women should definitely have an escort," he said, grinning at the both of them with long, narrow, grayish-colored teeth. The girls took an arm each and walked out the door. The door swung open again. Stohn walked in as I heard Lorelei's voice ask from the other side, "What time you gettin' here tomorrow, Chandler?"

"Around ten-thirty," I said.

Before the door closed again, Lorelei yelled back, "Okay, I'll be here no later than eleven."

Faintly, I heard Stevie Michelle say, "That's a good time for me, too." The door quietly shut after them, placing closure on the day.

I looked into Stohn's dark eyes and with an awry smile, I said, "If Mrs. Wilcox hasn't strumpetized you, will you walk with me to my car? It's been a long day, and the truth is I'm afraid of the dark and the boogeyman."

Glancing at me with a coy sparkle in his eyes, he said, "I'm at your service and defense, ma'am."

I activated the alarm and turned off the lights. Stohn put his arm through mine and we made the last few steps toward the door's threshold in the shadow of the street lamps. When we reached my car, Stohn unlocked the door and I got in. He handed me my keys. "Talk to you tomorrow," he said in a low, captivating voice.

I smiled and watched Stohn walk to his car, get inside and start the engine. I thought, *God, thank you for the opportunity to watch him walk away, knowing that he'll be back.*

Chapter 28

(Lorelei)

My shoelaces were untied. In the office of the restaurant, I sat behind the desk staring down at them. How did I leave without tying my shoes? I would have yelled at Three for not having his tied. I let Topper talk me into buying shoes that laced. I preferred slip-ons. As I bent over, I received another view of the desk. Smooth and shiny on the surface, it was old, discolored and dry underneath. At that moment I felt my heart tick in its cavity, jarring my stamina. I couldn't stop thinking about Walter.

The desk was another one of Chandler's great house sale purchases. She said it looked appropriate for an accountant with all the drawers and compartments so she had it loaded in a rented truck, with the chair, and brought it to the restaurant. It had to have been at least two decades since Chandler saw the inside of a furniture store. She said new furniture was a greedy waste, a sin, because there was enough used furniture to recycle. She had become very ecology minded in her old age. She said it started in the kitchen where she learned not to throw anything away. Point blank, she said, "If it's not spoiled, then there's a use for it." Her comment may have been misconstrued by many folks, but I've never eaten better, so I wasn't going to challenge her cooking methods.

Chandler spent her working hours in the kitchen and Stevie Michelle was in the dining room most of the time, but I was the one who worked in the office. A picture of my off-spring sat on the corner of the desk. That was the last time, in a long time, that my three children were together for more than an hour. They were growing older and separate. Oceanna had her own world, Topper was discovering hers, and Three occupied Mars.

I sat at the desk and attempted to concentrate on numbers, two columns at a time, but I couldn't stop thinking about Walter. They were good numbers, showing Maroon in the black.

Since the start of brunch on Sunday, Chandler's "widget" was in great demand. Everything and everyone was being paid, on time, including us. That was a good feeling, but I couldn't stop thinking, what about Walter? I wanted to call Chandler to tell her about him, but I couldn't do that. She would tell me how stupid it was to go to bed with him. But it felt good. No, it felt wonderful. It was—in between separation, divorce and Topper's braces—as if we never left the missionary position I loved so much. In the sex category, we picked up right where we left off.

What frightened me? What was Walter thinking? There wasn't a discussion about what had gone on before I rushed out. He kissed me passionately and I left, carrying his scent with me. The scent I thought would deteriorate, change with time, and with the other women after me. Feeling guilty, I called the children from the car. I didn't tell them that I had visited their father, my ex-husband, and had the most passionate thirty minutes in over two years. Why did I go? I thought it was to give him the insurance form for another one of Three's multiple visits to the dentist. He could have picked up the form with the children. He invited me in. I had never accepted one of his lame "come on in and have a cup of coffee" invitations before. But what pulled me in? Was it my ex-husband had aged like a fine Bordeaux? Chandler had taught me to appreciate good wine. She taught me the combination of aroma, taste and body—from the initial sip to passing the palate. Walter was from a good vintage that got better with age. He looked as good as when he stood in the doorway of his motel room in South Carolina, more than twenty years before—jeans, no shirt and no shoes. Or, was it that my raging hormones were no longer accepting of the mediocre sex I had attempted to satisfy them with? Whatever, I had gone where I hadn't been for a long time—in the hearth of passion. And Walter touched what hadn't been touched for a long time—the core of my soul.

I wondered how long I would be in the restaurant before the phone rang. What if I didn't answer? No one would know. The piercing ring wouldn't let me settle with the decision of not answering. Irritated, I picked up. "Hello, Maroon."

"Good. I'm glad somebody's there," Stevie Michelle said.

"Yeah," I sighed. "It's just little ol'me here, goin' over the facts and figures."

"Well, good morning to you, too."

"I ain't sure that it is," I quipped.

"Lorelei, is everything okay?"

Generously inhaling, I said, "Stevie Michelle, I— Stevie Michelle, Wal— Is there somethin' you need?"

"Lorelei, would you check out in the reception area on the shelf of the podium and see if I left my key to the restaurant there? I can't find it anywhere, and that's the last place I remember having it."

"Hold on." I looked down at my feet before I got out of the chair. Why?

The restaurant had no aura when it was empty. It could have been owned and run by anyone. There was no Chandler floating from table to table wearing one of her crazy, fancy chef coats that she had custom-made by the seamstress who worked at the cleaners on the other side of the tracks. She referred to Chandler as "Madame Chandler." That always cracked me up. I guess Chandler could just as well have run a whorehouse. There was no Stevie Michelle bending down to hug most of the "company" that came in, who were significantly shorter than she was—even the men, who nuzzled their heads between her bosom.

I reached in the podium and immediately felt the key ring. Pulling it out, I trotted back to the phone. "Stevie Michelle, you right, it's here."

"Good. Just leave it in the office in the bottom left drawer of your desk. I'll get it when I come in. If you're not there, I know Chandler or Jorge will be and I can get in. Well, that's all I needed. Are you the only one there?"

"So far. Hey, listen, Stevie Michelle, you got a minute? I need to—" I thought I heard it a few seconds earlier. "Someone's knockin' at the front door," I said. "It's a good thing Chandler ain't here. If it's a delivery, she'd go up one side of the delivery man and down the other, sayin', 'That's what rear doors are for, deliveries!' Hold on."

The knocking became louder and more urgent before I got to the door. It added to my irritation. "Just a minute, I'm comin'," I yelled.

The person standing there definitely was not a delivery man. The person was a woman. A well-dressed, poised woman. She was wearing a purple and black felt hat. It seemed forever since I saw a woman wearing a hat, unless it was Sunday at church, but it was Saturday, ten-thirty in the morning. She raised her fist again to knock, but hesitated when she saw me. I tried to recognize her through the window. The black brim of her hat obscured her face. Pulled low, it cast a deep shadow. A shadow of enigma. The dreary morning assisted in thc dimness.

"Welcome to Maroon," I said as I opened the door, realizing how programmed I had become. "How may I help you?"

Her voice calm and melodious, she said, "Lorelei?"

I hesitated because she seemed to be declaring my name. How did she know me? I didn't know her. It was rude of her to hide her face. "Yes, I'm Lorelei. Lorelei Garris."

"Lorelei you don't know me—"

"You right. I don't." I realized my attitude was brazen. "I'm sorry, ma'am. That was rude of me. Please, what can I help you with?"

"If you have the time, I'd like to talk to you."

"About what?" I asked as politely as I could.

"May I come in first?" Her voice distracted me. It was as if I had heard it before. The voice, pronunciations and pauses between words all sounded familiar. But I didn't know her. She said I didn't. I wanted to pull her hat off, look into her eyes.

"Yes, please come in." I stepped back out of the threshold of the door.

Graceful, the woman walked in wearing a deep purple, three-button suit and a colorful purple, red, black and yellow scarf. Draped elegantly across her shoulder, it was fastened to her suit with a pin, shaped in a simple square basket weave of brushed gold. She saw me staring at it. Embarrassed, I said, "Nice pin."

"Thank you. It's from Italy."

The woman pulled off her hat. With her eyes still lowered, and with an opened palm, she smoothed back the loose strands of hair that had been disturbed. The same color as my Aunt Ruby's, her hair was very gray, but not quite white. I had hoped to gray like that when I got older. Her eyes finally meeting mine, I looked into them. My heart fluttered. I wasn't staring in the mirror, so why did I see my own eyes? I gasped. Suddenly, I heard Aunt Ruby's voice. "Lorelei, you got Octavia's eyes." I gasped again, but with a deeper, more critical breath. The words emerged with effort like someone had punched me in the chest after each one. "My Mother," I stated with direct accusation.

"Yes, you're right."

All she said was, "Yes, you're right." What the *hell* did that mean? It couldn't be that simple. Forty years gone by and I hear, "Yes, you're right." It's like a murderer pleading guilty. There is no need for a trial. There is nothing to do but execute. After all the time and years I thought I wanted to find her, now that she had found me, I just wanted her to go away. There was no reason for her to be in the restaurant. I said, "I don't need you here."

"I understand that, Lorelei. I understand how you feel."

"No you don't, 'cause I don't understan' how I feel." Then I blurted, "I would never leave my children! I love my children."

"Lorelei, please—"

"Please!? There ain't no words. There ain't no—How did you find me? Who told you?"

"Ruby helped me."

"Aunt Ruby knows you here and she ain't called me? I don't believe—"

"I asked her not to. I know it was selfish of me, but I wanted us to meet without any forethought on your part. I had a feeling you would refuse."My Mother was articulate and when I said, "You got that right," I didn't give a damn how well she spoke, she was still a lowlife bitch for abandoning her children.

Looking around the room, she said, "Very nice place. Ruby told me how proud she is of you."

"Do my brothers know about you?"

"Do they know that I'm here? No. They didn't know I was in South Carolina, either." My Mother set her hat and purse on the reservation podium. "Lorelei, if we can sit down, I'll try to explain everything to you. I want to tell you all about it."

"No!" I exclaimed. I sounded like my ten-year-old son. I was helpless and defenseless. I wanted to scream for Aunt Ruby, but she had betrayed me. I needed Chandler. She would help. What was I doing? The resentment and anger were like arrows shooting into my core. They pierced. They stung. They ached. I wanted them to strike My Mother. I wanted her to feel the pain, misery, agony, hurt, and most of all, the grief. Aunt Ruby grieved for over forty years, only to deceive me with the very person who deceived us. "Aunt Ruby was the one who wanted to see you. I never wanted to. I ain't got no need to see you. Not then and definitely not now."

"Oh, Lorelei, please let me talk to you. I want us to talk. Ruby and I talked for days. Deep into the wee hours of the mornings, only to wake a few hours later and begin again. Please give me a chance."

"I told you I ain't got no need to talk to you. You no one to me. If you want to talk to somebody, talk to God and ask him to forgive you for abandonin' yo' children. You ain't nothin' but a—"

The door bolted open and Stevie Michelle rushed in, shouting, "Lorelei, are you all right!? You never came back to the pho—" Once inside, stopping on a dime, she stared first at My Mother and then at me, and then back at My Mother. "Oh, my God!" she whispered. Then Chandler rushed in, saying something when Stevie Michelle held out her arm, stopping her. Surprise and confusion clobbered Chandler. Her eyes danced amongst the three of us. It didn't take Sherlock Holmes to solve what was happening on that Saturday morning in Maroon. Chandler's mouth opened as she looked to Stevie Michelle for guidance. Who broke the silence? My Mother.

"Hello, I'm Octavia Garris. Lorelei's mother," she said, smiling for the first time. She smiled like Aunt Ruby.

Chandler's mouth widened and Stevie Michelle's eyes stretched.

"And she's just leavin'," I added, feeling assured about it.

Snapping her fingers, Stevie Michelle said, "The virtuoso trio to the office." Almost forgetting My Mother, she turned to say, "Mrs. Garris, please excuse us. We'll be back in a moment."

Before the office door shut, Chandler screeched, "Did you look at her!? It's like staring Lorelei in the face twenty years from now. Girlfrien', you got good genes. The woman is beautiful."

"Shut up," Stevie Michelle uttered to Chandler. "Okay, Lorelei, I'm asking you right off the bat, what are your feelings? You've got to verbally express them or they'll entangle you."

I was silent.

In a tone of authority, Stevie Michelle stated, "Talk to us, Lorelei."

"She ain't got no right," I said. "I can't believe she came here. I hate her. I hate—"

Stevie Michelle held up her hand. "Stop, Lorelei, and think. How can you hate someone you don't know? Have never known. You've got to dig deeper than that. Be honest with yourself. Not convenient. Don't use convenient analogies."

"Stevie Michelle, I don't want to think. All I been doin' this mornin' is thinkin'. I don't want to think no more. Then she shows up." I smacked the desktop with force. My hand stung.

Chandler added, "What Stevie Michelle is saying to you, Lorelei, is try to get past the superficial feelings and be conscientious about the situation. Stop treating it like a crisis. You're not being threatened by her, unless you place yourself in that position. The woman came to talk after forty years. Aren't you just a little bit curious? I know I sure the hell am. And you said in the Bahamas you wanted to find her. Well? Are you angry because she found you first?"

"I been thinkin' about that, Chandler. And I think— I hate to say it, but I think I wanted to find her in a grave. That way, it would've put closure on my feelings, on everything. But she's here—walkin', talkin'."

Chandler looked at me squarely. She said, "I want to know how she's ticked all these years, Lorelei. Actually, if you don't talk to her, I will. You definitely have to admit, she's an intriguing woman. There's mystery and history out there."

"You may be impressed, but I ain't," I said. "The woman abandoned me and my brothers when we needed her the most. There ain't no intrigue or mystery in that."

Stevie Michelle said, "Once again quoting my Grandma Shaky, Lorelei, it takes too much negative energy to hate. It will consume and destroy you, leaving little space for what's important—the love you have for the people in your life and your creative side." Sighing, she said, "C'mon, girl, be smart. Listen to what the woman has to say. You don't have to say a damn word. I think hearing her out will bring the finalization you need to this thing. I know when I wouldn't— Well, never mind that. But anyway, you owe it to yourself and just think what a great chapter for your memoir."

I was drained. I was functioning on overload. The circuits were going to spark and ignite at any second. I walked behind the desk and dropped into the chair. The phone was still off the hook. I placed the receiver in the cradle. "Okay, I'll listen."

My girlfriends' smiles let me know that they felt a victory in convincing me to talk to My Mother.

"We'll have her come in," Stevie Michelle said.

"No. I'll talk to her out there. At the 'conference room' table."

"Don't you want some privacy?" Chandler asked.

"I ain't got nothin' to keep private." I rose from the chair and walked out of the office. My girlfriends followed, leaving a respectable distance between us. My Mother stood in the reception area and as I approached, I saw what Chandler pointed out in the office. Just to look at My Mother, knowing nothing of her life, there was intrigue and beauty with no doubt that she was My Mother. "I got a few minutes to listen," I said in a low, coerced voice.

"Thank you, Lorelei," she said, nervously picking up her hat and purse off the podium, clutching them.

"Follow me," I instructed.

I sat in the chair I always occupied at the "conference room" table and she sat in Stevie Michelle's chair. I chuckled to myself. My Mother was the last person I would have dreamed of being at the table. Erect in the chair, I folded my arms.

My Mother straightened the scarf on her suit. "I don't know where to start," she said.

"How about the beginnin'."

Her stare was placid. "All right, the beginning it is, then. Some things I remember and others Ruby had to remind me when they occurred. I was so young and so were my children." After the first few labored sentences, My Mother's words flowed with easy, fluent articulation. Although the tale was tragic, I was lulled by her tranquil voice, querying only here and there. "All these years, Ruby said she only had one question, 'Why did I leave my children?' The answer was I couldn't take them with me. When Hammond left, even before you were born, I knew I didn't want to live without him, and I didn't care about the life that was in my belly growing from the little nourishment I provided. Then, when you came, I tried forgetting about Hammond, that I had a husband. I never mentioned him again once I realized he wasn't coming back. He left his family without warning or remorse. I was so in love with Hammond, I prayed every night that if I was going to be without him, for the Lord to take me. Well, Hammond did come back, but only for me and not our children."

Raring in my chair, I said, "Wait a minute. Aunt Ruby said you left in a black Pontiac with a man who looked like the devil drivin' you away. When did My Father come back?"

"That devil in the black Pontiac was Hammond, Lorelei—your father."

I gasped. "Oh, my God!"

"The choice I made was the best for me. I knew Ruby would take good care of you. She always did. When you were born, I didn't have the physical or emotional strength, so she took care of you, Manny, Aussie and Mike Ray."

It sounded peculiar hearing my brothers' names emit from a stranger who was also our mother.

"When the Lord brought Hammond back, I accepted it as His way of saying I couldn't have everything and to take what was being offered. As stupid as my thinking was at the time, that's how I justified being with the only man I had ever loved my whole life. I thought I could later convince Hammond to send for the four of you. High spirited and adventurous, your father was a different kind of man."

"Was?"

"Yes. He died about a year ago. A heart attack that didn't give me an opportunity to say goodbye. And when he died, I understood he was the only person in this world that meant more to me than my family. I had always prayed that I'd go before him, because I knew I'd have to face my regrets sooner or later. I wanted, so often, and so desperately, to go back to South Carolina, but one day I realized you were grown and didn't need me. All I remembered were the small children I left behind. Time does fly, Lorelei."

"What did you do all that flyin' time?"

"I traveled with Hammond. He started his own company of imports and exports. It wasn't a big operation, but it allowed us to travel and see things. Hammond didn't like working for anyone but himself, so, he made his niche in the import/export business and worked at it for more than forty years. I can see his entrepreneurial character in our children."

I sucked my teeth and rolled my eyes. "So, where are some of the places you been?"

"We traveled all through the United States and I saw a little of Europe, too—Paris and London." Smiling, My Mother said, "Do you know that the French don't have a clue what French toast is? I always liked French toast and I thought I'd be able to get the best there, but they've never heard of it." Her smile dissipating with her anecdote, she said, "Ruby showed me some of the letters I sent from different parts of the country."

"Why did you stop writin'?"

"I never stopped sending money."

"I ain't sayin' you did. I asked why you stopped writin'?"

"What was I going to write? I was tired of being a hypocrite. The bottom line was the money. It was the important thing. How many times could I write I was sorry and I loved everyone? I was selfish and loved no one more than I loved Hammond. Only the money mattered."

"You *are* selfish."

My Mother ignored my comment. "My sister is a good woman, Lorelei. She told me how she saved the money for you and your brothers. Her husband Simon is a saint, too. I regret missing all that." Sighing, My Mother slumped in the chair. For the first time since she'd been there, she looked fragile and exhausted.

"Would you like somethin' to drink?" I asked.

"Yes, please."

"Coffee? Tea?"

"Sweet tea?" she asked.

For a second, and only for a second, I felt a pang in my gut. She said it exactly the way I did. It was like hearing me speak. "I'll get it for you."

I deliberately walked slowly to the kitchen, giving myself time to think. I wanted to ask so many questions, but I felt she didn't deserve my curiosity. Chandler met me at the kitchen door.

"Can I get you two something to eat?"

"No. She wants tea. *Sweet tea*!"

"That's it?"

"That's it!" I said, giving Chandler the evil eye. I stood in the middle of the kitchen while she made the tea. There was always something unique about everything Chandler prepared. Instead of just pouring the tea in a glass with a wedge of lemon, she added a couple drops of peppermint extract and crushed ice.

"If she doesn't like it, bring it back and I'll pour a traditional glass."

"Thanks Chandler," I said, suddenly remembering that I had my girlfriends to depend on.

In the dining room, Stevie Michelle was behind the bar quietly sliding washed wine glasses in the rack above her head.

My Mother was writing in a small black leather book when I returned to the table. She unsuspiciously closed it and put it in her purse. "Thank you so much," she said as I placed a napkin on the table and then the tea.

"You welcome." Before she drank, I said, "Let me warn you that Chandler, my partner and chef here, added somethin' to the tea to give it a special flavor. I hope you like it, but if you don't I was informed to bring it back."

She took a sip and swallowed. "*Mmmm*, this is wonderful, Lorelei. It's cold and best of all, sweet. I understand Chandler is an excellent cook, also."

"Chef, Mo—" I caught myself. "Chandler prefers chef," I said, feeling fiery from the inside out.

"Okay. Fair enough. Chef it is."

My courage building, I asked, "If he hadn't died, would you have come back?"

"The truth?"

"I thought that's what you came to tell?"

"Probably not until I was old and feeble, and someone had to bring me. I don't know where I got the nerve to return other than I was alone and scared. I had never been alone before."

"Where do you live?"

"Arizona. We settled in Phoenix."

"I always wanted to travel. I mean, I been places, but travelin' abroad is what I always wanted."

"It's educational, Lorelei."

"Tell me somethin', how do they treat black people over there? I mean, did you feel, bein' in a foreign place, that you didn't belong? Did people make you feel uncomfortable like you wasn't welcomed?"

"Well, honey, there's prejudice everywhere. But I will say that it's not a priority in Europe. Everyone takes pride, even the poorest."

I hung onto her calling me honey. It was the way I talked to my children and what I called them. "I'm goin' to get there one day. Hopefully Paris. Stevie Michelle is datin' a guy who lives in London. Banning Morris. Did you meet any Morrises while in London?"

My Mother laughed. "No, can't say that I did. But I didn't get to know many people while we were there."

"Yeah. I guess it ain't like the south. Everybody knows everybody. Just mention a last name and that'll start a conversation of who's related to who."

"Lorelei, I'm not going to beat around the bush. I want to meet my grandchildren."

Once again, the heat inflamed my flesh. She wasn't ever going to stop catching me off guard. I hadn't thought that my children were her grandchildren. They didn't know anything about her. I mentioned Octavia Garris, their grandmother, to them once. They knew their grand aunt and their uncles, but there was no need to discuss a grandmother who didn't exist except in her sister's memory. "I can't do that," I said.

"Why not?"

"'Cause it will confuse'em."

"Do you really believe that?"

"Yes. Especially Three. He asks a lot of questions and if—"

"I'll answer any questions he may have. Even the embarrassing ones. Haven't I answered yours?"

"Not all of'em."

"Then ask me. Ask me anything."

"When you felt you didn't want to live without My Father did you ever want to kill yo'self?"

"I thought of many ways, but I didn't have the guts. Of all the questions, Lorelei, why that one?"

"'Cause when Walter, my ex-husband—but he wasn't my husband then—left me in Little River, I wanted to take Oceanna and myself and walk into the sea. She was about seven months old. The urge was strong and it was all 'cause of the love I had for a man that I couldn't be with. That has always bothered me. And to hear you express the kind of love you had for My Father, it must've been close to what I was feelin'. I know how dumb it is to want to die and I wonder if my love for Walter was similar to the love you had for My Father. What I'm sayin' is, I know it's just as bad to end a life as it is to abandon one."

"I know you're divorced, Lorelei. Ruby told me, but she doesn't have to tell me that you're in love with your ex-husband still. I can see it when you mention his name. Love is thc strongest of emotions. If it's real love, it's stronger than hate, guilt or fear. You will attempt the impossible. You'll try to get water from the moon to share love with the person you want it with. And before you ask, I'll tell you that if I had to do what I did all over again, I would do it. Either way, I'd regret something."

For more than two hours My Mother and I talked. We took restroom and iced tea breaks, but the majority of the time was consumed with conversation. Stevie Michelle was right. I couldn't hate someone I didn't know, so I listened, inquired and revealed. We aired our differences and explained our reasoning. We reflected. I even explained what I had done with Walter. My Mother laughed. All she said was, "Relax. Just think of it as you got what you needed and you don't have to cook his dinner or do his laundry."

Chandler, God bless her meddling heart, invited My Mother to dinner. Stevie Michelle wrote, "Octavia Garris" in the reservation book for six-thirty.

The last questions I asked My Mother before she left were, "What do you write in that little black book of yours?" and "What did you write earlier?"

Answering my first question, My Mother said, "Quotations and thoughts." Opening her purse to take out the book, she quickly indexed through the pages, the majority of them filled with blue and black ink. She stopped three-quarters into it and to answer my second question, she read, *"There's no difference between us. My hands are hers; we see the same things through the same eyes; she speaks with my lips and best of all, she thinks my thoughts."*

My Mother said she planned to be in town two days and had hoped to reserve one of them to meet her grandchildren. I, at the end of our talk, agreed she could. I thought about addressing the issue with Chandler and Stevie Michelle, but it had to be my decision. Besides, I knew what they would tell me. I told My Mother that I had to talk to the children first, though. I hadn't poisoned their minds about their grandmother, so I didn't have to detox them, but I did have to brief them.

I was baffled how easy it was for Octavia Garris to cross over from an unknown to maternal status. It didn't seem possible, but there she was, officially my mother. It was like receiving a degree through mail correspondence, never having classes, an instructor or tests.

By the time My Mother left the restaurant, Walter had called three times. The first two, Stevie Michelle took messages, but on the third, I asked her to ask him if the children were all right and if they were I would call him later. I wasn't ready to talk to Walter. The sex was good, but I was experiencing mixed emotions.

Before the restaurant opened, I sat at the "conference room" table with my partners. Stevie Michelle reminded me that I had control over the situation with My Mother. Chandler said, "I'm pleased with the way you handled yourself, Lorelei. You dealt with her with the objectivity and compassion that you deal with everyone."

"No, Chandler. What I was dealin' with was disbelief. Shock! Right before you came in, I was about to lose it. I thought I was dreamin'. When I looked into her eyes, I saw my childhood, my marriages, and the scariest part is, that's when I felt I knew her. I'm tryin' to decide if to call Aunt Ruby."

"My opinion is, you should wait. I'll put money on it that those sisters are talking right now, just like us. If she doesn't call you by tomorrow, then you do it," Chandler advised.

"I keep thinkin' and thinkin' about why Aunt Ruby didn't warn me. She knew My Mother was comin'."

"Lorelei," Stevie Michelle said with an astute tone, "don't question her motive or decision. It probably worked out the way she planned, and it definitely was destined to happen the way it did. So, don't think she didn't keep thinkin' and thinkin' if to call or not to call. Give her the benefit of believing she made the right choice. I believe she was under a lot of pressure to do what she did. So, when you talk to her, be kind and thank her for indirectly steering you. Because once again, I believe that if she had warned you, there would have been a significantly different outcome. This way was better. I'm sure of it." Looking at me straight on, Stevie Michelle asked, "And what is this with Walter calling?"

"I guess I might as well tell you. I told My Mother and I'm a hell of a lot closer to you than I'll probably ever be to her." Breathing deep, I said, "I slept with him this mornin'."

"*Aaah, sookie, sookie, now*! You've had a hell of a day, girlfrien," Chandler said, her grin so wide I could count all her teeth. She bragged often that she had all thirty-two.

"What happened? Your love come down on the way to work and Walter's was the closest?" Stevie Michelle's chuckle was of the devious kind.

"I'm glad you two think it's funny. I tried to laugh myself, but the bottom line is I had sex with my ex-husband."

"And?" Chandler asked.

"And I don't know what he thinks or is expectin'."

"What are you thinking and what do you expect, Lorelei? Once again, you have control. You're at the wheel," Stevie Michelle confirmed.

"Honestly, it was fantastic sex. Just the way I remembered it. But that's as far as I want to go. Here and now I'm goin' to confess that I still love Walter. I love him almost as much as the first time I went to bed with him, but I love my independence, too. I love doin' exactly what I'm doin'. As My Mother said, I ain't got to cook his dinner and he still got to do his own laundry. And that's the way I like it."

"Oh, I get it. He's on this year's *boy toy* roster." Chandler looked at Stevie Michelle and winked.

"Chandler, to hell with you and the broom you rode in on."

"Don't get mad at me for telling the truth. All I want to know is, was it worth it?"

When I began explaining the details, I had forgotten about it being a dilemma. "*Girrl*, I thought I had died and gone to Africa. Boyfrien' still got it goin' on. And it only took twenty minutes."

"You *were* horny," Stevie Michelle said.

"If it's done right, it don't take all day," I exclaimed.

"You got that right," Chandler testified.

Stevie Michelle's stare was thoughtful. "Lorelei, you've changed. You are not the same woman of a year ago. And I like it."

Chandler said, "We can't have two Stevie Michelle's running around here. Lorelei, I demand that you rethink this *new you*, because it's an old Stevie Michelle."

A knock at the door interrupted us.

I said, "I ain't gettin' that. I done had enough of what's behind door number one."

Stevie Michelle yelled, "We're closed. Come back at five."

Chandler slapped her wrist and got up to answer the door. Stevie Michelle and I sat giggling.

My laughter stopped when I heard the familiar sound of my son's shoes over the wood floor. The only way Three could be there was if Walter was with him. Stevie Michelle raised her eyebrows and eased out of the chair. I mumbled, "Shit."

Walter's voice rose above the sound of Three's squeal of, "Hi, Mommy. I bet you're surprised to see me."

"Lorelei, we were in the neighborhood, so I thought we'd stop by." Walter's gaze was contented.

"Where's Topper?" I asked.

"Probably still hugging and kissing Chandler," Walter said. "You know how she feels about her." He stared at me through goo-goo eyes.

Stevie Michelle said, "Three, why don't you come with me and we'll get some ice cream."

"Can we make a milkshake."

"Yeah. We'll make two."

"Topper waved and yelled, "Hi Mom," as she went through the kitchen door with Chandler.

I was alone with Walter. I said, "I can count the times on one hand you been here. What brings you today?"

"You know what brings me, Lorelei. Why haven't you returned my calls?"

"I was goin' to as soon as my meetin' was over. I done had a hell of a day, already." What did I say that for?

"Oh, yeah. You want to tell me about it, or do I know? And I don't know if I'd refer to it as a hell of a day. What, we had maybe ten or fifteen minutes together?"

"Twenty."

"It would be like you to know the exact time."

"Walter, I don't wanna argue. We need to talk, but I don't wanna argue. This mornin' was a—"

"Mistake?"

"No. I wasn't goin' to say that. I was— Aw, Walter, I just feel we need to think about this. I mean, you not obligated to me just 'cause we had," I whispered, "sex."

"Lorelei, the truth is I came here because I was so anxious waiting to hear from you. I need to know what this morning meant. You ran out so fast I thought you would trip over your shoelaces."

I burst into laughter. Walter smiled and then began laughing with me. I wasn't sure if he knew what we were laughing about. I said, "Come sit next to me." Still giggling, I asked, "You noticed my shoelaces?"

"They were trailing behind you like bike streamers." Walter had always been very observant. He informed me that I was pregnant with Topper and Three even before I felt any of the symptoms. He leaned over and kissed my mouth. "Lorelei, this morning was the best I've felt in a long time. When I picked up the kids, they asked what I was so happy about."

"Did you tell'em?"

"With tender details." Walter's goading of my rationale of thinking hadn't changed. "Lorelei, come on, what was I to say, 'Your mama and I had great sex this morning and I sure would like to do it again'?"

"Please don't bring the children into this," I asked. "At least not yet."

"Not until you make up your mind. Right?"

"I done already made up my mind."

"You have?"

"Yes."

"So, what's the verdict, Lorelei?"

"There ain't no verdict. I'll admit that I felt good, too. But Walter, we always had good sex. That was never a problem of ours. So, this mornin' only confirmed it. It don't mean that our problems have changed or that we want to have sex with each other again."

"Speak for yourself. I want to. As a matter of fact, I want to tonight." Taking my hand, Walter said, "I watched you this morning. I felt the passion. I felt your passion."

"I ain't goin' to deny that I wanted you, that I want you," I said, "but I want my independence, too. I want to keep my independence. It's very important to me, especially where I am now. I got a business. I ain't just Walter's wife who takes care of his books, him and his children." The words were spewing fast. "What I do is important. I need this. All of it."

"And you don't feel that you can have all of this and we be together?"

"Truthfully, no I don't. Right now, I believe I'll only become 'Walter's wife,' again. Not that you asked me, but I feel I'll lose, for whatever reasons, Lorelei, the accountant, the businesswoman, the restaurateur."

Walter looked at me, amazed.

"I know I sound selfish, 'cause that's exactly what I'm bein'."

"All right, Lorelei," Walter sighed. "At least you're honest. You know, you're not the Lorelei I remember."

"Why is everybody tellin' me that? I am the same Lorelei. Is it 'cause I got an opinion?"

"You've always had an opinion, but you're adamant about it now. There's no bending."

"Well, all I can say is, good! I like it like that. I like me. Hey, Walter, maybe that's what it is; I'm really beginnin' to like myself. Do you know how that feels? Oh, of course you do, 'son of Scott and Son'," I said in a low masculine voice. "Now, I'm 'Lorelei of Maroon' and other than my children, that is what I want to concentrate on."

Walter sat back in the chair. His smile was appealing. I knew he understood where I was coming from. "Well, can I at least call you and maybe have dinner now and then?"

"I'd like that," I said. "I really would."

"Okay, it's settled then. I'll pick you up around seven tomorrow and we'll go out for a little something."

"I'm workin' tomorrow. But I'll let you in on a little tidbit of information. I usually take Wednesdays off to do whatever it is I want to do. Call me."

"I think I could like this new Lorelei. She's definitely sassy. Or should I say saucy?"

"Call me, Walter."

"All right, bright eyes. The ball's in your court. But it always has been and now, for the first time, I think you know it." With a smile of respect, but defeat, he said, "I'll collect *our* children. I promised them Burger King. You wouldn't want to join us, would you?"

"I'm workin'." Walter stood and pushed the chair to the table. I did the same. Then I asked, "By the way, how was Three's dental appointment?"

"Oh, the same. No cavities and when we're ready, they're ready to put on the braces."

"Thanks, Walter."

"Don't mention it. They're my children, too." He raised my face and bent to kiss me. Slightly parting my lips with his tongue, I felt tingly, our connection running through my body. I did want to make love to him again, but I definitely wanted it to be on my terms.

Pulling away, I said, "Remember, no Coke for Three. The caffeine makes him bounce off the walls."

My ex-husband rounded up our children and he thanked Stevie Michelle and Chandler for keeping them occupied. Topper and Three gave me a big hug and left with Walter. When the door shut, I said, "Girls, that's what I'm talkin' about. I feel exonerated. I should have felt this way a lot sooner. It feels good."

Chandler whispered something to Stevie Michelle. They giggled, but I didn't care. "Whatever you say about me bounces back to you," I said.

CHAPTER 29

(Lorelei)

Chandler's dinner special was chicken and dumplings made with fresh dill, leeks and apple cider. I assessed that she had finally lost her culinary mind. But once again, she made a liar out of my palate. It was delicious and that was the word with our "company".

Mrs. Wilcox, Mr. Cooley and My Mother were at their reserved tables. When I stopped to talk with Mrs. Wilcox, she said, "Lorelei, I know my eyes aren't what they used to be, but if I'm not mistaken, that woman over there has to be a relative of yours."

"She's My Mother, Mrs. Wilcox."

"Your mother, and you didn't introduce us? Is she from out of town?"

"Yes. She's from Phoenix."

"You never mentioned your mother before. And why is she sitting alone?"

The next thing I saw, Mrs. Wilcox was out of her seat, headed for My Mother's table. I would have followed her, but at the same time Stevie Michelle called from the reception area. When I returned to the dining room, My Mother's place setting was at Mrs. Wilcox's table. They deserved each other. I chuckled.

Mr. Cooley left his seat to ask me, "Lorelei, who's the goddess in the brown and beige outfit sitting with Gertrude?" Did I hear him correctly? For the first time there was some semblance of life in his lifeless body. Then I imagined Mr. Cooley and My Mother together. Yuk!

"She's My Mother, Mr. Cooley." I found myself saying, "My Mother" a lot that night. Jorge, the cooks and the waiters were introduced, either by Stevie Michelle or Chandler, and sometimes by me.

The next day, My Mother met Topper and Three. Walter dropped them off at the restaurant and she had dinner with them. She introduced herself to Oceanna over the phone. Chandler even made an order of French toast because I told her the story about Paris that My Mother had told me.

Of course, my son is Walter's son. At dinner, Three asked My Mother if she had left more children anywhere else besides Little River. I think Walter was more shocked to meet My Mother than I was. He said, "The likeness is captivating. It's uncanny." Then he said, "When we're older, I want you to look just like that. Your mother only confirms how beautiful you are."

My Mother stayed an extra day. I was glad, because I had the opportunity to talk to her until a wee hour in the morning. I reminisced about growing up and she talked extensively about herself, her travels and My Father. I asked if she was going back to Little River to live. She said Little River was not home and that she'd visit and hoped Aunt Ruby would come to Phoenix. She said, "When I'm old and feeble, I'll think about it."

The afternoon she was leaving, Topper, Three and I took My Mother to the airport. Her ticket said Myrtle Beach, South Carolina. She wasn't going home. She was headed to South Carolina to meet my brothers and their families. Unlike me, Aunt Ruby prepared Manny, Aussie and Mike Ray for our mother's arrival. When she called the very next day after I met My Mother (as Chandler predicted), Aunt Ruby said, "I felt it was the only way, Lorelei. Please forgive me if I did wrong."

My response was, "Aunt Ruby, I love you and in my eyes, you can do no wrong. You got a knack for knowin' what's best."

I visualized Aunt Ruby's smile when she said, "Our lives are complete now. Our family will come together. The day Octavia called, it was a good thing I had a strong heart, 'cause I thought I was goin' to faint. It took her forty years, but my sister came and I'm thankful. I thank the Lord every day. Now, if we can get yo' brothers to be gentlemen, then the war is won."

Aunt Ruby and I agreed that Manny would be the most difficult, but the most appreciative. He needed closure on the issue of our mother as much as Aunt Ruby did, as much as I did—I discovered. I asked Aunt Ruby how she felt about My Mother not coming back to Little River to live. She said she was okay with it because she and My

Mother made a pledge that they would stay in touch and visit one another for the rest of their lives. Aunt Ruby announced she was going to Phoenix the very next month.

"I already made reservations, Lorelei. I'll be with my sister two weeks. I ain't never been to Arizona. Simon told me to go. Do you know I ain't never been away from him that long?" Shucks, come to think of it, I ain't never left to go no place without yo' Uncle Simon. Octavia tells me it's hot in Arizona. Hotter than the middle of August here. She says it's a dry heat, though." Aunt Ruby was happy. I could hear the joy and gratification dancing in her voice. She said to me, "Lorelei, there ain't enough time in my lifetime for me to finish gettin' to know my sister, but with God's blessin', you and yo' brothers will. Octavia's been around. She's got some good, tall stories to tell, and she needs to hear ours. So, what I'm askin' is for you to stay in touch with her. Do it for me, if not for Octavia or yo'self."

"Oh, you goin' to outlive all of us," I said, "but I promise just the same."

Aunt Ruby told me about the pictures My Mother brought and left with her. She said she had looked at them every day, sometimes four and five times. "I got out some old picture albums, too," she said. "And that's when Octavia cried. She cried for about fifteen minutes, if not longer. I knew that was my cue to leave her alone with the pictures of her children. I went to the market and came back before Octavia even knew I was gone. She was still sittin', bent over the table in the livin' room, turnin' pages, laughin' and cryin' at the same time." Aunt Ruby sighed. "She just kept mumblin', ' . . . please forgive me, please forgive me.' But you know what, Lorelei?"

"What, Aunt Ruby?"

"Octavia's already been forgiven. She was forgiven the day she ran off the porch. The Lord provides in mysterious ways, baby—even when we think it's strange or wrong."

"Did you think it was strange that the man who took her away was our very own father?"

"I always suspected it was Hammond. There was never nobody in Octavia's life except him. I couldn't know for sure, so I never said anything to anybody else. The fact was, she was gone and left willingly, not who she left with."

"Aunt Ruby, how is it that nobody saw My Mother when she came to Little River to see you, but you?"

"Well, she stayed in a hotel in North Myrtle Beach and I went there. I thought it was best. I brought her to the house once. That was the day we looked at pictures. But that was the only time. I didn't want her to feel uncomfortable. You know how Little River can gossip, Lorelei. Heck, Miss Mason—you remember Miss Mason down the road, don't you?"

"Hunh huh."

"Well, she was watchin' my every move. She asked where I was goin' every mornin' and why I was comin' home so late in the evenin'. I told her there ain't but two people I need to answer to and they were God and Simon, and ain't neither one of them asked me nothin'. It's goin' to be a heavy weight on Octavia when she comes, 'cause of people like Miss Mason." Aunt Ruby's voice trailed off. "Lorelei, I hope she comes back."

"Don't worry," I said. "She'll be back. You know us Garrises, we don't make the same mistakes twice. I think she's as comfortable with the situation as possible and is willin' to accept the consequences of her mistake. She'll be back."

Life returned to Aunt Ruby's voice. "And you need to think about comin' home to visit some time, too. I miss you and my grandnieces and nephew. They won't recognize their aunt."

"Aunt Ruby, how can you say such a thing? Me and the children were there five months ago."

"Yeah. For three days. That ain't no visit. That's a drive by with a wave." I could depend on Aunt Ruby to make a point—one to suit her.

"I'm sorry, but not bein' able to get away as much as I would like is a hazard of havin' a business. But, I'll try to get better."

"All right, honey. I ain't tryin' to give you a hard time. You a good girl, Lorelei." Aunt Ruby's final words before we hung up were, "I love you, baby," and, "Oh, by the way, I'm surprised it took you and Walter this long to get it on.

"Aunt Ruby!" I screeched.

* * * * *

The following Wednesday, Walter and I went to dinner at another restaurant. Topper and Three were excited to see us together. I told them we were going out to discuss plans for their college. Topper said, "Five years ahead of time? Yeah, right, Mom."

Through our meal, Walter brought out all his charm to persuade me to be his dessert. It was nice to hear him say, "What's one man's poison is another man's dessert," and, "What I call rich and sweet is across the table from me." He was on my dessert menu, also.

Chapter 30

(Stevie Michelle)

"Banning, Banning, Banning," I said, attempting a Cary Grant imitation. I didn't pull it off, but he laughed anyway. He was back in town, just as he had promised, and I was juggling my schedule to spend as much time with him as I could. Sitting on my sofa, my legs tucked, cuddling with him, I thought about what Chandler said one day. She told me that I had a severe case of "Banning on the brainitis". I told her I wasn't going to let Maroon be the only relationship I had, and I suggested that she consider the same. I said, "If Stohn Bradford was two inches taller, I'd have an international and national lover." Chandler's response was of streetwalker status—not very ladylike.

Banning had reserved a hotel room prior to his arrival, but spent many waking and a lot of resting hours with me. I offered him a room at my house, but he said in his sensuous English accent, "Stevie Michelle, you are a lady and I don't want your neighbors to have difficult opinions of you." He didn't understand that, except for Lorelei, I didn't give a damn about my neighbors' "difficult opinions".

"Banning, would you like to go to a movie and maybe take in some jazz later?" I asked as I wrapped my arms around his waist, looking straight into his dark eyes. "There's a little nightclub downtown that I like, and Marilyn Scott is performing tonight. I can't believe she's in Cleveland. The last time I saw her, she was at the Blue Note in New York. Chandler and I went to New York on a long weekend and there she was in living color, singing her heart out."

"I've never heard of her," he said, "but if you say you want to go, then I do, too. I love jazz and I trust your taste."

"Great! I'll make dinner reservations, check the movie and what time Marilyn is singing."

"You have to make reservations at your own restaurant?"

"We're not going to *my* restaurant, Banning."

"You're joking, right?"

"No, I'm not. You've eaten there every night. Don't you want to try some place different?"

"But, love, the food is awesome. And I feel so special when my entree is different from everyone else's, simply because Chandler does something fantastic, especially for me. And the company is magnificent. Not to mention Lorelei. I don't know if I'll be able to enjoy my meal without you and her desperately trying to work me in between seatings and phone calls."

At first, I took Banning's scenario very seriously, but realized he was kidding about not eating anywhere but Maroon.

"Trust me again, Mr. Morris. There are other good restaurants in this city. Besides, I think I've worn out my welcome at the divas' diner."

"What?"

"We're referred to as 'The Divas of Dining' by the media. A review was written that headlined—*Dining with Deity—not with one, two, but three divas of the restaurant world*. The article was more about us than the restaurant."

"How did you let that happen?"

"I didn't *let* anything happen, Banning," I said, feeling I was being chided. "When the final copy was sent over the fax, it got tossed with some other papers and I never saw it before the final deadline. That's how it got printed. Chandler and Lorelei haven't let me live that one down, yet. And speaking of Chandler—Banning, excuse me."

I had attempted to reach my girlfriend most of the morning and half the afternoon. She had not answered at home and Jorge said she hadn't been to the restaurant. It was very unusual for Chandler not to be reachable. I probably had no reason, but I was beginning to get concerned. It was three-thirty. She had always talked to someone by that time. I dialed her house again. Her voice mail clicked in. Frustrated, I immediately hung up. I called the restaurant. Lorelei answered. "Hey girl, what's happenin'?" she said.

"Lorelei, have you talked to Chandler today?"

"No. Have you?"

"*Nooo*. That's why I'm asking you. Has Jorge heard from her?"

"Wait. I'll ask."

I could hear their voices, although I couldn't decipher what they were saying. The phone crackled and knocked as Lorelei picked it up again. "Jorge said no, but he says he knows the menu for the night, so don't worry about that."

"The menu isn't what I'm worried about," I said. "This is not like Chandler."

"Maybe she's with Stohn. It ain't like she don't deserve the time," Lorelei said.

"That's not it, either. Listen, I'm trying not to overreact on this thing, but unless Chandler has lost her mind, she has no reason not to call to let us know what she's doing or that she's with Stohn. Has he called today?"

"I don't think so." Lorelei sighed.

I knew she didn't understand my concern and was becoming frustrated with my questions. But, one thing Chandler was, was consistent and focused. And those were the characteristics that had been altered. I noticed that she seemed preoccupied the day before and she never left the kitchen to come into the dining room. That only happened when we were so busy, we barely had enough time to get to the restroom, but the restaurant wasn't crowded.

"Do you know what time she left last night?" I asked.

"When Jorge and I left, she was still here. She said she wanted to work on some new menus. She was at the piano, Stevie Michelle, playin' it."

"Was the restaurant locked when you got there today?"

"I don't know. Jorge got here first. Stevie Michelle, you spookin' me and I wish you'd stop it."

"I'm sorry, Lorelei, but until I know where Chandler is, we'll both be spooked. Damn. I'll kill her if she's all right."

"Stevie Michelle, listen to yo'self."

"I know, but I don't know what else to do. I don't know Stohn's home number, but if I call the hospital, maybe he's there and if he's not then I'll assume that they're together." Banning came and stood by my side while I was on the phone. It felt good to have him near. I said to Lorelei, "Look, don't worry. I'll call Stohn and check back with you later."

Banning placed his warm hand at the back of my neck. "Is everything okay, love?"

"I hope so. It's just that I haven't heard from Chandler."

"Is that so irregular? She is an adult."

"Yes, Banning. It is *irregular* for Chandler." While we talked, I opened the phone book that I kept in a small wooden telephone cabinet. Taking a chance, I ran my finger down the Bradfords. Maybe Stohn's home number was listed? It wasn't. "Shit." Looking up the number for the hospital, I dialed it. Someone answered and before they could give me their spiel, I asked if Dr. Bradford was scheduled to be in and if he was could he please be paged. A nasally woman said, "Just a moment, miss; I'll see if he's to be in today." She seemed to take an eternity. Banning stood close. I leaned into his body. "What's taking her so long?" I said, irritated.

Banning whispered, "Stevie Michelle, take it easy."

The voice returned. "Yes, Dr. Bradford is scheduled. Would you like him paged?"

"Yes, please."

"And who should I tell—"

"Stevie Michelle Parks."

"Please hold, miss."

I wondered if all operators were trained to sound as if both nostrils were stuffed with bread pudding? I hated bread pudding.The music playing was from the *Phantom of the Opera*. Chandler and I had gone to see the play when it was in Cleveland. My girlfriend and I had done so much together over the years. I said to Banning, "Not only do I feel I've been on hold forever, I have to listen to the *Phantom of the Opera*. Not a good choice right now."

He didn't say anything, but held me closer.

The operator came back to the line. "I'll transfer you to Dr. Bradford, miss."

His voice was music when Stohn said, "Stevie Michelle, what a pleasant surprise. I was thinking about calling to get a table for tonight. I want to bring one of my colleagues. I've been telling him about Maroon and he asked if we could eat there. You didn't read my mind, did you?"

"No, Stohn, I didn't. I was hoping you were with Chandler. Have you talked to her today?"

"No, I haven't. I called this morning around eight, but apparently she was already gone. I didn't bother to call the restaurant. To tell the truth, maybe because I didn't want to know if she wasn't there."

I understood then how much Stohn cared for Chandler. She was a fool if she let him get away. He was handsome, a gentleman and willing to do anything for her.

"Stohn, I don't mean to alarm you, but I'm looking for her. It isn't like Chandler not to be either at home or at the restaurant. It's already four and she's nowhere to be found."

"You're sure she didn't have an appointment that you forgot about?"

"No. If I've forgotten," I said, "I'm sure Lorelei or Jorge would remember. Nobody knows anything. And I'm getting worried, especially now that I know she's not with you."

"Stevie Michelle, I'm making rounds, but as soon as I'm finished, I'll come by."

"No, don't. Let me do some more checking and I'll get back with you. In the meantime, call and make your reservations. Lorelei's at the restaurant."

"Are you sure?"

"I'm sure. I'm probably panicking for nothing. I'll— We'll see you tonight. Sorry to bother you, Dr. Bradford."

"No bother. I'll talk to you later."

"Okay."

"Stevie Michelle."

"Yeah?"

"If anything is wrong, you make sure you call me. Do you have my home number?"

"No. And I found out that you're not listed."

"Got a pen?"

"Sure."

Stohn recited the seven digits and I wrote them on the pad that I kept on the cabinet. "Thanks," I said.

"Call me!"

"I will." I hung up and stared into the blue wall ahead of me. I had almost forgotten Banning until he said, "Love, is there anything I can do?"

"Yes, there is. You can forgive me for acting like a nut, but until I at least talk to Chandler, I'll be on edge. Banning," I said, "I'm sorry, but can I drive you to the hotel and pick you up later? I hate to leave you like this, but I need to go by Chandler's."

As I talked, I walked into the kitchen. Banning followed me. I was thinking about where I had put the key to her house. The three of us had exchanged keys just for emergency purposes. I opened the draw in the kitchen where I kept everything and then some. Vacuum cleaner bags popped up. When I removed them, at the bottom were matchbooks, soy sauce packets, loose change, screwdrivers, a pair of pliers, pens and pencils, a bag of peppermints, business cards, and Chandler's key. It was attached to a white cardboard key tag labeled, "Chandler's house key". Lorelei's was there also. Pulling out Chandler's, I cupped it in my hand and turning to Banning, I said, "I'm sorry for all the chaos, but I need to do this. I'll drop you at the hotel and pick you up later for dinner. We may not make it to the movie."

"Do you want me to come with you?" he asked.

"Thanks, but no. If I'm going to make a spectacle of myself, I'd like to do it alone. Thanks, anyway."

He knew I was anxious to get moving, so Banning walked to the door and held out his hand for me to come with him. After I dropped him off, I drove like a bandit to Chandler's. When I pulled into the driveway, everything seemed normal. I got out of my car and looked through the garage window. Her cars were parked. My heart made a thud. If she was home, why hadn't she answered the phone? Maybe she just got there? Maybe she was sick and called the restaurant after I left to say she wouldn't be in? Oh, my God, maybe Chandler is—

I ran to the front door and rang the bell. I felt myself beginning to hyperventilate. I knocked hard. My knuckles hurt and were red. Looking at the windows, the blinds were closed tight. There was something wrong. Chandler never closed her blinds. She loved the natural light of the day. It didn't seem possible, but I knocked again even harder. Then I remembered the key. I took it out my pocket and put it in the lock. Before I turned it, I took a deep breath.

Although Chandler had given me the key, it felt as if I was breaking in. I turned the lock and the door opened. I didn't know what to expect, but I smelled lilies. In the living room on the table was a vase of Casablancas and stargazers. They smelled sweet, almost nauseatingly sweet. The mantle clock ticked away the silence. There were some pamphlets scattered over the sofa. I walked past the living room into the dining room. No Chandler. Peeking into her mini commercial kitchen, the stainless steel equipment gleamed. The coffee pot was empty and still no Chandler. The only other places to look were the basement and upstairs. I chose the upstairs. I didn't call her name. At the time, I felt if she was unconscious, or something worse, she wouldn't answer anyway. I tip-toed up the stairs. There were two bedrooms. Both doors were closed. Chandler's was to the right. I hesitated before I wrapped my hand around the doorknob, and then I decided to knock first. There was no answer. I could no longer feel my extremities. It was as if they were deprived of the oxygen that I had difficulty inhaling. Fathoming my fear of what may be on the other side of the door, I felt my stomach churn a vat of acid, weakening my body.

At that moment I wished I had let Banning come. He probably could have done what seemed impossible for me to do—open the door. I closed my eyes and tried to shove the tragic thoughts out of my mind. Opening my eyes and the door, I almost jumped out my shoes. I screamed, "Fuck, Chandler! Shit! You scared the damn fuck out of me." I had never sworn like that in my life. The words spewed common-like, releasing all the anxiety that had built up. My body trembled with fear, shock and anger. "Damn it, why the hell didn't you answer the fucking door!? I've called. Where the hell have you been, damn it!?" Suddenly I stopped.

My girlfriend was looking at me with an aimless stare. Her eyes were sunken, almost concave. She had been crying—no, sobbing hard and for a long time. I didn't want to go as far as to say she didn't recognize me, but there was no acknowledgment of my presence. On the table next to the Queen Anne chair she sat in were two wine bottles. One was drained and the other was three-quarters empty. The room was pungent with the odor of white fermented grapes. Chandler was in her work clothes from the night before. Her chef coat was stained with orange-pumpkin seed sauce and curry oil. She hadn't slept all night. The wine in the glass she held had lost its life.

"Oh my Lord, Chandler, honey, are you all right? What's going on here?"

I wasn't sure if she would answer until she finally said in a low, quavering voice, "Stevie Michelle, I should have known it would be like this. Just when I thought I could be happy. Do you know I've been unhappy for at least three-quarters of my life? No matter how hard I've tried, I've been unhappy. I was just beginning to feel good about life. I was just beginning to feel that maybe I had paid my dues. But maybe I hadn't paid for the wrong I've done." Shaking her head, she choked, "I haven't paid enough."

"Chandler, what are you talking about? You haven't done anything wrong."

"Yes, I have. A long time ago." The tears began to fall again. Chandler was suffering.

I went to be by her. I dropped to my knees in front of my girlfriend. "Oh, please tell me what's wrong, honey. Please. You're killing me. If I can, I'll make it better for you. Is something wrong with Kennedy or Alex?"

Between sobs she said, "Not yet."

"Damn it, talk to me," I said. "I can't help if you won't talk."

"There's nothing you can do. There's nothing anybody can do."

"The hell there isn't. Now, I demand that you tell me what the *hell* is going on. This is not fair. You're just being selfish. I've been worried all goddamn day and I'll be damned if you're not going to tell me something." I got up from my knees and stood over Chandler. She was still crying. Before I knew it, I had both her shoulders and was gently shaking her, demanding, "Don't do this to me. Don't shut me out." I pulled her out of the chair to her feet, hugging her. She was a weak bundle in my arms. "Oh, God, honey, whatever it is, we'll take care of it. I promise. *Pleezzz* tell me."

Her sobs turned to whimpers as she pushed me away. Chandler went to sit on the bed. Taking tissues from the box on her nightstand, I sat next to her, gently patting her red puffy eyes. She took another tissue and blowing her nose, she said, "Stevie Michelle, this is hard for me. So, what I'm about to tell you, you've got to promise you won't tell anyone."

"I can't promise you that. It depends on what it is. I won't even begin to say I won't say anything, because if I need to, I will. I know I will."

"Stevie Michelle," she said, picking at something invisible on the bedspread, her hand shaking, and her lips trembling, "I have— Oh, God—" She buried her face in her hands. Everything appeared to move in slow motion. Gathering as much composure as she could conjure, Chandler whispered, "I have a lump in my breast. In my right breast, underneath my arm there's a big lump."

"*Ohh, noo*!"

"And honestly, I've never felt more helpless and scared in my life." Her whole body began to quake when Chandler muttered, "I don't want to die."

A pool of tears settled in her eyes once more. I reached out to hold her close. She fell into my arms. I held her tight. "You're not going to die," I said. I rocked Chandler the way I used to rock Nelson when he thought his world had fallen apart. But she wasn't Nelson and her world was falling apart. No one had worked harder at establishing a decent life for herself and the people she cared about, and now she needed help, and whatever needed to be done for her, I was going to see that it was. "Chandler, have you been to the doctor?"

"I went yesterday morning. I had a mammogram and I'm scheduled for a biopsy tomorrow."

"What time tomorrow?"

"Nine."

"I'll be right there with you."

"Will you, Stevie Michelle? Will you go with me?"

"Try to keep me away."

Chandler's rolling tears turned into sobs. I couldn't hold her close enough. I felt her pain. And as much as I tried not to, as much as I wanted to be strong for her, the tears streamed down my cheeks, too.

We both held on tight. Then suddenly, Chandler laughed. It wasn't a mad, crazy laugh, but a subtle, discovery giggle. "Almost ten years, and it takes something like this for me to see you cry," she said.

We smiled at one another.

"I'm going to take good care of you," I said.

"Stevie Michelle, I feel so dirty. Real dirty." Her pity seemed to turn into anger when, with her jaws and teeth tight like a snarling dog's, Chandler said, "I wish I—" She grabbed at her breast and releasing a defeating moan, she then continued with, "I want to rip it out, Stevie Michelle. *Damn it*! I just wish I could yank this cancer right out of me!"

"You don't know that it's cancer. Four out of five lumps are benign, Chandler. And you're one of those four. I know you are." She had to be because if she wasn't, that meant I could lose the best friend I had. Then what would I do? "Remember," I said, holding my hand in a thumbs up as we whispered together, "the bestest of friends, through thick and thin, until the end." At that moment I thought of Lorelei. I had to make the decision of telling her, but I didn't want her to worry, at least not until the biopsy results. I told Chandler that I was going to call the restaurant because I had everybody on alert. "I'm not going to say what's happening. I'll just say you have a bad case of the flu and I want to stay with you."

"Thanks."

"Hey, what are we for? Lorelei will kill me later, but—" Picking up the phone, I went over in my mind what to say. Lorelei tried to ask all kinds of questions, but luckily the restaurant was busy and she didn't have time to talk. Chandler told me what to tell Jorge and he only had time to take instructions and get back to work.

The only other people to call were Banning and Stohn. I phoned Stohn first. I didn't tell Chandler before I made the call. "Stohn," I said, "I'm finally getting back with you." Chandler almost jumped to the ceiling in protest. I waved her down. I explained the situation to Stohn and he insisted on talking with Chandler. I didn't know what he said, but her tears developed into a rainbow of a smile. Handing me the phone, she said, "He wants to talk to you."

"Stevie Michelle, we'll get her the best care possible. I know a few specialists. I have a couple surgeries tomorrow, but I'll have them pushed back."

"You don't have to do that, Stohn. I'm not going to leave her side. Not tonight, not tomorrow."

"I need to be there," he said.

"I understand."

Before I hung up, I gave Stohn the details as Chandler gave them to me. She was to be at the hospital for outpatient ambulatory surgery at eight. No deodorant and no perfume.

Then I phoned Banning's hotel. He picked up on the first ring. "I've been waiting impatiently for your call."

"I'm sorry it took so long."

"Is everything okay with Chandler?"

"Not exactly. I'm going to have to postpone tonight, Banning. I'm sorry."

"Oh, but love, I was so looking forward to our evening."

"Me too, but Chandler is sick."

"Can't you give her a couple aspirin and come with me a little while."

It was like he had stuck a knife in my chest and was twisting it. Before I could catch myself, I quipped, "Obviously, you don't understand. My friend is ill; she needs me. Not tomorrow, not a few hours from now, but *now*! So, do you know where that puts you at the moment?" The line went silent. I realized what I had done. I wished I could have seen Banning's face. It was the only way to tell how badly I had hurt him. In an attempt to apologize, I stated as softly as I could, "I'm sorry. I'm as disappointed as you are, and I'll make it up to you."

I looked at Chandler on the bed. Exhausted, she was curled, her hands between her knees, resting on a pillow. "Banning, I have to go. I'll call you soon. Probably tomorrow. Please understand, and call Lorelei. Have dinner at the restaurant."

"Okay, love. I'll do that. And maybe take a cab down to the Flats. I've been reading about the clubs."

"That's a good idea. I'm sorry you'll be alone."

"Maybe not. Cindy's shift is over in a few hours. I think I'll ask her to go."

"Who's Cindy?"

"One of the reservationists."

That instant, I mouthed, "You bastard." But then suddenly I became very calm. I remembered what Chandler had told me one day. I realized what she meant when she said, 'Once you have the confidence in yourself and your independence, the dependence relinquishes itself.' "Please have a good time, Banning, and I'll call you." Before he could say another word, I quietly placed the phone down. I went back to the bed with my girlfriend and we propped ourselves on pillows. I got two cherry Lifesavers from my pocket and I handed Chandler one.

"I always end up chewing mine," she confessed.

"Me too, honey. Me too."

Chapter 31

(Stevie Michelle)

I didn't want to leave Chandler alone, but I had to go home to get a change of clothing. I promised her that I wouldn't be long. I left her getting dressed, reminding her not to wear any deodorant or perfume. When I got to the house, there was a message from Banning apologizing about the night before. I would talk to him later to apologize also. It was too early to bother Lorelei. She probably had been at the restaurant until closing. Was I using that as an excuse? I really didn't want to tell her, because I knew she would freak out. I decided I would call after Chandler was settled at the hospital. I was back with her in a matter of an hour. She was sitting on the sofa when I walked in. "You ready?"

"As ready as I can be."

"Okay, then let's get this thing done so we can take that vacation we need so much."

Chandler smiled a weary smile. I had never seen her so weak with exhaustion. She could work at the restaurant from sun up to sun down and beyond for days and never look the way she did then.

Just as we were walking out the door, Stohn called. He said he was on his way to the hospital to talk to Chandler's doctor and to look at her films. It was consoling to feel Stohn's presence. I needed as much support as I could get to be able to give Chandler the support she needed.

When we arrived at the hospital, Chandler's knight in scrubs was there waiting. Stohn Bradford's eminence dominated any fear I might have had. I hoped he did the same for Chandler. He took her hand and pulled her inside his grasp. He hugged her. She was very rigid, almost apprehensive, as if she was a leper and would make him one also. His grasp surrounded her. I read Stohn's lips as he quietly said in Chandler's ear, "I'm here, pretty girl. And I'll see to it that everything's all right."

Chandler's rigidity lessened and she rested her head on Stohn's shoulder. I looked at them wondering why an occurrence like this had to happen to bring two people together that always belonged together.

My girlfriend was registered in a flash and whisked away to the operating room. That's when I knew I had to make the call I had been dreading. Not until Lorelei answered the phone did I realize that I was muted. Swallowing several times, trying to activate my voice box, I finally spit, "Lorelei, I just called to tell you that Chandler's all right and—"

"I been tryin' to get you two," she said. "I would have called last night, but I was dog tired by the time the restaurant closed. I was callin' to see if I could bring Chandler anything. I wasn't sure what her symptoms were, so I didn't know if she needed a decongestant or just some plain old aspirin or Tylenol."

I was doomed. When I told her what was really happening, I was going to need General Patton and three bodyguards to protect me.

"Lorelei, can you be quiet for a minute? I've got something to tell you. I inhaled some serious air before I said, "*Aaah*, Chandler and I are at the hospital. And—"

"Was she that sick that you had to take her to the hospital?"

"Listen," I said. "If you'll just listen I'll tell you. Now, I need you to know that I think I handled this as best I could, so don't get upset with my decision."

"Stevie Michelle, I'm tryin' to be patient, but you—"

"All right. All right. Chandler's here because she's having a biopsy done. She has a lump in her breast."

"What the hell you talkin' about, Stevie Michelle? Did she have a lump yesterday?"

"Of course she did."

"Then why the hell didn't you tell me yesterday? What, I ain't a good enough friend to share somethin' like that with? You been—"

"Wait a minute. I told you I handled it the best I could, Lorelei. I didn't want you worrying until we— Well, at least until— Look, Chandler asked me not to say anything, but the real reason I didn't tell you is I needed you to keep things flowing at the restaurant last night. I didn't want you with this on your mind. Regardless of what's going on, Lorelei, Maroon has to still run, because that's the only way Chandler would have it. So, you've got to mind the store, so to speak."

"Where is she now?" Lorelei asked, her voice thin.

"In surgery. Stohn's with her."

"How long she goin' to be there?"

"In surgery?"

"No, in the hospital?"

"It's outpatient surgery. She'll be going home today."

"Stevie Michelle, I should be there."

"No, Lorelei. I told you that one of us has got to keep things functioning at the restaurant. At least for the next few days. But, one thing you can do is go over to Chandler's and get her room ready. She kind of left it a mess. There's a couple empty wine bottles and her bed should have fresh linen. Make sure she has that tea she likes. What's it called?"

"Sleepy time."

"Yeah, that one. Then we'll take it from there. Oh, and Lorelei, stop by the restaurant and get a bottle of Gloria Ferrer."

I didn't know how long Chandler was in surgery, but I waited two hours before anyone considered acknowledging my presence. Finally, a little nurse walked by the lounge I was sitting in and said, "Dr. Bradford asked me to tell you that he'll be out soon."

By the time Stohn appeared, I had wrung the circulation out of my hands. Before he said anything, I tried to read his face, but he was trained to leave his expression, expressionless. Then he said in a professional style, "It was a large one, Stevie Michelle. The size of a silver dollar. But, luckily, it's benign."

Stohn's smile matched mine. I don't know how many hugs and kisses I bestowed on the man, but he stood patiently until I finished. "Where is she?" Is she awake yet? Can I see her?" I asked.

"They're dressing her sutures now. I'll warn you, she'll be sore and there's some disfiguration. But the best part is she's healthy again. I'd give them another ten minutes and then you can see her. I've got some surgeries of my own today, so I better get going."

Stohn Bradford was one of the finest doctors on earth—both professional and personal. I kissed him once more. The same little nurse that stopped into the lounge was the one who showed me where Chandler was.

One arm through the hospital gown, the right chest and arm wrapped in bright white gauze and tape, Chandler was lethargic, but she recognized me. Her half smile was the most beautiful smile I'd ever seen. She said quietly, as if we were in church, "Stevie Michelle, I'm ready to go home. Stohn said I'm all right and I can go home."

I turned to the nurse and asked, "When can she leave?"

"As soon as she's coherent and she drinks what's in that cup." The nurse pointed to a medium-sized Dixie cup with what looked like a carbonated liquid in it. "If she keeps it down, she's free to go."

"Okay, Chandler. You've got to pass the test," I encouraged.

She reached for the cup. She was coherent enough to know she had to use her left arm. She couldn't grab it. I got it for her. Helping her sit up, Chandler sipped at the drink and swallowed slowly.

We waited another hour and then it was announced that she was able to leave. I helped her get dressed and pushed her wheelchair down the hall. Bending over the chair, I whispered in Chandler's ear, "You're going to have to hang up your Henckels for a while." It was the first time I'd heard my girlfriend laugh in twenty-four hours. She was going to be okay.

I called Lorelei at Chandler's from my car to tell her we were on our way. When we got there, she had everything in place. The bedroom had been freshened and food was waiting for us. That's when it was brought to my attention that I was hungry. We sat in Chandler's bedroom and Lorelei and I ate Cobb salads and French bread with butter, compliments of Jorge. Chandler, propped on pillows in her bed, sipped vegetable broth while we watched Oprah Winfrey. After the show was over, I went down to the kitchen to pour three glasses of champagne. Carefully carrying the pink sparkling wine upstairs, I handed each of my girlfriends a flute and toasted, "Today is tomorrow's yesterday and we have so many tomorrows to look forward to." I gave the thumbs up sign and we recited together, "The bestest of friends, through thick and thin, until the end."

Chapter 32

(Stevie Michelle)

Not until I had to, did I realize that I could. Chandler was sent home with instructions for exercises and the cleaning and dressing of her incision. I didn't know what type of scar was underneath her bandages, and I'll admit I was squeamish about seeing it. Stohn suggested that someone come in to help with her dressings and care, but I flatly refused, saying that between me and Lorelei, Chandler would have any and everything she needed. I wasn't going to let anyone else take care of her. The exercises were the toughest. The pain of movement made Chandler cantankerous. I had to help lift her arm, along with also lifting her spirits. My girlfriend was used to a flawless body, which, to her, had been defaced. Her scar didn't look as bad as she interpreted it, but it was like an anorexic looking in the mirror. She would see nothing but fat while the rest of the world visualized malnutrition. Lorelei made sure Chandler talked with Jorge daily. It was the only way we could keep her out of the restaurant until she was well enough to be there.

Stohn came by in the evenings bearing cute little gifts. One day he presented the book, *The Little Engine That Could* and read it to Chandler from cover to cover. She giggled through the end.

When I finally had a complete evening with Banning, he was leaving the next afternoon. We made the best of the hours, though. He upgraded his hotel room to one with a Jacuzzi and we spent time relaxing in warm bubbling water, drinking wine, eating and talking about our relationship.

When the words, "I'm in love with you, Stevie Michelle," flowed from Banning's mouth, my heart became a Fourth of July fireworks celebration.

For the first time in my forty-something years, I was in love, too. Carl was the closest I had come to that feeling—I loved and respected him, but I wasn't *in love*. I was *in love* with Banning. I was *in love* with the way we thought the same things at the same time. I was *in love* with the way he cupped my chin in his fingertips before kissing me. I was *in love* with the tone of his voice when he was vexed. I was *in love* with the way he said, "I'm in love with you, Stevie Michelle." And I wanted to tell everybody. I wanted to tell Mama most of all, because I never forgot her words of wisdom. 'When you're in love, it's a feelin' that you'll be unable to describe.' Personally, I didn't care to describe it. I was satisfied feeling it. And I felt it with Banning.

"Stevie Michelle, I just professed the greatest emotion I have to you," Banning said, grounding my soaring heart. "So, what do you think about that?"

Kissing him lovingly, I said, "Come with me. I can show you better than I can tell you, because words are unable to describe what I think."

In my bedroom, Banning sat in a chair with me on his lap. He brushed his fingertips over my exposed skin. The sensation was a bonding one.

Banning and I caressed and made love, slept, watched the sun come up, and made love again before I began to panic that he was leaving me.

"I know what you're thinking," he said, smoothing my hair on the pillow.

"You do not."

"Yes, I do."

"Then, what am I thinking?"

"You're thinking that you don't want me to leave."

"How do you do that?" I asked, my voice in giggles, moving closer to him, pulling the covers over us.

"I told you, I'm a mind reader, as well as a reporter."

"Oh, come on, Banning, really?"

"Okay, I saw you glance at the clock, so I made a good, accurate guess."

"You're sneaky."

"You're beautiful."

I thought I would blush myself into flames. "You're beautiful, too," I said, attempting to redirect my embarrassment.

The sheets were scented with Banning's cologne. I tried to inconspicuously bury my nose into them, sniffing the fragrance that I never wanted to forget. Closing my eyes, I murmured, "I love you. I love you very much." Banning didn't hear my affirmation.

"Stevie Michelle," he said, his voice slicing the silence, partially startling me, "I have a question, and I'm as— How do you say it?—as serious as my heart attacking me?"

"*Nooo*," I said, laughing so hard I could feel every muscle in my face. "It's as serious as a heart attack, Banning."

"You've got to stop laughing, Stevie Michelle. This is no laughing matter."

"Okay, I'll stop laughing," I said. But I couldn't. The more I tried, the sillier I became, not really knowing what I was laughing about.

"Well then, maybe what I have to say will help you. Stevie Michelle, I want you to be my wife. I want you to become Mrs. Banning Morris."

I stopped laughing. Sitting up in bed, holding the top of the sheet and my hand against my fluttering heart, I said, "Why now? I mean, why would you have me answer a question like that now? Couldn't you have asked me to commit murder or a robbery?"

"All you have to do is say yes or no," he said. "I'll still love you, whatever your answer. But if you say no, I want to hear an excellent reason. A reason where a rebuttal would be impossible."

"I'm not ready for marriage, Banning. It's as simple as that. I've done it three times and obviously with little success."

"And I've been in relationships, too, that didn't last, but I still want to marry you. I think about you all the time. When we're separated, I'm lost. Sometimes I think I'll go out of my head."

"I think you mean, out of your mind, Banning."

"No. I mean out of my head."

"We live in two different places," I said. "I have a business here and I'm almost sure you're not leaving your job. You love your work."

"Stevie Michelle, I can be a reporter anywhere. News sucks everywhere. And anywhere is paradise when you're with someone you love. I can understand you not giving up Maroon."

"Can you?"

"Yes."

"Then can you understand that right now my independence is part of Maroon and Maroon is part of my independence? I've been manipulated and taken care of by men most of my life, Banning. And now, I'm taking care of myself without the manipulation and it feels wonderful. Ecstatically wonderful."

"I wouldn't strip you of your independence."

"Maybe not, but you'll be a weighing factor in the equation that I've already worked out."

"Okay," Banning said, "but I hope you won't end our relationship because of my untimely proposal."

"Don't be silly. For the first time, I've never been more comfortable with a love affair."

"Good, because I'm going to ask again—a month from now or a year from now."

Banning and I had approximately two hours before his flight. We spent an hour of that saying goodbye. When we arrived at the airport, running up the concourse, I giggled and reflected that it was the first time I had ever said no to a marriage proposal. And the ironic thing was, I would have been marrying for the right reason—l-o-v-e.

Banning flashed me a smile and said, "Stevie Michelle, love will bring you around to seeing it my way. I know it will."

Chapter 33

(Chandler)

It was my first morning back in the restaurant after four weeks. The doctor said to take six, but I would have lost my sanity if I'd stayed home one more day. I was at Maroon early, before anyone else. I wanted to be alone to acclimate myself. Jorge, Lorelei and Stevie Michelle never missed a beat in maintaining quality control. The three of them ran the place without me, not that I didn't believe they could. Me being absent made me certain that we could open a second location. "Maroon, Too," or something like that. Jorge would chef for Maroon and I would work in the new one or vice versa.

I sat at the piano. Noticing the fingerprints on it, I rubbed the cabinet with the sleeve of my chef's jacket. It made me think about Marcus. I'd talked to him twice in the four weeks I was away, but I hadn't heard from him since. He had my home number, but I didn't have his. He was adamant about being secretive, even after he said I was his best friend. Maybe he didn't understand that best friends should be close. The fingerprints on the piano smudged, dulling the finish. *Where is Marcus*? I thought.

Lifting the mahogany lid, I tapped the eighty-eight keys, down the row, one by one. It needed tuning. I thought of Alexandria. As soon as she was old enough, she would learn to play the piano, especially now that Kennedy was talking to me again. My sister was angry because I didn't tell her about my surgery until after the fact. My illness had created a ton of distress for my friends and family. I felt bad about putting them through the anxiety, but at the same time, I was grateful that they were there. It was the first time in my life I felt I needed someone and that someone turned out to be four of the best people in the world. I couldn't've made it without them.

Everything was almost back to normal, and I was appreciative, thankful, and felt blessed. I thought, *Maybe God has forgiven me.* Never again would I take life for granted. I was going to spend more time with myself and with the people I loved and who loved me.

Subconsciously, I began to play *What a Wonderful World* on the piano. I chuckled and thought, *I better take lessons with Alex. I need the practice.* The phone rang, but I didn't get up to answer it. If it was Stevie Michelle or Lorelei, they would give me the third degree about what the doctor said and if it was anyone else, well, I didn't care.

I left the piano and walked into the kitchen. My tool box was where I had put it, on the side table. All my knives and decorating equipment were in it. Opening the box, I pulled out the largest of my Henckels. Gripping the knife handle, I was inclined to start chopping. In the corner, on the floor, was a bag of potatoes. I got a cutting board off the utility stand and a large potato out of the bag. With my knife, I sliced into it, using my style of a downward rocking motion. My arm felt strong. I got another potato and a bell pepper from the refrigerator. An onion out of the bin completed the medley. Staring at my work, I decided that home fries with scrambled eggs and toast were in order for breakfast.

I tossed the potatoes in a skillet with olive oil. I took a couple of eggs out of the refrigerator and some wheat bread from the pantry. I raised the heat under the potatoes and just as I turned on the CD player to listen to Joe Sample, I heard a knock at the front door. "Damn."

I made my way through the dining room into the reception area and smiled because I was familiar with the physique on the other side of the door. "Stohn," I said to myself. The doctor was holding a large fruit basket wrapped in golden cellophane with a purple bow.

"Happy birthday," he said as I invited him in.

Giggling, I said, "It's not my birthday, silly."

"Darn, and I bought you a gift and everything. Now I'm going to have to return it."

"No, you're not," I said, grabbing the basket. I set it on the podium and started tearing at the wrapper. I had my eye on a shiny red Delicious apple. I said thank you to Stohn and rubbed the fruit clean on my coat. Biting into the crisp, sweet fruit, my reaction was, "*Mmmm,*" as the succulent juice exploded across my taste buds.

Stohn's voice was sensual when he asked, "Chandler, how does an apple taste?"

Chuckling, I inquired, baffled, "You don't know how an apple tastes?"

"I don't know how an apple tastes to you."

I stopped chewing and stared at Stohn's strong features. I wanted to admit that I was drawn to his passion, but afraid, just as I was at seventeen. My gaze dropped, I swallowed and then answered, "It tastes like your first surprise kiss in the park. Sweet and tonic to all the senses."

Raising my head to his height, Stohn faintly brushed my lips with his. "You've run long enough, Chandler Elizabeth Cawthorne. I want you in my life. I want you for the rest of my life. I know that I know how to love you, because I've had more than two decades of practice. Chandler, please allow me—"

"Stop it," I said.

"Woman, what the hell are you afraid of? Just tell me what it is and I'll set your mind at ease."

"I'm not afraid of anything."

"Then if you don't want me being a part of your life—"

"You are a part of my life."

"No, Chandler. I mean a real part of your life. I don't want to be, 'this is an old friend of mine' any longer."

Under the pressure, I yelled, "Stohn, I have a scar. A nasty, ugly scar!"

"What you have is an opportunity to live. Scars don't intimidate me. I've seen deformities all my medical life. I've seen your scar. I was there with the surgeon, remember? I'm not shallow, and you can't use a scar as an excuse, because I'm blind to it. You are the most beautiful woman I know, inside and out. Flawless, as far as I'm concerned. And—"

The door opened and there walked in my chocolate Buddha.

"Marcus," I said to no one in particular. It was as if my prayer had been answered. Stohn gave me a look of, this isn't over. I wrapped my arms around Marcus and hugged him as tight as I could, feeling cautious of my arm. I looked into his eyes. They weren't bright and laughing the way I was used to them. He appeared ailed.

"What's happenin', Ms. C? Hey, Doc Stohn." His tone was languid.

"Marcus, are you all right?" I asked.

"I'm straight." He walked into the dining room. He wasn't limping, but he kept his left leg stiff as if he was wearing a splint.

"Are you all right, Marcus?" I asked again, following behind as he made it to the "conference room" table, easing into a chair. His leg was extended.

"Yeah. I had a little accident, that's all."

"What kind of accident?"

"Ms. C, I tripped, not watchin' where I was walkin', that's all. You can lighten' up now."

Marcus had never talked to me like that. He seemed agitated. I was anxious to know what was bothering him. I knew there was something, although he denied it.

Then I heard Stohn say, "What's that I smell, Chandler?"

"Oh, shit!" I rushed into the kitchen. Out of the corner of my eye, I saw Stohn following me. The kitchen was filling with smoke. I was surprised the detector hadn't set off. Stohn opened the back door. I grabbed a potholder and took the smoke-filled skillet outside. I set the burnt potatoes on the ground. If I'd had a blanket, I could have sent smoke signals. Going inside, I turned on the exhaust fan. My attempt at not coughing failed. Stohn's eyes were watering. "Let's get out of here," I said. I encompassed his hand in mine and led him out. Marcus was still sitting at the table. "Well, I guess we'll have to go out for breakfast," I said as I accidently stumbled over Marcus' outstretched leg.

His eyes rolled back in his head. He made noises of a wounded grizzly bear. Blasphemy filtered through his groans. "Goddamn, Ms. C. Fuck. Shit. Oh, it fuckin' hurts."

It was as if Marcus was possessed. For the first time, his existence frightened me. He grabbed his leg and rocked back and forth. His grimacing face indicated pain. I had bumped his leg, not amputated it.

Stohn and I were silent, staring at one another and then back at Marcus, when the left leg of his khaki trousers turned a deep red, almost purple. I gasped. "Marcus, what happened? I only bumped you."

Stohn acknowledged that the crimson color was blood. The doctor moved into action. He began asking Marcus grueling questions. "Is it a stab or gunshot wound, Marcus?"

Stab or gunshot? What was Stohn talking about?

"It ain't nothin', Doc," Marcus managed.

"Look man, I'm a doctor. Been aroun' the block a few times, so you can cut the crap."

Pellets of sweat formed and then rolled down Marcus' forehead. His once round, jolly face was raging with pain.

"Chandler, get a knife," Stohn commanded.

"Naw, man. You ain't cuttin' my pants."

"What difference will it make, Marcus. They're stained with blood. Get the knife, Chandler."

I thought, *So much for everything being normal again*. I ran into the kitchen and cleaned the knife I used to cut vegetables.

"Now give me the 4-1-1," I heard Stohn ask Marcus as I returned to the dining room. I had never heard Stohn talk that way. I didn't know he could. Slang wasn't something he was taught in medical school, and I was sure he hadn't been on the streets of late.

Marcus' jaw was as tight as a vise. His teeth clenched, he said, "I caught it in the leg. We was just kickin' it when the bullets started flyin'. One of my homies got it in the chest. He got it in the chest, Doc, and I watched him die right there."

"When was this, Marcus?" I asked. "I didn't see anything on the news or in the paper."

"Everything doesn't make it to the news, Chandler," Stohn confirmed. He was right. I instantly thought of Spoon. I remembered the little article in the newspaper about his murder. He was "just kickin' it", too, when he was shot, except he wasn't as lucky as Marcus.

Stohn's tone was professional when he said, "Marcus, I'm going to take a look at that leg." The size of the knife and the way Stohn held it was unnerving. It sliced into the material as if it was tissue paper. The blood stained pant leg opened to reveal Marcus' ballooned limb. It looked swollen enough to split.

Gasping, I declared, "It's infected." Stohn attested my conclusion.

"When did this happen?" he asked Marcus.

"Last Friday."

It was Saturday.

Stohn's bedside manner unfolded. "You've got to get to the hospital, Marcus. This is serious."

"Naw, man. I can't go to no hospital."

"Do you want to lose your leg?"

"Naw, man."

"Well, if we don't stop the infection, then that's what's next. Infection, gangrene and then amputation."

Marcus' round face contorted. "Doc Stohn, they'll ask me all kinds of questions. Makin' police reports. I don't know nothin'. I was just there."

"Are you sure about that?" Stohn questioned.

"Yeah, Doc. I'm sure."

"Then you've got nothing to worry about. I'll take you to the hospital myself. You tell them what you know and we'll get you fixed up like new. What do you say?"

Marcus stared at the floor. I was hoping he would agree. His leg oozed with pus and blood.

"Is Ms. C comin'?"

"If she wants," Stohn said.

"I'll come," I confirmed, taking off my chef coat. Somehow, it had been stained with blood.

Stohn and I helped Marcus from the chair. His pants were ruined. I would buy him another pair if he needed me to. The blood was now trickling into his sock. I went into the kitchen to get a clean laundered towel. Dampening it, I went back into the dining room. Marcus' leg was tender to my touch. My eyes filled with tears. I thought about his lifestyle. I wanted to change it. I *would* change it.

"Let's go, Chandler," Stohn said. I took hold of Marcus' other arm and Stohn and I were his crutches.

When we walked into the emergency room, Stohn was greeted with smiles from the nurses and doctors. The receptionist at the desk asked, "Who do we owe for this pleasant surprise, Dr. Bradford?"

"Natalie, we've got a trauma to the left leg, here."

Miraculously, I thought about Marcus' guardian. He was under age. He would need consent. I whispered into his ear, "Where is your mom, Marcus?"

"What, Ms. C?"

"They won't treat you without your mom's permission. Can you get her to come?"

"No. I told you I didn't want to come. Now you want to bring her into this. She won't come. She can't come."

"But, Marcus—"

"She won't come, Ms. C. I know she won't."

I interrupted Stohn's conversation. "Aah, Dr. Bradford, may I speak to you in private for a moment, please?"

"Sure, Chandler. What is it?"

I pulled Stohn further from the desk before I began. "Aah, Marcus needs a guardian's permission to be treated."

Stohn massaged his chin before he said, "You know, I hadn't thought of that. Maybe because I don't think of Marcus as a juvenile. We've got to call his—"

"I'll be her, Stohn. Marcus says she won't come."

"Chandler, what do you mean she won't come? She's his mother."

"That's what Marcus tells me."

"Is it that she won't come or he doesn't want her to come? Have you thought that maybe he's hiding something, Chandler. Obviously, he hasn't told her about his leg. I think he's afraid of being punished if she finds out."

"I don't think so," I said. "There's some underlying factor here."

"Well, Chandler, the bottom line is he can't get help unless someone signs for him."

"I'll do it."

"Honey, you can't."

"Yes, I can. I'll be his guardian. No one will know but us."

"Chandler. . ." "I won't bring you into this, Stohn. As far as you're concerned, I'm who I say I am. Please?"

Stohn's nod was apprehensive, but a nod of acceptance just the same. He went back to the desk and I went to sit with Marcus. He was physically exhausted. I presented him with an affectionate smile and a gentle kiss on his fat cheek. I hoped that someone would take care of him soon. From nowhere came a young lady with a clipboard and pen. Hesitant, I took it from her. I didn't feel comfortable with what I was about to do. The lady walked away and I explained my plan to Marcus. He just said, "Thanks, Ms. C." He leaned on my shoulder and I braced myself for his weight. I would have held him up for as long as he needed it.

Filling out the form, under insurance I wrote none, and if Marcus had any, I certainly wasn't going to attempt to use it. I had a feeling that this was definitely a criminal offense. Stohn watched me from across the room. When he thought I had completed the information, he came over, took the clipboard and gave it to the receptionist. I watched her examine the data. When she placed the board into a slot on the wall, I looked into Marcus' face and said, "It's going to be all right, honey." His tough guy image had faded. Marcus was as vulnerable as a newborn baby, and I was going to protect him as if he was.

"Marcus Taylor," a voice rang into the emergency room.

"This is it," I whispered to him.

Stohn said, "Wait, we'll get a wheelchair for you."

The wheelchair arrived and we helped Marcus into it. The gurney in the room that the transporter pushed him to was surrounded by buttons and valves protruding from the pale pink walls. Stohn helped Marcus onto the cot. I left the room while Marcus was prepared for an examination. His pants were removed and a resident listened to Stohn as he explained his diagnosis. The resident examined the leg and made notes. Then he and Stohn left the room. I went in. "How are you feeling?" I asked Marcus.

"Ms. C, thanks. My leg's been killin' me. I ain't been able to sleep or nothin'."

"That explains everything," I said. "I'm just thankful it didn't get any worse before you came to me. That's why you came today, isn't it?"

"I don't know. I guess so. I don't have anybody else to go to."

"I need to ask you something, Marcus. And I want you to answer me. No trying to get around the question."

"All right," he said. "I owe you that, at least."

"Where do you live?"

"Down the hill."

"No, Marcus. What's the street? What's the address?"

A defeating sigh escaped. "Twenty-six, thirty, a hundred and first street."

"Where's your mom, Marcus?"

"You're getting' a little personal, now, Ms. C."

"Marcus, I'm not playing with you. I've done something unethical here. I signed as your guardian. If something goes wrong, I'm in big trouble."

"She could be anywhere. The last note she left me, she was goin' to Columbus with some dude. Probably another no good, drug usin' motherfucka."

"Marcus!"

"Well, you asked. It ain't pretty, Ms. C."

"Neither is your vocabulary."

"Okay. I'm sorry."

"That's better, young man. Now . . . what's her name?"

"Bernadette."

"When was the last time you saw her?"

"I guess it's been three days."

"And she just leaves you like this?"

"I can take care of myself. I been doin' it a long time."

"Yeah. We can see how well you've been doin' it."

"Aw, don't be a hater, Ms. C. I don't criticize you."

"I'm not criticizing you."

"Then what do you call it?"

"I call it being concerned about a good friend of mine."

"Look. My name is Marcus Anthony Taylor, Jr." Marcus chuckled as if he was laughing at himself. "And I don't know where the junior came from. I ain't never met my father, Ms. C. Can you believe it? There's got to be a senior in order for there to be a junior. There ain't no senior. I ain't got no father."

"You have a father, Marcus. You just don't know him."

"I don't know him and I don't want to know him. He's probably just like my mother. Not worth a good shit."

"Marcus!"

"I can't help it, Ms. C. I'm tired of tryin' to run away from the truth."

"Not running is a good concept. But you've got to understand," I said, "that there's no one on this earth who's perfect."

"You're perfect, Ms. C. You got it goin' on."

"Thanks. I'm flattered, but your compliment couldn't be farther from the truth. I used to want to be perfect. Thought I could be. I used to hate my mother for not being a perfect parent. But not until I got older did I understand that parents have problems that their children don't have a clue about. And that's part of being a good parent, keeping your problems and frustrations from your children. You say your mother uses drugs. Well, mine was an alcoholic. She drank herself to death because she was lonely, although she had a husband, and I think she wanted to die." I had never expressed myself about my mother with such depth as I was explaining it to Marcus, a thirteen-year-old.

The three doctors who filed into the room included Stohn Bradford. A nurse soon followed with a cart of needles and bottles. Stohn explained to Marcus who the people were that surrounded him. "This is Dr. Byers and Dr. Henig," he said.

"Dr. Henig, a bald, tall, lanky man in a lab coat spoke next. "We're going to get an x-ray of your leg, look for fractures and hopefully find the bullet. If it's not in a precarious position, we'll have no problem removing it. Nurse McKinley will start the antibiotics. Then the anesthesiologist will put you to sleep and when you wake up you'll be on your way to recovery."

Marcus was nervous. I thought my voice would help him relax. "Sounds like my surgery, Marcus. It'll be a piece of cake."

"Think so, Ms. C?"

"Know so."

Stohn chimed in. "The pain of rehabilitation will be nothing compared to the pain you're having now."

"Then let's get it over with, 'cause my leg's sendin' a message to my brain that I need to put myself out of the agony I'm in."

"All right, Marcus. Your agony is going to end today. Drs. Henig and Byers are two of the best. And I'll be there, too," Stohn said with modesty.

"Time for pictures," Dr. Byers announced. It was the first occasion she had said anything. Her voice wasn't what I expected. She was petite, freckle-face with red hair and a deep, vibrating voice.

We all left the small room together, Marcus was being wheeled out with us surrounding him. I kissed his forehead and said, "I'll be waiting, so don't be too long."

"I was thinkin' we could have ribs for dinner," he said.

"That's a good idea," I said, thinking that if food was on his mind, he wasn't worried.

Stohn stood next to me. "Chandler, I would like to continue what we—"

"Hold that thought," I said. "I have to call the restaurant. I didn't leave a note. Lorelei and Stevie Michelle are probably looking for me."

The sigh I heard emerge from Stohn's diaphragm was definitely one of frustration. I thought, *I'll take care of it as soon as I talk to Stevie Michelle and Lorelei.* I perused the area for a pay phone. "I'll be right back," I said to him. I headed in the direction of the phone I spotted on the other side of the emergency room.

Stevie Michelle answered after what seemed the thousandth ring. "Chandler, where the hell are you? Do you know what you've put everybody through? Lorelei was just on her way to your house. *Girrl,* if—"

"Stevie Michelle, shut up. I'm all right. I was there this morning. If you checked the kitchen, I left burnt potatoes and chopped vegetables in there."

"Oh yeah. Burnt food. That's a good clue, Chandler. Aaah, excuse me for not getting it, but Jorge could have done that. Where the hell are you, anyway? You're supposed to be at home recuperating."

"I have recuperated. I'm in the emergency room."

"What!?"

"If you don't let me explain, I'm going to hang up on you," I said.

"You know the rule," she said. "We don't hang up on each other."

"Then shut up so I won't be forced to." We knew when to be obedient. "I'm here with Marcus and Stohn's here with the both of us."

"What's Marcus doing there?"

"He had a little accident, as he refers to it. But the truth is he was shot in the leg. He didn't have it taken care of, so now it's infected and he needs surgery."

"What next?"

"Hopefully nothing, Stevie Michelle, so tell Lorelei what's happening and I'll be at the hospital for awhile. I want to be here when he comes out of surgery."

"Chandler, it may not be any of my business, but where is his mother?"

"If it's the truth, she's in Columbus. Look, I've got some things I need to talk to you and Lorelei about. I've got some decisions to make, but now is not the time to tell you about them. But what I will say is when Marcus is discharged from the hospital, I want him to stay with me until he's better."

"Chandler, think about that. You're not his mother."

"Neither is his mother," I snapped. "Listen, we'll talk about it later. Stohn's waiting for me. I'll call back to tell you how Marcus' surgery went and to see how things are going at the restaurant. I love you."

"I love you, too."

It was a relief and a plus to express myself with my girlfriends. Most times they listened and were honest with me. I hung up the phone and stared at it for a few seconds. Voicing my thoughts, I said, "He's the child I never had."

Stohn wasn't where I left him. I looked through the emergency room, but no Dr. Bradford. I sat on the bench, indecisive as to which way to go. The cafeteria was my choice. I stopped at the newsstand in the gift shop and bought a *Gourmet* magazine for myself and a get well card for Marcus.

Lunchtime in the cafeteria had it filled to capacity. Standing in line, I read the menu on the wall and decided a Coke and small salad was all I wanted. I didn't have much of an appetite. Besides, the menu wasn't much to whet the appetite.

I sat at a table with a woman who seemed to be in mental deliberation. She emerged from her thoughts long enough for me to say, "Good afternoon," and to ask if it was all right that I sit with her.

"Be my guest," she said in a soft sensual voice.

I looked at the woman and for some reason, I started assessing her appearance. She may have been in her late twenties, early thirties, and wasn't beautiful, but her brown skin was smooth and unblemished. The makeup around her eyes was subtle and her lips were full, with a thin natural ridge defining them. On the table in front of her was a tray with cookies, ice cream and a Coke on it.

She startled me when she said, "I have my moments when I don't want anything but junk food, especially when I'm nervous."

"I get that way sometimes, too," I responded. I prepared my salad with salt and pepper and opened my magazine.

"You like to cook?" the woman asked.

Chuckling, I said, "Yeah. I guess I do. I'm a chef."

"Really, an honest to goodness chef?"

"I sure am. I have a restaurant, too."

"A restaurant, too. Really? A honest to goodness chef with a restaurant. What's the name of your restaurant?"

"Maroon."

"I can't say I've heard of that one."

"Well, we've been in business a couple years now, almost three. I have two partners, who are also my best friends."

"I have a best friend, too. That's why I'm here today. She got real sick about eight this morning and I brought her to the hospital. She couldn't breathe. The doctors think its pneumonia, but they want to run some more tests to be sure. I'm so tired, I could pass out right here."

"My name is Chandler Cawthorne," I said.

"Oh yeah. How rude of me. I'm having a conversation with you and haven't even introduced myself. My name is Honey. Honey Bonet."

I thought, *What a provocative name*. "It's nice to meet you, Honey."

"You too. I haven't ever met a real live chef before, who's a sister, and who has her own restaurant."

I blushed. "Thanks for what I think's a compliment."

"Oh, it's a compliment, all right. I admire people who are somebody."

I didn't know what she meant by that, and I didn't have enough guts to ask. I also didn't have the nerve to ask what she did for a living. The low neckline of her tight, red knit sweater displaying her cleavage, seemed a little risqué. *And in the middle of the day*, I thought. I couldn't help to think of Scarlet O'Hara when Mammy told her it wasn't respectable to show her bosom before the sun went down. Honey's chestnut hair was styled in a French roll, while long, narrow, silver earrings dangled from her ears. Her fancy acrylic nails were dressed in red polish with rhinestones at the tips. I didn't know if she was wearing slacks or a skirt, because I couldn't see under the table, but I was positive that whichever it was, it would complete the rest of her ensemble.

"I wanted to be a teacher, but I never got any further than junior college and didn't finish that," she said, biting into a cookie.

"Have you ever thought about going back?" I asked.

"All the time. I just can't figure out the right time."

"I went back and I'm glad I did. Now I'm doing what I want to do."

"And that's the key, ain't it?" Honey said. "Doing what it is you want to do and not what you have to."

I was even more curious as to what she did, but I still didn't have the courage to ask. I wished she'd just tell me.

My friend, Ginger, the girl I brought here, went to cosmetology school, but she didn't finish either. We said we'd go back at the same time, but she doesn't want to be a cosmetologist anymore. She wants to be an interior decorator and antiques dealer."

"You know, when your girlfriend is feeling better, I want the both of you to come to the restaurant for dinner. I think I have a business card with me," I said as I searched in the zipper part of my purse where I kept some. "Yeah. Here's one."

Honey Bonet took the card and said, "Maroon. Where did you get that name? It's interesting."

"Well, as we both know, maroon is a color, but it was also the name given to slaves of the West Indies and Guiana when they escaped to the mountains for refuge."

"Whoa. That's deep, Chandler. And you thought to name your restaurant that? It's amazing how one word can have so much depth to it. I'm impressed."

"Thank you, Honey."

"Well, I guess I better go check on Ginger. And I will take you up on your invitation. As soon as she feels like eating again, Ginger and I will come to your restaurant. Do we need reservations?"

"It would be better if you call to make sure we have a table available when you get there."

"Whoa. A restaurant where I need reservations. I got a feeling this place ain't no Ponderosa."

She may not have known when to show cleavage, but Honey Bonet was a breath of fresh air. She stood and I could see she wore skin-tight jeans. Her sweater tucked inside, the black leather belt accentuated her neat waist.

"Thanks for the company, Chandler. I'll be talking to you."

"Honey, I want to ask you something."

"Okay. Go ahead."

Standing, she towered over me and I felt awkward, but I inhaled and said, "What do you do?"

With a half smile and half a smirk, she said, "I'm a call girl. A real one."

I didn't know what she meant by "a real one," as I thought about it for a few seconds.

She must have read my expression. "You know what I mean. With a little black book and everything. I entertain the big boys. Politicians and celebrities."

"I've never knowingly met a call girl before," I found myself saying.

Honey Bonet's stare was poignant. "So, I guess we're even," she said, lifting the tray from the table. "We're like other people, Chandler," she informed me. "Dysfunctional as dysfunctional is."

Call girl or not, I liked her style and openness. "Honey, please come to the restaurant. I want you to meet my partners. They'll love you."

"Do you believe they will?"

"I know they will, especially Stevie Michelle."

"Do all three of you have strange names?"

"I've never thought of us as having strange names."

"What's your other partner's name?"

"Lorelei."

"See? What did I tell you? I've been places and I've never met a Chandler, Stevie Michelle or Lorelei before. But there's always a first time for everything. And I hope to learn and see a lot more before I die. Ginger and I are going to Africa next month. We saved a long time for it. That's why she's got to get better. It's one thing to be sick, but another to be sick that far away from home."

"It sounds exciting. I hope to get there one day," I said. "What part of Africa?"

"Ghana."

"You'll have to tell me all about it when you get back."

"Deal." Honey seemed anxious. "I've gotta go, Chandler. I'm sure Ginger's having a fit. The girl is so impatient. But I loved talking to you and don't be shocked when we show up at your place."

"I won't be. I'll be ecstatic."

"See you soon."

Honey Bonet had the stride I expected her to have. Her hips, like a regulated pendulum, swayed to and fro as she walked in black heels. The men in the cafeteria bull's-eyed her red sweater and the voluptuous mounds in it. I wondered if they were real. I smiled and at the same time I thought, *There goes the strumpet Mrs. Wilcox described.*

Signing Marcus' card, I wrote a little note of adoration on the blank side and then attempted to read my magazine.

Chapter 34

(Chandler)

At the time, the most difficult thing I felt I ever did was call Marcus' mother. Before he was discharged from the hospital, I threatened that he'd be left there if he didn't give me a phone number to contact his mother. Reluctantly, he cooperated. When I finally reached her, the voice that answered sounded desiccate and lethargic. I introduced myself and explained that my call was regarding Marcus.

Her words to me were, "What has he done now?"

"Mrs. Taylor, Marcus hasn't done anything," I said, irritated by her indifference."He came into my restaurant the other—"

"Oh, you that chef lady he talks about?"

"Marcus talks about me?"

"Yeah. He says you have a restaurant up the hill and it ain't no joint. It's a fancy restaurant with all kinds of fancy food."

The flattery had clouded my reason for the call. I snapped out of it and said, "Mrs. Taylor, getting back to Marcus, I took him to the hospital day before yesterday because he had been shot in the leg and an infection set in."

"Is he all right? I just got back in town this mornin'. I had been callin' while I was in Columbus, but he never picked up the phone. I'm glad you called 'cause I was gettin' worried."

I thought, *So, Marcus was telling the truth. She was in Columbus.* "Mrs. Taylor, do you leave Marcus alone often?"

"Who the fuck are you, missy, a social worker? 'Cause if you called here tryin' to start some trouble—"

I was shocked at her sudden change of demeanor, but uncultured defense could be handled with uncultured offense. Sternly, I said, "What I am, *missy*, is concerned about Marcus, which obviously you don't give a shit about, so don't fuck with me, because my middle name is *trouble*—"

I thought she hung up until her crackling voice sputtered, "Are you goin' to call welfare on me?"

"No, Mrs. Taylor. That is not the purpose here. The reason I called was to tell you that Marcus is with me, resting. He's been through a lot, but he's also getting better. I wanted to let you know where he is and to also say you are more than welcome to come by and see him." *Although, I don't know if I want you in my house*, I thought.

I could sense she was thinking and that she didn't know what to say. "Is he all right?"

"Yes. He's fine. I'm giving him the best attention I can."

"I'm glad, 'cause that's more than I can give him." That time she did hang up.

I listened to the dial tone for what I felt was forever. I eventually hung up and went upstairs. I needed to have Marcus in my view. He was propped on pillows, the television remote in his hand, when I walked in. His smile was like a sunbeam in the room. "*Heyyy*, Ms. C. I was wonderin' if you were gone. I didn't hear you downstairs."

Tears hydrated my eyes, but I refused to let them fall. "Marcus," I said, "I've got to go to the restaurant, but I'll be back as soon as I can." He could use his crutches to get to the bathroom, but it was difficult for him to go down the steps.

"Okay, Ms. C. Setting me up with the cooler was a good idea."

I had brought my cooler, filled with ice, upstairs and put it next to the bed with water, juice, fruit, and smoked turkey and cheese sandwiches in it. It was like Marcus had his own portable refrigerator. I said, "I called your school to let them know you'll be out all week. You've got to work like hell to catch up with your school work. I'll help, if you need me to."

"I hate I got shot, Ms. C, but bein' here with you is better than a thousand dollars' worth of video game tokens."

I chuckled. "I'm flattered, Marcus. You sure know how to make a girl feel real good." I wanted to mention that I had talked with his mother, but I didn't know how to explain the conversation, or that she'd hung up, not acknowledging that she wanted or didn't want to see her son. I inhaled deeply and then decided not to ruin the mood, although I felt it was strange that Marcus never asked for her. Every child asks for their mother. At least I thought they did.

"Call the restaurant if you need me," I said. When I reached the bottom of the steps I yelled, "And those books on the nightstand are for reading, young man."

Chapter 35

(Chandler)

"Well, look who the wind blew in," Lorelei said, rearranging the newly delivered flowers in the reception area. It was good to see her, too. Stevie Michelle was helping one of the waiters put tablecloths on the tables. Jorge and the other cooks were already busy prepping for the night. I felt guilty not being there earlier. I apologized and took one of my coats out of the tiny closet where two or three clean ones hung.

"Chandler, the veggies that were delivered this morning are fresher than fresh. I thought we'd do one of your famous stir-fries for the special tonight," Jorge suggested.

"Sounds good. Did we get shrimp and scallops, too?"

"Sure did. Jumbo ones." He sounded excited about the catch of the day. "Then how about shrimp and scallop stir-fry in a ginger and curry sauce over jasmine rice?"

"How about a teriyaki and sesame sauce over soft noodles?" Jorge countered.

"That sounds even better," I said, thinking Jorge's culinary savvy may be surpassing mine. Or, maybe I hadn't concentrated on my business of food preparation like I should. I shrugged off my thoughts, gave a final okay to the menu and went to join Lorelei and Stevie Michelle in the dining room. They were at the "conference room" table.

"Chandler," Stevie Michelle said. I knew that tone. It was the one she used when we needed to talk.

I said, "*Whaat*? I didn't do it. I swear."

Sit down, she gestured with a point of her long finger to my usual chair.

I sat, and the seconds she and Lorelei stared at me felt as if I was transparent. "Okay," I said, "what's on your minds?"

Lorelei spoke. "Oh, we just need to bounce some things off you."

"How's Marcus?" Stevie Michelle asked.

"He's getting better. He's in good spirits."

The superficial chitchat was making me crazy. I knew my girlfriends, and there was more on their brains than how Marcus was. Lorelei had the stare of a mother about to give sound advice and Stevie Michelle looked like she was effervescing with a bulletin news flash.

She said, "Chandler, have you talked to Marcus' mother?"

"Before I got here, as a matter of fact."

"*Annnd*?"

"And she hung up on me."

"She did what?" Lorelei asked.

"She hung up on me. She asked if Marcus was all right. We had a few more words and then I listened to the dial tone."

"You sure you didn't get disconnected?" Stevie Michelle inquired.

"I don't think so. It sounded like a deliberate hang up to me."

"So, where are you going from here?"

"Stevie Michelle, I wish you would stop beating around the damn bush and tell me what's on your mind."

"Okay. What's on my mind is how you're handling this Marcus thing. It's all wrong. First, you illegally sign documents at the hospital and now you're harboring him."

"Harboring him? That's real dramatic. You've been watching too much *Most Wanted*. Besides, he's not a criminal."

"What he is, is someone else's child."

"I damn well know that," I said. "And how can I forget it when you remind me every day."

"Stevie Michelle, you promised," Lorelei spoke out.

"Promised what?" I asked. "Obviously, my ears should be burning."

"Listen, Chandler," Lorelei started, "Stevie Michelle and I been talkin' about a lot of things that involve you, and the three of us should discuss'em. And yes, Marcus is a subject. We both know how you feel about'im. We all like Marcus."

"Lorelei, just get to the point," I said.

"The point is we got a business to operate and you been pretty distracted."

"Why the hell don't you just say it? You don't like what I'm doing with Marcus, so quit using something else as an excuse, Lorelei, because there's nothing else distracting me. I don't have a life, except here. You two tell me I need one and when I try, you tell me it's the wrong life to have. Marcus needs me. After talking to his mother, I'm even more convinced. And the truth is I think I need him, too. The both of you have children. I'm not that fortunate. I know I have Alexandria, but she's Kennedy's baby. I'm just her aunt. Besides, I know I can help Marcus. I'm relieved that we're getting this out in the open. I can't think of a better time to talk about my feelings and tell you what I plan to do."

Stevie Michelle and Lorelei settled in their chairs. I suddenly felt like my mouth had been swabbed with calcium chloride. The lump in my throat hindered my speech. I cleared it. "His mother's worried about losing her welfare," I said. "Marcus is a monthly check for her. I'm not saying she doesn't care about him, but I think there are more pressing matters in her life, like drugs and men. She's treated Marcus as if he's an adult. He has survival instincts, but he's a child. He acts like a child when he's permitted to. He's tough on the streets, but he knows he can be vulnerable when he's with me. Marcus is smart, guys. If I can get through to him with the things he likes, I don't think there's a limit to his achievements. He says he wants to be a zoologist. A dummy doesn't think with such magnitude. A dummy doesn't even know what a zoologist is. I want custody of him. He'll become another statistic if I don't help."

"His mother will never let it happen, Chandler." Stevie Michelle's interruption irritated me.

"I can't be afraid to try. Maybe I can get her to understand the benefit. It's just like this restaurant. I was frightened to death, having cold sweats and nightmares about all the things that could go wrong. Nothing happened that we couldn't handle or conquer. Remember?"

Reminiscent smiles modified my partners' faces.

"Yeah," Lorelei said. "I remember the banker that told us we should think about a daycare center, 'cause we'd have a better chance gettin' financed."

"And you told him if you needed career advice, he'd be the last person you'd consult, because he was white, therefore prejudiced and biased," I stated.

Stevie Michelle added, "That's when I knew our chances of a loan from that bank were zilch."

"But the fact is, regardless of where we got it, we did get it because we didn't give up," I said. "And that's why I've got to think positive. I don't want to hurt Marcus' mother, but at the same time I want to give him a future. I have a lot to share, guys, and he's like a sponge, ready to absorb."

Lorelei said, "Chandler, you got a two-bedroom house. One bedroom is yours and the other is Alexandria's. It's full of all kinds of little girl stuff. There ain't nowhere for Marcus to sleep."

"I've thought of that, too. I'm going to make a private area for him in the basement. He'll have his bedroom, bath and recreation space all to himself. You know I've talked about finishing the basement anyway. "

Stevie Michelle continued the interrogation. "What about school?"

"Catholic or private."

"That's costly, Chandler."

"I know. But if Marcus and I convince them that he's dedicated to his studies, maybe he'll be able to get some type of financial aid or something. I don't know, Stevie Michelle, but I want to try."

Then, without a sign from the kitchen or above, Lorelei's next inquiry almost knocked me off my chair. "I know we talked before about many personal things," she began, "but Chandler, I always wanted to know, but never had the nerve to ask, why you ain't never had a baby?"

Answering Lorelei would take our friendship to a greater level; a height beyond any rain forest canopy. There was so much we knew about one another that we'd take to our graves, never sharing with the outside world our personal intimacy of being best friends. We had discussed our sex lives, our fears, our idiosyncrasies, and only slightly judged one another. But we understood that judgment was good, when everybody involved knew the rules, how to keep score and where the judgment stopped, and either assistance or butting out began. So, I had been caught off guard with Lorelei's unexpected question, but I was also comfortable and actually ready to talk.

"I'm amazed it took either one of you these many years to ask," I said. "Only Wade knows the details," I confessed. "I'll begin by saying that before Wade and I were married, we agreed that our marriage would be childless. He didn't want any and I— Well, I—"

"Chandler, if you'd rather not—"

"No, I'd rather I do. I need to, Stevie Michelle. Lately, I've felt guilty about my past and things deep in my past. It's like I've just developed a conscience."

Lorelei chuckled. "Chandler, you always had a conscience. Yours just functions a little differently than the rest of the world's. You one of the kindest people I know, but at the same time one of the most rigid."

"I'm relieved you said that, girlfrien', because your perception will only confirm what I'm about to tell you." I inhaled and slowly released the air. "When I was sixteen, I was very much in love— No. Let me start again." I stared into Lorelei's inquisitive face and said, "Remember the birdhouse that hung from the porch at Mr. Van Horn's cabin?"

"Yeah. The one when you saw it, you broke down?"

"That's the one. Well, that birdhouse was made by a boy that I had lost my virginity to. He was also the father of my aborted babies." Lorelei's eyes widened. Stevie Michelle, uneasy, fidgeted in her chair, crossing and uncrossing her legs. "Yes, babies," I confirmed, as if they didn't hear my initial confession. "The first time it happened Spoon and I had unprotected sex and my mother insisted on an abortion. The second time I got pregnant, the protection failed. I was so frightened of my mother that I thought of nothing else but another abortion. Then Spoon was killed. I knew that was part of my punishment for what I did. I often asked God why him and not me, because at the time I didn't mind dying. As a matter of fact, I thought it was the solution to everything. Then one day, I realized it wasn't Wade who had convinced me not to have children, but my fear of being a parent, because I didn't feel I could be a good one. I felt I would make all the mistakes my mother made. As they say, you are a product of your environment. I hadn't been taught how to be a loving, considerate mother. Also, I never thought it was a natural instinct. So, if I was any kind of mother, I would be a bad one. Stevie Michelle and Lorelei, I had a fucking shitty, miserable, sad childhood. Can you imagine I never heard my mother say she loved me? The words were always negative when she spoke to me. So, I was scared to assume the responsibility of another life, especially a baby. And when Wade said he didn't want children, it was fine, too. But, not until Alexandria was born did I realize I could handle it. I could love and feel comfortable with a baby and know the right things to do and say. But, by that time, Wade and I were divorced and I was standing in forty's threshold. I know I've been blessed, but at the same time I feel I've been condemned, too."

"How so, Chandler?" Lorelei's voice stabilized my thoughts.

"Blessed in the way of indirectly receiving Alexandria and condemned by Wade being the person to confirm that children didn't need to be part of my life. I still don't understand if God sent him to punish me or if the devil did. Either way, I've been punished. I've lived in denial for a long time. And when I think of the sins I've committed, I go even deeper into denial."

Stevie Michelle asked, "Do you ever go to la la land?"

"I've heard you mention la la land before, but I never inquired what that meant."

"For me, it also means denial. It was a way I used to protect myself from the thoughts of *my* fucking, shitty, sad childhood. And, I did hear I love you, Chandler. But it was from a man who violated me. I was a victim of incest. And the only way I found I could cope was to go to la la land. In that place, I was anyone I wanted to be. I was a model. I was an actress. I was even a princess with everything—money, clothes, people who adored me. As the years progressed, it became more and more difficult to get there. My imagination had diminished, but the smells and colors and the feel of the man who molested me remain."

Stevie Michelle's stare was nowhere. I knew she had traveled back to the period in her life where she needed to go to la la land to escape. I quietly asked her, "You all right, girlfrien'?"

That's when she focused on me and said, "I don't think I'll ever be all right, but I've learned to cope. Uncle Lucius is dead. Mama said his heart attacked him. I don't know why it pumped life through such a worthless body for as long as it did. I didn't go to the funeral. And I know he's burning in hell, and if that's the only satisfaction I can have, then so be it."

Lorelei included, "We all got skeletons. Some are our faults and others we couldn't avoid. When I talked to my mother yesterday, her main concern was if I had forgiven her. I said that there was someone greater than myself that she needed forgiveness from. I know it is a sin to hate and to commit adultery, but I'm guilty of both. So, to answer her question, I said, 'I'm sittin' next to you in the pew of forgiveness.' Self-righteous, I ain't."

"Okay, we've established that you don't agree with what I plan for Marcus, and we all have skeletons in our closets, so where do we go from here?" I was determined to close old doors and open new windows.

Lorelei bellowed, "We go south."

"What?" I asked.

The subdued atmosphere of moments before had been replaced with excitement.

"Chandler, I been talkin' to Manny and he tells me that land, lumber and interest rates are at their lowest in South Carolina. He said that if we were serious about buildin' a cabin down there, we should really start thinkin' about it. My brothers are willin' to do the work dirt cheap if we hurry up and give'em the go ahead."

"I'm out of the loop for a few weeks and look what happens. Stevie Michelle, do you know about all this?" I asked, giggling inside.

"Aaah, Lorelei mentioned it. She said something about the land's already available. She described it to me. It sounds beautiful."

"You mean Mr. Van Horn's land, don't you, Lorelei?"

"Yeah."

"Lorelei! I haven't talked to Sam Van Horn since we were in Bluffton."

"But I have."

"When?"

"You want the truth?"

"Yes, I want the truth."

"Well then, you goin' to have to stop yellin'."

"I'm not yelling."

"Then what do you call it?"

"Lorelei!"

"Okay. I talked to him yesterday, a week ago and three weeks before that."

"And where the hell was I?"

"Gettin' well?"

I sucked in some deep breaths and then collected my thoughts and emotions. "All right. So you talked to Mr. Van Horn and he *saaid* . . ."

"He said that when we were ready to talk business he was more than willin' to sit down with us. The offer still stands, Chandler. He wants to sell some of his land. About two acres."

"Well, I'm going to throw a wrench in the works. I've been thinking we should open another restaurant," I said.

"*Ohh*," Lorelei said.

Stevie Michelle squealed, "Another restaurant?!"

"It came to me while I was recuperating. You guys handled everything so well while I was off, another restaurant should be a piece of cake. Jorge can run the kitchen with a blindfold on. As a matter of fact, I think he's gotten better than me."

"We got a dilemma," Lorelei said. "I say, heads we do the cabin and tails we do the restaurant."

"Just like that?" Stevie Michelle asked. "We're not talking about which movie to see."

"But some things can be settled with the toss of a coin," Lorelei stated. "We have two issues here, a restaurant or a vacation home. Either one costs money and we can't afford to do both."

"Speaking of money, Lorelei," I said, "do you feel we can swing it and is now a good time?"

"It's timely," she said with business confidence. "Mr. Hunt called Tuesday to say our credit line has been extended and whatever we need he's sure he can get it for us. That's when I started givin' serious thought to the cabin. You said so yo'self, Chandler, that we would like to have some place to relax when we needed it. And it would be ours. An investment, part of the assets." Lorelei sounded like a professional salesperson. "We'll put it in the corporate name."

"And you don't feel the restaurant is a good idea?"

"I think we are very busy with the one we got. Another one, unless you talkin' franchise, means larger capital, depletion of time, and quality control and more employees, and we still need a vacation. I feel we should give ourselves another two years or so before venturin' out."

"The cabin is a heavy price also," I said.

"That's true, Chandler. But, real estate would be a good diversification. With the low cost of financin' and labor, it's temptin'. It's a sound investment, not to mention the smell of pine, the fresh air, the blue skies and stars at night."

I chuckled and said, "Sounds personal to me."

She smiled. "It is."

Lorelei's description of Bluffton transported me. I was convinced, but Stevie Michelle was the third peg that stabilized our foundation. I asked her, "So, what do you think?"

"I think you're both treating this as if we're playing Monopoly, but what do I know? I'm just the PR person around here. But, a vacation with pine trees, fresh air, blue skies and stars sounds good to me."

"Then forget the toss," I said. "It appears this vote is unanimous."

Lorelei said, "That was too damn easy. I'll call Manny right now before somebody changes their mind."

"Not so fast," I said. "There's one minor detail that hasn't been discussed."

"What?" Stevie Michelle and Lorelei said in unison.

"What are we going to name our little vacation spot?"

"Hunh?"

"You know. There was the Ponderosa, the Lonesome Dove, High Chaparral. I think we should name our cabin."

"Yeah. Maybe 'Little Henhouse on the Prairie' or 'Over Forty on the Range'," Stevie Michelle said.

Our laughter brought Jorge out of the kitchen. "Am I the only one who works around here?" he said as he went behind the bar to get a glass of Coke from the fountain.

Just as I was about to answer him, the phone rang. Jorge answered it. "Yes, she is," he said. Then he said, "Chandler, it's for you."

"Probably Marcus," I mumbled. Jorge laid the phone on the back counter. "Hello," I said into it when I picked it up.

"Chandler, this is Stohn."

My heart thumped. I hadn't heard from him since the hospital. He was gone and Marcus said he had just left when I went up to recovery to see him. I thought, *Has it been four or five days*? Then I whispered, "I know who it is. How are you?"

"I'm headed your way. I want to stop and talk to you. That's if you can spare ten or fifteen minutes?"

"Yes, Stohn. I can spare ten or fifteen minutes."

"I'm pulling in the lot now," he said.

I chuckled and said, "Okay." I stood at the bar with expected anticipation. I knew I had missed him, but I didn't realize how much until he called.

Stevie Michelle looked at me and said, "Who was that?"

"Stohn."

"Something wrong?" Lorelei asked.

"No, I don't think so. He called from his car. He's on his way in."

That was Stevie Michelle and Lorelei's cue to scatter. They began doing little miscellaneous things around the restaurant, rearranging the bud vases, straightening tables and chairs.

The door opened and I stood stiff. Deep down, I thought Stohn had given up. He walked in and said hello to Stevie Michelle and Lorelei. I couldn't move, but I didn't have to. Stohn came to me. His arms encompassed my waist and I could smell the scent of lime, orange blossoms and black musk. He pulled me tight. I relaxed in his arms. He whispered, "I wasn't going to call, but the bottom line is I'm in love with you, Chandler. I've deduced that I have everything in my life that I need, but when you feel true love, everything in your life isn't what you need. I need you to talk to, Chandler. I need you to grow old with me."

I felt the weight of the loneliness lift. I felt the denial release me. I felt the fear vanish. And I found myself asking, "Are you sure?"

"Well, it's not the constant wild and crazy sex we have, so it's gotta be love. Nothing but pure love, baby."

Stohn and I had never had sex and it didn't matter. I felt close to him. Closer than I had felt to Wade and I had made love with him many times. "Where do we go from here?" I asked.

"First thing, you've got to believe that I'm sincere."

"I believe you."

"Then you've got to be sincere."

I hesitated.

"Okay, Chandler. What are you afraid of, commitment, being hurt, what?" Stohn had us face to face.

"Nothing," I said.

"Then let's try it. We'll take it slow. Maybe a movie now and then. PG of course, with your own popcorn." Stohn watched as my smile developed. "After we're comfortable with the movies, maybe we can graduate to candlelight dinners and then the ultimate—French kissing." My giggles were childlike.

"All right, Stohn. We'll take it one step at a time, and you can have some of my popcorn."

Then to my surprise, Stohn yelled into the restaurant, "Hey everybody, I think I got myself a girlfriend."

I thought I'd blush to ashes.

Chapter 36

(Lorelei)

We chose an acre across the creek from Mr. Van Horn's cabin and my brothers built us a four-bedroom log cabin—three up and one down. Chandler and Stevie Michelle concurred with me that the cabin was as beautiful as we had anticipated. The fourth bedroom was a "bonus room," as Manny called it. Supplies and lumber cost less than estimated, so he was able to include it at no additional charge.

Chandler and Stevie Michelle decorated their bedrooms in an Aztec style with pottery, kilim rugs and pillows, and other rattan furniture. My room was done in African motif. The hardwood floor was covered in a large coir rug that was excellent for scratching the bottoms of your feet when they itched. I looked high and low for a wooden platform bed. I found one at a little shop in Conway made of solid alder with a deep brown stain. I placed it in the center of the room surrounded by African carvings and art. The curtains I chose were of natural twill that matched the spread for the bed. Chandler, Stevie Michelle and I agreed that the colors throughout the cabin should be stone, russet, tan and hunter green. Earthy was our goal.

We had a huge living room/dining room combination decorated in an oversized sofa and chairs with tan linen slipcovers. The dining table was of sturdy, rustic walnut with hunter green chairs. Stevie Michelle found brass, iron and copper pole lamps, topped in intricate silk, glass and copper shades, that provided warm, subtle lighting. And like Mr. Van Horn's, Aussie installed a large ceiling fan in the middle of the cabin. Off the dining room, three steps led into a small corner study that Chandler filled with hardcover novels and oil and pencil portraits.

The most discussed and fussed over room in the cabin was the kitchen. Chandler went as far as customizing a recipe cabinet that had a combination lock. Glass panes and satin nickel hardware dressed the wooden cabinets. Diner bar stools surrounded the breakfast-bar island. A big glass pane window framed Chandler's herb garden and the Douglas firs that we planted.

As a warming gift, Mr. Van Horn had a twenty-five-foot bridge built that connected one side of the creek to the other. I imagined Three leaning over the rail with a pole, fishing for mullet and spot.

It was Chandler's idea that we have a four-day, family/friend reunion at the cabin. She made all the plans and sent out the invitations. The list was endless. My family and Stevie Michelle's family made up a platoon, but Chandler found inexpensive hotel rooms and Stevie Michelle suggested that whomever wanted to camp out on our acre, could. Six rented tents were erected on our land. It looked like a gold mining camp. Manny's children, my Three and Marcus all had tents, and the shocker was when Stevie Michelle and Banning decided to camp out. Of course, their tent was as far as possible from the children. Stevie Michelle explained that her first night in camp was the most seductive, romantic night of her life. She said, "I have a whole new perspective of the outdoors. The fresh air and stars brought out the animal magnetism in the both of us. Banning roared and I purred."

Walter and I were seeing a lot of each other, but I remained adamant about my independence, and he seemed to like the new me. Our relationship felt as if we had grown closer instead of apart since the divorce. We were definitely sexually active.

Chandler didn't pursue custody of Marcus, but she did receive permission from his mother to participate in his life. She even tried to help Bernadette receive counseling for her drug addiction. Bernadette was invited, but she didn't come to the reunion with Marcus.

Stohn came down to Bluffton a day early to look at some prospective property for himself. I felt he would go to any length to be close to Chandler. One day, as he leaned over the bar at the restaurant with his favorite cocktail in hand, Stohn said to me, "Lorelei, do you know I kept a post office box for twenty-five years hoping she'd write to me?" When I told Chandler about his confession, she said, "I still have the address number folded in my wallet."

With a chuckle, I said, "I wanna see a piece of paper that's been folded for twenty-five years."

Oceanna persuaded me to give her permission to have a boyfriend visit while she was in Bluffton. I made sure he was escorted to his motel every evening before I went to bed, even though Oceanna assured me she was still a virgin. But like Stevie Michelle said, it was something about the air and the stars that brought out the animal in a person.

Mrs. Wilcox and Mr. Cooley came to our reunion, too. They said that since the restaurant was closed for the week, they had no choice but to come. They drove down together.

Jorge brought his family and Chandler was grateful that there was someone else to take the meal shifts. Breakfast and dinner were prepared at the cabin, but lunch was up to each individual. Usually breakfast was so abundant that no one wanted to eat until dinner time.

The third and last night at "Halfway to Heaven," as we decided to call our little getaway place, we had a big barbeque with kegs of beer, bottles of wine, lots of corn on the cob, watermelon, music and laughter.

Chapter 37

(Stevie Michelle)

There was Banning, Lorelei's brothers, my brothers, and even Mr. Van Horn—I had never seen so many beautiful black men on one acre. For that matter, I had never been on one acre that I could call my own. The first time I saw it, Lorelei, Chandler and I drove to Bluffton to finalize the paperwork for the land with Mr. Van Horn. Everything was so green and manicured, I thought I had stepped into a landscape portrait. When the acre was staked out, I said, "All this for five hundred dollars?" That was Mr. Van Horn's asking price. We, Lorelei, Chandler and myself, tried to say we didn't feel comfortable with the gift, but he insisted that it was the least he could do for us.

He said, "There's plenty of land to go around. I've talked it over with my sons and they've already confessed that if and when something happens to me, they will sell. So, it is, I feel, my prerogative to give it to people I know appreciate it. Just promise me you won't let anybody put a development on it."

My sisters, Barbara, Connie, Roslyn and Faith came to the reunion with their children. Joseph and Isaiah visited without their clan, but Faye had a schedule conflict and couldn't come. Mama, though, came with Al Norton and said she was never going to leave. She said it was the most beautiful place she'd ever seen. "Yo' Grandma Shaky would've loved this place," she said while inhaling deep cleansing breaths.

I enjoyed the company of my family, but the best company of all was Banning Morris. I confessed to Mama that for the first time I felt

I was in love. She asked me to describe the feeling and I said, "I can't, Mama," and that's when she said, "You're in love all right."

Nelson was invited to the reunion and accepted the invitation at the last minute. He and I had never talked about his homosexuality, because maybe neither one of us had anything to discuss. He knew he was, I knew he was, and finally I asked Chandler and Lorelei if they knew he was. Chandler said in a low, respectful tone, "Since he was about ten."

Lorelei, obviously uncomfortable with the subject, asked, "Can I just say that I recognize somethin' different about'im?"

I tried reading a book on homosexuality, but it was difficult to be biased when your son is "the different one." Anyway, Nelson came, and I had to admit that my son's taste in men was as good as mine. They were intelligent and sexy.

Chapter 38

(Chandler)

Lorelei and Stevie Michelle surprised me with the three rockers they ordered from Ernest Lee Carter. They were in a perfect line on the porch when we arrived for the last inspection. Our names were engraved on them with, "Halfway to Heaven" and the date our cabin was built. Lorelei said they got the idea from when I had the key chains engraved for the restaurant.

Kennedy, Cornelius, and my favorite niece, Alexandria, were having a ball at Halfway to Heaven. They stayed in Stevie Michelle's room and Lorelei's mother stayed with Mr. Van Horn—in separate rooms, of course, although I could see lights on late into the night. Mr. Van Horn and Mrs. Garris hit it off right away. So did Alexandria and Marcus. He carried her around on his shoulders wherever he went. Lorelei said her brother Manny used to do the same thing with her. Marcus was good with Alex and she was happy. Alex could look at Marcus and would giggle. There's nothing like a baby's giggle.

Marcus was in heaven at Halfway to Heaven. There were more critters than he could collect. He caught a snake, crabs, a frog and even a lizard. He kept them all in his tent and I asked him to keep them away from the baby, but Alex liked playing with them as much as Marcus. He promised to let them go after the reunion. I told him there would be a body and bag search before he left.

When Stohn Bradford drove up the road of Halfway to Heaven for the first time, I felt everything was complete. He was well worth the twenty-something years wait. He made me feel secure, worshipped and loved, just like he said he would. He assured me that he'd never leave me again, although I knew promises were made to be broken. But it felt good just the same.

After all our guests had left the reunion to go home, Stevie Michelle, Lorelei and I stayed one last night alone together. It was a perfect scene. The sunset, glasses of champagne, good old-fashioned girl talk, and a friendship that would last long beyond eternity, was our wonderful private world. It was like a pajama party.

"So, should we be makin' plans for a weddin'?" Lorelei asked.

I replied, "Not unless it's for Oceanna. I like Stohn's and my relationship just the way it is."

"Well, I'm just glad you two got it together. I was tired of watching two ships pass in the night." I could always depend on Stevie Michelle to have something smart to say.

"And what about you and Banning? You two looked like Siamese twins this weekend," I said.

"We were joined in places all right. This may be the last time you hear this, so listen up, girls. I love him. I don't plan to marry him, at least not right away, but I do love him."

I said, "I've got a feeling you'll marry him, but make sure there's a prenupt. For the first time, girlfrien', you can end up paying. Neither Halfway to Heaven nor Maroon is negotiable." Our laughter drowned out the crickets' love songs.

"Chandler, did you believe we'd do it?" Lorelei asked.

"Do what?"

"Be here. Don't you remember when we sat on Mr. Van Horn's porch wishin' for this?"

"Oh, I remember it all right. I remember it very well, like it was yesterday. I pinched myself an hour ago just to make sure I'm real and all this is, too. I asked the universe if I could now say I'm successful."

"And what did the universe say back?"

"It said, not yet. I've got some soul searching left to do, and a few more cooking workshops, and then I can say I'm successful."

"Well, I'm satisfied with my success," Stevie Michelle said. "What else could I want? I have good friends, a business, and for the first time in my life, after. . .well, never mind how many men, I'm in love."

"You're right," I said. "What else could you want? How about you, Lorelei? Do you feel successful?"

"I feel blessed. Our destinies have been good to us, ladies. I questioned mine a few times, but so far, it's been right on."

"I believe everything has happened the way it was meant to," I said. "There's as much to be thankful for in the bad as there is in the good stuff that happens. I feel guilty and ashamed about some things in my life, but I also feel stronger because of them."

Stevie Michelle added, "We all do, Chandler."

I got up from my rocker and went into the cabin to get my journal and pencil. When I returned, I wrote the day's events in by the last of daylight.

In the distance, Stevie Michelle, Lorelei and I watched Buster slowly cross the bridge. Since it had been built, he didn't swim as much as he used to. He walked up on our porch and flopped between Lorelei's and my rockers.

"Chandler," Lorelei said, "Anita Baker and Al Jarreau are comin' to Cleveland."

"Together?"

"No, but I thought we'd get tickets and also try to get'em into the restaurant."

"That's Stevie Michelle's job."

"I'm already on it," Stevie Michelle said, as we lazily rocked in our chairs.

The sun was a ball of fire that balanced on the pointed tips of the mighty pine trees. It would soon fall off and disappear until the same time the next evening. The difference would be we wouldn't be there to see it. Maroon and its "company" were waiting.

Closing my journal, I shouted into our acre, "God, thank you!"

Lorelei sang, "Amen."

"Yes, thank you," Stevie Michelle echoed. "We've been blessed."

Stevie Michelle, Lorelei and I sipped our champagne and listened to the crickets' and frogs' serenade. I knew their songs were dedicated to us.

Then, without provocation other than I could, I asked, "Hey, Stevie Michelle, by the way, how many men have you had?"

"Shut up, Chandler."

Lorelei said, "Don't you two ever stop?"

CPSIA information can be obtained at www.ICGtesting.com
Printed in the USA
BVOW020522171212

308401BV00002B/5/P